The House Kat

ZUGSWANG

A Kat Fernando novel

By Hugh Russel

This novel is a work of fiction. Any references to real people, events, establishments, organizations, or locale are intended only to give the fiction a sense of reality and authenticity and are used fictitiously. All other names, characters and places, and all dialogue and incidents portrayed in this book are the product of the author's imagination.

Cover design: Hugh Russel
Lisbon Image by Freepik
Toronto image by Freepik
Rome image by Freepik
London image by Freepik
Hugh Russel's portrait by Denni Russel Photography

Published February 02, 2020
Library and Archives Canada
Paperback ISBN: 978-1-7773671-3-8
e-Book ISBN: 978-1-7773671-4-5
For information about this and other books by Hugh Russel Contact Negative Space Publishing:
email: negative.space.publishing@gmail.com

For Zina

Elzina Grace Allen Russel
Thank you for everything.
1922-2022

Acknowledgements

My thanks to readers, Rose Dotten and Barbara Besse for their friendship, expertise, comments and enthusiastic support for my story telling and for their help getting my work ready for publication.

I can't say enough about my wife Cheryl, but thanks will have to do here. She reads everything I write. Not only that she edits, advises and suggests things when I'm brain dead and she's tough too and boldly tells me when I have just written utter crap. No kidding, she reads it all. The only one other person has done that and that was my mother.
Love you Cheryl.

"Life is what happens to you while you're busy making other plans."
 John Lennon
Sadly, that held true for him as well as Kat.

And for those of us who went off to find ourselves during the 60s …

"Remember, no matter where you go, there you are."
Buckaroo Bonzi

Part 1

Rome

Chapter ~ 1

Righetti's Little Black Book

The concierge, Nicolas Righetti, kept a little black book that had it all, the favored guest, their special tastes and unique appetites, whatever they might be. The wealthy and powerful clients knew that when they needed something special, all they had to do was follow the instructions on the young man's business card … 'For something special, day or night. Call Signore Righetti.'

What she needed was access to that book, access to the section that recorded the purveyors of pleasure that could satisfy those late-night appetites and peccadillos.

Setting up this meeting with Righetti was the easiest part. She had said it was important to meet privately and that would awaken his curiosity. She chose him as her source because she was counting on the chance that he was young. Hopefully, he was old enough to remember Anita's sexsational fame as the Happy Widow of Ibiza, and young enough to have missed that Anita Franco had assassinated the crime boss Delph Petros. The risk was worth it as he agreed to meet her at 11:00 am.

Righetti was a stout, pleasant looking little man with wavy black hair and a broad smile. He offered her a seat then sat down at the desk.

"Yes, Signorina Franco, how may I be of service to you?"

"Signore Righetti, I am new to Rome ..."

"Benvenuto."

"Uh yes ... thank you ... I'm setting up a business providing a special and very exclusive service."

His naturally animated round face became serious. "I see, go on."

"I believe what I am offering will be of mutual benefit."

Even though he thought he knew what she was talking about, he wanted her to confirm it. "I am intrigued. What sort of special service are you providing?"

"I tailor my business to the special needs of my clients," she said, crossing her legs suggestively. "I am eager to make a name for myself in Italy. I believe you know what I am talking about."

"I believe I do." Apparently, that was as close to confirmation as he would get. He became aroused merely by the suggestion.

"Perhaps you could help me."

"If I can. First tell me how I would benefit from your service."

"I assume that you receive a percentage of the service fees."

"Generally, 15% of the gross."

"That seems more than fair. I would be prepared to offer you a signing bonus, for want of a better term, and a premium on top of your usual percentage."

"That sounds very generous. How much would the premium be?"

"Say another 5%."

"I like it. You understand that I would need to sample your special services before I make my decision."

"Oh, of course, that goes without saying. But before I take care of you, there is something I need from you."

"Ah hah," he said, preparing for the inevitable catch, "and what would that be?"

"I want a list of the girls you have already given access to and the names of their regular clients."

"That is impossible," he said resolutely.

"Nothing is impossible, Signore."

"But why would you want that?"

"It's just good business to know with whom, and what I am working. I'll make it worth your while, of course."

"Of course." Leaning forward and putting his hands together as if in prayer. "How much are you offering?"

"We could start with this." She carefully placed an envelope on his desk.

"I see an envelope with bank notes, but it does not tell me how much."

"Ten thousand euros." His eyes widened. "Does that appeal to you?"

"Oh, it does."

"Wonderful. Then if I am happy with the list, I'll let you have a bonus." He was overwhelmed. "A second bonus?"

"My personal attention." He would have thought that was a given, but he didn't say that. His job had provided him with the opportunity to become an expert in selecting the most desirable women for the hotel's guests. "Would you mind standing up, so that I may have a good look at you?"

She did.

"Now would you turn around for me." She began to turn. "Slowly please." She smiled. He studied her with a critical eye and concluded that this woman was one of the better ones. Oh no, she was the best. But during their interview he had neglected to insist on knowing what her service was. She towered over him. His eyes were level with her shoulders making it perfect for a view of her cleavage. In bare feet, she must be at least six feet tall. His general professional assessment was that the dress and shoes she wore were perfect.

They showed off her beautiful body without being too obvious. The neckline revealed just enough cleavage to draw in the eye without being vulgar. He knew that his more discerning guests would love the look of her, and the names of affluent guests quickly came to mind.

"You are so thoughtful, Signore. Do you like what you see?"

"You are beautiful…" His voice trailed off.

"I hear a 'but'."

"More of a question actually. I wonder, what sort of things will you do for them?" That was the right question, but they were talking about two entirely different things.

"I am a professional, Signore. I recognize the same quality in you. I do whatever it takes to finish off my client. And I don't kiss and tell. None of my clients has ever complained." How could one be more truthful than that?"

"I like the way you put that." She nudged the envelope closer. "Do we have a deal?" He took hold of the corner, but she pressed on it with a fingertip. "Ah-ah-ah, not so fast, Signore Righetti. First, you must give me what I want. A printout of that list, if you please."

"Yes, certainly." He took a little black book from his pocket. "I'll scan it for you."

"No-no-no, Signore. I need it typed. Double spaced, and don't forget to link the clients to their favorite girls. Also, I need the client's preferences. That is very important."

That elicited some sarcasm. "Is that all?"

"No." He raised his eyebrows. "You must see to it that I won't have any trouble with your security when I come to visit my clients."

He relaxed. "That will not be a problem at all. We have a system in place for just such situations."

She knew that of course, that was why she asked for it. He opened the side drawer of the desk and took out a golden disk with his signature engraved on the face.

"When you are invited by one of our guests, you will show this token to the security people as you enter the hotel.

"It is my personal guarantee that you are a trusted, … uh, service provider."

"How simply perfect. Thank you. I will wait for you in the lobby." Returning the money to her purse, she turned to leave.

"Ah, I thought you would…"

"What, here? Are you mad?" She smiled. "No-no-no, there is a time and a place for everything Signore Righetti. What I will provide for you will be special, dare I say, unforgettable." *A confident whore*, he thought with a momentary touch of anger soon replaced by eager lustful anticipation, "I'll start on the list right away. It shouldn't take too long."

"That's a good boy." She tapped the end of his nose with her fingertip and withdrew from the room without looking back.

He set to work copying the names he had so diligently collected since he arrived at the hotel as a bell hop. It looked unimpressive printed on plain paper, so after placing it a plain white envelope, he happily erased the file from his hard drive. He couldn't see her in the lobby and anxiously called out, "Signorina Franco?" With no response, so he called once again, "Anita Franco?" People turned, as people so often do, to see if they could identify the person who would eventually answer. One or two of the hotel guests knew that name and remembered the glamorous woman vividly. They also failed to locate her.

Hedda was well pleased by their reactions. Not wanting them to put her together with that name, she sat quietly watching Righetti in the marbled mirror. When he seemed to give up his search and everyone relaxed, she moved quietly towards him and tapped him on his shoulder and put her finger to her lips.

The gesture did two things. Forcing his silence made it seem that she was not Anita Franco, but someone with an unrelated question. Also, it encouraged Righetti to recall that their business was not open to public scrutiny. "Do you have the list for me?"

"Si, Signorina Fra..."

"Shush now, let's try to employ a little discretion, Nicolas."

"Scusa. The information you requested is in this envelope. Now you have something for me?"

"Of course. You have been most helpful."

"Yes, yes, but when will I receive my unforgettable reward?" His impatience was a bonus for her if she could make him hand Desrosiers to her on a platter.

"That depends on who is coming to stay here, doesn't it?"

That was all it took. Eager to please his new madam, he handed the politician's head on a golden token. "There is a very special someone on my list who would appreciate your services. His preference is for a particular brunette with dark eyes and tanned skin. But one look at you and he will forget there was ever anyone else."

"How flattering. When will he be here?"

"The day after tomorrow."

"And does he have a name?"

"Of course, Monsieur Desrosiers. He is the French Minister of Defense, a very important man."

"How absolutely thrilling. His favorite woman, what is her name?"

"Clarissa. You will find her name near the top of the list along with her address and phone number."

"Perfect. I'll make some special arrangements for Clarissa, so that I can take her place when the minister requests a visit."

Just the mention of the name Anita Franco was enough to spark renewed interest among some of the guests. She was thought to be dead, but an official at the hotel, especially someone like Signore Righetti, who should know about these things, was looking for her in the hotel lobby. Word began to spread out from there. A tabloid picked up the rumor. All that was known about her outside of the criminal underworld, was that she was a wickedly glamorously woman who had a series of tragic relationships with rich old men.

***

Righetti's list was exactly what she needed, and her first order of business now was to meet Clarissa Aubertin and find a way to get her quietly out of Rome. She soon discovered that the list provided that solution as well. She called her man in Zürich and gave him the list of Clarissa's clients. As soon as the name came up Siggi recognized a fellow Suisse and made contact with the man.

Ibrik Stromboli was a flamboyant German millionaire, living in Zürich. Kraft had done a special favor for Stromboli and the old party animal was now indebted to him. Kraft called the man and suggested that it was time for one of his famous celebrations and mentioned that he had a special request. Thinking that this favor would clear his debt, Stromboli was delighted to agree.

Kraft suggested he invite Clarissa to a party and keep her entertained for a week or so. It was as simple as that.

Stromboli was delighted, saying that Clarissa could never turn down a party. But there was a problem, she had a cat that was too old and frail to travel. Clarissa would need a cat sitter.

That cat became Hedda's key into the woman's apartment.

"Ah hah," said Kraft, "I have the perfect solution. As it happens, I have a friend visiting Rome for a few days. She is unhappy with her present accommodations and wants to leave her hotel and rent an apartment."

"Wonderful, then I'll arrange it right away." Stromboli called Clarissa and told her about the party and his dear friend who was in Rome.

"Does she like cats?" asked Clarissa.

"That's just it, she loves them." Stromboli had no idea if that was true, but he would say anything to get Clarissa out of Rome to clear his debt with Kraft. I'm sure she would be happy to look after your Clio. I could arrange to have her meet you this afternoon. Would that be acceptable?"

"Yes, of course it would! How wonderful, then I can come to you party!"

It all seemed to happen so naturally. Preparation for the Minister's first night in Rome would be a simple matter of introducing herself as Anita Franco when she showed the token to the guards.

Then be prepared to fight.

***

They met at the Caffè delle Palme, Clarissa's local, just up the street from her apartment. Hedda had an instant and rare emotional reaction when she saw her for the first time. Her almond shaped, dark chocolate eyes latched onto Hedda's like a tractor beam and the connection was complete. Both women were bi. Making love to another woman, especially an experienced, Mediterranean beauty like this one would be very satisfying.

Beyond that first impression, it was amazing how closely the woman resembled the real Anita Franco. Though Clarissa was an inch or two shorter, her facial features and body were similar. Her brown olive skin was smooth to the touch and her black haired gleamed in the hot Roman sun.

9

"Ciao Anita," she said, taking hold of Hedda's arms and kissing her on each cheek. She felt so warm and inviting. "I can see why you are a close friend of Ibrik. He has always been partial to beautiful blonds. Come, we can get to know each other over a cappuccino." They took the small table at the front of the café.

"Ciao Clarissa, who is your lovely friend?"

"Anita Franco, she is visiting from Spain. Two cappuccinos please Helena."

After Helena left them Hedda commented on her introduction, "Ibrik must have told you all about me."

"Only a little, he said I would like you."

"Was he right?"

"Come Anita, you know that Ibrik is always right. It is a shame I am flying out tonight, we could have spent some time together."

Never one to let an opportunity for pleasure to pass her by Hedda had an answer for that. "We still have all afternoon."

Clarissa smiled happily. Though Hedda was perhaps ten years her senior, Clarissa felt like she had met a kindred spirit.

"I am so glad you like cats. He can be difficult; it takes a cat person to make him comfortable."

"Don't worry, I adore cats."

"How lucky it was that Ibrik sent you to me."

"Yes, wasn't it? Dear old Ibrik."

They lay in bed perhaps a little longer than they should have. Clarissa packed quickly, kissed Hedda goodbye and left with her girlfriend Ester on Stromboli's private jet.

Clarissa's apartment suited Hedda very well. It was small, but tasteful, and very comfortable. Her business was obviously very rewarding. With the first phase of her plan completed, she turned her attention to the more difficult problems.

A gossip columnist picked up the rumor that Anita Franco was in town and penned an article titled, Do you remember the Happy Widow of

Ibiza. It ran on page five with a small low resolution photo of Anita from the paper's archives. Very few people took the time to read it.

****

Chapter ~2

The days of investigation and antiterrorist activities in Europe were over. Although it had taken some time to get used to life as a new Canadian and a civilian. It was the life she had always wanted. However, the adjustment to the slower pace and benign activities was proving more difficult than she had imagined. Kat Fernando was a stay-at-home mum now and although that was a truly happy experience, she couldn't help feeling the need to keep looking over her shoulder.

Would her paranoia ever go away? That unfortunately was still an open question.

Her daughter Sara was a wonderful child, a typical four-year-old, the most beautiful, amusing, mischievous, and of course, brilliant child there ever was. She was also precocious to a fault and sometimes more than a handful. Rosario, her nanny had a way of dealing with her occasional tantrums and the seemingly constant demands for attention. Also, Kat was in love again. Early on, she had accepted that she couldn't keep Deacon at arm's length any longer. Yet, she was adamant about resisting marriage. And for the first time she was enjoying the affection of a few good friendships.

However it didn't take a lot before the memories of old battles returned in the form of flashbacks and dreams. She sought help for her PTSD issue and found that EMDR (Eye Movement Desensitization and Reprocessing) handled a great deal of it and keeping busy was good for that as well. To stay fit and keep her reflexes sharp, she had been working out in the near-by dojo after her daily twenty-minute run.

Her therapist questioned the decision to use a martial art to stay in condition and she just looked at him. "What I mean is, doesn't doing that just take you back into the memories and flashbacks?"

"It's just the way my body works. What's wrong with that?"

"Hey, I'm just saying it could cause you some problems down the road."

Kat's husband, Harm Toucksberry, left her an enormous fortune. She used some of it in her fight against the major crime syndicates before retirement but that was a drop in the bucket. The problem with that much wealth, if one could call it a problem, was that it was always increasing. Jasper Cleveland had a similar fortune when he died and left it all to his old friend Deacon. In turn Deacon used it to start a philanthropic enterprise called the Cleveland Foundation. That was the source of funding for several charitable groups around the world. Following his lead, Kat created the Harmon Toucksberry Foundation to quietly use her enormous wealth to support a number of projects, including women's health, start-up businesses for woman, and literacy programs.

She had a staff of good people to take care of that, so that she could keep busy enjoying her life with Sara and Deacon.

***

On the same Tuesday that Hedda met Clarissa in Rome, Kat had been out for a run and heading for her dojo. It should have been a pleasure, but it wasn't. It was late spring, the air was a pleasant 20° C, and Sara was at home asleep in the care of Rosario.

In Toronto there are only two seasons, winter and construction. As usual the city was under construction, everywhere. Jarvis and the Esplanade were a mess which made crossing the street hazardous.

She was nearly hit by a dump truck that clipped the cone barrier at her heels. Dodging that put her in the path of a taxi that just missed her by inches and the driver had the audacity to hurl insults at her.

When she arrived at the dojo just off King St. She was tense, anxious and a little angry. Perhaps she should have gone straight home, but she felt she had to work it out.

She had intended to sweat out stress by doing the essential exercise groups, but she hadn't anticipated running into Taylor Harding, a young overly ambitious day trader. He was a cliché straight out of the Karate Kid, the cocky son-of-a-bitch who was always trying to prove how good he was.

To be ignored, especially by an attractive woman of any age, was just plain insulting. She was doing her weight training and purposefully ignoring him. He moved over to the weights, so that he was right beside her to put on a show. She continued to ignore him.

At last he had to say something. It might have been something nice like, it's a beautiful day, or did you have a good run, Kat? But that wouldn't have been in character for Taylor. No, he had to get right to it, the challenge. His intention was clear, "If you think you're the best," he said, "Why don't you and I spar together?"

She stopped and calmly glanced his way. "Not a good idea, Taylor."

"What's the matter?" Harding was always annoying, but this morning he seemed particularly aggressive. "Are you afraid of getting bruised?"

"Yeah, that's it. Now go away."

"You know, I don't think that a black belt on a woman is equal to a man's."

"That's nice," she said.

"You're afraid to prove me wrong?"

"Two for two Taylor, very good. Now please, go away."

"Come on bitch." As he said that, he started hopping around on the mat like a lemur.

"There's no reason to be rude," she said.

He gestured his response with his hands. "Bring it on, bitch!"

"Are you sure?"

"You know it, bitch."

"You said bitch three times, you know that's how you call the devil up."

"Ha!"

"You said spar, but I'm guessing what you really want is full contact."

"Yeah. Yeah," he said impatiently, "full contact. Let's go."

"Alright." She moved onto the center mat and kept her eyes on him as she bowed. The moment she lowered her head he leapt right into a high-flying kick. With three quick strokes she blocked the kick with her forearm, struck him under his arm with a half fist, then a quick palm thrust to the chest while he was still in the air. The blows were extremely fast and far harder than he expected. With the air knocked out of him, he dropped to the mat clutching his chest, and writhing in pain.

She stood over him. "That was a stupid opening, Taylor. You should learn to control your urges."

He tried to sweep her legs, but she sprang up and came down with her knee on his thigh, adding a punch to the gut. He couldn't get up after that. Sam Yu, the master of the dojo, had been watching them fight from the other side of the room. He was concerned that she was about to do some serious damage and put a stop to it.

Walking calmly over to stand beside Kat. He reached down for his hand and helped him up onto his feet. "Come on Taylor, face it, she's way out of your league. Your opening was stupid, and your rudeness is unacceptable. I don't think you belong here anymore, so clean out your locker and don't come back."

As Taylor limped away, he placed his hand on Kat's shoulder, "Can I speak with you in my office for a moment?"

"Sure Sam." Dusting off her hands, she followed him. Opening the door, he stepped aside and let her go in first. "I'm sorry about that Sam. He was pushing my buttons and I…"

"Hey no, it's not about that, Kat. I'm glad he's finally out of here."

He closed the door and walked by her and sat on the edge of the desk. She looked around the room, noting everything, a professional habit. A coffee maker a small bar fridge, a pile of clothes on the file cabinet, cups and dishes on the windowsill. A futon rolled up behind the desk. "What's with the futon? Are you living in here now?"

"Yeah, but not for much longer. I'm going to have to shut down the dojo. That's what I wanted to talk to you about."

"I don't like the sound of that. What's the problem?"

"It's the rent. The landlord is selling the building. I heard the new owner wants to turn it into condos."

"The whole city is turning into condos. I think the City Hall is next." He wasn't in the mood for humor. He just stared out the window looking totally defeated. "Yeah."

"Hey, sorry Sam." She paused as an idea quickly popped into her head. "I have some money to invest."

"Kat, come on, we're talking millions here. It's a nice idea, but if you were thinking of buying the building, dream on."

"But…"

"No, I've just got to face it. It was a good run, but it's over."

"We're friends, right? We help each other. I wasn't kidding about the money, I set up a foundation to help small businesses, and there's more than enough to do it."

"Really?"

"Uh huh, I'll have the foundation look into buying the building. Have you got the landlord's information handy?"

"Yeah." He just sat there for a moment. "I just can't believe that you're serious."

"I'm perfectly serious. Let's have that name."

"Alright, it's in this file."

She took it and had a quick look inside. "Great. I'll make some calls."

"You'd really do that for me?"

"Sam, before you get all squishy, let's see if I can buy the property first, then you can gush and throw flowers at my feet. OK? In the meantime, cheer up."

***

Early Thursday morning, the day before Gérard Desrosiers's big finalé, Hedda visited the hotel. Having studied a plan of the hotel supplied by Kraft, she used the code he supplied to open the employee's entrance and made her way to the staff area.

She was dressed in the typical garb of a French secret service agent, the dark gray suit, white shirt, black tie, and carried a badge, DGSI (*Direction générale de la sécurité intérieure*) identification card, and a large briefcase. The effect was enhanced by the dull brown wig she wore tied back in a ponytail.

She completed the look with pilot style sunglasses to obscure her face. The room looked tired, olive-green lockers lined the drab, chipped paint on the walls. A single, long, metal table with five, uncomfortable looking metal chairs, filled the space at the end.

It looked like a set designer decorated it to keep the staff breaks as short as possible. Sitting alone in the gloom on the sixth chair at the end of the table was a small, round, middle aged woman.

As Hedda entered she looked up but chose to remain silent.

"Ciao," Hedda said.

"Ciao." It was a weak response carrying a hint of a question in it. Hedda couldn't have cared less. "I am Special Agent Anita Franco, DGSI," she flashed her badge quickly, "are you with maid service?"

"Si."

"Good. Name?"

"Renata Parma. What is this about?"

Hedda wrote that down in a small notebook. "I am with the French Minister's security team doing an advanced inspection. I need to have a look at his rooms before he comes."

"Big shots, always causing a fuss. It's a hotel suite, what for does he need to have it inspected?"

"So that he knows he is a big shot, I suppose. Renata, I need to use your master keys."

"That is forbidden Signorina. I cannot do that."

"This is official government business, and I must ask you to cooperate with me for the sake of security."

"How long will you need them?"

"I would think twenty minutes would be enough."

"My break is over in fifteen minutes."

"Then we should hurry up, shouldn't we?"

"Signorina, you are sure I won't get into trouble?"

"You can trust the word of Anita Franco."

"Very well, here they are. This is the master room key. This one will get you into the elevator."

"Thank you, I'll be back in fifteen minutes."

She found her way to the special service elevator and rode up to the fifth floor. There was plenty of time to set up her entertainment. It took only ten minutes to place her traps starting with removing the flowers from the large ceramic vases in the hall next to the elevator. She cradled a cellphone IED attached to a small brick of C-4, in each vase. That would take care of his bodyguards and cover her escape when the mission was done.

After burying the explosives in a deep layer of ball bearings she replaced the glass beads and rearranged the flowers. Moving into the President's Suite she placed a third cell phone, disguised to looked like a TV remote, in the center drawer of the living room desk.

Pressing 449 would set off the bombs. Her murder weapon had been Anita Franco's favorite, the SIG 226. She would drop it by the body when she was done. Adding details like that to the mound of evidence would surely link her nemesis to the killing. The gun was sealed in a plastic bag with a suppressor and an extra clip which she taped inside the toilet tank.

Her preparations were complete, and the stage was set for the event of the year. She returned to the lounge and handed the keys back to Renata.

"Is everything as it should be?"

"It is, thanks to you."

***

Deacon joined Kat for burgers, fries and milkshakes at the George St. Diner just around the corner from her home. They, meaning she and Deacon, decided to have some grownup time to talk. They took the long way back to her apartment down Adelaide to Sherbourne, discussing among other things, the purchase of Sam's building. Deacon wasn't particularly interested in that, but the subject of real estate had always been his lead in when working his way up to her housing situation which was his ever-present concern.

He wanted her to marry him and to move into his home. She wasn't ready for marriage, she said. She wanted to build another house in Mulmur. He said she was just being silly, why go backwards when her future was inevitably going to be with him. That made her a bit testy. A man's attempt at domination was a sore point with her. "I am just not ready for that Deacon, so let's drop it OK.

"You're just afraid to commit."

"Perhaps." But there was no perhaps about it he'd hit the nail on the head. She was certain that if she made that commitment somehow it would complete the pattern of her life.

The men she had loved, her father, Harm, and even Paul, they had all died and somehow it was her fault. She wasn't just afraid, she was terrified that she would lose Deacon as well.

She didn't want to talk about it. He wasn't sure which of the options it was that she couldn't commit to marriage or moving in together.

Was he going to give up?

In a word, no.

But that was another fear she had, though she couldn't talk about that either.

"I'm going to give up on you soon."

"I don't believe it."

"Really? I'm not kidding Kat, the day will come when I'll just stop asking you."

That made her angrier. "Promises, promises."

"You are incorrigible."

"And you're not?"

"Alright, change of subject. We should do something this afternoon."

"Sure, what did you have in mind?"

"How about we go back to my place and make out."

"Deacon, is that all you think about?"

"Pretty much all the time, yeah. So how about it?"

"OK." That got her over the anger rather quickly. So, it was the promise of sex that calmed his Tiger. Who knew? They turned the corner and headed down to King St.

"Let's get that cab." His hand shot up. "Taxi!" The driver saw him, so Deacon turned his attention back to Kat.

"I'll call Rose and tell her we're having coffee at the palace, and you can send Jim down to pick them up."

Ignoring her tendency to issue orders he took umbrage with her choice of words. "Must you always call it a palace?"

"Hey, it's a palace, what do you want me to call it? We can have dinner and a sleepover. Sara will like that." The cab pulled up beside them and they got in.

The drive looked back as Kat made her call. "Where we going to, sir?" Deacon gave him the address.

"Oh, the Japanese palace, I've always wanted to see the place. Do you guys live there?"

"See!" she teased. Deacon shook his head, and she went back to her phone call. "So, we'll see you around four ish?" She paused to listen. "Uh huh, OK, terrific and tell Sara mommy loves her. Bye."

****

The attractive woman with the motor scooter was watching from across the street as the diplomatic motorcade paused at the intersection of Via Vittorio Emanuele Orland and Via Parigi. Friday afternoon traffic was always heavy and had backed up for a great distance behind the motorcade.

One of the two lead motorcycle police peeled off and hurried beyond the hotel to block the oncoming cars from the east. The other remained to block the traffic coming from the south.

The two officers following the procession, stopped on the crosswalk at the corner of the hotel to block off the traffic behind the procession. That small part of Rome was not thrilled with diplomatic privilege.

A small group had gathered with her to see what all the fuss was about, but elsewhere, Romans couldn't have cared less.

With the streets secured, three black sedans turned left and proceeded up past the narrow island of trees that separated the street from the hotel. They turned left again onto the driveway at the side entrance to the St. Regis Hotel, Rome.

The cars stopped at the Diplomatic Entrance under the shade of the large plane trees, positioning the middle car, a Mercedes limousine with a French flag fixed prominently on the front fender. Security personnel jumped out of their cars in front and behind and moved into position around the official's car. Their automatic weapons were held in their right hands out of view under their jackets.

Two impeccably dressed men in white tie and tails hurried out of the building to greet their important guest.

The elder man stepped down to the narrow curb and bowed smartly as the minister stepped out of the car. She couldn't help smiling when she saw Desrosiers. He looked like a ridiculous old Marabou stork in a three-piece suit and a Homberg.

M. Gérard Desrosiers, France's exalted Minister of Defense was a pompous, arrogant ass. He was from a very old family that traced its roots back to pre-revolutionary aristocracy who somehow escaped the guillotine. The right-wing population of France seemed to have changed their minds about the value of such people.

Fortunately for Madame Desrosiers, she no longer traveled with him on these trips.

Having seen what she came for, Hedda gracefully mounted her Vespa and tucked a lock of blond hair behind her ear, tightened the scarf under her chin and sped off.

The call that would begin the destructive chain of events would come from the concierge that evening.

***

Back in the 50s, when the city was called 'Toronto the Good,' bar windows were blacked out so passersby couldn't see the people with loose morals inside drinking. You couldn't drive a truck, buy a drink, or go to a movie on a Sunday where they rolled up the sidewalks at 6:30. And the neighborhood now known as Don Mills was a horse farm owned by millionaire E. P. Taylor.

As the city became the 'Big Smoke,' that farmland transformed into the suburb and other millionaires built mansions in a neighborhood called the Bridal Path. It all used to seem so far out of town but in no time it too was surrounded by the expanding GTA (Greater Toronto Area). Then, along came multi billionaire, Deacon Loats. The reason for this amazing project was grief brought on by the loss of the woman he loved.

The same grief that gave us India's Taj Mahal and Toronto's Casa Loma.

He thought Kat had died in a terrible gun battle while protecting him. Deacon bought up a large portion of the land owned by Toronto's super-rich and tore their monster homes down. The land was then sculpted and transformed into a private park with a lake, ponds and streams. Near the center of it he built his palace, a revised version of the famous historic Rokuon-ji (鹿苑）Deer Garden Temple and Kinkakuji (金閣寺）Golden Pavilion, which was built for the shogun, Ashikaga Yoshimitsu, back in the 14th century.

As luck would have it (and Deacon certainly had his share of good fortune), he discovered that Kat was alive and living with her baby daughter Sara in Toronto. Their reunion changed the tone of the palace. It became a celebration of their lives together, except for except for the fact that they weren't actually living together .

Their cab arrived at a security hut, build into the wall at the north gate. The guard pressed a button to open the gate to let them in. The cab driver was amazed to see that is wasn't as big as everyone had thought. Instead, it had a quiet, peaceful Zen-like quality and was extraordinarily beautiful.

Janet met them at the front door. "Hello, Ms. Fernando. Dr. Loats, I received a call from Jim. He said he'd have Sara and Rose here at about four."

"Thanks Janet. Anything else?" asked Deacon, as Kat joined him.

"Yes, Rod Bartel from the London office wanted to speak with you. At your convenience, it's not urgent, and there are some messages for you, I left them on your desk."

"Thanks, I'll call Mr. Bartel tomorrow." He peeled off his shoes.

Kat left her shoes with Deacon's in an open cupboard at the entrance and stepped into the stone floor of the ante room.

"Have you planned anything for dinner, Janet?"

"I thought of doing something simple. How does roast chicken sound?"

Kat answered for him. "That sounds perfect."

"Wonderful. I'm going shopping, I should be back ..." she looked at

Deacon for a clue and got one, "in about two hours. I hope you will be able to find something to do while I'm gone."

Slightly embarrassed by her inference, Deacon said, "Uh … thank you Janet. Don't let us keep you."

Kat winked at her, and she hurried off smiling to herself.

Alone at last they made their way through the house to Deacon's bedroom which overlooked the lake.

They kissed in the open doorway to the veranda, with the magnificent pavilion in the background. Slowly, they began to move their bodies together, dancing without music.

When they parted Kat continued the dance undoing the buttons of her blouse. He backed away from her to watch. She followed, making him feel the momentum of each button's release as if it was pulling him closer. He took a step towards her, but she held him back with a gesture.

"No touching."

The last button was undone, setting the blouse free and as it rolled off her shoulders, she watched him melt a little more. He licked his lips.

How wonderful, she thought. To have him want me so much. The sleeves fell from her arms and the silk shirt floated to the floor. Sliding her hands across her breasts she pinched the shoulder straps of her bra and slipped them to the side.

His groan of excitement sounded more like a whimper.

She reached behind her and undid the hooks and held the bra in place for a moment, knowing how eager he was to see her. Her sexy, come hither smile stoked the fire within him.

He groaned, again, and she almost giggled, enjoying his desire. First, she revealed one side, just a peek, shedding the garment as if in slow motion, having more fun teasing him than he was having being teased.

There was no need to wonder what he was thinking.

As each item was released his eyes would follow its progress to the floor just like a cat would watch its fluttering prey.

She took a step closer to him until their bodies almost touched. She waited, staring into his eyes, daring him to do something, but he couldn't move. "What's the matter?"

"What do you mean?"

"You still have your clothes on."

"Oh-god … Uh… I uh…"

"Never mind, I'll help you." Her hands moved to his belt. He backed up unexpectedly. She hesitated. "What's wrong?"

"Nothing. It's just that …"

"What?"

"Sometimes when you look at me like that, it scares me silly."

"How am I looking at you?"

"Like a tiger stalking her prey."

Her smile intensified. "You know something?"

"No, what?"

"I am."

***

Reaching the landing, the day manager, Signore Faletti, moved to the oversized glass paneled doors which he and Signor Negi held open. The security men hurried forward to secure the passage as Desrosiers and his private secretary followed. Once again, Signore Faletti scuttled ahead to call the elevator and hold the door for his guest.

The Minister and his secretary, Mademoiselle Simøne Ferrara, rode up with Faletti and two guards while the other two remained in the hallway to cover their exit. When the door slid open at the fifth floor, one the bodyguards drew his weapon. One stayed with the minister while the other went with Faletti to inspect and secure the suite. "I assure you sir, everything is quite safe and secure.

No one has been inside since housekeeping prepared the room."

The housekeeper hadn't said a word to anyone about the Secret Service visit yesterday.

"Nevertheless, I will do my job. Please remain here while I look around."

"Of course, Signore."

After clearing the rooms, the guard allowed Faletti to escort M. Desrosiers and his secretary into his suite. When the minister was settled in, the young woman left him and went to her room next door. She had work to do to prepare for the upcoming meetings and wasn't expecting to see him again until then. The elevator returned to the main floor where the two security guards had taken their positions. Their duty was to ensure that no unauthorized people could enter. The remaining six men boarded the lift with the luggage and rode it to the Minister's floor. They took up positions on either side of the door next to two large Venetian glass vases. On the other side of the hall the second pair took the luggage inside and then stood out in the hall guarding the door. The last two took their positions by the doorways to the stairs at opposite ends of the floor.

***

The Concierge's phone rang. The caller was Richard Perrin, head of security for the minister and the nature of the call was just what Righetti expected it would be. "Of course, sir," he said, with his usual confidence, "I will take care of it for you."

"See to it that it is the woman I asked for." Perrin's rules were simple. When making the arrangements, don't mention any names, make sure the woman was punctual, and no changes; that was crucial. But there was a problem. Righetti fumbled with the coil of his telephone. "Sir," he cleared his throat, "there is one slight change…"

A former Legionnaire, Perrin had earned his battle scars in Algiers. He was as hard as steel, quick to anger and violent.

Righetti described his voice as being as coarse as desert sand and seasoned with scorpion venom. He had a vocal range that could be heard over a sandstorm and then drop all the way down to a whispered curse. According to him, there were few things quite as threatening as hearing that man speaking quietly, and that was just what he was doing now. "We agreed that there would be no changes."

"Yes, we did but…" Righetti's gut twisted as he tried to avoid sounding panicked. "Signore Perrin please, this was just one of those unavoidable situations. His usual hostess is not available and…"

"I have told you about this before. I will not accept substitutions."

"Yes, yes, I know. But I have not failed you yet, have I?"

"Your point?"

"I have found a lady that fits his requirements perfectly … and in fact, I believe that she is at least five levels of quality higher than Cl-… ah… than his usual companion."

"Alright, but remember this, if he is not happy, I will bring his complaint to you personally." Truthfully Righetti knew that when he used the pronoun '*he*', he wasn't talking about his boss. Perrin didn't care what the old shit wanted.

"I guarantee that he will be delighted."

"We shall see, Signore," he said, managing to make that sound like his life hung in the balance. The line was disconnected. Righetti returned the receiver to its cradle as if it might bite him. Drumming his fingers on his desk he cursed the day he said he would meet with that woman. How could he have let himself put his life on the line for a hooker?

✳✳✳

Gérard Desrosiers could have stayed at his country's Embassy where he would be safe and could have saved the French government a small fortune. But he was a man of insatiable appetites. He preferred the fine

27

old hotel with its gracious décor, and a resourceful young concierge with old-world discretion.

It was the words *Diplomatic Entrance* that he relied on. They not only described how the hotel's special guests were greeted but also the way in which the 'entertainment' was discretely escorted in. He sat in a golden upholstered chair closed his eyes and fantasized about his evening with Clarissa. Hedda sat on the window ledge with Clarissa's ancient cat curled on her lap. Absent mindedly, she stroked the back of his boney neck and he purred happily. For Hedda's part, she enjoyed the sensation of his soft fur on her fingertips. Feeling very much in control, she smiled contentedly.

She gazed out at the city knowing with some regret that the time was almost at hand, and she had only just discovered a new sensation. What would her life be like if she could have lived as simply as this?

To have a comfortable place to live, in such an enchanted vibrant city, would be idyllic. Wouldn't it be wonderful to have nothing more serious to think about than to be sweet, and pretty, flexible, and pampered? She was feeling comfortable and remarkably relaxed in Clarissa's small but tastefully furnished Via Treviso apartment. It reminded her of the house in Spain where she was born. In fact, she hadn't felt like this since she was a teenager.

For the moment, the purring cat was the perfect companion.

The sound of approaching voices drew her attention to the street below. Two middle-aged women carrying groceries, stopped to gossip on the street below her window. She looked down supposing that these women were Clarissa's neighbors. They were near her Vespa and that sexy old Alpha Spyder she bought for this one night. As their conversation continued, their shadows stretched down the sidewalk and eventually spilled over onto the street. They tossed stories back and forth about their grandchildren, their useless husbands, the unbearable heat, the price of bread, and the state of the neighborhood.

She had never been a part of a conversation like that, though years ago when out shopping with her mother in the nearby town of Nerja, she remembered hearing women babble on just like that.

The mundane acts of everyday life generally meant nothing to her, but there were the odd times when she either found it informative, or entertaining.

A noisy pigeon landed on the ledge above her and cooed. The cat lifted his head, looked up and hissed loudly.

One of the women was startled and look up to see her watching them. That brought on an angry response that amused Hedda. The woman knew who lived in that apartment, in fact, all the women in the neighborhood knew what she was. Obviously, their hatred must have been because their husbands knew about the slut from Naples.

"È la puttana," she said to her friend. "Basta!" She made a rude gesture and encouraged her friend to move on.

The insult angered Hedda, and as her impulse to seek revenge awoke, her grip momentarily tightened on the cat's neck, who complained, and the impulse faded. Instead, she just said, "Ciao," and laughed. "Oh, did mean old Auntie Hedda hurt you Clio? I'm sorry."

She resumed gently petting the cat. "Hush little man, there's nothing to worry about; it was just a couple of old hens."

The purring resumed and she turned her gaze back to the cityscape. It was a pleasant evening to watch the sun go down behind the hills spiked with the silhouettes of villas and ancient cypress.

The call would come soon. She was ready, a little excited as well. But until then, she was happy to spend a few peaceful minutes drinking in the view.

✳✳✳

Righetti hung up and sat for a moment staring at the phone as if it might bite him. Forcing himself to follow through, he lifted the instrument and dialed Clarissa's number.

"Buena Sera." Hedda used her most seductively sweet voice.

For some reason that sound made him feel reassured that everything would be alright. "Buena Sera… is that…"

"Why Signore Righetti, who else would it be?" He could feel her smile as she spoke.

"Signorina Franco, your client has invited you to visit him at midnight."

"Wonderful. I shall not be late"

"Good …" He was losing his nerve again. " …but…"

"Calm yourself Signore, there is no cause for concern. We have an understanding, no?"

"Si, it is just that his security man, he is French, you understand? The French are always … difficult.

"Don't worry yourself. I know how to deal with the Frenchman, I will be sure to take care of his concerns. It will all work out perfectly."

"Mille grazie Signorina."

"Not at all, my little chubby friend," she said, and put down the phone. Returning her attention to the cat "Such a lovely old fellow aren't you?" he purred.

***

Righetti decided that he should be elsewhere when Anita Franco showed up. He called the night manager to say he was ill and there would be a substitute for Clarissa. "Her name is Anita Franco." He hung up and left immediately.

At 11:55, Hedda pulled up in her Alpha Romeo Spyder and stopped in front of the Diplomatic Entrance. It was the correct time, so the night manager assumed that this must be the Frenchman's call girl.

Reluctantly, Signore Negi set down the latest Donna Leon mystery, and went out to greet her. "Buena Sera, Signorina." She was hardly what he expected. This undeniably lovely woman was certainly not the well-known Clarissa. For a moment, he stared into her cleavage as she gracefully lifted herself out of the low sports car. But then he was drawn to her dark amber eyes and could not look away.

"Signore…?"

"Negi. uh, Signore Negi. Buena Sera Signorina. Mi scusi, ma chi sei?"

"Oh, has Signore Righetti not spoken to you about me?"

"Uh, Oh si mi scusi. You are the girl who is to replace Clarissa uh…"

"Anita," she paused waiting for the man to catch up, "Clarissa's roommate? She was called away to Switzerland, quite suddenly."

"Oh, is that what happened? He said it was some sort of emergency. This is something that I will have to talk to him about in the morning."

"Oh, I think you two will have a lot to talk about in the morning, Signore Negi." She smiled and showed him Righetti's gold token.

"May I say that this is a welcome surprise, of course." The coin was really all the proof he needed. After smoothing down the jacket of his suit he extended his hand.

She accepted it with a gloved hand, and he affectionately covered it with his left hand, and asked, "Is it just Anita?"

"No, it is Anita Franco." She smiled a coquettish smile, and gave his hand a little squeeze, "I guarantee the name will be quite familiar at the hotel soon, Signore Righetti will see to that."

"As will I. I am delighted to meet you, Signorina Franco." Snapping his fingers, he summoned a young valet who rushed out to remove the car. "For some reason, your name is already familiar to me. Why is that Signorina?"

Anita simply smiled. She dipped her hand into her large shoulder-bag for her wallet, then handed the valet a ten euro note, saying, "You will take good care of it for me, won't you?" The she handed Signore Negi a hundred euros. He smiled broadly and escorted her up the stairs where she was met at the top by two of the minister's security men.

Familiar with the women his employer entertained, the first man was quick to demand. "Signore Negi, where is Clarissa?"

"Out of the country, I'm afraid." He presented Anita as if she was a close personal friend. "M. Hûbert, This is Signorina Anita Franco, Clarissa's roommate. I'm sure your employer will be delighted to meet her. One can never have too many beautiful friends, non monsieur?"

"As you say. Good evening mademoiselle. Do you have it?"

"Oui," she said, and showed the token to him.

"Bien." He promptly lifted her arms up and began searching her from her fingertips to the pit of her arm. "Pourquoi les gants?"

"Do you not find them a little bit arousing, monsieur?"

"Maybe," Hûbert said, and started by rolling down the blue kid leather gloves that covered her arms beyond her elbows.

Finding nothing in them his eyes went straight to her breasts. The sheer blue silk of the dress did little to hide what was beneath.

"Do you think I could hide anything there?" she asked. He shrugged and began to fondle her. "Enough monsieur. Find something else to fondle."

While his partner searched her shoulder bag, Hûbert moved down her body. The partner Sanjib found her negligée. Holding it up he grinned imagining what she'd look like with it on and. "Regarde Hûbert, not bad eh?" Then with a raised eyebrow he checked the change of clothes she brought for the getaway.

Idiot, she removed Hûbert's hands and pushed him away. Anticipating Sanjib's question, she said, "Pour après la fête, Monsieur."

"Bien." The guards exchanged glances before he continued his inspection, looking in her wallet and the small, zippered makeup bag. He checked the hairbrush, presumably for a hidden knife, took the cap off her deodorant stick and smelled it. Satisfied at last he said, "She's clean," and handed back her bag. As she rolled the long blue gloves up again Sanjib touched his earpiece.

The security chief from the exclusive floor answered, "Perrin."

"The woman is here."

"How does she look?"

"She is unbelievable. I think the boss is going to enjoy himself tonight."

"He'd better. I'll be down in a moment."

"Bien." Turning back to her he said, "M. Perrin is coming down to see you."

"How wonderful. I can't wait. Is he as charming as you boys?" She made it clear that she was not amused. In truth, if there was the slightest problem she would attack and kill them all with her bare hands.

Perrin stepped out of the elevator a moment later and took one look at her. Speaking in English he said, "Where did you say Clarissa Aubertin was?"

"I didn't, but she has gone to Switzerland to visit an ailing relative."

"Signore Negi, do you know this person?"

She answered for Negi, again in flawless French. "My name is Anita Franco. I assure you that I can give your minister everything he could wish for."

Ignoring her, he repeated, "Do you know this woman?"

"To be sure I know her well, Signore. In all of Rome, she is the crema della crema." Negi boasted. She smiled seductively.

Perrin studied her for a moment and the guard who groped her enthusiastically nodded his approval. That gesture irked her, making her sorry that the man would not be upstairs to receive the surprise she left for the others. "Very well. Come."

The guards stared as she led the way into the lift and turned around so that they could ogle her one last time. It was a sight they would always remember.

Perrin pressed number 5 and the door closed. Just as the car began to move, he pressed the stop button. Continuing in English, he said, "You are wearing a wig. Why?"

"You have a good eye monsieur. I understand that M. Desrosiers prefers brunettes, I am a natural blond."

"I see." Then looking at her chest asked, "Is there anything else that is unnatural that I should know about?"

"I am wearing contacts, my eyes are actually blue." She took out a contact lens to show him.

He smiled. "Ah-h-h-h. Take the other out. I think he will prefer you as you are."

"You say the sweetest things M. Perrin," she smiled sweetly, then made a show of straightening her dress."

"Are you ready now?"

"I am."

He started the lift again. When the door opened, she took her time crossing the hall imagining how much better she was going to feel when they were all dead.

She looked to the left and right locating each man and was satisfied that they were exactly where she thought they would be.

Perrin knocked, then used his keycard to open the door. Holding it for her, he put on a display of courtesy.

"Merci," she said, and entered the room as if it were her own. She'd already selected a spot in the center of the magnificent Persian carpet she had admired yesterday. Now she imagined what the rug would look like when the job was done and, once again, smiled brightly.

Everything looked just as it had when she did her prep work, but the lighting at night made it seem so much more exotic.

Poised like a dilapidated ancient emperor the mark sat on the gold upholstered armchair, the antithesis of his beautiful surroundings the,. The night lights of Rome twinkled through the window behind him, but even that couldn't improve the look of the man. The moment she placed herself on the carpet before him he shot up from the chair and demanded, "Where is Clarissa?"

"Clarissa was unavailable Monsieur," Perrin replied, in a tone without color, "This one's name is Anita Franco, Monsieur."

Gérard Desrosiers looked at his security chief as if he had spoken out of turn. Then studying her more closely, the old stork changed his body language and tone. "Is it now?"

He sounded intrigued. "Where have I heard that name before?" She instantly tensed as a stream of thoughts raced through her head. There had been a chance that he would have met with Anita, or at least known about her.

If that were so, then she would have no option but to take on the guards now. It was certainly doable, she had defeated men like this before. But the dress was not designed for fighting.

She knew where Perrin's gun was and planned how to take him before he took it from its holster. As soon as she had it in hand the others would not be a problem.

Desrosiers had been watching her intently. He had met the real Anita before but as she was a simply a functionary, all he could vaguely remember was a name from the past with no associations. She took a deep breath and held it. That lifted her breasts, distracting the old man, and the question he had been pondering, was forgotten.

To her enormous relief, he flicked his finger at Perrin as if ridding the room of a mosquito. "Leave us."

She relaxed. Perrin was obviously used to that sort of treatment and left without comment. "Do you like what you see?" she said, very quietly.

"Oh I do, most definitely." His stare seemed oddly hostile, but she realized that it was simply the geography of his face. Like the stork, the eyes showed one expression, that of a creature looking for nourishment. "Come closer so that I can see you better." The translucent gown, the matching shoes and gloves had obviously stirred the loins of the men outside, but they were in rut like a randy bull, and easy to read. This man's emotions were more difficult to decipher. She moved to him.

The change in lighting did the trick, he was able to see that the sheer fabric left little to the imagination.

Desrosiers couldn't take his eyes off her. "That dress is …" he couldn't find the words he was looking for. "Turn for me."

She gave him a profile and then turned around so he could see everything. "Do you like the dress?" She took a deep breath lifting her breasts again. The tighter the material became, the easier it was to see the nipples beneath.

"I do indeed. It is very chic." He stared at her for an uncomfortably long time, then finally spoke. "How does it come off?"

"With a little champagne, everything comes off Monsieur." She turned around and lifted her hair, so that he could see the bow.

"Ah hah, how marvelously simple. Shall I undo it now?"

"No-no Monsieur. You will sit down. While I entertain you."

He collapsed into his chair. "Oh yes, continue."

"Perhaps we could be more comfortable on the sofa and have a little music to heighten the mood."

"Oui."

As he moved to the couch, she selected a recording of Revel's Bolero CD from her purse, it was guaranteed to arouse him. She placed the disc in the machine and pushed play. Before she began to dance, she removed her TV remote from the desk drawer and set it down on the surface. The dance began slowly with the music. She turned lightly following the building tempo. Her skirt billowed out as he imagined Shahrazad's veils had, exposed Anita's beautiful legs. As the music's intensity changed, she moved seductively to the center of the carpet.

As he watched her, his expression was reminiscent of someone who had just suffered a stroke. His eye lids lifted slightly, and his upper lip tightened as he followed her swaying body.

Soon he was humming along. "You are an excellent dancer." She smiled and continued to dance in the center of the room. "But I would like us to get much closer."

"Patience Monsieur, patience." She reached behind her neck and untied the bow. The sight of her naked breasts caused him to jerk forward with his chin on his chest. He could hardly sit still, and his legs began to tremble. She began to wonder if just dancing naked for him would be enough to kill the old bastard.

He was fully aroused his breathing was labored. She intensified her movements, and she drew closer to him. There was a bottle of Champagne in a bucket stand near his chair and crystal flutes on a tray on the side table.

She swayed over to it and taking the bottle she rolled it across her chest then slid it up and down between her breasts.

He was ready to burst as she made a show of opening the bottle with a pop and the champagne splashed up on her. She licked her lips then lifted the bottle high over her chest and placed a glass between her breasts spilling more of the bubbly wine into it, allowing the froth to overflow, and spill over her body.

She leaned towards him letting droplets of the wine fall from her nipples into his mouth. He began to lick at her. "Patience Monsieur, patience."

"Why are you being so cruel?"

She handed him the glass and danced away.

"This is torture Mademoiselle."

"You will appreciate it all the more … when the time is right," she said, catching a dribble on her gloved finger and touching it to her lips.

"You are a wicked-wicked woman, Anita."

"Oh Monsieur, you have no idea how wicked I am."

"Anita." He paused and looked away for a moment. "You know, you do remind me of someone."

She missed a step. "Do I?" She was not prepared to go through that again.

With a wide smile it came to him. "Yes. With those long gloves, and the long hair you remind me of that pretty little nude drawing from the Playboy humor page. All you are missing are the bunny ears." He began to snort like a rutting bull. It sounded revolting and it was all she could do not to sneer with disgust. It had never been her intention to let any part of the old lecher touch her body.

His grasping hands would soon become a problem, so the time had come. "Would you give me a moment to wash this off?"

"No-no, let me lick it off."

"You would like that, wouldn't you?"

"Oh yes, yes I would."

"Well then give me a moment and I will let you pour wine all over me and drink it up to your heart's content," she said, pressing her breasts together and squeezing them. It was sticky and she didn't like the feeling at all. With that tantalizing teasing she backed away to the bathroom. He tried to speak but once again, words failed him. As she spun though the opening she said theatrically, "It will all come to you in just a moment." Then closed and locked the door.

She washed the wine off her chest, retrieved the gun and affixed the silencer. As she dressed in the street clothes, he began banging on the door. "Anita, what is taking you so long?"

"Patience, my love."

"I have been patient Anita and I am tired of being patient!"

"I will be just a moment. Would you do me a favor?"

"Anything, if it will get you out of there sooner."

"How sweet you are. Will you remove your clothes and stand in the middle of the carpet?"

"I am already undressed."

"Perfect, now go to the center of the carpet and close your eyes." She unlocked the door and came out, wearing the summer dress and pumps. Still wearing the gloves, she held the shoulder bag in her left hand and behind her back was the gun in her right hand.

"Now you can look." The moment he saw her his face went blank.

"What the devil is this? Wait, Anita Franco, of course, she was that American Colonel. I met her in The Hague, what was her name …?"

"Anita, you old, fool." She brought up the gun and fired a shot that removed that offending little member between his legs. He screamed, then she sent two more hollow points into his head. He tipped back, and fell flat on his back, landing in the mess that was once his brain.

She was right. It did make a terrible mess of the carpet.

In no time, Perrin was pounding on the door. Then joined by the other man they put their shoulders to it.

The heavy oak door threatened to break down. She took cover in the bathroom and pressed 449 on her device.

The building shook slightly as the IEDs exploded in the hall. The door burst open sending the two men into the vestibule. All six men died instantly, their bodies torn to shreds as ball-bearings, glass marbles and fragments of the glass vases spread throughout the kill zone. She put the remote control in her bag and zipped it up.

The fire alarms sounded, and the sprinkler system switched on spraying freezing cold water everywhere.

As Hedda left the room, Simøne Ferrara emerged from her room. Wiping the water from her eyes she stepped out into the carnage.

Anita quickly lifted her gun and fired hitting her in the nape of her neck dropping her like a stone.

Hedda tossed her gun back into the room and quickly padded over the sloppy carpeting to the fire exit.

Once in the stairwell, she joined the other guests as they ran down to the main floor, all cold and soaked to the skin. None of them had any idea what had happened, and never gave her a second thought.

She stripped the long gloves off and sent them into the bag with everything else. As she made it to the ground floor, the men guarding the ambassador's elevator were on their way up to find out what had happened. By the time they discovered the massacre, she was in the street. Perrin and the dead guards on the fifth floor were the only ones to see her as she really was. No one would be looking for a blond, blue eyed tourist.

Emergency vehicles, fire, police and ambulances began arriving from all directions. As part of the flood of guests being escorted to the far side of the street, the police paid no attention to her.

Hedda crossed to the parking lot and with the distracted crowd watching the unfolding drama at the hotel, she deposited her bag into a dustbin chained to a drainpipe.

Anita the assassin, had struck again, then vanished leaving nothing but a gun, bodies and chaos behind as she had done so many times before. Hedda Jäger left Clarissa's apartment neat and tidy making sure that the cat had some food and water, then she hopped into a taxi and headed for the airport. At 2:00 am, as she boarded the plane, the remote control in the bag containing her costumes burst into flames.

****

Chapter ~3

Edward and Hedda's father had told them this story a dozen times or more. "Have I ever told you the story about how we came to Nerja?"
Yes Father.
So, it began just after the war, I remember it so clearly, as if it were just yesterday, he would say. Eventually it became a tradition with him as he wasted away from drink and depression. He repeated it so many times that when he had drifted off to sleep the children could pick it up from where he left off, reciting it word for word.

"It was April, the 18, a terrible day, children, you can't imagine how bad it was in 1945. Simply to find something to eat, anything, the taste of the glue from the back of the wallpaper. There were fourteen starving people to feed, and we had to go out at night to steal food. It was the last time I saw my mother. She did not want me to go, but Rupert said I was a man, nearly seventeen and should have been in the army defending Germany. There was no one else well enough to come with me.

"She finally relented and wrapped her coat around my shoulders. At first, I refused to take it, but she insisted. I remembered how strong she was. My older brother Ähern was too weak to go.
He had a birth defect and mother hid him from the Nazis because he was not normal. His head was too big for his body. Rupert wanted to get rid of him, but mother wouldn't hear of it.

There were no tears when we left, just a kiss good-bye, as she returned to the huddle to keep warm.

"With only the pale moon to light to show the way my father and I set out. It was a cold, damp and dangerous journey that only father and I were strong enough to make. My father's name was Rupert. That is what I called him, Rupert Jäger. He had been away fighting the war for so long that when he finally made it home, I did not know him. He frightened me.

"Leaving the Soviet controlled Eastern Section, we crossed the bombed-out city, keeping out of sight. The Soviet soldiers were monsters who would kill any Germans they found wandering the streets at night. We avoided them at all cost. Then there were the English, the French and the American soldiers patrolling the streets and manning the check points. They weren't much better, but sometimes we could steal from their garbage.

"That night your grandfather carried a suitcase that we hoped to fill. We had heard rumors that the Americans had more food than they could use and would share with us. We didn't know if it was true, and we searched all night trying to find where these generous soldiers were."

The next part of the story was not his to tell, but it happened, and this was how it went.

Germany had been split in two by the Soviet Military Administration in Germany. West Germany under Allied occupation and East Germany under Soviet authority.

The Soviets created an ever increasingly hostile barrier between them. Churchill called it the iron curtain, and nothing got through. The Soviet Military Administration instituted the Beria-order No. 00315 and Soviet soldiers began arresting people at random.

They said it was because of alleged ties with the Nazis, or that they were anti-Communist hindering the establishment of Stalinism.

Without a trial, they were taken to Buchenwald, a Nazi concentration camp that the NKVD called a special filtration camp. The Soviets denied the camps even existed and inmates were permitted no contact with the outside world, so they became known as the Silence Camps.

"I remember heading home in the daylight with the empty suitcase when American soldiers stopped us at the barrier. We had no idea that anything had happened until that moment. They had split Germany in half, and we would never be able to cross to the other side. Rupert took me back into the western half and found a place to live. Rumors began to filter through. Life was not so good on the other side. We heard stories of the Russian camps where Nazi sympathizers had been taken that were as bad as they were when Germany ran them for the Jews."

Until Ähern arrived to tell his story, Peter thought that his mother and Ähern had made do much the same way that they had.

The reality was a terrible shock and there was small comfort knowing that there was nothing he could have done had he known the truth. As he told it, somehow Ähern had managed to keep them together during those first horrendous months in the prison. But the conditions were so poor that their mother became ill and eventually died of starvation. He said he was there by her side protecting her till the end.

What he left out was that while he did whatever he could to ingratiate himself with the Russian guards and won many concessions from his Russian guards, his mother was not willing to turn on her own people. Ähern told her she was a fool and let her die.

Having provided the Russians with anything they wanted he was given everything he needed. He turned eighteen in 1948, and as a birthday gift he was released and given a low-level government job. He showed promise and steadily worked his way up.

Peter's story continued from 1952 when Rupert heard of work to the south and moved with Peter to Stuttgart and found jobs at the Mercedes-Benz factory.

"Rupert bought a house and he and I planted a garden to grow vegetables and fruit. Rupert renewed friendships with some of the soldiers from his old unit. I was never a part of their group, so I didn't know what they talked about. They met in secret in the basement to reminisce about the glory days of the Nazi Party."

Peter knew full well what his father was doing, but he kept quiet like the rest of Germany, everyone kept quiet.

Ähern arrived unexpectedly in 1958. He said he had gained a great deal of freedom as he worked for the East German government and finally was able to track them down. Peter was stunned to learn of the agony Ähern and his mother had endured. On the other side of the reunion, Ähern knew quite a bit about how things faired in Stuttgart and was angered by the comparative luxury they had managed to build. The small house and garden were so far beyond anything he could have had in the East, and it made him bitter beyond reason.

Ähern's joyous reunion was nothing more than a pantomime. He swore that the tables would turn some day and he would make his father and brother suffer as much as he had.

"I was overjoyed that Ähern had survived and was able to join us, but his stories of their suffering in the concentration camp made me feel guilty. Ähern confessed that the only work he could get was with the communist government. Eventually, he earned the privilege to cross over to the west to visit us. He said his visit came at a great personal cost, but it was worth it to see us and know how well we were doing. He said, it was the greatest thrill of his life, but I am saddened to say that it was a lie."

Ähern failed to mention what government department employed him; the importance of his position in the department that allowed him to own an apartment just for himself.

Nor did he mention the type of work he was doing that gave him the freedom to cross into West Berlin and elsewhere whenever he liked.

"Our easy life changed without warning when a Nazi hunter from Israel was given Rupert's name in connection with Hitler's teenage division of the SS death squads. I had no idea that that was what he did near the end of the war. The boys he pressed into such terrible service for the

Führer had been my age. I suppose it was my mother's influence that made Rupert pass me by. Those boys who survived would have to live the rest of their lives with the shame of what they had done. "The man arrived at our door with the police and an arrest warrant. They took Rupert and his friends away and, one by one they were put on trial for war crimes. Rupert's death sentence was commuted to a life sentence. He became ill and died alone in his cell after only serving two years of that sentence.

"It didn't matter how the Nazi hunter had found him so easily. When I learned the truth about what Rupert had done, I was glad that justice had finally found him.

"I stayed in the house alone and carried on at the factory. Ähern came to visit often and before too long I suspected what he must have been doing. Ähern was a spy working for the GDR, I was sure of it, but he had become very opinionated and overbearing and I became too frightened to say anything to him."

In fact, Ähern was more than a spy for the GDR, so much more. While they were confined in the camp his true nature was given a chance to emerge. Without the slightest twinge or remorse, he became an informant. He claimed that his only wish was to offer his life in the service of the Soviet administration. To prove his loyalty, he identified the so-called 'Nazi war criminals' who were hiding amongst them. Turning on his own people convinced the Russians that he was a committed Stalinist. As a reward, he was permitted to join the ranks of the Stasi, GDR's secret police. He was ruthless and by the time of his first visit to Stuttgart had quickly worked his way up to captain, a position of importance and privilege. He continued to gain momentum and used his growing power to extort and murder.

He created an organization that spread beyond Germany into the Soviet Union. He bought legitimate businesses in oil and gas production, machinery and weapons manufacturing through entrapment, extortion and murder and eventually became a German Oligarch. While Ähern had become cruel and hard, Peter remained a gentle man.

"I met your mother in Stuttgart. She was so beautiful, Hedda you are just like her. What I loved about her was that she was uncomplicated, she said what was on her mind and we were happy. When Metra and I got married we decided to leave Germany and move to some place warm. We chose Spain and with my savings and the sale of his house, we purchased this land on the Costa del Sol, where we could look out and see the Mediterranean Sea."

***

Kat was up early for her run. She returned, glistening with sweat and slipped silently back into her apartment to shower. She dressed in street clothes and then joined Sara and Rosario for breakfast. It was waffle day, Sara's favorites.

As usual, the princess led their breakfast conversation, and she decided that they should all go for a walk to St. James Park.

They had lunch in a restaurant next to the St. Lawrence Market then Kat left them at home and went to a meeting with the foundation lawyer. She learned that the owner was happy to sell at four hundred thousand over asking. It looked like it was a done deal and all they needed to do was get through the paperwork. Kat decided to let her lawyer deal with it. Deacon was at his office building off Dundas and called to see if she could join him for coffee. "I'm on Bay Street, where would you like to meet?"

"How about that coffee bar over on Richmond St.?"

"You mean, *Appelle-moi?*"

"That's the one."

"OK. I'll see you there."

The cab driver was talking to a friend on the phone in Arabic, so she listened, but only because it had been some time since she had heard the language. They were talking about a terrorist attack on a hotel in

Rome. "No-no-no, it was not Al Qaeda, Hajji, I told you, it was some crazy white woman. Don't get all upset…" Kat was no longer interested in the details of terrorism, so it went in one ear and out the other.

She met Deacon and the talk quickly turned to the dojo building. She filled him in on the visit to the park and the latest miracles that Sara performed. As always, Deacon listened with the patience of Job. After all, Sara thought of him as her father, and he adored her.

When she had told him all about her morning Deacon asked Kat if she had heard anything about the attack in Rome. "Well, I heard the cab driver talking about it. Apparently, a woman was involved somehow."

"They say she was acting alone and that it wasn't a terrorist attack, it was an assassination. She blew up half the hotel to get the Defense Minister from France."

"Desrosiers?"

"Yeah, that was the guy's name. Did you know him?"

"I met him once, in the Hague. He was an unpleasant bastard. I'm not surprised that someone wanted him dead."

"It's stood Europe on its collective ear."

By the end of the day Kat was exhausted and declared that she was going to bed early. As she slept soundly, the 11:00 o'clock news carried the developing story from Rome.

"And now a special report from CBC's foreign correspondent, Phyllis Daniels in Rome."

"Thank you, Peter. Authorities here in Rome are stumped following the assassination yesterday, of the French Minister of Defense, Gérard Desrosiers. Witnesses questioned at St. Regis Hotel reported that they had actual contact with the woman calling herself Anita Franco, and positively identified her from police photos.

"You may remember Gérard Desrosiers' name mentioned in connection with a multi-national coalition, formed by Interpol in 2009, to stop a murderous, terrorist threat against Americans in Europe. The efforts of the coalition culminated in an unprecedented American military missile strike on the Italian mountaintop fortress belonging to the self-proclaimed leader of the EU, German billionaire, Ähern Jäger.

"Authorities are now connecting the murder of General Mario Giancarlo in Genoa, also part of that Interpole Coalition. Eyewitnesses in that case have also identified Anita Franco as the assassin.

"The name Anita Franco first hit the headlines in 2005, as a minor celebrity, following the accidental drowning of her millionaire husband, Paulino Franco, on their wedding day. Suspected of his murderer, she was detained by Ibiza authorities, but later released and cleared of any wrongdoing.

"After inheriting her husband's millions, she went on a European shopping spree with the media following her every move. Spanish newspapers nicknamed her the Happy Widow of Ibiza. Her lavish spending ended in Berlin, when she disappeared at the same time as German crime boss, Delph Petrus, was assassinated.

"Police have a video from the Petrus estate's security camera which they refused to make public. Then, an unnamed source at Interpole revealed that the recording clearly shows that the assassin was in fact Anita Franco. Working alone he said, she overcame his security people with frightening ease and then murdered Petrus and his staff. The video also shows that she was mortally wounded during the attack.

Though her body was not recovered experts claimed that she could not have survived such a wound. The investigation was closed.

"Political experts say that the Kremlin is applying pressure to keep the incriminating video under wraps. The man who released the story has returned to say that he had found a section of the video that was thought to be deleted.

What Putin wanted to hide was that Anita Franco had a backup team. Russian SF soldiers landed before she arrived at the compound and took out the Petrus security force guarding the estate clearing the way for Anita Franco to murder the German crime boss. When she was wounded, they evacuated her from the scene."

"Phyllis, where does the investigation of the Desrosiers murder stand now?"

"Peter, when put together with evidence collected in Rome this amazing added information lends credence to the theory that Anita Franco is alive and back in the business of political assassination and may be working for Russian President Putin. Authorities are taking no chances, a continent-wide search is on for her now. Peter."

"Thank you, Phyllis. Phyllis Daniels in Rome. In other news…"

***

It was late evening when Hedda drove the 1985 Ford Europa up the Av. De Andalucía. It had been a long, exhausting flight from Rome to Malaga and then the drive home along the coastal road. At the north end of Nerja, she turned away from the Med., heading up into the foothills of the Sierra Nevada mountains.

She had been up and down that mountain road so many times as a child, she could close her eyes and see every curve. She could picture the young artists, refugees from Rhodesia, that lived just there on that bend in the road. All of the old milestones that once lined the road were gone because of them, Belinda and Arthur Helmsley. Arthur had confessed to her that the stones were perfect for carving, and he had taken them all.

Then there was the English writer further up the road, Hal Fotheringham a friend of Hedda's father. He had taken her to visit Mr. Fotheringham several times. He was a nice old man who read magical stories to her and Edward.

They were all gone now, the artists, their houses, all the people who remembered those times. All gone but her.

She looked up and could see the white walls of Fragiliana's old buildings huddled together above the terraced fields and gardens. It was a place steeped in history, from the time when the Romans arrived in the 19th century BC and then the Moors here from 711 until they were driven out in 1492 with the fall of Granada.

Her father used to go on at length about how Fragiliana was the last of the Moorish villages to fall during the Uprising and then survived the Reconquista. She loved the history of it all and because of those stories, history became the focus of her life. But now she was disturbed by what Fragiliana had become. It had been changed forever by developers and none of it, as far as she was concerned, was for the better.

Her parents had come to this part of Spain, the Costa del Sol, from Stuttgart. He chose a bit of land in the valley below the ancient village and built the house she grew up in. He called it Villa de las Palomas, and planted an orchard of orange and pomegranate trees. She and Edward, her older brother, loved everything about it. They loved the rawness of it all, from the tanned earth of their farm to the jagged mountains behind them and the stark blue sky over the Med.

Apart from her house and the orchard, everything had changed. Her parents, her brother, her uncle and the carefree life she had known, all gone. There were many to blame for that, like that sickening Frenchman in Rome. There were so many things she could have done with her life instead of this, but it had become her mission to make them all suffer. There was one person who deserved to be punished more than any of the others. First, that woman had to be tormented to distraction, utterly destroyed emotionally. Then the ultimate revenge would be to have her terminated by her own people.

Hedda used the assassin's name so that her guilt would be written across the sky, so that there would be no place on earth for her to hide. When Hedda was done, Anita Franco would rot in hell.

The narrow, winding road that led up the mountain to the sleepy little village, was a highway now. As Hedda drove around the new traffic circle to take the western fork, her head ached and all she could think of was how tired she was. She turned left again, off the main road and stopped to pick up a cardboard tube that lay by the side of the road and tossed it onto the seat beside her.

The car moved over the lip of the hill, then turning off the engine she shifted into neutral and let it roll quietly down into the valley following the trail that took her home. Thanks to her, the pavement ended at that trail. She refused to allow her road to change.

The old Ford kicked up a faint cloud of red dust as her headlights picked out the white stucco walls of her home. Like the old car, the house her father built was a sort of time capsule, a reminder of her childhood. Memories of family vacations spent in the foothills, and weekends on the small beaches of Nerja haunted the place. Her innocence and all her childhood joys were wrapped up in that place. The woman she might have been, the things she might have done, all of it had been stolen away by family tragedy and Cold War politics.

Stepping inside that house was like stepping through a portal into a world where those childhood joys still existed. Then, Nerja was a small town, about eleven thousand people. Like most of the towns and villages along the coast, it had a thriving German community. They spoke German, read German newspapers, ate in German restaurants and shopped in German shops.

There were other nationalities too, virtually closed off in their own little ghettos. The largest was probably the English one. But those other communities, including the core of Spaniards, could have been on another planet as far as the Germans were concerned.

For their part, the Spaniards were just as happy to maintain the ghettos. They were not fond of foreigners at the best of times. In their own fashion, they tolerated them but did not accept them.

Within limits, they tolerated the intrusive cultural peculiarities, ignorance and bad manners. But they vehemently resisted integration.

Resist! That, she thought could have been a Spanish motto. It was something she totally understood now.

That resistance, her father explained, radiated from the Spaniards in rings of isolation. Like a closed matryoshka, the Russian nesting dolls, outsiders could never get near the core. The outsiders held little interest for them. The Spaniards were fine, so long as the outsiders stayed outside.

Hedda's father fervently believed that he could be the exception. Through positive effort, he would be allowed to assimilate. And, for a time, he believed that he'd succeeded. But no matter how fluent his Spanish was, or persistent his efforts were to be one of them, he would always be German. Spain was for the Spaniards.

That was the thing that broke him down, the realization that he would always be a foreigner.

What ended Peter's life was the cumulation of tragedy, the death of his wife, the constant harassment, and the disloyalty of his brother. The final blow was when Ähern stole his children away. She and Edward went with him willingly because her father was weak. She stopped at the gate and wondered why she kept the place. Was it to show her father that she was stronger than he? That she could survive where he could not. Was she that sentimental? After entering the coded sequence to disarm the security system, then a second sequence which opened the gate, she drove into the compound. The precautions were necessary as Hedda expected to be attacked sooner or later. The defenses she had installed were deadly. There was a sign on the gate in ten languages, Danger, do not enter. If someone tried to get in without turning off the security system, they were going to die.

Leaving the car at the side of the house she slowly set her feet on sand, stood up and stretched. "Reach for the stars," Her father would say, "and grow big and strong."

It had been a while since she had begun her campaign. It was a struggle she could win and now she had. Her attack in Rome had been successful, the name Anita Franco was writ large around the world. All she had to do now was step back and let the world collapse on the woman's head. It should have felt good to be home again, to be surrounded by the warmth of familiar things.

But it didn't.

"Hedda-a-a-." A voice called out from the dark.

She turned. "What?"

She thought she heard something, someone calling her name. Was it a man's voice? "Edward?" Hedda shouted, then paused waiting for an answer. "Is … is that you, Edward?"

She heard the voice again, He-e-e-dd-a-a-a.

"Yes?" she said, breathlessly. She listened for it again but there was nothing. "I hear you, Edward. Edward … are you there?"

In the silence that followed, all she heard was the sound of the wind rushing down the mountainside.

"Fuck! I must be losing my mind."

She unlocked the house and carried her things inside. The cardboard tube contained a copy of the International Herald Tribune for Monday, April 16. She placed it on the hall table and put her suitcase by the stairs. After getting a cold San Miguel from the fridge, she tipped it into a tall glass. Returning to the table to collect the paper, she continued to her office. A few moments later her computer began to purr, and the monitor lit up. Hedda drank the beer and stared at the newspaper. Its delivery meant that the paper contained a job offer. She didn't have to take it, but she did have to respond.

So Siggi, what do you have this time? She settled into her chair, brushed a lock of hair from her eyes and took a sip of beer. Putting the glass aside she quickly stripped the pages away discarding everything but the Classifieds. Then sliding her finger down the entries in the personals, she scanned for her personal message.

Her finger stopped on an item in the third column. "Ah-hah, there you are." It began, 'My darling daughter.'

'My darling daughter, Elizabeth C. London. All is forgiven. We miss you, please call home.'

The coded message meant that a contract was offered from someone outside her organization. The name Elizabeth referred to England, the C told her that the contract was from a civilian, and London told her where the target could be found. 'We miss you' meant that the contract was exclusive, and 'all is forgiven,' told her that the client had been vetted and verified.

She turned to her computer, clicked on the video-phone icon then typed in the address. A few minutes later the connection was made, and she had her second cold beer on the desk beside her. She was trying to decide if she was done with the campaign now. She had accomplished what she had set out to do, Anita was guilty and being pursued by every police organization on the planet. The public was sure she was guilty, and the police would shoot her on sight.

"Hello Hedda."

"Siggi. Why have you sent a contract in England? It doesn't have anything to do with my brother."

Her abruptness alarmed him, but he controlled his expressions. "True, but it is paying a lot of money."

"You know I'm not doing this for the money."

"I know that, but I do. This hit is to settle a domestic dispute."

"I don't care about the money, and I am not interested in domestic disputes."

"My dear Hedda," he said, placing his fingertips together as he began his short lecture. "It is important to include these unrelated contracts to prevent the authorities from spotting the thread that links your chosen victims. Should they discover that, they will move to protect those who remain, and it will be over."

"To that point …"

"You should reconsider, this issue is important. Are you are interested in survival?" It was phrased as a question, though delivered like a threat. She would have challenged him if she had not been so tired. She couldn't be bothered to fight with him now.

"Fine, give me the details."

"The client's name is Samuel Williams-Blake."

Oh God. "A stupid double-barrel name. How very British. He wants to terminate his wife?"

"Exactly, yes."

"What have you got on Mr. Williams-Blake?"

"He lives in London, married for money and he's tired of her now. What he wants is to get out of the marriage and keep her seven-figure bank account."

"And, in your infinite wisdom, you thought I'd be interested in canceling an innocent woman to Enrichen a greedy pretentious husband?"

"If you want to put it that way, yes. You are having a problem with this, why?"

"The nature of my moral dilemma is none of your concern. Tell me about the wife."

"Her name is Sandra Tammering. He says she's having an affair."

"Is that true?"

"Yes, it has been thoroughly researched and verified."

"I would like to know why she's having an affair."

"Now how would I know that?"

"Perhaps your research was not as thorough as you thought."

"Hedda, this is a trivial matter. The fee is one-hundred-thousand euros, be reasonable. Kill the woman, collect the money and move on."

"I don't like repeating myself, Siggi. I don't care about the money. No, this contract does not interest me, I won't do it, move on."

"If you don't, then someone else will and the woman will be just as dead." She stopped to think about it, as Siggi watched impatiently.

"Alright, I'll look into it. What is her address?"

"So, you will do it?"

"I said, I would look into it."

"Very well. But keep in mind that the agency that supplies your information, etcetera, does not run without funding."

"And I would like to remind you that I own the agency, that I pay the bills, and am well aware of our operating costs." She was not pleased with the little worm's attitude.

"Of course," he said, "But there are certain …"

"You said that the money is hers?"

"Yes, she is very wealthy."

"The man she is with now, does he have money?"

"He does, perhaps more than she has. They live on Canary Wharf."

The more Siggi told her the less interested she became. "Where on Canary Wharf, specifically?"

"The fifteenth floor of 1 West India Quay. A large two-story flat. It is in his name."

"Alright, tell me about the client, this …, Samuel Williams-Blake. Does he have an issue with the man she is living with?"

"The man, no. He is not included in this contract. But if you like, I can reopen the negotiations to include him. Would you like me to do that?"

"No. Does the client have any particular date in mind?"

"He requested that it be done as soon as possible."

"Everyone is in such a hurry these days."

"Hedda, will you do it?"

"Siggi! …, I have already given you my answer. Send me the details and include photos of Williams-Blake, his wife … and I should have one of her paramour as well. I'll let you know what I have decided in a couple of days."

"Very well. I will send the information at once," he said, and she closed the connection. He had made her angry. She shut the computer down and went outside for a walk.

Siggi had become increasingly irritating, overstepping his position, beginning to think that he was giving the orders. That was not the case at all. He was a functionary, nothing more, and was thoroughly dispensable. But not yet, there were still names on the list, people who had to pay. This was not why she went into the killing business. These personal squabbles didn't mean anything to her, so why should she get involved?

As she strolled through the orchard, memories of her family flooded her mind. The further she walked, the angrier she became. Angry because her family was gone, angry that Siggi, the insensitive slug, was pushing her. She would push back, there was no doubt about that.

Then this Samuel Williams-Blake business made her angry. Not that she cared about the life of the woman. It would be fitting to end her career as Anita Franco by killing Williams-Blake and Siggi Kraft. That made her smile.

***

When the orchard he had planted came into flower, they had their first child, Edward. Three years later Hedda was born and as they grew, she and Edward were inseparable. Hedda recalled her surprise at seeing her Uncle Ähern for the first time. Though he looked odd, almost grotesque, he was very kind to them and after several visits during the late seventies, both she and Edward became fond of him and remembered those times with great affection.

Usually, he came in the spring and fall when it wasn't too hot and stayed in a small cottage that Peter built for him near the main house. He would visit for a month or so and then be off to who knew where. She was too young to understand, but it was impossible for her father and mother to ignore why he came so often. He was using those visits to expand his business interests in the west, with meetings in Malaga, Marbella and Gibraltar. Peter complained that Ähern's business interests were putting his family in danger.

He resented having his house used as a front for a criminal communist organization. But Ähern was too busy to care. Hedda and Edward found life on the Costa del Sol idyllic. However, in January of 1985, when Hedda was fourteen and Edward seventeen, quite suddenly it changed. It happened on the winding highway to Malaga. A tour bus coming from the east strayed into oncoming traffic, and sideswiped Marta's car sending it over the cliff's edge into the sea. It was a senseless tragedy. She had been the glue that held the family together and her death sucked the joy out of their lives. The loss changed Peter; he drank to forget but it only served to drive a wedge between him and his children. He neglected his responsibilities, and the children became virtual orphans. For a time, they depended on each other for everything. Edward was ashamed of their father and was desperate to be free of him though he couldn't leave Hedda to fend for herself.

Edward had written to tell Uncle Ähern what was happening, and he rushed down to offer his help. Peter resented the intrusion and told him to leave, but Hedda and Edward protested. His arrival was like Christmas in July. He brought gifts, things they could never get in Spain, wonderful food, wine from West Berlin and clothes from Paris. He and Peter argued constantly about what was best for Edward and Hedda. Ähern wanted to take them back to Germany to go to good schools and be proper Germans. Peter refused to consider it and their battle raged for more than a week, until finally Peter had had enough. He forbade Ähern to have any further contact with his children, told him to go away, and never return. Hedda couldn't understand why her father was being so unreasonable. It was obvious to both children that what Uncle Ähern was offering was far better than anything he could give them. As she thought about it later, it seemed that that was precisely the opportunity that Ähern had been waiting for. He countered Peter's dismissal by filing a petition with the courts in Spain and Germany claiming that Peter was an unfit parent. Edward took his side on that point, and Hedda agreed without reservation.

Their father couldn't believe that they could turn against him like that. Especially Hedda, with whom he had such a close relationship. He believed that they had become bewitched by his brother, and perhaps they had been.

They went to live in Germany with their uncle leaving Peter alone and devastated. After they had settled into their uncle's fine house in Berlin with a full staff, their transition from the absent father to the doting uncle was complete. They had never realized that such wealth existed, but soon became accustomed to it.

There was something that neither Hedda not Edward would ever know. The family crisis which appeared to be the result of unavoidable and unfortunate circumstances was far from unavoidable.

The truth however was that Metra's death and Peter's disintegration had been planned down to the timing of the bus on the highway and the excessive drinking. Ähern had almost settled the score with his father and brother by taking the children. Then, in October of 1994, Peter died, an apparent victim of suicide. Distorting the cause of death to suite a certain story line was a skill Ähern had picked up at work. That was the coup de gras, bringing him the justice he been planning since he and his mother were abandoned in Berlin.

Edward immediately regretted what had happened, feeling that it was his fault that Peter killed himself. But it seemed that Hedda felt nothing. It was as if Peter had meant nothing to her and Ähern found that very interesting.

There was one last detail that Ähern wanted to settle to complete the icing on the cake. "I suppose you will want to sell the place as soon as possible," he said.

Hedda bridled. "No! I won't ever sell it."

"Hedda really, Uncle was only..." Edward began.

"No Edward, I don't care what anyone says. It's mine, I was happy there and I want to keep it."

Ähern was astute enough to read her mood and accepted that arguing with her would be counterproductive. It would be more beneficial to be generous. "If that is what you want my dear, then it's yours to do with as you please."

"Good." She felt no sentiment, or gratitude, just acceptance. She had always been loving and generous with her brother and felt it necessary to include him. "It is yours too Edward."

Edward felt the farm would forever remind him of how he failed his father. "No Hedda, it's all yours. I'll never set foot in that place again."

"Fine."

With Ähern 's complete support, Edward went to *Humboldt-Universität zu Berlin* and Hedda attended an expensive private school. He gave them bank accounts, clothes, anything they wanted. She and her brother were beautiful children, tall, blue eyed and blond, and with maturity, Edward would become strikingly handsome and Hedda would grow into the very ideal of Aryan beauty, unlike their uncle.

Over time, as he observed the girl's behavior, he began to see the problem. They shared a similar emotional disconnect, neither being able to respond to the feelings of other people. The older she got the more self-absorbed she became. Often, he would throw jealous barbs subtly disguised as compliments at Hedda. Do you know that the two of you remind me of Richard Wagner's Tristan and Isolde?"

"Do we Uncle?" Hedda would was always eager to hear compliments.

"Oh, absolutely every once in a while, but other times you are just like one of the Valkyries."

"Oh Uncle, what an awful thing to say!" Not surprisingly, while his relationship with Edward blossomed, he and Hedda were becoming emotionally distant. While visually stunning, she was also a remarkably intelligent and talented woman. By the time she entered university she spoke several languages fluently and put that talent to work in her courses. Her primary interest had always been the history of war and *War Through the Ages* became the subject of her doctoral thesis.

Through her studies, she developed a strong and rather unique sense of justice and ethical morality. While her brother was exempt from her increasingly judgmental attitude, Uncle Ähern was not.

Edward had been completely won over by him and was willing to accept anything Ähern said. He was a brilliant student, earning a law degree and a doctorate in economics. Early on, he knew what his uncle was doing and was keenly interested in how the business worked.

On the day he received his degree, his uncle asked him to come to work for him. He accepted immediately.

TALEN was the entity that Ähern Jäger had created to control his vast holdings, both legitimate and otherwise and Edward fit right in. Ähern's ambition to be the Chancellor of Europe captured Edward's imagination. Together they began to map out their campaign to the government palace. The operation needed two things to become successful, first it needed money, lots of it. Second, it needed to be free of American interference. Herr Doctor Edward Jäger became the master planner, working behind the scenes, he orchestrated the ingenious scheme to corner the world's gold market.

Then together they put those resources to work indoctrinating the people who would become the army to oust America from the continent once and for all and they chose the name Rote Faust (the Red Fist).

Unlike her brother, Hedda had no interest in her uncle's business, politics, or his lust for continental domination. All she saw was the public side of Ähern Jäger, the interviews on radio television and in publications. She was too preoccupied with her own interests to associate him with the terrorist activities across Europe, and both he and Edward made sure that it stayed that way.

Perhaps Ähern was too self-involved to worry about Hedda's interests. As long as she didn't present an obstacle to what he and Edward were doing he felt safe in ignoring her. In a very superficial way, he supported her academic career by giving her all the funding she could ever asked for and applauded her field work.

After her doctoral presentation was accepted, she chose to leave Germany and follow her passion for the art of war. She traveled extensively, mostly in the Far East to learn the techniques employed by their civilizations from the beginning to the present. Her doctorate became her key to the treasures locked away in the libraries and museum around the world.

Access to knowledge and situations few people would ever experience. She embedded herself with American combat troops in Afghanistan to experience battle firsthand. Her ambition to immerse herself in her subject went far beyond the academic study of war; she wanted to become a warrior, like the fabled Ninja. She used her wealth to train her mind and body in the art of killing. What she did was of no concern to Ähern or Edward as long as she was out of the way. What he failed to notice was that she was not that far away at all. In the process of studying her new avocation, Hedda began to learn a great deal about her uncle and her wealth allowed her to infiltrate TALEN's activities.

She knew that what they were doing would inevitably fail and the repercussions would put Edward in jeopardy. She attempted to protect him by creating a sort of fifth column within the Kroner Agency, her uncle's intelligence network. Her inside man was a greedy, unscrupulous man by the name of Siggi Kraft.

She was in Greece when the bomb hit the Golden Fortress, killing Edward. There was nothing she or anyone else could have done to save him. As far she knew Uncle Ähern had died in the explosion as well, but she was only concerned with the murder of her brother.

There had to be a way she could avenge Edward's death and it was Siggi who came up with the way she could do it. He knew who killed his former employer Kroner, and he knew that she was responsible for the devastating attack on the mountain at Peredicci. She was going to find Anita Franco and kill her. But Siggi had another idea. He wanted her to kill the people who sent her to kill Edward and blame the assassin for it.

At first it didn't make sense to her. "No. I'll just find the woman and kill her."

"And all you would be doing would be killing one woman. What message would that send?"

"Why do I have to send a message?"

"Because she didn't act on her own."

He didn't care about Anita Franco other than she could be used as a vehicle under his control to continue the idea of European domination. "There were several people involved to make that possible, people high up in their governments. They were the ones who killed your brother. If you want to avenge Edward, then they are the ones who must pay. And wouldn't it be perfect if the woman they hired to kill him was the one who killed them?"

"The world would be out for her blood."

"Exactly. Now, I will find them for you and supply you with the intelligence to get to them. All you will have to do is kill them."

"Oh, is that all?" she scoffed. "How many are there?"

Dozens, he thought, *all the people who got in the way of Jäger obsession.* People that Siggi wanted out of the way to allow him to do the things he wanted to do. Here was his chance to make her work for him. "Never mind that now, I will give you their names. But you must convince the authorities that the assassin is back in business, you must assume her identity. And it would be a good idea to add a few unrelated clients to the list and allow her reputation to grow."

"I don't see how that would help in the slightest."

"On the contrary, that part is vital."

"I won't kill innocent people."

"I hadn't noticed that you cared about other people before. Why the sudden conscience?"

"To kill without reason is barbaric. There is no honor in that."

He almost laughed. "I assure you, Hedda, I would never give you a contract against an innocent human being. We must trust each other in this enterprise. Let me take care of everything."

It was Sigismund Kraft who passed the security recording from Kroner's Glass House the night when Anita Franco stole into the compound and captured Kroner. He showed it to Hedda to sharpen her taste for revenge. It was also instructional, to show how Anita operated.

Of course, there wasn't much of Anita in the video, Hedda understood that part, it was how she was trained to kill. The real education came at the end when Anita forced Kroner to talk. Also, Siggi had compiled a dossier about Anita Franco from her first appearance on the beach at Valencia to the surveillance video of the attack on the hunting lodge where she killed Petrus. He finished off with her first appearance at the Golden Fortress. That was when Hedda's blood turned to ice. After witnessing that, she determined that she would stop at nothing to see that Anita paid for what she had done.

With his guidance and her enormous wealth Hedda had made an outstanding first move. Kraft was a greedy man, the last thing he wanted was for her to stop the killing. Siggi's knowledge of Anita Franco was extensive, and he shared it all with Hedda except for one important detail. He couldn't tell her who Anita Franco really was.

***

Chapter ~ 4

The analysts at Wiesbaden Army Airfield in Germany and at Fort Belvoir in Virginia were going over the information they'd received from the French Intelligence and the findings were disturbing. There had been five assassinations in quick succession since the beginning of the year. Two were prominent civilians, an American in Prague and a judge from Mumbai about to speak in Paris. Two were high ranking intelligence and national security personnel from the Netherlands and Belgium. Then, the most recent murder of the French Minister of Defense. All were obvious political assassinations, but other than Anita Franco's name being linked to each of them, they had no idea what tied them together.

Interpol was working on trying to identify what linked the killings. Wolfson couldn't understand why they didn't get it. He had picked up on that right away. The link was the destruction of Rote Faust. The victims were all active with the Joint Task Force campaign against the anti-American terrorists. The big question that the Europeans seemed to be missing was why was she being so obvious? The motive had to be revenge against the task force, and as Kat was in that task force and now unmistakably retired, there was no way she would have gone after them. He could prove that. Kat was at home in Canada while the assassinations were carried out.

The woman the French identified as his former special agent was a phony, and clearly, she was out to blame her crimes on Kat.

***

As usual, Samuel Williams-Blake left his Mayfair townhouse early morning, to walk his dog, Clifford. They strolled down Berkley Square, then after a long wait for a break in traffic they crossed the street to the sidewalk to head for home. Williams-Blake was a dandy, short and slight, the perfect build to wear Savile Row suits. He was overdressed with an ascot round his neck, a fedora from Woodrow of Piccadilly rakishly tilted over his ear, and brown and white brogue shoes. A handsome looking man, she thought, in a very British sort of way.

His two-year-old standard poodle had as much muscle mass as he and was a bit of a handful on the lead. As he walked along looking up at the ancient plane trees he was unceremoniously jerked to a halt as Clifford paused to sniff, then mark a pole. The dog moved on perhaps a yard or so, when once again Williams-Blake was jerked out of his reveries. Clifford had selected the location to do his business. "Oh! Well done you, Cliffy-my-boy! It's a short walk for us today, thank god."

Dutifully, Williams-Blake stooped and scooped, then holding a hot bag of shit at arm's length, the soon-to-be-single and eligible-man-about-town, searched for a bin in which to dump it. There was one over in the park and he thought about crossing the busy street again, but his mission was abruptly changed. He suddenly noticed a very attractive woman walking toward him. Why hadn't he seen her before this? Thinking that he was the attraction he smiled a casual smile and doffed his cap. She ignored him, for it was the handsome dog Clifford that she was drawn to. The reason for having a dog was that it would be the babe magnet when all else failed. Compared to the dog, Williams-Blake's success rate was abysmal. He pushed the bag through the bars of a wrought iron fence and let it go.

The bag fell with a plop down onto the sub-landing where there was an entrance to a law office. Wiping his hand on his jacket he looked up at her. Pretended she not noticed the disgusting thing he'd just done, she said, "What a lovely doggie." He noted that her accent was German. "What's his name?"

"Uh … it's Clifford actually."

"How sweet, like the big red dog?"

"I suppose so."

"How delightful. Is he friendly?"

"I'm sure he'd lift a paw or two for you." Clifford was very friendly. The beautiful blond woman bent at the knee to pat his woolly head. "Oh, but he is such a sweet thing, isn't he?" Clifford enjoyed the attention, wagging his tail furiously and licking her hand. She stood and looked at Samuel with a rather inviting smile. "Is this your neighborhood?"

He nodded and gazed about, as if to say it was all his. "It is, indeed. I walk around here every day. Say, I haven't seen you before, are you new to the area?"

"I wish, but no. I am from Hamburg. I will be in town for just the weekend."

"Business. or pleasure?"

"You are very nosy." She smiled and stroked Clifford's head. "Always it's business. Lately, I have had little time for pleasure."

"Are you seeking pleasure right now?"

"I am not sure how to answer such a mischievous question. Since I am alone, I walk, but I have come much further than I had planned. My feet are tired, and I was about to take a taxi back to my hotel." She lifted her leg to adjust her shoe. "These heels have become quite uncomfortable."

"Heels were not made for long walks."

"No." she smiled so he hadn't blown his chance yet. He tried again though this time he presented an invitation that sounded less desperate. "You know, a-as it happens, my house is quite close. Yes, and I haven't had my morning tea yet. I wonder if you would like to, well that is to say, …”

“Are you inviting me in for a cup of tea?”

“Very awkwardly to say the least, but yes, that is what I was trying to do. Would you care to join me?”

“Why not? That would be very nice. Thank you.”

“Well Cliffy-my-boy, it looks like we have company. Come on then, we’re just around the corner.”

They walked around the corner and down to the end of the short block. “This is my humble abode,” he said, with false modesty, while fishing the key from his coat pocket.

“It is far from modest. You appear to be a very wealthy man.”

“Oh, I don’t know. I’m comfortable, I suppose.” He closed the door.

“Yes, I’m sure you are with your wife’s money.”

“Excuse me.”

He released Clifford from the lead as she dropped the German accent. He looked up at her just in time to see her take out her gun. “What the hell are you doing?”

“Isn’t it obvious?” She was in no hurry “You put out the contract did you not?”

“I did yes, but surely you can’t be that stupid that you think I would hire a killer to kill me. The contract was for my wife.”

“Yes, I am fully aware of that.” Then she began to screw the suppressor on to the threaded barrel. “Sandra will be so happy to get you out of her house at last.”

“What?” He backed away.

“You heard me.” She aimed the gun at his chest.

“Wait! No, no-no w-w-wait. L-l-listen to me, you’re making a mistake!”

“No, you made the mistake.”

“I’ll double your fee.”

“You are too late.” She fired the first shot through his left lung.

Staggering back clutching his chest he looked at her in disbelief. "But I ..."

She put the second bullet through his eye into his brain. Without feeling rushed she removed the suppressor and put it and her gun in her purse. Two brass casings were on the floor nearby. She scooped them up and dropped them in with the weapon.

Clifford watched silently from the stairs and, amusingly, he didn't seem to mind at all.

***t

The woman was just putting her scarf around her neck to go out, when the phone rang. "Hello, 7238-****."

While she waited for her flight, Hedda thought she should give the woman a call to explain what happened. "Hello, am I speaking to Sandra?"

"Yes, who is this please?"

"Sandra, my name is Anita Franco. You may have heard of me."

"No, I don't think so. Are you a friend of my husband?"

"Hardly. I know this is going to sound strange, but please bear with me for a moment. I was hired by your husband to kill you."

"What?! If this is some sort of sick practical joke, then ..."

"No, I'm perfectly serious."

"Oh my God!"

"Please, don't be alarmed. I am not coming for you."

"I can't believe this! What do you want?"

"I am simply calling to tell you that dear Samuel wanted you dead and paid me one hundred thousand pounds to do it. He just offered to double it if I went after you. Adding insult to murder, he has been dipping into your money to pay me. I have already returned the money to your account of course."

"But ... I ... I ..."

69

"I completely agree, it was a despicable thing to do. You are a decent woman Sandra and didn't deserve to die. But he did, and I'm afraid that his lovely dog has been left alone in that big house in Mayfair and he needs looking after."

"He's dead?"

"Your husband? Yes, he is very dead. So, call the police and tell that he's a good gentle dog. Will you do that for me?"

"I don't know what to …"

"I know, it's all a bit of a shock, but I'm sure you already knew that William didn't deserve you. I wish you better luck with Greg. He's a lovely man, I'm sure. Oh, and I understand that you are pregnant, congratulations it's a boy. Good luck, Sandra."

"William is dead?"

"Yes." The silence seemed to drag on forever and Hedda needed to push on. "Oh, please Sandra, there's nothing to cry about, we all die eventually, his time just came earlier than he expected."

***

MGen Wolfson wished to God that that grave marker in Arlington cemetery actually had Katrina Fernando under it. It would have saved him a whole lot of problems.

With that on his mind, he wondered why the Europeans hadn't publicly put Anita Franco and US Military Counterintelligence together. He was delighted that they hadn't of course.

Shit, he thought, when they do ……. Oh God ……. when they do, I'll be the skunk at a wine tasting party. It'll ruin my reputation.

There was no doubt that he could produce evidence that the original Anita Franco, in other words, Katrina Fernando was innocent. That both Katrina, who is no longer in the Army, and Special Agent Devlyn, who is dead, had cooked up the mission on their own.

In fact, he could show that he believed that Katrina Fernando was dead and that he delivered the eulogy at her funeral.

The scheme they cooked up to publicize Anita Franco was going to change her title from the Happy Widow to the Evil Widow of Ibiza. Her face on the bedroom walls of every post pubescent man-child in Europe. Then, after she took out Delph Petros, her face was on a wanted poster in every police department across the continent and the story ended with her supposed death alongside the crime boss. She re-emerged some years later in connection with Ähern Jäger who manufactured the terrorist outbreak against Americans in Europe and was assumed to have been killed when a US missile destroyed Ähern's mountaintop headquarters in Italy. But then he'd have to explain how he knew that she was alive. Then why the US Government contracted a known assassin to be a vital part of the Operation Rote Faust. Oh yes, it will be messy. Apart from Wolfson and a few others, no one knew that Anita Franco had survived that bombing.

It was broadly believed that Ähern Jäger and Jesús Maria Etxebarria had perished in the destruction of the Italian fortress. But then a year later Etxebarria was spotted at Toronto's Pearson Airport and then followed to Bartica, Guyana where he and Ähern were hiding.

Wolfson wondered what if he was forced to admit that he knew Anita Franco was alive, and that he brought her back out of retirement. And further that he had personally given her the unofficial orders and the means to go down to Guyana to commit sanctioned murder. The moment he heard Anita Franco's name again and that it was attached to the assassination of General Mario Giancarlo in Genoa, Wolfson had an agent assigned to watch and report on the status of Katrina in Toronto.

He didn't know who was sent and didn't care, he just wanted proof that Kat Fernando wasn't involved. With the death of Gérard Desrosiers, priorities changed. The optics weren't just bad, they were devastating. It no longer mattered that he had proof that Kat wasn't involved.

The fact that she had been the notorious Anita Franco and had worked for him was enough to sink his canoe.

It would be so much easier if she was well and truly dead.

Wolfson switched on the intercom to his Aide-de-Camp, Capt. John Gradin. "Call Col. Manx over at JAG, tell him I need to see him ASAP."

"Right away, Sir."

A few minutes later the captain came over the intercom. "I called the colonel, Sir. He said he would be here within the hour."

"Very well."

Fifty minutes later the JAG officer was in the outer office. "Send him through."

The colonel entered and offered a casual salute.

"Christ, thanks for coming so quickly. I've got problems Bill. Take a seat."

"Gradin said you were upset. What's going on?"

"We have a situation brewing over in Europe."

"Something to do with the Six-Six?"

"No. Have you heard about the assassination in Italy?"

"Yes, a terrible tragedy, I hear he was a fine man."

"He was a pompous dick."

"I stand corrected, General."

"This is more than a tragedy; it's turning into a fuck catastrophe."

"Does it impact on M-CI?"

"Big time, and I need your legal opinion." He stood up and walked around his desk then perched himself on the corner of it to peer down at the lawyer. "This must remain strictly need to know."

"Are you asking me to represent you in this regard, Sir?"

"Why?" That question startled him. "Did you hear something?"

"No, I'm saying that if I am your counsel, everything you say to me is considered confidential, and covered by client attorney privilege."

"Right. Yeah, that's some comfort I suppose. Yes, I want you to represent me. The French are tossing around the name of the assassin…"

"Anita Franco, yes I've heard."

"OK good. At one time she was one of our people."

"You're referring to Katrina Fernando."

"Jesus Christ, who the fuck are you working for, JAG or the CIA?"

"It's still JAG, but I have hidden talents in case you're interested. I read the file on Colonel Paul Devlyn and it described the take down of Petrus and then Operation Rote Faust. It included some of his field notes about his black ops missions."

"Black ops, my ass. That first one was way off the reservation. This office had nothing to do with it."

"Understood. But it is true that Special Agent Katrina Fernando used the name Anita Franco as her cover?"

"Yeah. What do you know about her, Fernando?"

"I am quite familiar with her career. I've read her jacket. She was a good agent but went off the rails in Canada. Then there was the question about the Petrus murder. The Pentagon was curious, and asked JAG to look into your possible culpability."

Shocked and mortified, he practically jumped off the desk. "Christ! I didn't know that."

"It's OK, you were cleared, and it didn't go beyond the Joint Chief's."

"Thank God for that. Alright, to the best of my knowledge Katrina Fernando has nothing to do with what has been going on in Europe. I've put surveillance on her, and she hasn't left the country in years."

"Are you absolutely sure?"

"What do you mean by that? Of course I'm sure."

"I hope you're right, because if she was involved in any way, it will blow right back in your face."

"Tell me something I don't already know. I want you to be straight with me Bill, what is my level of exposure vis a vis this impostor bitch?"

Manx frowned as he took a few seconds to answer. "Um-m-m, OK, as I recall, the decision to bomb Perdellacino was made jointly with our European allies."

"That is correct."

"And that President Lake and President of Italy signed off on it."

"Right again, President Lake negotiated a generous compensation package to cover that."

"Then, in my opinion, you have nothing to worry about. Your exposure is zero. Just keep Fernando's name out of it."

"Good." He was relieved at first but then hesitated, "OK. I have another question. Hypothetically now, let's say that one of my retired agents was unofficially called back to do some wet work in a foreign country as a private contractor for M-CI?"

"Would he be working for one of the companies like Eagle's Nest or Blackwater?"

"Something like that. Then someone trips over it and discovers that I may have ..."

"Let me stop you right there. OK, from this moment on you cannot tell me about any crimes…"

"Whoa, who said anything about a crime?"

"Tucker listen to me, your involvement with that former agent, whomever he/she may be, was over and done with at the end of Operation Rote Faust. Do not receive or make communications with her in any form, ever again."

"Yes, but ..."

"I know where you were going with that, and I'm certain that you acted in the best interests of the service and the nation. It's water under the bridge. Forget about it."

"OK, got it. So where do we go from here?"

"There is nowhere to go. If the EU authorities link the assassin to Fernando, then that's her problem."

"Sure, and what if Fernando drags us into it."

"Deny it."

"What if they ask to view her official record? How do I respond when she gives evidence that she and I met to discuss her role in Operation

Rote Faust? That meeting was on the record."

"That would certainly be detrimental."

"Goddammit ..." He paced the room. I wish to hell that bitch was dead."

"I didn't hear that, and there's no fairy godfather to grant that kind of wish. As a JAG officer, I cannot offer any advice that might appear as instructing you to do something illegal."

"What are you talking about?"

Manx held up his hand "Wait a second. …….. I can say that I will defend you, should any charges arise from any (using air quotes) ' prophylactic,' actions you might take to nullify the problem."

"What the fuck does that …? Jesus Bill, are you telling me to…?"

"As I said, I can't advise you to do anything illegal Tucker." He stood up. "Think about what I just said and remember that I'm on your team now. When you need me, I will be in my office." He turned and left the room. Wolfson was left unsure about what he was told. "What did he mean by 'prophylactic'?"

He picked up the phone again. "Cpt. Gradin, come in here."

***

The point of this campaign was not at issue. Revenge trumped everything. No matter what the cost, the real Anita Franco had to be destroyed.

She returned to her office, rebooted the computer, and opened Skype to call Zürich again. As usual, Sigismund Kraft picked up quickly. "Hedda, have you made a decision?"

"I have."

"Good. Now if I could, I wish to discuss your mission in Rome."

"Go ahead if you must."

"It was a complete success. The French security agency has been very aggressive, as we expected. They have been moving faster than the

Italians and traced your activities before the event. As you predicted, they all identified Franco from the media photos. Brava."

"You are too kind," she said, without trying to hide her sarcasm. "Did the witnesses bring it up, or did the police ask them specifically?"

"They all said they heard you identify yourself as Anita Franco. There was a woman in the café where you had coffee with that prostitute, that said she heard Clarissa mention the Happy Widow of Ibiza and then called you Anita Franco. She confirmed her identification after being shown the photographs of your nemesis."

"Perfect."

"The prostitute also said you were sweet to her, and very kind to her cat."

"How would the woman know how I treated the beast?"

"Maybe the cat talks to her."

"Or maybe she had a nanny cam in her apartment. Damn, I never bothered to look for one."

"Are you getting careless, Hedda?"

"Your characterizations of me, and my methods are as unnecessary as they are unhelpful."

"Forgive me, Hedda."

She ignored his apology. "What other information do you have for me?"

"There was no clear image of you recorded on any of the surveillance apparatus. They showed just enough to reinforce the inevitable match up with the real Anita Franco. The mission was perfection."

"Wonderful. Is it certain that she is being blamed for everything?"

"Yes, the clues you left have made that very clear, the assassin Anita Franco is back."

"Brilliant. Then I have finished my campaign and that is the end of it."

"No, Hedda, there is more to do. Remember the people who conspired against your uncle. They have to be dealt with."

No, it's over, I'm tired of it, and tired of you. That's what she wanted to say but she didn't. "I don't care about them, Siggi I wanted to get Franco and I've done that. It's finished"

"No. There are people out there who gave the Americans the approval to drop the bomb. They allowed Anita Franco to go in and kill Edward. Hedda, you mustn't let them go unpunished."

Did it really matter to her? Would killing them give her any more pleasure than killing Desrosiers and the others? It was a game, of sorts, like the game she and Edward would play when they were young. Damn Siggi. He had given her the perfect excuse to end this and then snatched it away. Was he playing a game with her? Probably, it was always mind games with him, games he consistently lost. Why didn't he realize that he was fencing with a stick while she held a rapier.

"Hedda?"

"What?" she growled.

He jerked back from the screen, surprised, and truth be known, a little frightened. "You do understand how important this is, don't you?"

"To whom Siggi, to you or to me?" she said angrily. "Truthfully, I couldn't care less about your list of people."

"These people killed Edward." Not wanting him to see the indecision on her face she turned away from the screen. "Your next hit is in Spain. Your target is one of the three Director Generals of CNI (Spain's National Intelligence Center), Olivia de Taddeo. She lives and works in Madrid. May I send you the file now?"

She couldn't admit to herself, or him, that he had won this one. "You may as well."

"Of course." Another icon appeared on the lower right corner of her screen indicating that the file had been received. "How will you handle this one?"

"I'll read the reports and call you."

"Thank you."

***

She entered her code, her desktop appeared, and she clicked on the second file icon in the lower right corner.

The PDF s were encrypted in a sub-folder and required another password. It was impossible to remember what it was, so she gave up and opened another hidden file that stored her passwords.

The Madrid contract was a long document with pictures, diagrams and photos. As she skimmed through the contents, she became more engaged in the game. This part was what she loved, to become absorbed in the research and planning. She opened the images and the first few photos showed a two-building complex surrounded by a concrete and steel-grey glass walls.

The headquarters for Securitas Direct España S. A., the *Centro Nacional de Inteligencia*, CNI was placed it on the north edge of the city, off the A6 Motorway. There must have been a reason they placed it so far from the center of Madrid. The buildings themselves were innocuous looking industrial structures, three-stories of the usual colored metal cladding, glass, and concrete. There was nothing to identify that the agency was in there. But the security shack at the gate suggested they were protecting more than just the companies whose names appeared prominently at the top.

It was a very busy area, practically surrounded by large commercial projects with perhaps thousands of employees. The ingress and egress were limited to large volume highways with traffic circles and diminishing curved ramps.

She didn't like the layout at all. Every exit-strategy she could think of would run the risk of a chase on the ground and from the air. There was no upside to that.

It was frustrating to be handed such a ridiculous plan. He must have known she would turn that down. She closed the file and pushed away from her desk. She needed a drink and kept a few bottles of her favorite sauvignon blanc in a wine cooler. After pouring a heavy nine ounces into a fine crystal glass, she walked slowly back to her desk thinking about the problem.

Her mind glided peacefully over the city she had visited several times as if she were a predator bird looking for prey. Her glass emptied before her flight was finished so she returned to the cooler and took the open bottle back to her desk.

Oh-damn! I've been drifting again. She refilled her glass for the second time and resumed her imaginary flight.

Siggi would have known that if she attacked the headquarters that would be the end of her, and her fortune would be his. That was not going to happen, and he would pay dearly for that deception.

There had to be another option in that information. All she had to do was concentrate. She returned to her computer and tried to focus on the next bit of information. Eventually as she read the target's address, it came to her.

She looked at the calendar on the desk and there it was. The solution to her dilemma. She picked it up and drew on her knowledge of Spain's troubled past. She'd studied this at university and published a paper on the incident.

"I've found my prey."

Olivia de Taddeo lived on the Calle Divino Pastor, in the district of Malasaña. It was one of the most famous parts of Madrid. It was the site of an incident on the 2nd of May 1808, that eventually lead to the Peninsular War. That Incident became the reason for one of Spain's most important fiestas.

Leaning back in her chair she let the details run through her mind like a movie. First, there was the portrait of the pretty fifteen-year-old seamstress Manuela Malasaña, one of the key names associated with the uprising. Hedda, then typed in the event and along with the story came images of Goya's paintings of the executions of the Madridlianos. There was another painting as well of the pretty young Manuela.

In the aftermath of the uprising, Manuela was found by the French troops sitting on a pair of scissors. She said she used them in her work. They saw them as a weapon, linked her to the rebellion and executed her. She became a martyr and a symbol of the struggle.

As the history came to life in her mind, she entered the address into Google Earth and zoomed in on the street.

When the image cleared, her face brightened into a wide smile. It was just as she had remembered. Amazingly, the Plaza del Dos de Mayo was just a block away from the target's house.

At the time of the uprising, the Plaza was the barracks of the Monteleón artillery units, the only Spanish troops to disobey the French orders to stand down. Instead, they joined the uprising.

Hundreds died in the fighting and hundreds more were executed for taking part in it. Some say that the girl was found helping the soldiers load their cannon. Others say she was just sitting there, an innocent girl who died because of a pair of scissors.

Either way, she became a hero, and that day was proclaimed Bando de la Independencia, the day of the Declaration of Independence. And every year since, Madrid became Fiesta City.

Hedda thought how appropriate it was that a Director of the Spanish Intelligence Service would choose to live there.

Olivia's three-story house was magnificent. Traditionally, as with the Moors before them, when possible, the Spanish build their homes behind high walls, placing a barrier between their family and just about everyone else. That was the case with Director de Taddeo's house, hidden behind an innocent looking, graffiti covered wall.

Inside the enclosure was an oasis. There was a paved courtyard for parking, but the rest was a cool, green garden under the shade of fig trees. Every true oasis had to have a water feature or well and this one had a swimming pool. She wrote to Siggi asking for the details of this woman's house. She wanted everything he could find.

Siggi's detailed description of the house included the security system.

How he managed to get this sort of information was unfathomable. Alarms, triggered by invisible laser beams, protected the courtyard entrance and the tops of the walls. Her security system included the narrow, tree-lined street, where cameras were hidden inside the streetlamps. They covered the entire length of the block.

Everything was visible, from the church on the eastern corner to the furniture store on the west. The security specialists must have thought that was a sufficient deterrent, but Hedda's keen eye for detail locked on the weakness. A sniper could see into the courtyard from the top apartments across the street. It afforded a clean shot through any of the third-floor windows. Which was probably why those buildings had been converted into office space for government workers. Siggi had covered that too but failed to see the advantage. His report stated that at least one of the offices was occupied by NCI employees. Undoubtedly, part of her security protocol. There was no conventional pedestrian door in the outer wall.

The only access was the wide overhead door to the courtyard and further down to the west, while behind another overhead door was the entrance into her underground parking. Siggi's intel suggested they were linked, though he had no way of proving it.

As she studied the aerial images on Google Earth, she began to think that the best way to take an assault team in was by invitation, posing as tradesmen.

When she finished the report, she called Zürich and, as usual, it was answered on the second ring. "That was quick. Have you decided what you want to do?"

"For the Madrid job, I am going to need three, possibly four people to go in with me."

"You are thinking of the party she has planned for Dos de Mayo?"

"I am. We would go in as part of the catering service, or after party cleanup. I'll need to know specifically who will be doing the catering. Will the same company do it all, or will there be subcontractors providing the food and wine?"

"Subcontractors I think."

"That's good. When I select the service, I will need the IDs of all the employees as I want to select the ones we will be replacing. I'll also need to know how de Taddeo's security will be screening the contractors. That's all I can think of for now."

"What about egress?"

"The celebration out in the streets will provide all the distraction we are going to need. I'm considering the removal of all security personnel. Perhaps some explosives would be useful for that."

"Of course, I'll supply anything you need. Keep in mind that we only have ten days to prepare the plan. That doesn't leave us with much time."

"You'll just have to put more people on it. I ..." she began, then hesitated.

Siggi was just recognizing that her attitude had improved since their last conversation, but that hesitation sharpened his apprehension. "Is there a problem? I sense that something is bothering you."

"I was just wondering about the Americans. Have they moved against her yet?"

"You mean Anita Franco?"

"Of course I mean Anita Franco, you idiot!"

"There's no call for rudeness. And the answer is no, not that I am aware of."

"Damn. Why not?"

"I can only speculate. Remember, that she was with Counterintelligence a senior special agent, one of their top people.

"You mean she had infiltrated counterintelligence, don't you?"

"Yes, but they would never admit something like that. They won't be quick to do anything that would damage their national pride."

"Is there no one in Europe that will make that connection?"

"Don't entirely dismiss the Americans. They do have their uses from time to time. I trust that their European partners will eventually pressure them into taking action against her."

"I am losing patience with this campaign. It would have been more satisfying to have just gone after her."

"Hedda, I designed this campaign to punish them all. Try to hold on to that ambition a little while longer. After the Madrid contract is attributed to her, they will have no other choice."

"That's what you said about the Frenchman."

"They just need a little more incentive. She will be convicted in the international media and the Americans will be forced to go after her."

"My-god, haven't I given them enough incentive?"

"Please try to maintain your composure. Military intelligence did a good job of keeping her existence secret."

"The longer it takes, the more risk there is for me."

"Yes, understood, but only those who worked with the Americans on the Emergency Council are alive to expose her. When they begin to feel personally vulnerable, they will force America's hand to save themselves."

"I hope so. Call me the moment you have what I asked for."

"I have already put my people on the problem. Have you made a decision about Mr. Williams-Blake?"

"Mr. Williams-Blake? Oh, good grief, Siggi, that business was cleared up days ago."

"Then she is dead?"

"No, he is." She ended the call.

***

Chapter ~ 5

His face appeared on her computer screen. "Siggi, have you found the men I need?"

"I have men on standby that I trust completely. They will meet you in Madrid at any location you choose. I just have to know how many you require."

She split the screen, pulled up Notebook and began taking notes. "Let's hear what you have found out about the caterers."

"She has engaged two caterers for the party. The one that is interesting is the wine merchant. They have arranged to have one of their employees manage three temp workers to deliver and serve the wine. The only one who will be on the security list is the woman in charge."

"That sounds perfect."

"Wonderful, I have already sent you her information. She has photo ID, which can be created for you. But she may be familiar to the target's staff. You will have to do some minor alterations to satisfy the security check. A wig and some makeup should suffice. Oh," he said, as his face slipped into a lecherous grin, "and note that she was not blessed with the same physical attributes God gave you."

"Meaning?"

"She is flat chested. But I'm sure as uncomfortable as that might be for you. Can you manage to deal with that problem?"

She closed her eyes and expelled a heavy breath of exasperation. "Why do I put up with you?" He merely shrugged. "Is there a schedule for the delivery?"

"It is all in the package I have sent you. Hedda ... one thing before you go." His hesitation suggested he had taken issue with something she had done.

She knew what was coming, so she just let him get on with it. "There was a problem that must be brought to your attention."

"Yes?"

"You are aware that you made an error in London."

"I don't recall making an error."

"Hedda, good God! You killed the client! How will that look to future clients? What will they think when there is the possibility that you would turn on them as well?"

"If you'll recall, by his own admission, his wife, Sandra Tammering, paid the contract. I thought it only fair that she benefited from it."

"You are playing with fire, my dear. There could be serious repercussions."

"From whom, Siggi ... From you?"

That caught him off guard, even though it was true. "Certainly not. I would never do anything against you. Can you tell me what happened?"

"I didn't like the client."

"You knew that before you went."

"But I didn't know he had a dog named Clifford."

"A dog?

"My father once said that a dog can be a very good judge of character."

"Hedda..."

"Clifford didn't like the client either."

"You killed him because of his dog?"

"I trusted the dog's assessment. Don't worry about it Siggi, there is one less rat in London. He will not be missed."

"When did you catch this sudden case of morality?"

Her voice turned cold as ice. "Siggi … I will kill, or spare whomever I like." Her meaning was clear.

"Uh … Of course my dear. I was merely …"

"Let's get back to Madrid. What hotel did Anita Franco use while she was in Madrid?"

"I believe it was a boutique hotel, the Only You, on Calle Barquillo."

"Perfect. Book a room for me there. The same room she had if possible."

"Unfortunately, the hotel was bombed during the terrible hostilities against the Americans just before your uncle's tragic loss. The rooms were all redesigned during the restoration."

"I see. Nevertheless, book me a room there and use the name Anita Franco. I'll need three men. Have them meet me there in the lobby on the 29th."

"I shall see to it."

✳✳✳

The picnic at Cherry Beach had been a great success. Sandcastles had been made under the brilliant, hot sun, lunch had been eaten with some exceptions, and it seemed that they were all ready for some time inside. A female special agent from M-CI followed them down and had been watching from a safe distance. Her orders were to observe and report and under no circumstances was she to make contact. So far, she had enjoyed the assignment. It was easy and, at times like this, she really enjoyed watching the little family at play. Kat and the nanny behaved more like sisters than employer and employee.

She admired Kat a great deal, her profile had been used as the class subject for many days of her training. There were a lot of examples of do's and don'ts, but it was mostly about how she had operated when on assignment. Her mission in Honduras, then working with the 66th Brigade out of Wiesbaden, Germany as a field officer at the embassy in Rome and later in Paris. Also, her work undercover with examples of her mission in St. Petersburg, Russia; and during the Operation Rote Faust in Europe. The special agent thought her assignment was a waste of time. It was obvious that Kat had nothing to do with what was going on over there.

***

Wolfson had given this a lot of thought "Captain, I want to send an asset to Toronto to check on the activities of a woman by the name of Katrina Fernando." He concluded that he had to lay the foundation for a solid defense.

"Sir? If you will recall, you have already sent an agent up there to do that."

"Oh right. Dammit, I had forgotten about her. There is too much going on. Who did I send?"

"Special Agent Raini Hanamansingh. She's a good agent, thorough and totally loyal to you."

"Yes, I remember her now. She studied Fernando at Huachuca as I recall."

"If you say so, Sir."

"Is there any chance that she may … be persuaded to go over to the dark side?"

"Do you mean to take part in a black ops, General?"

"No, I mean, could she be corrupted by Fernando?"

"I have no idea, Sir. Is that a concern?"

"Hell yes, it's a concern. Fernando has a way of twisting our people to do what she wants. I don't want that to happen now."

"Should I pull Hanamansingh and send a replacement?"

"Let me make myself clear, Captain. I have recently heard things about Katrina Fernando that have given me some concern. She has gone rogue before. I don't believe she's involved with these assassinations, but if she is, she may drag MI into some serious trouble."

"Yes, Sir. What are your orders?"

"I want to eliminate anything that could possibly come back and bite us in the ass. Do you follow me?"

"I'm not sure that I do, Sir."

"Then let me make it clear for you." He typed the orders on his computer, printed it, then handed it to the captain.

The Department of Defense hereby issues this warrant to the appointed agents of the office of Military Intelligence, for the arrest of Colonel Katrina Fernando, Retired. The agents are authorized to use any means necessary to place the subject in custody and return her to the United States for prosecution. They are also authorized to enter said person's residence to search and seize any and all documents, and related evidence that are, or may be related in any way, to the assassin Anita Franco.

By order of G-2, Military Intelligence,

Major General Tucker Wolfson

"Are you saying that you want us them to eliminate Katrina Fernando?"

"Did I say eliminate her, Captain? No, I did not. It's right there on the paper. It says, and I quote, 'The agents are authorized to use any means

"Uh Sir ..."

"Those are my orders. I am putting you in charge of seeing to it that this is taken care of. Do you copy?"

"Copy that, Sir. I'm in charge of this operation. Yes Sir."

***

Chapter ~ 6

As always, Friday night's fireworks display in the Jardines de las Vistillas was magnificent. Hedda was there to watch as Madrid veritably throbbed with excitement. The Dos de Mayo Fiesta would officially begin at noon. The bars and restaurants were already filled with Madridlianos in full party mode.

As daylight crept over the city, things had quietened down. Drunk and exhausted revelers began to drag themselves to bed, while the sane and sober ones were just getting started.

The Spanish military began marshaling for the big display that afternoon in the Plaza de Oriente. That would be the official beginning to the celebration of the victory over Napoleon's troops.

During that quiet, but busy time, Olivia de Taddeo was preparing for her private fiesta. The caterer had arrived with vans loaded with tables and chairs and began setting up in the courtyard. The food truck was due to arrive soon. She wanted enough to feed at least fifty people for eight hours or more, so things had to move smoothly on a tight schedule.

One of Siggi's worker bees had researched each of the companies that would be delivering services to the party.

Hedda chose the one she thought would give her the most mobility. The security would be tight, and she had to get their weapons into the compound undetected. Hedda had already gathered her small invasion force of four.

The van was loaded with wine, guns and explosives and Siggi's three men, were ready for action.

Usually, she worked alone but now she was working with strangers, not a perfect situation by any standard but she really had no choice.

Werner Brans was a pleasant looking man of medium height, a typical Aryan blue eyed, blond. He showed that he was in excellent physical condition by easily loading the equipment into the truck. Like everything about him, his power was subtle.

By contrast, Tag Fritz was a swarthy man slightly shorter than Brans at about five-five. His personality matched the dark complexion, his eyes were like lifeless lumps of coal peering out from beneath a thick, black uni-brow. He too was in excellent condition but liked to show off his attributes wearing a very tight t-shirt with the sleeves rolled up high on his biceps. To complete the renegade look, he kept a pack of French smokes rolled up in one sleeve.

Olaf Bönweld was a marathon runner, tall and slim with bright intelligent eyes. He was an ordinary looking man that people would walk by without taking notice and ignore at social gatherings. Always the unsmiling man in the background of the crowd who looks the other way just as the photo is snapped. He didn't talk much, and she suspected that he didn't miss much either. He had been a sniper in the German special forces Command, KSK. In fact, Siggi got them all from Kommando Spezialkräfte.

They were obviously a seasoned team, and Siggi promised that they would do whatever she wanted, without question, but she had no illusions about where their true loyalties lay.

The wine merchant, TadéoVino, was supplying the fine wines. Hedda ordered special deep boxes ahead of time to transport her materials.

They all had false bottoms but only four would be needed to accommodate the machine guns, pistols and explosives.

The wine distributor had subcontracted the delivery to a small logistics company. Hedda's team intercepted their van after the wine had been picked up. She had no intention of killing them so she had them locked in a warehouse where they could be found later. Her men took their IDs, and then replaced the distributor's wine cases with hers.

While Hedda left to change her appearance for this mission, Fritz returned to the warehouse and quietly murdered the logistics team.

To look like the woman in charge, Hedda applied a spray tan to change her skin color, bound her chest flat and donned a frizzy black wig to hide her blond hair. The makeup was applied artfully to accentuate her nose and darkened the color under her eyes so that she looked like she had not slept in days. The final touch were the brown contact lenses to hide her blue eyes.

To protect their wait staff clothing during the delivery, they wore long grey pin-striped coats with the logistics company logo on the breast pocket.

The ever-popular HK45 Tactical handguns and MP5K submachine guns with suppressors and extra clips were hidden in two boxes. The other two were packed with a dozen explosive devices and a remote detonator. When the false bottoms were covered securely, the boxes were sprayed with a sealant that eliminated the smell of the explosives, so that even sniffer dogs wouldn't find them. To ensure that they would be the first to be unloaded those cases were placed in the van last.

✷✷✷

CNP (Cuerpo Nacional de Policía), the national civilian police force of Spain, was handling the security for the event. Six uniformed officers blocked the street and with them was a very alert Belgian shepherd. Hedda's transport was stopped just outside the overhead door. After being thoroughly frisked and their IDs checked out, they stood back quietly while two guards and the dog searched the van. A third guard remained by Hedda's men.

He tried asking Olaf a question, so Hedda had to explain that her men were new immigrants without much Spanish. They were just there to carry things and serve. "So, if you have any questions you have to talk to me." He seemed to be fine with that. The small shepherd climbed over the boxes, sniffing everything while the guards looked on.

"Will this take long?" Hedda asked.

"It will take as long as it takes. Have you someplace else to be?"

"As a matter of fact, I do," she said irritably. "Inside, setting up the wine. The white wines have to be chilled before they are served, and the hostess was very particular about that."

"I see, OK." He backed down and told her that the caterer's food truck had arrived twenty minutes earlier and they were still in the courtyard unpacking it.

"Would it be permitted for my men to get out and have a smoke?"

"Yes, have them stand over there by the wall where I can watch them."

"Nun, lass uns Freunde gehen." They headed for the wall but only Fritz lit a cigarette. As far as the police could tell the men seemed relaxed, men well used to the moments before an action. Hedda hated smoking and stood up wind from them in the shade of a small tree. She bided her time watching the traffic go by on Calle Fuencarral.

Dos de Mayo was the city's largest celebration, the perfect cover for her operation. Crowds of tourists flocked to the barrio of Malasaña by the hundreds to join the Madrileños. Swarming down the street in waves, they made it difficult for the guards to watch her people.

At last, at 11:00 the big overhead door rose up, and the food truck began its departure.

"Alright, get your people back in the van. We will be letting you in soon."

"Finally," said Hedda.

The whole community had become a madhouse, with music, dancing in the street, and the odd bang of fireworks set off by children. As soon as the catering truck pushed into the swelling crowd, her team was allowed to enter.

The tables and chairs were set up and the caterers were covering them with tablecloths and flowers. The arrangement left only enough room for her van to back in and squeeze into the opening. There was just enough room to open the side and back doors.

As always there were curious tourists looking for a party and trying to see what was going on inside. The guards struggled to keep them back and hurried them along. The pressure eased a bit when the door was closed.

The food services people were running around making the final preparations. There was too much activity for anyone to notice what Hedda's men were doing.

They had only just begun to unload the wine when Director de Taddeo came down to see that it was being handled carefully. "Do you have the Champagne I ordered?"

"Of course, Señora, ten cases."

"Excellent. Where are they?"

"There, the first to come off the truck."

"Bueno, I want them inside as soon as possible. It must be chilled before the guests arrive."

"I will see to it myself, Señora. Can you have someone show me where to take it?"

"I will take you there myself, follow me. And you men there ... See that you are careful with the cases. I will not accept any breakage."

"They will be very careful, Señora, I assure you." She picked up a case, filled only with Champagne. "I am ready, Señora." The Director nodded and strode off with Hedda following.

The hostess led her into her house via the lower floor, allowing Hedda to take note of everything. At the front there was a grand staircase leading to the main floor. At the back of the large room was a stairway to the wine cellar.

"The cold room is down there on the right. Unpack the boxes and place the bottles on the shelves." Hedda scanned the room looking for problems. "Oh, be sure to keep the wine you bring in separate from my personal stock. I don't want you to become confused and serve my vintage wines."

"I assure you that there will be no confusion, Señora. Thank you."

"Good. Well then, I'll leave you to it." She started to walk away then changed her mind as she thought of another detail. "What is your name?"

"Renetta Bolario, Señora," replied Hedda.

"Fine, Renetta there is a bonus for you if your people do their jobs well and as quickly as possible."

"Thank you, Señora. I promise, they will take care of everything. My people are very good at what they do."

"Excellent." She went upstairs and met Brans at the top with the second case. "Down there," she said, needlessly. Then she crossed the room to take the grand staircase to the upper level.

All but one of the Champagne cases had been taken down and Hedda said, "I'll bring the last box. Get set up, I want to do this now, before the place fills up with guests."

"Some have already arrived," said Werner.

She was amazed. "Already?"

"Ja."

"Then that's their bad luck. Get those cartons opened and set up. We go the moment I return."

The men quickly armed the bombs and strapped on their guns. She returned, set the last case on the floor, and was handed her weapons. "Ready? Let's move."

With their guns hidden beneath their coats the three men began moving about the courtyard, garden and house appearing to be helping with the preparations as they placed the explosives.

They concentrated on the areas where the guards would be posted. Hedda took Olaf aside and pointed out the small west facing windows on the top floor. "That's where I want you." They had gone over the plan in detail earlier, so that was all she needed to say.

Hedda went up and scanned the courtyard from the middle floor, the security people were where she thought they'd be.

She went downstairs and said, "It's time. Olaf, go. Signal me from that one on the right when you arrive. As soon as the charges go off, take out the man on the roof then come down. Shoot anyone who gets in your way."

"Ja."

"Werner, I want you to watch my back. We will go into the house and find the target."

She turned to Tag and placing her hand on his chest, she said, "You have the trigger?"

He nodded. "Ja."

"Stand in the far corner by the overhead door. When we get to the top of the stairs I will raise my hand to my face, as if to touch my nose." She demonstrated. "When I drop my hand, you take cover and press the trigger. Shoot anyone left standing."

He nodded. "Ya."

She slapped the weapon beneath her coat for reassurance. "Alright."

Olaf had already left the main staircase and, without being noticed, was heading up into the private part of the house. Halfway up he met Director de Taddeo coming down.

She was talking on her cell phone. He stopped, pushed his back against the wall and kept his head down, until she passed. She paid no attention to him.

Hedda was waiting in the courtyard for Olaf's signal. When he waved from the window, she turned and nodded to Tag.

She and Werner headed for the stairs.

With the detonators armed and the trigger ready in his hand, he crouched down behind a table and watched for her signal.

They stopped on the landing; she looked around to see if anything had changed. Nothing had.

With her right hand she brushed a stray hair from her face, then gave the signal. Tag tipped the table, ducked down and covered his face as he pressed the trigger.

The courtyard erupted in a series of explosions throwing ball bearings and nails everywhere. Their van was riddled with holes and began burning. A part of the barrier wall came down opening the courtyard to the street and the whole area was filled with flames and smoke.

Inside, safe from the shrapnel and shattered glass, Hedda and Werner pulled their submachine guns into position and opened fire on the hysterical people in the big room. Every one of them died in seconds. A heartbeat after the explosions, Olaf placed a well-aimed shot into the face of the CNP sniper on the roof opposite, then killed two other men who appeared in the window below.

Terrified people ran for cover as the police outside moved in. Tag opened up with his machine gun killing three, reloaded and continued firing as they breeched the wall. Even the Belgium shepherd fell in the hail of bullets. Olaf switched the shot selector to automatic then headed downstairs. Two men appeared on the second floor below. Without stopping, he killed them with a quick burst. The suppressor had kept the sound down, so that the woman coming out of a bedroom a moment later had no idea he was there. She died before her scream left her lips. On the main floor, three guards were just turning toward Hedda with expressions of horror. She cut them down and while she changed her magazine, Werner shot a caterer coming through the kitchen door on the left. The CNP officer who came out behind her also died without firing a shot.

Hedda ran forward through the rooms firing on anything that moved. When her clip was empty, without missing a step, she reloaded for a second time.

Bursting into a small study at the back of the house they found Olivia in a meeting with five members of the National Intelligence service.

They were huddled in the back corner behind the Director.

"Who are you people?" demanded Olivia. "What do you want?"

Hedda took off her wig paused and said, "I am Hedda Jäger. You helped kill my uncle."

"Who?"

Hedda realized that her name meant nothing to the woman, it was as if she'd never heard the name Jäger before.

Suddenly, nothing seemed to make sense. She had never identified herself to a victim before, never thought to explain why she was doing this. Why had things changed so much? Did it matter if they knew why they were about to die?

As those thoughts raged in her mind, she realized that she was speaking to Olivia. "You people killed Edward! You destroyed my family."

"And now it's Edward?" Olivia said, angrily. Unable to comprehend what Hedda was saying. "Who the hell is Edward?"

"Shut up and kill them," Werner shouted.

"My brother! The nephew of Ähern Jäger, the man who would have unified Europe ... if ..." Every face in the room showed the same look of shock and astonishment.

"Woman, shut up!"

"You mean the idiot who pushed that Pan European movement?" Hedda felt as though the earth was beginning to crumble away beneath her feet. "That terrorist who was the head of Rote Faust?" Olivia said. "You are doing this to avenge a barbaric terrorist?! My God woman, you are insane! He was an animal! He had to be stopped! If your brother was with him, then he had to be stopped as well!"

"There's no time for this!" Werner shouted as he opened fire. Hedda just stood there and watched as his bullets ripped through Olivia's body sending her twisting and jerking into the others. They all died flailing about like puppets in a macabre dance, their blood splashed out like water.

Werner stripped off his coat, dropped his machine gun, and ran from the room. After a hesitation that seemed to last an eternity, Hedda replaced the wig and followed him.

Olaf was waiting for them on the balcony, and they charged down the stairs, heading for the hole in the wall. Using their handguns, they eliminated the last witnesses in the courtyard, people who hadn't had the good sense to stay hidden.

When they were the only ones standing, they dropped those guns and ran through the hole covered in blood to meld with the survivors. Tag was already waiting outside for them.

There were many civilians on the ground, some dead, some bleeding, victims of the blast that destroyed the wall. Apart from them, the street was empty now. The rest of the people had taken cover around the corners.

The air was filled with the sounds of approaching sirens. Police, medics and firefighters all trying to move through the fiesta crowds.

Hedda and the others followed Olaf to the escape vehicle that was parked on Calle Manuela Malasaña, the street named for the heroine of the uprising. They squeezed by the police who were fighting against the terrified crowd to get to the house.

In a few minutes they were three blocks away, driving north to Calle Corranza where the traffic was moving well.

They turned west and were gone.

The people behind them in the Plaza del Dos de Mayo thought it was fireworks, so the music continued, and the people danced. Few, if any, realized that something terrible had happened just a block away.

Having ditched their overcoats, Olaf piloted the car to three predetermined intersections and one by one the team members got out and vanished.

They were to take cabs to the airport and meet her at her private plane.

"Happy Independence Day, Madrid," she whispered through the taxi cab's window to the dancing crowds, as she fled to the airport. This was the end of it for her. She had satisfied her obligation to avenge her brother and may her uncle be damned.

The Learjet 45XR was fueled and ready to go. While she waited for the men, she tried to calm down as she began the pre-flight. She'd just finished that and was starting the engines when the first man arrived. The others were close behind him. They flew down to Malaga and then Olaf sat behind the wheel of her father's old Ford and drove them up the coast to Nerja. No one spoke about the operation, but she knew that Werner had told them what happened in that room. They were not happy with her.

She left them at the Balcón de Europa Hotel at about four and drove herself up the mountain for home, confused, exhausted and thoroughly depressed.

***

Chapter ~ 7

For a short time, early in her career with Counterintelligence, Kat worked at Fort Belvoir, a sprawling facility which covered a peninsula that reached out into the Potomac. To the north was Arlington, the site of the Arlington National Cemetery. For some inexplicable reason, there was still a headstone with her name on it. It stood beside a cross bearing the name of her partner, George Flynn. She remembered that he was easier to get along with if you just called him Flynn. To the east, across the Potomac, was Washington D. C., which was, for the moment, still the seat of the greatest power on earth.

Fort Belvoir was an important part of that power. It was the home of several departments of the DoD, a branch of the US Air Force, a National Guard unit, a detachment of Marines and the Army Corps of Engineers. More people worked in Fort Belvoir than at the Pentagon and the work that went on there, affected just about every branch of the military.

Tucked in amongst all those sturdy institutional red brick and limestone buildings, was the comparatively unassuming Museum Support Center Building. And hidden within it was INSCOM, the Army's Intelligence and National Security Command.

A lot of what went on there, stayed well below civilian radar. Even so, as far as MGen Tucker Wolfson was concerned his office was the center of the universe. Though he was struggling now with his back to the wall he was prepared to do anything, to avoid getting hit.

What had just happened at 11:20 in Madrid hit the airwaves throughout Europe and with the six hour difference it made the major Friday morning papers in America.

Above the fold and beneath the headline, was the picture of a very beautiful woman. Images form the security cameras showed that one of the terrorists was a tall, agile, dark skinned woman with black hair. Though the images were grainy that's all the authorities needed to identify her as Anita Franco. The caption read: *The Assassin*, and next to her was a handsome portrait of Olivia de Taddeo's with the caption: *The Victim*.

The fact that the expertly airbrushed picture of Kat was taken by a paparazzo, and the woman in the grainy photo was shot by a tourist in the crowd and had nothing in common, other than hair color and height, seemed unimportant. As far as the authorities were concerned it was the same woman.

Wolfson had thought that the assassination in Rome wasn't going to touch him, but after Madrid he realized that people on his side of the pond had to know that Franco was Fernando. She had become the anchor to the chain tied around his neck. If he didn't cut that chain, she'd sink him. Gradin brought in a Spanish newspaper and laid it on Wolfson's desk.

"Holy Mother of God. Get Manx in here, *now*!"

"Sir, the JAG office doesn't open until 08:30."

"I don't give a fuck when it opens, I want him in here now!"

"Sir."

Half an hour later, Col. Manx was standing by G-2's desk re-reading the article the general had pointed out. Then he tossed another paper onto the desk.

It was EL PAÍS from Madrid and the headline read, *Asesino Americano!*
"That just came in from Madrid." Then he pushed the front page of the Washington Post across his desk. Under her picture they'd written, *Former US Military Intelligence Agent Katrina Fernando linked to assassination of Spanish Intelligence Director.*

"How did they find out Franco was Fernando?"

"Someone from here must have leaked it."

"Oh God, am I totally fucked?"

"It's bad, but it hasn't touched you directly yet."

"Hasn't touched me? It's all over the fucking continent. The Spaniards are screaming at the President. The French have been leaking this information to the press since the incident in Rome. Now they're pointing right at me. My picture will be on that page by this afternoon."

"Even so, the Top-Secret file detailing the incident in Guyana is sealed. It can't be opened for fifty years."

"Really? Well then how the fuck did you get hold of it?"

"Sir, trust me, you are going to ride out this storm without a speck of dust on you. Providing ..."

"Oh yeah? Providing what?"

"You have to take care of that business we did not mention the last time we talked?"

"What? ... Oh, that. Yes. Yes, I've already taken care of that."

"Good."

"So, I'm going to have to ..."

"You haven't taken any direct action, correct?" Wolfson shrugged but confirmed that he had with a nod then showed him the warrant he had drafted.

Nonplussed Manx stammered. "A-and you ... gave that to someone?"

"Yes, to Capt. Gradin."

"Christ. You signed it."

"Well yeah, it works better that way."

"Sure it does. OK then. My advice for you is to burn that copy right now and delete it and anything else you have written about it on your computer. Assign someone you don't know, someone way down the food chain to deal with it. Tell them to destroy the warrant as soon as they have served it. Have them attempt … and let me emphasize the word attempt … to bring her in for questioning. There is a strong possibility that under the right circumstances, she will resist. Are you following me?"

"Yes, I follow you."

"Then I'll say no more."

"Wait a minute Manx. Are you sure that'll work?"

"I can't build a plausible defense based on the language you used there. If the people attempting to make the arrest are seen as crossing the line, then it is possible you won't be found culpable."

"A possibility?"

"That warrant has to disappear. Do you have anyone in mind to put in command of this … what shall we call it? An arresting squad?"

"That works. And as a matter of fact, I do." He printed the name and handed it to Manx."

"There you go writing again. You've gotta stop doing that Tucker." He took out his lighter and set the paper ablaze then dumped it in the trash bin. "Just out of curiosity General, where did you come up with that man's name?"

"It's from a report submitted by one of my senior agents. I guess it just stuck with me. It was unusual because according to the report that guy was the only agent who had ever shown open hostility towards Fernando. I thought I might try to take advantage of that."

"Interesting, have you ever met this agent?"

"No."

"Have you ever had any knowledge of, or direct communicated with that man prior to this?"

"No."

"Then, I agree. He's a good choice."

Wolfson called in Cpt. Gradin. The captain entered and acknowledged the lawyer with a nod. With a subtle, reassuring lift of his chin, Manx nodded in response.

Gradin smiled. "Yes, Sir?"

"Have you come up with a squad to follow the orders I gave you?"

He looked questioningly at the colonel. Manx raised an eyebrow and very subtly shook his head. "I'm still working on that, Sir."

"Then stop looking. I have chosen the man I want." He gave the captain the special agent's name.

Gradin confidently shifted his eyes from the general and then to colonel. "Call in this man and tell him to pick his own squad. I want this done ASAP. Clear?"

"Yes, Sir." He saluted. "Right away, Sir."

"Oh, by the way. In your report you will simply say that a special team has been dispatched to apprehend Katrina Fernando."

"But Sir, you just gave me orders to ..."

"I am fully aware of what I said, Captain. A special team has been dispatched to apprehend Katrina Fernando. That is all you need to write down. Am I clear?"

"Clear, Sir"

"Good. That is all."

When Gradin left the room, Manx said, "I didn't hear any of that."

"You're either with me, or against me, Manx. What's it going to be?"

"Oh, I'm with you General. And as long as we're doing this, I would also suggest that it would be good optics to assist our allies in Europe with the hunt for the assassin."

"Yes, I was just about to suggest that." He picked up the phone and said, "Captain, get me BG Renfrew, 66th Brigade on the line."

It took a little time to place the call to Germany, but the moment Renfrew picked up the phone, Wolfson began. "Brad."

"Tucker, hello, what can I do for you?"

"What have we done over there to assist the Europeans with this Anita

Franco fiasco?"

"Not much, I'll tell you that right now. We're just processing the intel we got from the NCP. It's a real mess, Tucker. It's too early to draw any conclusions about what took place there. But we're denying that any Americans were involved."

"That's good."

"Yeah, but it's not flying here. They're saying that's bullshit. I have to say that the evidence they're coming up with is pretty convincing. We're denying it, of course. Hell, I know that woman Tucker; I've worked with her, I know what she's capable of, and I don't believe for a second that she has anything to do with it."

"I agree but we can't sit on our hands. Have you offered any help to find her?"

"Our office in Madrid has offered to work with the NCP, but they're not all that interested in US cooperation right now."

"Well, make some noise over there, let the press know that we're doing all we can to assist our allies, and all that crap."

"Oh, believe me Tucker, we're all over this one. As soon as we have something to report, I'll call you."

"Outstanding." He put the phone down and looked up at Manx. "Happy?"

"We can work with that. I've got to get back to my office now. Let me know what happens in Toronto."

***

Chapter ~8

She knew all about his attempt to take over Europe, to be the all-powerful dictator and she couldn't have cared less. She had no idea that he was behind the terrorist attacks on Americans. Even for her, that revelation was stunning. Purposefully killing innocent civilians was against her code. Yes, there were innocent people who died in Madrid, in war time, civilians die, it's unavoidable. But you don't go out with the express purpose of murdering them. That is barbaric. The vendetta was over. Siggi made a video called. "About Madrid."

"What about it?"

"I was told you had a problem."

"The woman said some things about Ähern."

"What did she say?"

"How well did you know my uncle?"

"What?" He looked puzzled. "Has something happened, Hedda? The mission was a success, no?"

"Answer my question."

"Are you injured?"

"No, there is nothing wrong with me. Now answer my question. How well did you know my uncle?"

"I never actually met the man. I was just an analyst working for Kroner during that time," he said, purposefully obfuscating.

"So, how did it go?" He was so fucking Swiss. She could never tell what was going on in his head. Was anything he uttered true? Or was it all lies to manipulate her?

"She is dead, and I'm done with this business Siggi. You know, I believe what she said to me. Ähern Jäger was a terrorist. This whole campaign has been an act of vicious of terrorism to further his plan for European domination."

"Hedda, it changes nothing. They killed your brother, and you swore revenge, and you are so close to completion, you can't stop now."

"The hell I can't. You just watch me."

"Then perhaps I should have said I won't let you stop."

That caught her by surprise. "What?"

"There are still people who must be eliminated. Only when they are dead can you stop."

"How could you possibly force me to go on?"

"You forget, Hedda, I know you, I know what you are. You are a psychopath just like him. He thought he knew everything, could do anything he wanted, but he didn't plan ahead, he couldn't see that his methods were wrong."

"I am not like him at all."

"Of course you are. You want what you want. You don't really care about anyone else, do you. It's why you have been able to do what you have done your whole life. You take what you want without regard for the cost, or what it may cost other people. You are a killer without conscience. You have no emotional connections, no empathy, no sympathy, no remorse.

"That's not true."

He smiled and chuckled. "Yes, it is. You asked for truth. Well, there it is, you are a spoiled selfish child Hedda. That was your uncle, and you have made the same mistake. You have left yourself open for attack."

"And who would be attacking me, you?" she said sarcastically.

"Of course, since the very beginning." That floored her. "You will carry on with the work as I give it to you, or I provide evidence, anonymously of course, that Anita Franco is Hedda Jäger, the real assassin and that the woman who used that name before no longer exists. They will end you and she will be free. What do you have to say about that?"

"I will kill you Sigismund Kraft. If it is the last thing I do on this earth, I will kill you."

He smiled. "There is no doubt that you will try, my dear."

***

Chapter ~ 9

After Kat's morning run, she was heading down King St. with Sara in her arms. Rosario was beside her carrying her gym bag in it. "Are you sure you don't want to join my exercise class?"

"Oh-my-god no, Kat. What you do in that dojo is not exercise, it's combat."

"Rose come on; I lift weights. How is that anything like combat?"

"It doesn't matter, I'm not getting anywhere near those crazy people, so no thank you."

"They are not crazy people; they're exercise junkies and a girl's gotta keep in shape."

"There's nothing wrong with my shape, thank you very much. And I've seen you spar with your instructor, and it scares the hell out of the poor guy."

"I don't scare him! He's just horsing around."

"Oh really? Kat, I feel his pain. and by the way, to tell the truth, there are times when you scare me too."

"I do not."

"Yes, you do."

They crossed the street and upon reaching the other side, a cell phone rang.

Both women checked to see if it was theirs. Kat cursed. "Damn, it's mine." She read the caller ID. "Shit, Rose, can you take Sara please. The gym bag hit the ground and the child changed hands.

"Hi, can you hold on for a sec." Then putting her hand over the mic. "Listen why don't you guys just go. I'll catch up."

"Sure. Sara, do you want to walk?"

When she was alone Kat went back to her phone. "Hi Ramsey, I can't believe it. Is that really you?"

"Oh, it's me alright, Kat."

"How the hell are you?"

"I'm good. And you?"

"We're fine, Sara is terrific, growing like a weed and won't shut up. When are you and Bernice going to come up for a visit?"

"I'll let you know."

"Alright but don't wait too long, OK?"

"Yeah, we'll come up as soon as we can. Uh, Kat, I'm curious about something."

"Curiosity is good. What about?"

"Have you made any trips to Europe lately?"

"Europe? I'm a house Kat with a kid. Who has time to go to Europe? Why do you ask?"

"I was talking to someone recently who said they spotted you in Rome." She laughed. "Rome? Jesus, Ramsey. If I did take a trip, it sure wouldn't be to Italy. You can tell that person you were talking to that they need glasses. I've gone totally domestic all the way. Domestic food, domestic wine, domestic me. I drink B.C. wines. They're domestic right?"

"I think they are, yeah. Anyway, I thought he was full of crap, but I had to check."

"Spill Ramsey, what's going on?"

"There's nothing to spill, I was thinking about you, that's all."

"Ramsey, for Christ's sake, tell me what is going on?"

"Alright, I just can't believe you're so calm now."

"About what?"

"How it's possible that you don't know about it.

"Ramsey darling, you are driving me nuts."

"Sorry, but it's all over the news. The French Minister of Defense has been assassinated and they're saying you did it. Witnesses say they saw you there."

"That is ridiculous. I haven't been out of Toronto in four years."

"They have witnesses who swear to it that they saw Anita Franco in Rome."

"Ramsey, Anita Franco doesn't exist, the French are idiots. Thank you for worrying about me, but seriously ..."

"Kat, shut up and listen to me. Wolfson told me they have positively identified Anita Franco. They now have wanted posters with your picture on them plastered all over Europe."

"So, I should expect an attempted rendition?"

"That would be my guess."

"Shit. OK, I'll deal with it."

"How?"

"Jezzus Ramsey, I can't tell you that."

"Right, and whatever you do step on it. You're running out of time and lives, Kat. You're down three already and I'd hate to lose you."

"Thanks."

He had triggered the alarm. Clearly, something was going on in Virginia because Ramsey's warning had come directly from Wolfson. Kat was instantly in combat mode again.

About to cross the street she checked for traffic, and subtly took stock of the people around her. It was a basic field-craft, the people who weren't interested in her because they were obviously involved with other things. The people who were watching her, often tried too hard to look disinterested and stood out.

That was precisely what that person was doing over to her left, on the other side of King.

She took a fraction of a second too long to look away. A rookie mistake. Kat took out her phone and while pretending to make a call snapped a picture of the woman. The woman was being more careful now.

She would remember everything about that person now. South Asian, probably Sikh, young, late twenties, tall, slim, attractive. After what Ramsey had said, it was likely that Wolfson had sent someone to check up on her. Glancing at the reflection in a shop window she saw the woman walking on a parallel course. A moment later, she had crossed the street and was right behind Kat suggesting that she intended to intercept Kat. It was time to go on the offensive.

Pushing on, Kat turned onto Sherbourne and hurried down the street before the young woman had made the corner. Kat ducked into the alley across from the dojo and waited.

She didn't have to wait long; the agent was casually looking over at the dojo as she walked by then she stopped just to the right of the alley. "I understand that you want to buy the building," she said. Kat did not see any weapons, so she relaxed a little. Perhaps this was another warning from Wolfson, the head of Military Counterintelligence. "Shit. I'm slipping, aren't I"

"Not at all. You don't know anything about me, and yet I've made a point of finding out as much as I could about you."

"Should I be flattered or frightened?"

She smiled, thinking that was a compliment. "Your choice, I'm not about to put words in your mouth."

But what if it wasn't a compliment? she thought. "OK, I have some ground to make up. Let's start with who the hell are you and who do you work for?"

"Sure, I'm Special Agent Raini Hanamansingh, M-CI, a big fan by the way. Big-big fan. That's why I volunteered to come up here to see what you were up to."

"Wait a second, you volunteered?"

"Yeah, strange eh? Actually, it was a special request. There were some guys who wanted to do this detail, but they were sure you were guilty, and I wanted it to be an unbiased appraisal."

"Unbiased eh, and you just said you were a big fan."

"I am, but if you were dirty, I'd put you down."

"Whoa," Kat stepped back, "with friends like you … you know what I mean?"

"Calm down, I knew you weren't guilty. I was thrilled to report that you've been good as gold."

"I'm glad to hear it. So, that means that Wolfson has let the Europeans know that I wasn't involved?"

"Uh huh. I'm guessing that's what you were told on the phone."

"But you'd be wrong. I was told they have my picture posted all over Europe."

"What? I filed my report last night and it has been received. So, you should be in the clear."

"My information seems to have put the lie to that. I don't like this at all. Thanks for telling me." She headed back to King St.

"Where are you going?"

"I am going back to my house. I don't know what you're going to do, but I'm going to prepare for war."

"Oh Christ. Ms. Fernando."

Kat was distracted as she pulled out her phone. "What?"

"What about Sara and the nanny?"

"I'm texting Rose and tell her to follow me."

"Oh. Uh, follow us, you mean."

"Are you nuts?" She sent the message. "You're not coming with me."

"You'll need backup."

"Yeah, you and who's army?"

"Don't underestimate me."

"OK, sorry, but you don't look old enough."

"I'm twenty-seven, and it's coming up to three years since I graduated from Huachuca."

"Impossible." Kat thought about that, then said, "So, you've been in the army for nine years?"

"Yup, since I was eighteen."

"No kidding?" that cheered her up a bit. "Any combat?"

"Two tours in Afghanistan."

"Respect," Kat said. "Are you armed."

"Of course."

"Then you're my backup."

***

By Friday evening the news of Dos de Mayo Madrid Massacre was the lead story everywhere. Videos taken from the cc cameras of the attack, beginning with the explosions, were running across the networks. Kat, Sara, Raini and Rosario sat stunned looking at the television screen.

Raini couldn't understand what had happened. She had made her reports, they were accepted, but somehow the message wasn't getting through. As far as the media in France, Italy and Spain were concerned, Kat had now been identified as a rogue American agent.

The Americans obviously denied any connection to the assassinations and the assassin. They would only say that the woman in the Madrid videos was tall and had dark hair like one of their agents. That was as far as the similarities went. When the Europeans pushed, they responded, "Yes, at one time there was an agent who used that name.

Yes, it was the same woman shown in those popular magazine photos from years ago. She was a special agent using the alias for undercover work. It was not her real name, and she has since retired from M-CI. She could not possibly have anything to do with the attacks."

But as the 66th Brigade commander said, "That didn't fly with the Europeans."

Sara seemed to know that something was wrong, and she couldn't settle, so Kat read her three stories and sang to her until she fell asleep.

The TV stayed tuned in to one of the news channels all night. It was a constant stream of talking heads, but in all that time there was no new information.

When they awoke Saturday morning one of those old sexy photos of Kat as the Happy Widow of Ibiza showed up and was now the omnipresent backdrop for news shows.

From that, she knew this wasn't going to go away. Watching Sara play gave her the feeling of being in a crowd on a sidewalk as a bus came smashing over them. She couldn't escape the feeling that no matter what she did, something bad always came along to screw it up.

She was so tired; it was impossible to shut down that little voice in her head. The voice that dredged up all the pain and sorrow from a lifetime of abuse. And now Sara was facing the possibility that she going to lose her mommy too. How could she protect her from what was coming? At that point she couldn't hold back the tears. Rose had been watching her. It was as if she could see the nightmare taking over her mind. "Kat?"

Trying to regain control she looked at her. "What is it Rose?"

"Is there something I can do?"

"Oh Christ, I wish there was." She took a deep breath. "But really there isn't. I'll be OK .... I'm sorry about the water works. I was just thinking ..."

"... about what's going to happen to Sara" Rose finished.

"Am I really that transparent?"

"Sometimes."

"I don't know what to do now. I feel like I'm drowning. I don't want Sara to have to go through what I did."

"That would never happen Kat. Never, I wouldn't let it."

"Oh ..." She stopped and began to look around her as if she was looking for an escape hatch. "I just don't know what to do. Can't we just run away from all of this?"

"To where, Kat? They'll keep coming after you no matter where we go."

"I know." She paused for a long time as visions of secluded locations raced through her mind. "I hate this ... Oh god, it's hopeless."

"The best thing to do now is try to put it out of your mind. You are here in this magnificent house you built; we are safe ..."

"Yes, but for how long?"

"No one can answer that. But those people you worked for; they know you're not responsible for what's happening. Raini tell her"

"They do," Raini said emphatically. Kat was once the icon of bravery, strength, and perseverance, at the pinnacle of her profession which Raini had followed and admired. This was something she had never have expected. Had she become exactly what she had always wanted to be, experiencing the normal life she had always wanted? Had she become a homebody, a house-Kat, a woman at peace with herself, and with hope for the future?

Perhaps it was just a matter of being overwhelmed by what was being done to her and she would snap out of it.

Or perhaps it was something more profound, the tipping point into the abyss. After all the things she's had to endure, has she come to the point where it has completely overwhelmed her?

Obviously as Kat's closest friend, Rose, had also seen the change, but she didn't want to admit it. "See? Everything will be alright. I know we'll be alright. I'm going into the kitchen to fix us a snack."

"OK."

Raini got up from the floor. "I'll help you." When they were alone in the kitchen Raini asked Rose what she meant when she mentioned this magnificent house.

"It's just an apartment above a shop. What's so magnificent about it?"

"I hope you will never have to find out." Leaving Raini speechless, Rose made a mountain of cinnamon toast and large pot of tea, then brought their snack into the living room on a tray. Kat looked up smiled, gratefully and reached out her hand to Rose. When she took it, Kat gave it an affectionate squeeze. "Rose, it's amazing what you've been able to put up with. I don't know what I did to deserve you."

"You've made me part of your family, that's what you did."

***

Chapter ~ 10

It was ten Saturday evening; she'd spent the whole day trying to come to terms with her dilemma before she made the call. The campaign wasn't making any sense to her now, but Siggi's threat compelled her to continue. "Guten Abend, Siggi."

"Guten Abend, Hedda. Are you feeling rested now?"

"Does it matter? I'm ready to hear about the next contract."

"I knew you would come around. His name is Holt von Grimmelshausen, he is the German ambassador to the UN."

That didn't shock her at all. Just another important man who was doing his duty. Was she finally developing some sort of empathy? "What has he done?"

"He has been in league with the Americans from the beginning. He was one of the men passing information on to them from behind the scenes."

That was a lie, of course, it was meant to help convince her to do what he wanted. In fact, the reason he wanted the man killed was that he was one of the few, truly sane men who was helping to guide the European leaders at the UN.

"He also negotiated the terms of reparation between the Americans and the Italians for the bombing of the Golden Fortress."

That was a lie too, but Siggi held up some pages she couldn't really see, suggesting they contained the proof. "It is all in here."

The fiesta was still carrying on all around her. She had been listening to the fireworks and the sounds of the frenzied Flamenco guitars, and strident gypsy voices tumbled down into the valley like a rockslide. The people of Fragiliana were being royally entertained. Hedda was in no mood for celebrations. "Have you heard any news about Franco?"

"As we had hoped, the Americans have begun to react. My sources in US intelligence have told me that they are preparing to try to arrest her. His exact words were, 'by any means necessary.' My understanding of that phrase means dead or alive, preferably dead."

"At last."

"Yes, it is very good news. If they find her, and I'm sure they will, your crusade will come to an end, Hedda. In the time we have left, it is vital that we deal with von Grimmelshausen."

"Very well. Send me everything you have on him." She looked away from the screen to the window on her right. The village that clung to the side of the mountain was ablaze with colored lights and fireworks. There was a time, not so long ago, when she would have been up there with them singing and dancing like a normal person. Now she wished those times had never come to an end. The file came through. She printed it and she scanned the pages looking for the right way to approach her target. "I see some options already. I'll study the files. When I have a workable plan, I'll let you know."

"Call me if you need assistance."

"The team you sent me will be sufficient."

"As you wish." That bit of news delighted him.

"Perhaps you should call them. Tell them it may take a few days to get the items I need together. They can do what they like until then." With a quick tap on the keyboard, the screen went dark. After reading over the files the plan began to emerge. There was a river, the house was on the riverbank. There was a small airfield close by the river.

There was a safe and secure way in and out, her small twin prop Baron G58 would make that easy. She needed a boat to carry them across and a skipper who wouldn't ask too many questions.

***

Kat dreaded another sleepless night, watching her little princess happily play with her monkey doll, while the wolves were practically at the door. It almost made her cry.

Don't do that, she told herself, not now. Sara looked so incredible in her teddy bear jammys, with her coal black hair up in a ponytail and big blue eyes shining up at her. Those blue eyes had definitely come from her father, but everything else was directly from her. "Aren't you sleepy-tired yet, Honeybun?"

"No," she chirped, yawned, and rubbed her eyes.

It was half past eleven. "OK you little monster it's time." Rose stood and stretched. "How about a quick bath and then bed?"

"Will Mommy read me a story?"

She looked at Kat and read the signs. "No, I'll read you the story tonight."

After they had gone upstairs, Kat and Raini just stared at the television screen in silence. Raini became increasingly anxious as the silence stretched on. She began to fidget.

"OK, spill, what's on your mind?"

Raini got up and went to the window. "I have a really bad feeling about where this is going."

"Are you worried about your job at the agency?"

"No, I don't care about that anymore. I thought they'd have cleared you before any of this. I had expected that I'd be recalled. Now that I'm here they must know that I disobeyed orders. I wasn't supposed to have any contact with you at all."

"Did I know about that?"

"Honestly, I can't remember if I told you."

"I'm sorry."

"It wasn't your fault. I was with you the moment we spoke out there on the street."

"I don't know what to say. You know they're going to try to bury this as deep as they can. I've been through this with Wolfson before and there's a tombstone in Arlington to prove it."

"You're kidding!"

"You didn't know that?" She laughed. "I thought you studied my record."

"I guess that proves your point. What if..."

The phone rang and Kat reached for the instrument in her pocket. Looking at the caller ID she whispered, "Shit!" Then brightening her voice, she said, "Ramsey hi! Is there a ...?"

"Kat! Stop talking! You have to get out of there now! They are coming for you."

"Who?"

"A kill squad. Get out of there fast. I don't know how soon they'll get to you, but they are on their way, and they have orders to use any means necessary."

"What?"

"They're going to kill you, Kat. Get out now." The connection ended.

"Ramsey ... Ramsey?!" She put the phone down. "Oh-holy shit...! Rosario!"

She was upstairs in the hallway. "Yes?"

Kat was already running up and Raini wasn't far behind. "We've got to get out of here now. Get Sara dressed and bring her into my office. Hurry please!"

As Rose dressed Sara, Raini followed Kat into her office. "I don't understand what's happening. Who called?"

"An old friend. He said company is coming and trust me, they aren't coming up for coffee, so we're leaving by the back door."

That phrase spoke volumes to Rose. "Oh my-god, no."

"Who's coming?"

"Wolfson has sent a kill squad."

"Oh shit. Where's the back door?"

"You'll see."

"Rose, is this what you meant about the magnificent house?"

Rose had gone through several escape drills, basically the same thing as a lifeboat drill on a cruise ship. People had to know what to do in unlikely event that the ship was sinking. "But they're just drills, right?" she asked at the time, "I mean, those ships can't really sink, can they?"

"Remember the Titanic?" That was during the first drill. She had been with Kat for four eventful years waiting for this ship to sink, so she had paid attention.

"Yes. Lord help us."

"Don't waste your breath on him, Rose. He's not going to help us out of this."

"I'm frightened, Kat."

"So am I, Rose. But we've planned for this, right?"

"You planned for this?"

"Raini, just pay attention and follow my lead."

Before they came down to the city from Mulmur, Kat knew that her past would eventually catch up to her. It was a certainty. That's why she bought a block of King St. buildings and spent a fortune on renovations to prepare for this moment. Protecting Sara had become the most important job of her life. She came up with this innovative backup plan for the safehouse. During the construction they were living in a large house in Mulmur a township north of Toronto, and she figured that there was time to prepare for disaster.

On that score she made it just under the wire. A security company pulled out all of the tricks of the trade to design a safehouse that couldn't be breached. But in the event of a Titanic-esque event and the security system was activated, it would provide a way to escape and cover her tracks.

They thought she was crazy, but you don't say no to a client with money and Kat had lots of it. What she wanted was a fire box built inside, but independent of the existing building. Special materials were employed to suspend the massive structure away from the shell, so that during a raid the outer building would remain unharmed.

"Follow you where?" asked Raini.

"You'll see. Rose, we're going to be alright. I promise."

"OK. Maybe I should get some warmer clothes for her."

"No time." Kat moved away from the desk to stroke Sara's face. "We're OK, Honeybun. Rosario, I've everything she needs in her go bag."

"Sorry, I forgot. Of course, you do."

"What's the matter, Mommy?"

"We are going on an adventure just like we practiced."

"Goodie! Through the tunnel?"

"That's right, through the tunnel and there's going to be a lot of noise. Don't be scared, OK."

"OK Mommy."

The phone rang again but the ring was different this time. Three quick trills, then three more, then three more again. "Holy shit."

"What was that?" Raini's professionalism was getting shaky.

"That means they're here!"

"Holy shit, and we're leaving through a tunnel in the roof?"

"The attic, yes."

Taking Raini's hand, brave little Sara said, "It's OK, you can hold my hand."

"That's my girl, you take care of her. Now don't panic, but our full-on defense systems have been activated automatically."

Rose looked horrified. "We're sinking?!"

"Uh… Well, yeah, I suppose the house is sinking, but we're OK, it's on hold for the moment."

With increasing alarm, Raini asked, "On hold? W- hat does that mean and w-w-what's this full-on defense thing?"

"It's a sort of self-destruct program."

"Uh… a WHAT?"

"We have five minutes to get out, so we have to move."

"Oh, OK. And what happens in five minutes?"

"Don't worry, we have plenty of time."

"Yeah, but Kat, what happens in five minutes?"

Kat demonstrated with a graphic hand gesture and sound effects. "KA-BADA-BOOM!" Stepping back around her desk she reached for the keyboard. "'HOLD' is like the 'SAFETY' on a gun." Hitting Ctrl+ Esc three times will unlock it."

Raini's eyes widened. "Wait, did you just take it off the 'SAFETY?'"

"Yup." The image on the screen flashed red three times, then remained red as the computer began a countdown. "The flashing screen means that all the defense systems have been activated, and the countdown is going. Listen to me, Raini. They don't know you are in here with us. Once we get out of here you can resume whatever it was that you were doing, and they won't know about this."

"That's not going to happen."

"What are talking about?"

"I'm not having anything else to do with them. You are innocent and they know it. Yet they still want to sanction you … and them?" She said, pointing at Sara and Rose. "No. No way. If you'll let me, I'm staying with you."

Kat studied her face and saw that she was perfectly serious. "I don't think you really know what you're letting yourself in for, but I'm glad you're here."

"Uh Kat … the countdown … T-04:34."

"Right. We'll talk about this later."

The images from the exterior cameras appeared on two other monitors above her desk. "Oh shit, look at the screens." Rainy looked and saw men at both front and back doors. There were eight of them. No uniforms for these guys, this was black ops, wet work.

They were dressed like regular Joes, ball caps, windbreakers, jeans and cross-trainers.

It was impossible to see their faces under those caps, but it was what they were trying to hide against their chests that revealed why they were down there. They were carrying what looked like SIG MPX submachine guns with suppressors. How did Ramsey know?

T-04:28.

Two men were crouching down by the locks at the back door and the front with their picks working away. The man at the front door started first, it was his picks that closed the circuit and switched on the first tier of her defense system. Even so, they both got burned at the same time as a chemical reaction superheated the locks, making them glowed white-hot. As the tumblers began to melt, they welded the picks in place and the doors to the jamb. The men lurched back in agony with serious burns to their hands. They had all backed off expecting an explosion which did not come.

"Serves you right, you bastards," Raini said.

T-04:21.

Kat tapped Delete, Delete, Delete, on her keyboard which turned off sets of rare-earth magnets that had locked two hidden doors in her office paneling. "Alright Rose, are you ready?" Rose nodded and holding Sara tightly she pushed on the panel and the door popped open.

The first secret cupboard held their go bags, three backpacks with their emergency travel kits containing money, documents and clothing.

The first one was for Rose, the second was Sara's. Rose hesitated. "Try to keep focused, Rose. Are you alright?"

She nodded.

"Raini, you and I are sharing this one. Do you still have your gun?"

"Yes."

"Good. OK take this." Raini slung the backpack over her shoulder.

T-04:14

"Why is it so heavy?"

"Among … other things, my gun and ammunition are in it."

Raini didn't attempt to figure it out. "Copy that. Do you think we're going to have to shoot our way out?"

T-04:08

"No, but by the look of those guys, you never know. Rose, you can give the bookshelf a push now."

T-04:05

Holding Sara on her hip, Rose pushed the case aside, revealing a heavy steel panel which opened with a touch of her hand. Rose hesitated again.

"Go on through, we'll be right behind you." Kat glanced back at the monitor in time to see their leader looking directly into the hidden camera above the door. It was as if he knew she was there watching him. He pointed at the camera, his handgun and fired.

"Oh, shit. You bastard!" That was a face she would never forget. She hit rewind then pause to freeze the image. "You *son*-of-a-bitch!"

"You know him?" asked Raini.

"Oh yeah, that's Jamie Nunez, a walking, talking, brown sphincter."

"Sphincter," said Sara.

Kat almost laughed, "That's right, Honeybun, he's a sphincter."

T-03:58.

Behind the second door was a tunnel lined with the same material used to protect the space shuttle upon re-entry. It led to the east end of the city block. "Raini, it's your turn, I'll follow in a few seconds."

"But …"

"We still have lots of time. I'll be right there, go on."

T-03:51.

T-03:49.

The men were applying plastique to the hinges and handle.

T-03:48.

The street was quiet.

T-03:47.

Apart from a lonely cab heading west there was no one else around. Nunez had been looking up into the corner of the door frame sure that what he saw was a tiny camera. He was right of course. He imagined that Kat was watching him, and he was right about that too. The shot he fired broke the camera, but it was nothing compared to the destruction that was coming.

He wanted the doors opened front and back, so his team set the charges and backed into the entrance of the shop next door. "Fire in the hole." Eight small, simultaneous explosions blew off the hinges.

This was the second time Rosario and Sara had lost everything to an explosion. They all felt the loss. Rose had left behind things her family had given her to replace what she'd lost when their house was destroyed. Every photo of Sara since she was one, her books, her clothes, her toys. All the things they'd collected over the past three years to try to restore some semblance of normalcy, everything had to be left behind. There just wasn't enough time.

Everything inside the insulated steel box was turned into ash in minutes. Rosario trusted Kat implicitly. She understood what staying with Kat would be like and she was prepared to endure the hardship to be part of a family she loved. She had taken Sara through without question, and now they were waiting for Kat to join them at the far end.

T-02:20.

There was one thing Kat couldn't leave behind. Before she followed Raini, she saved her data on the exterior hard drive, unplugged it, leaving the CPU and monitor to continue the countdown.

T-02:10.

Dropping the hard drive in her purse she stepped through the opening then turned to close the door with the touch of her hand. As it clicked into place, it began to lock itself. That simple looking portal was in fact a sophisticated blast-door, designed to withstand the fire, as well as the possible explosives that might be used to try to open it.

T-01:47

Eight solid steel rods slid out from the four edges of the door and slid home in the surrounding steel structure. The thing was designed for a single use. The rods moved into place breaking glass vials containing the chemical which welded them in place. No one could follow them through now.

T-01:30

The men outside backed off and prepared to set off the charges.

T-01:20

While the kill squad was working on their plan 'B,' Kat, Sara, Rosario and Raini were standing by a special elevator that didn't exist on any official plan. They boarded the lift and went down two floors to a small room with a door that opened onto George St.

Safe at last in that sheltered room Kat made her first phone call on a throwaway phone.

T-00:50.

Deacon answered guardedly. "Hello?"

"Deacon."

"Kat it's nearly ... midnight, is something wrong?"

T-00:40

"Yeah, something's wrong alright. There is an M-CI kill squad outside, trying to break into our apartment."

T-00:30

"A kill squad?" That took a few seconds to sink in. "Why would M-CI want to kill you? You were on their side, for Christ's sake."

"Time has a way of changing relationships," she said philosophically.

"Say what?!"

T-00:20

"Deacon, we need your help."

T-00:18

128

"Of course."

T-00:17

"My car's a write-off and we need transportation to get away from here."

T-00:14

"Your car? What ..."

"Deacon don't worry about the car; we need a place to hide.

T-00:12

"Then can come here."

T-00:09

"Absolutely not. They'll come looking for me there and I am not putting your life at risk."

T-00:05

T-00:04.

Deacon heard the small, muffled explosions in the background as the kill squad blew the door's hinges off the frame.

T-00:03.

"What the hell was that?"

T-00:02.

"That was their C-4 door-crackers."

"My God!"

"Hold on guys it's boom time."

T-00:01.

KA-BOOM!-WHOOSH-BOOM.

The shockwave shook the whole block, and the sound of the roaring fire was deafening.

"Jesus Christ, Kat! What the hell was that?"

"What? I can't hear you."

"What the hell was that?"

"Ah ... that would be my self-destruct system going off. My apartment is currently an easy bake oven."

"You blew your building up?!"

129

"Yeah ..., well not the *whole* building. I'm hoping that the fire is fully contained in the apartment. The rest of the buildings should be safe."

"You're hoping?! Are you crazy?! How can you joke at a time like this?"

"I wasn't joking"

"You've got to get out of there."

"I was hoping you'd help with that."

"I'll call the fire department."

"They're already on their way. We can't leave here until they've gone."

"Jesus!"

"Don't worry, we're safe where we are for a while."

"For a while?"

"We're safe Deacon, I know this is asking a lot, but can you come and get us?"

"I'm calling Jim right now, he's at a club in the entertainment district. He should be able to get to you in a few minutes."

"Thanks, tell him to come in from the east. The road will be blocked off at Jarvis."

"OK." He had to think for a moment. That pause made Kat fear that she might have lost him. The noise of the fire was amplified as the insulated steel box began to expand. It was all taken into consideration; the exterior walls were safe. Sirens could be heard faintly over the roar of the fire, and they were getting closer.

"Deacon, are you still there?"

"Yeah. Yes, sorry, I … I had to take care of a couple of things here. Right, I've got a place for you and Jim is on the way. I have a building downtown with an apartment you can have.

"Jim will show you how to get into it. I set it up to…"

"Oh, hang on a second," she said, cutting him off. "I have a monitor with cameras on the streets around us. The fire trucks are here, so the special team must have bugged out. I can see the police are too. They're blocking off the road now. Is Jim on his way to us now?"

"Yes, he'll be in own his car, it's his old green Buick."

"Yes, I know it. Tell him we'll be at the side door on George St."

"Are you going to be OK?"

"Yes thanks, we're fine I just want to get us away from here. We'll talk soon Deacon, OK?"

"Yes. Please call me as soon as you're in the apartment."

"I will."

***

When the ground shook, Nunez and his boys scurried back across the street. Alarms went off everywhere. In an instant, Kat's apartment had become an inferno and all they could do was stare at it with their mouths open. They all were thinking the same thing.

No one could survive that. Obviously, it was suicide.

The blaze seemed to be completely contained in Kat's apartment. How was that possible?

Soon sirens could be heard moving towards them. There was nothing more to do, she had taken care of their job for them. Apart from the two injuries, it had been a successful mission.

The rest of the team came out from the lane behind, and they gathered on the corner of George Street. Nunez pointed to their van down the street, and they ran for it and departed with squealing tires. People in neighboring apartments, wakened by the explosion were at their window and were horrified by what they saw. They all knew Kat in some way or other and couldn't believe that anyone would want to harm her and her child. They described what they saw to police. Eight men had set fire to Kat's apartment and took off in a dark colored van. The firetrucks, four of them, arrived from the west just moments after the van faded into the distance. The police cars came in from everywhere. What they found was one for the books, like nothing they had ever seen before. The fires from hell, were completely contained in the two floors above the furniture store. It looked like a crematorium;

131

the very effect Kat was hoping for. The building's exterior was cool to the touch. There were special chimneys installed on the roof to let the smoke and gases escape, so that it wouldn't blow up.

In any event, the firefighters hooked their hoses up to the hydrant down the block and started dousing the building even though the water didn't touch the fire that raged on inside.

The police blocked off King at Jarvis. A policeman drove his car to the intersection at George St. and closed it down.

The firefighters working at the door began to wonder why it had been so difficult to open. Not only that but the fire hadn't migrated to the store below or next door. The fire crew just stood back helplessly and watched it burn.

Perhaps ten minutes after they arrived the place miraculously filled with fire retardant foam and in seconds the fire was out. No one on the street could believe what they were seeing. There was no doubt that it was arson, but why? Who were the men that started it? How did they manage to contain it? And where did the foam come from?

Kat, Sara and Rose and Raini watched the monitor. A crowd had gathered on King St. to watch the M.T.F.D. do their stuff. Just another night of danger and excitement on the job in the Big Smoke.

***

Chapter ~ 11

All the attention was on the apartment above the furniture store. The monitor beside the elevator brightened as the camera picked up the flash of headlights heading west on King. A police officer stood in front of his cruiser, blocking off King and waving the cars to go north and south. All but one went north. Behind him was organized chaos. Soon it was Jim Cotter's turn and the police officer signaled for Jim to turn left. Kat watched as the Buick followed his directions, then the officer turned back to watch the fire.

Jim stopped at the curb by the door and a moment later the graffiti stained side portal swung open and Rosario cautiously stepped out with Sara in her arms. When she saw the way was clear, she ran for the car and ducked into the back seat. She sat Sara down then dragged the go bags in after her. Raini went next tossing her go bag through the open front door and held the back door for Kat then she got in beside Jim.

"Hello, and who might you be?" Jim asked.

"She's a friend, Jim."

"OK."

"Raini Hanamansingh, hello."

"And hey, thanks for coming." Kat said, closing the door. While buckling her seatbelt she added quietly, "I wish I had a car seat."

"If wishes were horses ...," Jim quipped, and pulled away. "Just hang on to her and I'll be as careful as humanly possible."

No one was paying attention as the steel door closed, and for the last time, it locked and sealed.

Timing couldn't have been better because as the car reached the end of the street four firefighters came out of the alley onto George St. on their way back up to King.

"Did you see any suspicious looking men hanging around on King street?" Kat asked.

"Hey, there was a bit of a crowd forming. The collected media is out there doing their thing, so no, I couldn't tell you if there was anyone suspicious lurking about. Funny thing though, I did notice that the fire is already out. Those M.T.F.D. guys worked really fast."

"Good, I was worried that the tech guys might've screwed that up."

"What tech guys?"

"Never mind. Poor Graham, he had some really nice pieces in the furniture shop. I hope nothing got damaged."

"He'll be insured. What started the fire?"

"A phone."

"A what?" he asked.

She didn't respond. She was more concerned about not having a car seat for Sara. She and Rose held her securely between them. When Sara settled, Kat stared out the window, but she wasn't looking at the city.

Jim was about to say something, but Raini sensed that Kat had had enough. She reached out and, touching his arm, stopped him with a subtle shake of the head.

Silently, he turned onto The Esplanade and headed west to Jarvis.

Rubbernecking motorists slowed to gawk as the drama unfolding on Kat's block, created a bottleneck at King.

The light changed three times before they had an opportunity to get through the intersection. As far as Jim could tell, no one was following them.

***

Sara eventually fell asleep on Kat's lap, with her head lolled to one side. It was just as well because Kat wasn't there anymore.

Unwillingly, she had drifted across time and the Atlantic, to relive a part of her nightmarish past. The scene played back as if it had just happened. It was the day she met that man she'd just seen shoot out the door camera. The man who, if he had the chance, would have killed not only her but Sara, Rosario and Raini.

She had taken a break from the war on Rote Faust to see a doctor in Paris about her pregnancy. Meanwhile Col. Paul Devlyn Sara's father, had gone on ahead to Zürich to assemble a new team in a secret CIA operations base he borrowed. They were there to get Helmut Kroner, Siggi Kraft's old boss, the man giving the orders to the terrorist cells. This operation was working out of an apartment building on Zypressenstrasse in the 4th District.

It was the tipping point, the moment when Kat was struggling to separate herself from her alter ego, Anita Franco. When she finally arrived at the safe house and peeked up at the building from the edge of her umbrella she saw that man, Special Agent Jamie Nunez. It was the look of hostility on his face that ensured Kat's alter ego would soon be in complete control of her mind.

He didn't really know her and yet he did everything he could to get in her way. She had no idea why he did what he did then. And here he was

again trying to kill her. What the hell was his problem?

***

Kat had been lost in the past, but when they bounced over the streetcar tracks at Church and Richmond it jolted Sara awake. She rubbed her eyes and tried to get up, drawing Kat back to the present.

Jim turned onto Grenville St, and she knew exactly where they were now. "Jesus, Jim, are you turning me in?"

"What?" Then he got it. "Oh shit, no! No-no-no, I thought you knew that the Headington Tower is kitty-corner from the top cop shop. Sorry about that. I should have warned you. Don't worry it's not going to be a problem, I promise."

"That's easy for you to say," she fired back.

"I think Dr. Loats was thinking that no one in their right mind would choose to hide out across the street from the Toronto Police Headquarters."

"Yeah, I'd say he got that right."

"Here's the thing, first, they aren't looking for you, and second, virtually no one knows that Dr. Loats owns this building, let alone that there's a secret apartment up there. So, relax."

"It is possible, that sooner or later the police will be looking for me."

"They think you're dead."

She wasn't having it. "When they do, I'll be the proverbial girl next door."

Jim laughed as the garage door opened smoothly and he drove straight in without stopping. When the door closed behind them her concern began to fade. They coasted down the ramp to the bottom level, P3. He pressed another button and a second overhead door opened. He parked in a Service Vehicles Only spot in the northwest.

It was next to a utility room that jutted out into the circular parking area. The outstanding feature was the much used and abused garbage container, sitting near a door. On the door was a sign that read:

Staff Only

Electrical Room

Danger

High Voltage Unit

"This section of the floor is reserved for the Foundation employees. The main elevators are around on the other side of that wall. There's a door through it but there are special keys for it.

Security has one, I've got the one and the rest are in the apartment."

"Wow, do the tenants know what they're missing?" said Raini. Rose got out of the car with Sara in her arms, and Kat stared at the garbage container.

"The gate back there was the first security gate, the electrical room door is the second," Jim said. "The bin is just to discourage the curious."

"Trust me, it's working," Kat said, as she got the backpacks from the car.

Above the latch was a keypad. "There's one code for maintenance workers, and another one that unlocks the door. He entered the code reciting it aloud as he tapped the keys, 5-5-3-7-6. The door clicked open, and a light switched on, revealing a neat utility room.

"The third gate is the door on the other side of that." He pointed to the electrical transformer. "That one takes a special key. I'm told the lock is pick-proof."

"Jim does someone come down here to clean this room?" asked Kat.

"Yeah, once a month a janitor opens it up to get rid of the cobwebs and check the systems." He held up a brass key and said, "And as an extra precaution, this key only works on this door *if*... you've entered the correct code on the pad outside."

"Aren't the maintenance guys curious about what's behind that?"

"I don't think so." He tapped the sign on the door which said, Elevator Maintenance.

"It's supposed to be an access port to the elevator shaft and elevator maintenance, it's not part of their job description."

He inserted the key and turned the knob. This key doesn't turn in the lock. You just insert it and pull it out. It transmits a coded signal to the security system which unlocks the door. If you try to turn it, it sets off a silent alarm and you'd be locked in here until someone comes to let you out."

"Got it."

"I'll write down that code for you when we get into the apartment."

"No need, I have memorized it," Kat said.

"Really? Remind me not to let you look over my shoulder at the bank machine."

"You're always safe with me, Jim," said Kat solemnly. He and Raini smiled.

"You can write it down for me," Rosario chimed in," And they all laughed.

Beyond that door was something totally unexpected. It was like walking into Dr. Who's Tardis. The floor was a checkerboard of black and white granite tile, the walls were gleaming black granite, polished to a mirror finish and the frosted glass ceiling was illuminated as if it had a direct link to the sun. The single stainless-steel elevator door was a work of art, engraved and embossed with a gold-inlayed Phoenix, the logo of Dectron International.

Kat was astonished. "Whoa, I didn't expect anything like this."

"Yeah, it's a bit over the top, but this place was designed to impress and intimidate."

"Really," said Raini, well tell him it works."

"It was designed by a psychologist/interior decorator."

Rose put Sara down and shook her head "I didn't know there was such a thing."

Sara went over to the door and placed her hands in it. "I'm leaving my fingerprints here for Daddy."

"Good for you honey, Daddy needs a little more mess in his uptight tidy life." Rose took Sara's hand and pulled her away from the door.

Kat pressed the call button and the door immediately swished aside. Inside the elevator was just a smaller version of the lobby and there were only two buttons on the panel, UP and DOWN.

"It only goes to the 30th floor."

"Big surprise."

Rushed in. "Can I push the button?"

"Sure Sara, we're going up now."

"I know. I'm four you know."

"Kids," Jim said, with mock exasperation. "I heard they start off cute so parents don't throw them in the garbage." Sara gave him a look that made him stand back out of reach.

Kat smiled. "Spoken like a true bachelor."

"Why do they call this the Soup Can?" Rosario asked.

"That's just one of the many unanswerable questions about this building. All I can tell you is the architect borrowed the idea from Warhol's Campbell's Soup Cans. The building has an atrium in the center that reaches up 28 stories. The offices and apartments are on the outer ring, there's a glass faced hallway to view the atrium's forest in the center. The first 22 floors are devoted to office space and the top 6 to apartments.

The ceiling of the atrium is like the one down in the secret lobby. Basically, it's a huge grow lamp mimicking the movement of the sun.

"Above that, are 2 more floors but they're not listed on the directory in the lobby. You need a resident's card to operate the elevators The main elevators will only go down to the parking floors and up to the 28th floor. A special card allows you up to the 29th. Part of it houses the air conditioning and heat systems for the building. It has restricted access for maintenance workers.

Everyone thinks that above that is the roof. But wait, there's more."

The elevator stopped, and the door swished aside to reveal a semi-circular space surrounded by glass. It was huge. "This is segregated from the rest of the building.

This elevator is one of only three ways that'll get you up here. The 2nd is a stairway in the H&AC maintenance room. Only workers with a special security pass can come up here. The third is a secret staircase to the Cleveland Fund offices. It's never been used, so I doubt that anyone knows it exists. Now this is your new apartment. The windows are one-way glass, we can see out, nobody can see in."

"Holy ...! You're kidding, right?" Kat was overwhelmed by the place. "You could put a dozen families in this space."

"What can I say? This was the space left over, so he used it all."

"Why would anybody build something like this?"

"Dr. Loats is probably one of the richest men in the world. He has similar buildings in just about every city where Dectron does business. To be honest, I think it has more to do with the intimidation factor than anything else."

"That's not the Deacon I know."

"I've been on business trips with him. He likes to set the tone for the discussions with an *informal* meeting in a space like this."

Kat's jaw dropped, "I had no idea. Does it work?"

"It worked on you, didn't it?"

"Point taken." She began a walk about with Raini, while Rose and Sara went off to find the bedrooms. "He doesn't bring his business guests up in the elevator, does he?"

"There are secrets about this place that even I don't know about."

"Stop joking around."

"It's true, the designer went nuts when she saw her budget, and Dr. Loats has yet to bring anyone here. So don't expect visitors."

"Good," Kat said.

"By the look of your go bags, if you're going to be here for a while you'll need to do some shopping."

Rosario joined them and said, "I'll take care of that."

∗∗∗

Kat's first impulse was to call Ramsey. He picked up on the seventh ring. "Do you know what goddamn time it is?"

"Ramsey, it's me."

"Holy-Jerusalem, Kat."

"What the hell is going on, Ramsey?"

"So, they did come after you. I wasn't sure if I was being played. Are you someplace safe now?"

"Yes, for a while. How close are you to this?"

"I feel like I'm watching this from the moon, Kat. I just got a call from someone who said he was a friend of a friend."

"Who in the world would that be?"

"I have no idea, maybe it came from Wolfson. Anyway, he told me to tell you they were coming to get you **by any means necessary**. You know that's basically a kill order, don't you?"

"I got that impression, yeah."

"I'm sorry, I have no idea what's going on."

"I don't understand any of this, Ramsey. They've had an agent watching me, so they know I didn't do any of it."

"You know about the agent?"

"Let's just say we discovered each other. I think we can count on her being on Team Fernando now."

"Do you know for certain that M-CI is behind this?"

"Yeah, it's got Wolfson written all over it and he knows that I'm innocent. I recognized one of the guys too."

Ramsey's voice was tight with stress and worry. "Things are so screwed up; I don't know who I can trust now."

"Kat, you have to believe that the European authorities are going to catch the imposter. This will be over, and you'll get your life back."

Kat heard Bernice in the background. "Who are you talking to?"

"Bernice, it's just Kat. now go back to sleep. Honey, it'll be OK. I promise."

"I hope you're right. Meanwhile you should take Bernice and go visit Vlad for a while."

"Do you know how hot it is in Arizona this time of year?"

"Ramsey, you could be in real danger."

"Hey, I'll think about it."

"Fuck that, Ramsey! Get Bernice out of bed and go now, tonight!"

"Take it easy, Kat. I don't see that I'm in any danger. Let's just concentrate on ..."

"If this is the beginning of a cover up, then loose ends are going to be cut off. Trust me, Ramsey, you are a loose end now."

"Huh, you're paranoid."

"It's not paranoia when someone is actually trying to kill you. I'm being set up, and they've pulled you into it now. This isn't just a copycat criminal; the woman wants to destroy me.

"Go on."

"OK, Wolfson knows that I'm not involved, yet he sent up the goons. That means he's covering his ass. Why?"

We don't know that it was Wolfson."

"Oh, come on, sure we do. The leader of the goon squad just happens to be Nunez, a guy who has a big hate on for me. God knows why. Now he can use these killings in Europe as an excuse to …"

"Jesus, Kat. I'm …" Kat could hear some pounding and yelling in the distance. "Shit! Wait a second, hang on will ya, there's someone banging on my door."

"Oh, for Christ's sake, Ramsey, don't go down there. Just hang up and call the cops."

"Kat relax, I told you, they're not after me. Now I'll get rid of them and be right back."

A voice in the background said, "Who's at the door, Ramsey?"

"Jesus Bernice, I won't know until I open the damn door, will I?"

"Ramsey!" Kat shouted into the phone, "Don't, don't go down there! ... Ramsey!"

Kat listened to the pounding while Ramsey descended to the foyer. She was terrified.

Bernice was frightened too, she picked up the phone.

"What's going on Kat?"

"I don't know Bernice."

"Well, I'm going down to find out."

"No Bernice, stay in you room! Lock the door!"

A minute stretched into two and then five before Bernice finally came on the phone crying hysterically. "Kat, are you still there?"

"Yes Bernice, what happened?"

"They took him Kat; they just took him away."

"Who took him?"

"The Army, the Army took him. They wouldn't talk to me. They just grabbed him and dragged him out to their car. What have you done? He's gone, Kat! Ramsey's gone! What did you do?!"

"Hang up and call the police. Hang up right now Bernice and call the police."

***

Chapter ~12

Raini didn't know it, but her mission had been over since the moment they received her report on Tuesday. She'd expected to be recalled but she hadn't heard anything from Virginia, and it had been nagging at her. She had to find out what the hell was going on down there.

Kat sensed that it was bothering her and told Raini to go over to the police station to make the call. "If they ping you there, they'll think you're asking for help. That should hold them off for a while."

"Do you want me to come back?"

"Raini, listen to me. We really don't know each other at all." Raini opened her mouth. "No, don't argue with me, we don't. I have to go to Europe and clear my name and I may not survive. This is not your fight."

"And you think you're going to be able to do that alone. Well, you can't. You need me, Kat."

That offended her. "I've worked alone before."

"You haven't been in the field for years, Kat, and there's something different about you."

"Don't be ridiculous."

"She's right Kat. I've noticed it too. You are not as …" Rose had to choose her words carefully now because she could see that Kat was getting very angry. "… confident as you used to be."

She knew that was true, and she couldn't say anything to refute it. This experience had practically unhinged her. "I think you need to go to bed. We can talk about this in the morning."

After a few hours of restless sleep Raini announced that she was going to call in.

"Here, use this phone and then junk it."

"OK. I won't be long." She made the call standing just inside the doors of police headquarters. If they searched for her that is where her signal would place her.

"Virginia Heating and Air Conditioning, how can I help you?"

"Special Agent Hanamansingh, 68238."

"Section Chief Hernandez, Special Agent Hanamansingh. Where are you?"

"Still in Toronto."

"We have been trying to reach you. Why haven't you answered your phone?"

"I haven't received any calls, Sir."

"This phone you are using is not the one we issued. Where is it?"

"There was an explosion at Fernando's apartment. I lost it there in the crowd."

"Your current location is the Toronto Police Headquarters?"

"Correct."

"Why have you gone to the police?"

"Like I said, Fernando's apartment just blew up. What's going on. Did you send out a hit squad?"

"Don't be ridiculous. I am sending agents to pick you up."

"Don't bother, I won't be here."

"Stay where you are. We are bringing you in for a debrief. I have dispatched Special Agent Nunez to pick you up and he… " There was silence.

"Special Agent Hanamansingh …. Special Agent Hanamansingh?"

Until this mission Raini was a special agent with a future now that future was gone. Sending Agent Nunez was a death sentence.

Kat had no choice now, like it or not Raini was going with her.

***

The Charlottesville police responded to the 911 call from Bernice and found her standing at the door side light with the phone in her hand. They had to knock several times before she realized they were there and opened the door.

When they determined that that it was a kidnapping and that she wasn't in any immediate danger they called in the FBI and an ambulance. As soon as the FBI arrived the local cops left leaving the Feds to deal with her.

She was given a tranquillizer and taken to the hospital. Later that morning Brennan and Daniel, the FBI special agents handling the case were at her bedside waiting for her to wake up. They wanted to start right at the beginning, but there was little she could give them. Bernice didn't know what had gone on before Kat called that night. Ramsey didn't talk about that sort of thing. All she knew was that Kat had called and that Ramsey was very agitated. While he was on the phone people came to the door and he went down to see who it was. They just took him away.

"Who had called him?" asked Daniels.

"Katrina Fernando. She was married to Ramsey's oldest friend from the Army. She has a child now, Sara. She's such a darling ..."

"Mrs. Hershoff," the agent cut in, as delicately as he could. He wasn't interested in grandchildren. "Could you tell us what your husband and Mrs. Fernando were talking about?"

"Oh, Harm's name wasn't Fernando, dear, it was Toucksberry. She never took his ..."

"Yeah, that doesn't matter now. What I'd like to know, is what they were talking about."

"Well, I couldn't hear what *she* was saying, of course, I was on the other side of the bed. But I heard what he was saying. He was concerned that she wasn't safe."

Brennan perked up and said, "Safe? Safe from what?"

"Well, that's the thing, isn't it? I have no idea. Oh dear, she is always in trouble, the poor thing. It seems like he's forever helping her out of one disaster or another."

"Do you have any idea what kind of disaster she was having last night?"

"Not at all. Then she touched her lips with her finger and said, "Well, perhaps I may have remembered something after all. Ramsey had mentioned that he had called Kat ..."

"Kat, that's her name?"

"Yes, it's what her friends call her. Anyway, earlier he'd called Kat to ask her if she had been to Europe lately."

"Why would he do that"?"

"Oh, I don't know, they hadn't talked to one another for quite a while. I suppose he was just catching up. Someone in Army Intelligence, a friend of a friend, he said, called him to say she was in trouble and that they were to take her by any means necessary."

"That was the phrase they used, by any means necessary?"

"Oh yes. I have no idea what it means but Ramsey was very upset by that."

"Can you remember anything about what he told her?"

"Let me think for a moment. I don't remember exactly what he said."

"Do you have any idea why the Army wanted her?" asked Daniels.

"Well, I'm not sure I do, Agent Daniels. He had been going on about those killings in Europe, something about the killer using Kat's alias."

"Anita Franco?"

"Yes, that was it, Anita Franco. It was very odd you see because we knew Kat hadn't left Toronto in years."

"Does she work for the Canadian Government by any chance?"

"Heavens no. She used to be with Army Counterintelligence, she was a lieutenant colonel I believe. She retired years ago to raise her little girl."

"Did your husband have any connections with any other foreign power?"

"Well, I don't know what work he was doing. He did work with NATO before Desert Storm. He was a Russian expert you know."

"No, I didn't know that."

"Oh yes, he was very important. He was a handler for a Russian defector. Kat work with Vlad too. They were very close."

"Mrs. Hershoff, is there a chance that Gen. Hershoff was working for the Russians?"

"What? Do you mean like a spy? Oh, good heavens no! Why would you ask a thing like that?" she demanded, with a raised voice. "No, he and Vladimir Mogilevski were friends, Ramsey helped him defect to America."

He raised an eyebrow. "Are you sure about that?"

"Of course I am. If you don't believe me, you can ask them at the Pentagon. Now I think I've answered enough of your questions. I'm tired and I'd like to rest."

"Please, just a couple more questions then we'll let you rest. You said he was getting information from someone in Army Intelligence, what information exactly?"

"Well, I already told you that, didn't I. He was told she was in trouble …"

"By she you mean Katrina Fernando?"

"Yes, and that uh … now what did he tell her? He said they were going to bring her in by any means necessary. And then he said, You know that's basically a kill order, don't you?"

"Are you saying that Military Counterintelligence put a kill order on an American citizen?"

"That's what Ramsey said."

"We're going to go now, Mrs. Hershoff and let you rest. We'll keep you informed."

"Thank you, Agent Daniels."

Their case had been elevated to a threat to National Security and they had to bring the CIA and DHS into it. Even though the possibility of any contact from the kidnappers was practically zero, they set up a surveillance post in the house with the equipment to record and trace the caller. They also notified the RCMP and CSIS that Kat was only a person of interest, not a suspect. They also said that her life was in danger.

They dug out Kat's Army records and realized how incendiary this case had become. They linked her to what was going on in Europe and in concert with the Canadian agencies began an investigation into the recent activities of Army Lieutenant Colonel Katrina Fernando, retired. The question they had to answer, was M-CI trying to cover up some wrongdoing? Was that why they snatched General Hershoff in the middle of the night?

It was illegal for any department of the US government to sanction a hit on an American.

***

Chapter ~ 13

Three hours after he'd been taken from his home, Ramsey Hershoff was approximately 147 miles away in the cellar of a small building in Arlington. They'd strapped his hands together behind his back and covered his head with a hood during the ride, so he had no idea where he was.

They sat him down on the steel chair and released his hands for a moment to cuff him to a hoop in the middle of a steel table. The hood was jerked off his head and the light was so bright he had to turn away and close his eyes. Gradually they began to adjust to it, and he looked around the small, windowless cell. He wasn't alone, he could sense his jailer standing behind him.

"Where the fuck am I?"

The man said nothing.

As he waited for an answer, a terrible feeling swept over him, this could be his home for the rest of his life and there probably wasn't much of it left. "Talk to me, you son-of-a-bitch!" he yelled and got no response. "It's freezing in here. Do you want me to freeze to death, is that it?" The cold was telegraphed through his body by the chair, and he couldn't stop shivering. The absence of a bed seemed to confirm that his stay wouldn't be a long one.

Ramsey was scared, but he wasn't going to show it. "Come on, you want something from me, so let's get on with it!" He couldn't see the man. "Hey scumbag, I'm talking to you!"

The man left the room without uttering a word and the light went out. The elderly general sat in total darkness for another hour before he was visited again. The blinding light came on and burned his eyes. The door opened, and a different man walked in.

Definitely military but in civilian clothes, trim, late thirties, mean.

"Finally. Maybe I can start getting some answers now. Let's start with, who the fuck are you people? And why was I brought here?"

"Let's get a couple of things straight right now." The man spoke quietly but there was an edge in his voice as sharp as any knife. "You are no longer in charge, General. You don't need to know where you are, or who I am. All you need to do, is answer one simple question for me. If I like the answer, then you're out of here."

"What's the question?"

"Where is Katrina Fernando?"

"Haven't a clue."

The man struck him across the face with the back of his hand. It felt like he'd loosened a tooth or two. "Wrong answer. You were on the phone with her when my people picked you up. We were listening in, so we know you know where she is."

"You don't know shit." He spat some blood on the floor. "If you were listening in you would have heard that she didn't tell me where she was."

"You're done General. The only choice you have is make it easy and die quickly or make it hard and painful."

"I'll make it easy for you, asshole. I don't know where she is."

The man put on brass knuckles and slammed him in the gut. "That's just a taste. Your option is still on the table. Think about it."

The man returned three hours later. Ramsey was on the verge of hypothermia and parched.

The conversation was a repeat of the first, but the violence was scaled up a notch. Ramsey was bruised and bleeding, ribs were broken and his hand was crushed, but he simple repeated that he didn't know where she was.

Another three hours passed before the next visit. "OK. I've had enough, she's in Montreal. No sorry, Vancouver, or was that Ottawa? Nope, it was Toronto. Yup, Toronto. She called me from Toronto."

"Was she with Hanamansingh?"

"Who? I don't know who that is so how the fuck should I know that?" The man left without comment or punishment this time. He returned twelve hours later. "I'm giving you one last chance, Hershoff."

"Well, thank fucking-H-Christ for that because I have to take a piss really bad. Would you come a little closer, I don't want to miss."

The man pulled gun from his belt and said, "Is that your final word?"

"No, these are. Go to hell!"

***

Raini stepped out of the elevator looking seriously worried. "Jesus, what happened?" Kat asked.

"I called in. They lied about the squad at your apartment. They were able to ping the burner and placed me at the police station. By the way that was a brilliant idea. Kat, they told me I had to come in and were sending Nunez to pick me up."

"That means you're coming with me whether I want you to or not."

"I already figured that, but thanks for the vote of confidence."

"Oh, come on, I didn't mean it that way." She stopped to think about what Raini had said last night. "Hey, I'm sorry, you're on their hit list now too."

"Yeah, I figured they'd want to clean up their mess. What do you want to do now?"

"To start, we steal a car. We'll pack up and go down to the garage and look for a car with some dust on the roof."

"Classic." Raini went looking for a car. She found one almost immediately. Under a thick layer of dust was a spanking new Mercedes.

There was a parking slip on the dashboard that read, Long Term Parking. Property of Dectron R&D. Without attempting to break-in, she ran back to Kat and told her what she found.

"Then there might be keys in here somewhere." It didn't take long for her to find them. Kat and Raini were in the private office hovering by a monitor. They were scanning the outside of the building using the surveillance camera system and could scan the entire street.

Rose came into the office in time to see Nunez and three other men across the road at the police station.

"They just arrived and went inside. A moment later they hurried out and stopped a policeman at the curb. Nunez spoke and the policeman shook his head."

"I told the guy that I wouldn't be there when Nunez showed up, but I didn't expect them to get there so quickly. Well, they're getting back into their car, and they're gone."

"OK, let's get down to the car. Quickly now."

Sara carried her own go bag, while Rose handled the other two. They loaded up the trunk of the car and headed out. Once they were out into the daylight, Kat saw that the dust made the car stand out. As they crossed the sidewalk onto the street, they saw Nunez and his goons parked across from the police building. They were deep in conversation. One could not ask for better karma. They weren't spotted. Kat drove away sedately, and no one paid any attention to them. It took four city blocks before her heart stopped racing.

"I must be getting old, this is harder than I remembered."

Raini didn't say a word.

∗∗∗

Sitting across the street Nunez pulled out his phone and called in.

"Virginia Heating and Air Conditioning, how can I help you?"

"Special Agent Nunez, 49568."

"Section, report."

"She wasn't here."

"What do you mean she wasn't there, that's where her signal came from."

"What can I tell you? Maybe she called from outside. I was told that nobody of her description had been in the building."

"Her signal came from inside the building. That can't be faked. Maybe they are keeping her in protective custody."

"So, they might say that she wasn't here."

"It's a possibility. I'll try to find out from this end. What is the status of your team?"

"Two men were hospitalized with 3rd degree burns to their hands; the rest are good."

"Copy that."

"Any further orders?"

"We are assuming that the target has been eliminated."

"Affirmative."

"Alright, we're calling this mission accomplished. Return to base."

"Copy that."

***

Part 2

Chapter ~ 14

It took some time to find a carwash, so Kat pulled off the road and turned the driving over to Raini. With Rosario's phone she called Deacon for help. He was expecting the call.

"How is the apartment?"

"It was great Deacon, a bit over the top but hey, when you got it, flaunt it right?"

"Uh …"

"Listen sweetheart, we have to get away from Toronto and I'd be really happy to do that today. The problem is they will be watching the airports and we're driving a Dectron car."

"Never mind about the car. Where do you want to go?"

"I've been thinking about that. The last assassination was in Madrid, I'd like to get somewhere close by …"

The discussion continued as they drove around looking for a carwash. As it happened, Deacon was scheduled to have a meeting in Lisbon in two days and he thought perhaps he could go earlier. That was the seed from which their plan for absolution sprang. The first issue was getting through customs in Portugal.

As passengers, they would pass through customs and immigration and their names would be out there for anyone to pick up. But as company pilots there was a good chance that they'd be overlooked.

Both Kat and Raini were pilots checked out on multi engine jets. Deacon happened to have one or two, so that was the method they chose to make the crossing.

The second issue was that he said he would agree to that part of the plan on one condition. "And what condition would that be?"

"That Sara and Rose stay at my house until you've done whatever it is you are going to do." Kat accepted that condition gladly.

"What size is your friend?"

"What are you thinking, Deacon?"

"There are some uniforms at the airport, maybe there's something that will fit you."

"I'm a twelve," Raini said.

"Yeah, that works for me as well, but I don't think men's jackets would fit us, we carry extra baggage."

"Never would I refer to the bumper you have as baggage."

"Gee Deacon, you say the sweetest things."

"And for your information we use women pilots too. I think we can find something to fit you both."

"Great. We're going to stop and put Sara and Rose in a cab and send them to the house now, is that OK?"

"Perfect."

"And we will wait for you at the airport."

"That too is perfect. I'll make arrangements to have the plane fueled and ready and see you when I get there. You know the setup at the fight office so you can log a flight plan while you wait for me. Oh, by the way, if you want this business trip to look normal, then I'll have to ask Janet and Jim to come too."

"Not a problem."

"OK, we'll meet you at the hanger."

"Thanks Deacon."

Raini found a gas station with a drive through car wash and pulled in. "Who are Janet and Jim?"

"Janet Ireland and Jim Cotter are Deacon's security team, ex-military, Jim doubles as his chauffeur ..."

"That's the guy that picked us up last night."

"Yup, and Janet pretends she's his housekeeper, but she's got hidden skills. And she's an amazing cook."

"So, are we a team of four now?"

"No, they'll stay with Deacon. It's going to be just you and me, kid."

"Kat?"

"Yes Rose?"

"How long will you be away?"

"Can you manage here on your own for a while?"

She looked stricken. "Of course I can, but how long is a while?" Kat just looked at her. "It could be forever, couldn't it. Oh-god, I knew this would happen."

"I'm sorry, Rose, I have to do this."

"Yes, I know, it's fine," she said sharply. She was angry and frightened, and with good reason. The last time Kat went away, Sara was just four months old, and Kat nearly didn't make it back. "We can manage for a few days. Just make sure that you come home to us."

"Home. Damn, I hadn't even thought about that till now. That's two you've been burned out of."

"But who's counting?" she shot back.

"I haven't had a very good record, have I Rose?"

"Not with homes Kat, but we'll survive, and you have to too. You will come back and get us another place, right? Maybe a nice city house this time, one with a garden."

"If that's what you want, I'll buy a house in the city with a garden. I promise."

"Just try to come home in one piece, promise me that." Rosario couldn't come to terms with the possibility that Kat could leave and never come back.

Would she and Sara ever know what happened to her? This kind of situation wasn't in the job description, and the stress was terrible. But she had made a commitment, and she would never let Kat down. "I'll be here for Sara as long as I live."

****

Things had been coming apart so quickly that other than realizing that she had to fix this herself, she hadn't had time to consider how to do it. Getting to Europe was being handled, but what was the move after that?

All she knew was that it was a woman, and that she had access to classified information about Anita Franco. Now that Raini was with her, perhaps she could begin to figure out who was doing this to her. Deacon kept his plane in a charter hanger on the southwest side of the airport. Kat drove them to the Flightservice terminal on Midfield Rd. E. and left the Merc in the visitor's parking lot. The limousine arrived with Jim at the wheel, Janet sat in the back with Deacon. Kat watched with amazement as Jim unloaded the luggage. "Guys, there's enough to last a month. Are you moving to Lisbon?"

"Good one. No," Deacon said, oozing sarcasm. "Janet went through your closet at my house and brought a few things for you two." He paused to move his attention to Raini. "Hi, you must be Raini, I'm Deacon."

"Yes. Hi Deacon. This is amazing." Janet was pulling a couple of suitcases and said, "Hi, I'm Janet. By the look of you, I'd say Kat's things would fit you too. You could be her body double."

"I'll take that as a compliment, thanks. Hi Jim," she said, smiling brightly.

"Raini."

Deacon picked up the conversation while the others shared the load. "It's hard for me to get excited about dropping you and Kat off in Europe.

She's been treating this as if it's no big thing, but I know firsthand how these things can end, and I don't mind telling you that it scares the hell out of me."

"I have to admit that I'm having qualms about it too."

Kat listened to them talk but she kept out of it. It was best to keep her emotions in check and her mind on business before the flight.

Janet showed them where to change into their flight uniforms and the three of them talked while they changed. The news was full of 'so called expert commentary' from people who claimed to have in-depth knowledge of Anita Franco's history. But it was all speculation and lies, there were no solid facts.

Raini was astonished. "How could she know anything about you at all?"

"I don't know. The only people that knew who Anita really was, and what I did, are either dead or working with M-CI. Jamie Nunez may be the source if he made a study of my file after I retired, but there wouldn't be much about Anita. That was never M-CI business."

"So, there is a big question mark hanging over that info."

"What's your connection to the two latest victims?" asked Janet.

"There is none, apart from Desrosiers I didn't know any of them."

"Then why would killing the French Defense Minister or the Spanish Intelligence Director mean anything to Anita Franco?"

"There doesn't need to be one, assassins don't choose their victims they just ..." the germ of a thought stopped her. "Unless ..." Kat thought about that for a moment. "Oh, that can't be it?"

Raini couldn't stand the suspense. "Unless what?"

Kat had to drag herself out of a nasty mental image.

"The French, the Belgians, Dutch, Germans, Italians and the Spaniards, they all worked on the International Task Force against Rote Faust."

"Yes, so?"

"What if it wasn't destroyed with Jäger? Rote Faust, I mean. What if it's like a weed, you think you've destroyed the thing, but you never get all of the root, so it comes back again, and again.

"What if this Anita Franco is punishing the task force? What if they're starting it all over again and …?"

"And they're using this Franco imposter to destroy you because you worked with the ITF."

"It's gotta be something like that Raini."

Janet suggested something that opened up the question to another whole hornet's nest. "Could Rote Faust have planted sleepers in M-CI?"

"I can't see how they could have done that. I doubt that they would have been thinking that far into the future."

"No, I suppose not."

"Although … the imposter is getting her intel from someone inside M-CI right now. Raini, who sent you to watch me?"

"Jesus. The orders came directly from Gen Wolfson. It was handed to me by his adjutant Captain Gradin. I hadn't thought of him. Oh …"

"Wolfson didn't choose me specifically; it was Senior Special Agent Song. He said he was asked to select someone who knew about you but couldn't have had any dealings with you. As I was one of the newest agents and I'd spent time studying …"

"Song," Kat said, interrupting her. "I remember him, a pompous ass."

"Yeah, that's Song."

"I don't mean to be insulting but maybe you were chosen because you were … Uh…"

"Disposable. No worries, I know I'm unimportant."

"Don't beat yourself up honey, we're all disposable. Yes, I think you're right Janet. This has to come from inside."

Raini picked it up. "So, how does this woman fit into it? Is she just an assassin, or does she have a personal stake in these killings? I mean, it could be about revenge, so could know about you and have some reason to avenge Jäger?"

"Was there a girlfriend who's pissed at me for killing him," Kat mused. She meant it as a joke, but it wasn't impossible.

"Wait …, you terminated Jäger?"

"Yes, him and his Basque bombmaker. They nearly killed Sara." She suddenly pictured Jäger. "On second thought, that guy couldn't buy a girlfriend."

They came out of the dressing room looking very much like corporate pilots. Deacon gave them a one man standing ovation and then asked if they were ready to go.

They'd filed their flight plan, had their weather and landing permits in a folder, so they were all ready to go. Kat asked Deacon if he had a laptop they could borrow. He did and as she appeared to be the one who would be using it, he handed it to Raini. "OK, so let's see if your bird will fly."

It was all flight business from then until they got their clearance and were in the air. The subject of their search didn't come up again until they were out of Toronto airspace and leveled off. Raini opened the computer and began with a search for Ähern Jäger. He was easy to find, there were a number of sites devoted to him. Raini opened the Wikipedia version first.

"What about a relative?" Kat asked.

"It says he was never married, and there's nothing about illegitimate children. But it's Wikipedia, so what do you expect."

"Have you ever seen a picture of the guy? He was a bubbleheaded, sadistic, perverted, narcissistic, megalomaniac ... Crap, I've just run out of adjectives.

"Oh, here's a picture of him here. Ouch!"

"Exactly, who would marry something like that?"

"Maybe if she was really into marrying for money."

"Raini, come on. Can you imagine a woman that desperate?"

"I don't know. It makes my skin crawl just thinking about it, but Trump is on wife number three, isn't he?" She closed the computer.

"Those women must have been brain dead. The guy is a bad joke." Kat had no time for 'The Donald.'

Kat stared out the window at the clouds and the little bits of Quebec that were visible down below. It was going to be a very long flight and she thought that it might take all that time to get that image out of her head. An hour passed by without a word between them.

The Raini broke the silence "What about siblings?"

"Yeah, did he have any that lived?"

Raini went back to the internet. There was another site in German and the Germans were known for meticulous record keeping.

"Here we are. Yes, one brother, Peter. They were separated when the Russians closed off the Eastern side of Berlin. There's nothing more about Peter here. Maybe he died during the war."

"Yeah, but maybe he didn't." Raini did a search for Peter but couldn't find anything. Kat leaned back and closed her eyes for a moment as she combed her fingers through her hair. "What do you know about Rote Faust?"

"We studied it of course."

"Oh, come on, how is that possible? You must have graduated before that."

"Yeah, from Huachuca, but I took some additional courses. There was a lot about you."

"Was there? Anybody I know who was in that course with you?"

"I wouldn't know. They said you were in the Abbey's dungeon when the bomb hit. I can't imagine what that must have been like."

"There were three of us down there. Jäger and his buddy wanted to watch while his bodyguard gutted us. The guy was a fucking troll."

"You're kidding me? That was metaphorical, right?"

"Uh-uh. There was nothing metaphorical about being sliced open from pubic to throat. Apparently, he was into disembowelment. Luckily, a couple of Delta Force guys got us out of there just in time."

"Jesus." She tried to push that out of her mind. "They told us about the executions and bombings, but how did it start?"

"You mean, from the beginning?"

"If you don't mind. We weren't given any specific details, just the headlines and the mission debriefings from the ITF."

Kat retold the whole story from the first meeting with Deacon to returning to Toronto from Guyana.

"Jesus, it was a one-woman war."

"Not at all. But that's what it felt like to me too. I thought I'd ended that war for good. Apparently, I was wrong. You see where this is going? Just when I think I'm free it starts all over again. It's a curse and I need it to stop."

A long silence followed that story as they flew over Labrador and headed out over the Atlantic. Again, it was Raini who ended the silence.

"I was just thinking about Peter Jäger. Did he have any children?"

"I guess if he'd survived the war he could have. But you said you couldn't find a link to him,"

Raini picked up the computer again and began tapping keys. "Maybe I didn't look hard enough. If he did, and he had a daughter, then she could be the counterfeit Anita."

"We never thought to look for a family when we went after him. That could be a real possibility. Except that if she looks anything like Jäger then there's no way she could pass herself off as me."

"Maybe Jäger was the anomaly, and his sib was normal."

Kat allowed for the possibility. "I guess that could happen."

She began searching the name Jäger. There was a lot about the Pan European revival and the Rote Faust terrorist campaign. Skipping through two dozen people named Jäger, she found something promising. It was a report in Malaga's English newspaper Diario Sur, from 1985. A fatal collision on N-340, the coastal road between Malaga and Nerja. The victim was Metra Jäger, a resident of Fragiliana. Her husband was Peter Jäger. They had two children, 17 year-old Edward and 14 year-old Hedda.

"That sounds like a Bingo to me," said Kat.

"Peter is a common name. They might not be related."

Kat looked at her expectantly.

"OK, still looking." Next, in the same paper she came across a story from 1994 about a drowning in the Med. The victim was Peter Jäger.

"My God, here's the clincher. There's a family picture." She turned the screen so Kat could see it. "Look at this. There's Peter Jäger with his wife Metra, there's Edward and there, my friend, is Peter's brother with his arm around little Hedda's shoulder."

Because of the prominence of the fifth person in the photograph, the same story appeared in the Berliner Morgenpost. That famous person was Ähern Jäger.

"The article says that Peter was laid to rest beside his beloved wife Metra at their farm near Fragiliana."

"I've been past Fragiliana a couple of times. Never went up there, but I know where it is," said Kat. Fragiliana is a farming village in the mountains just above Nerja, right on the Med. The whole coast has been a tourist haunt for years."

They had a name now, Hedda Jäger. That was the name Raini looked up next. They had the location of a family farm, but there was nothing yet to suggest that she would be there.

"Ähern Jäger became Edward and Hedda's guardian and it says they live with him in Berlin."

"Shit. So that eliminates Fragiliana from the picture."

"Don't be so impatient Kat. I'm finding more stuff here.

More information on them started turning up all over the place. Over the years, there were articles about their successes and excesses. There was a short piece in the Berlin Kurier, about a young lawyer, Edward Jäger PhD who having received his post grad degree, went right into his uncle's firm, TALEN Industries.

"So, he was in the building when it blew up."

"Yeah, and here's a photo of him in cap and gown. He was a nice looking guy and standing next to him is ... wow! ... Was his beautiful younger sister, Hedda Jäger."

"Let me see her." Kat took a look and with a critical eye she compared her body type to Hedda's, and yes, it was possible that if one couldn't see her face clearly, she could be mistaken for Kat. Once again, the man standing behind them was their uncle, Ähern Jäger. "Jesus, what are the chances?"

"Obviously, Ähern's genetic 'oops' didn't carry on through the family."

"Here's another article with a photo. They loved these people in Berlin. It's Hedda's graduation, and look, here's another about her receiving her doctorate in history. They were academic rock stars." She showed the picture, this time Hedda was wearing the cap and gown standing between Ähern and Edward. "Kat, I'm telling you, she's the one," Raini said.

"Yeah, but come on, a PhD in history, next to geology that's got to be the most boring subject on earth. She's an academic. Oh, uh and look there." Kat pointed to the next paragraph. "As soon as she was handed her degree she turned into a jet setting bimbo."

"OK," said Raini pointing out the topic of her doctorate, "but don't you find it interesting that her subject was History of War?"

"Not particularly. What does that tell you?"

"Why would a girl who looks like that become an expert in a subject like war."

"That means nothing. Hell, I studied ..." her voice trailed off as she realized she couldn't deny it any longer.

"Look at the date of her brother's death."

"That's the day that Jäger's fortress was destroyed."

"Yes. Losing your brother and your evil uncle at the same time would tend to fuck you up."

"It would fuck me up."

***

Chapter ~ 15

Halfway across the Atlantic, Deacon entered the flight deck to asked how things were going.

"We're making good time."

"I'm delighted to hear that." Raini smiled but didn't comment. "Kat, can I take you away for a bit? There are a few things we need to discuss. You don't mind do you, Raini?"

"No. I've got this."

"Thanks."

Kat followed him past Janet and Jim who were playing cards. Janet asked, "How's your new friend shaping up?"

"I really like her, she's going to be great partner."

"I'm glad you found her. I'd hate to think of you doing whatever it is you're doing on your own."

They went to the back of the plane and sat down facing each other.

"Kat, now that we have a few minutes to talk, are you going to tell me what you're up to?" he asked. "Why are we going to Lisbon?"

She paused to try to come up with a way to ease into it. "The thing is, I have no idea how long it will take to do what we have to do."

"Which is, exactly?"

"Deacon, I'm going to find this woman who is pretending to be me and I'm going to stop her."

"Do you even know who she is?"

"We do now. We just don't know where she is. I wanted to start in Lisbon because she hasn't done any work there yet, as far as we know, so the chances of being recognized are slimmer there."

"Kat, come on, that woman is all over the news. People think it's you and they're trying to kill you. The moment the police see you, hell, the moment a customs officer sees you, you'll be arrested."

"I've worked out a simple plan to get by that. It was Raini's idea first. We're going in as Muslims, wearing hijabs and veils. We'll overdo the eye makeup and hang on to you like you're God's gift to humanity. They won't see anything else."

"I hope to hell you're right. And you know you can count on me to help in any way I can."

"I think I am right, Deacon. But after we leave you in Lisbon, we will have no further contact with you. There's no way I am going to let you get involved any further than you already are. Look what happened to Vlad when he helped me. It's too dangerous for you."

"No way! What about you, Kat? I don't want to lose you. You're the only person in the world that I care about. I..."

"Deacon, listen to me. We have a lead on where to find her."

"Where is she?"

"No! Please we are so close. I just need you to stay out of it. I'm asking you to wait for me. Can you do that? When I've caught her, and have proof that she is the killer, then I may need your help to get people to listen."

"I wish you could have just stayed in that apartment and let me look after you."

"They found it in a day. There is no place where they can't track me down. Don't you see, I have to keep moving."

"So, OK, I get it. I'll just wait until this is over and hope that you survive."

"Thank you for understanding."

"Oh," he sighed. "No Kat, I definitely do not understand, but there's bugger-all I can do about it, is there?”

“You know I love you ..., it’s just that ... What can I do?”

“We could have tonight in Lisbon.”

“I’d love that.”

“Good, that’s something at least.”

✳✳✳

Chapter ~ 16

They arrived fifteen minutes early and anticipating trouble at Portuguese customs they donned full hijabs to further confuse the officials. They were much relieved by the deference paid to Deacon. He and his entourage experienced nothing more than a friendly greeting and a wish for a happy stay.

Having cleared customs, they were taken out to a waiting Limo bus and whisked away to the Olissippo Lapa Palace Hotel.

Deacon had made the reservations before they left Toronto, booking the largest Villa suite on the sixth floor. The manager was notified that they'd arrived and was waiting to greet them at the door. He wanted to be the one to escort Deacon to the Villa wing and was surprised that Deacon's companions were two female pilots, wearing hijabs with their face covered. He didn't mention his dismay as he handed Raini her room key. She said goodnight and disappeared. Jim and Janet weren't far behind.

Before they went up, Kat stopped at the concierge desk to ask about transportation. Being fluent in the language opened a level of service not usually available to the average foreign tourist. "Tell me, would you be able to get a car for me today?"

"Certainly, I can arrange a Mercedes for you. How long would you be needing it?"

"No-no, I want to buy a car, nothing fancy and it must have Spanish plates. Do you think you could do that for me?"

"Spanish plates, that I think would be very difficult to arrange. And you would you need it for today?"

"Yes, if possible, say around noon," she said, handing him two-hundred euros.

He looked at his watch and raised his eyebrows. "It is already twenty minutes to six, Senhorita. It will take time."

She responded to his suggestion with another two hundred. "Do the best you can, I don't care what it costs."

With four hundred in his pocket just for talking, he had become highly motivated "Ah ..., yes ...," he said cautiously, "I think I am positive I can find you something, Senhorita."

"I would be most grateful."

"I don't mean to be rude Senhorita, but may I ask how grateful you would be?"

"I tell you what, if you can find a good car for me, ... without gouging me you understand ... I'll pay you same as I pay the owner of the car. Does that help?"

With a broad smile, he said, "I'll have a car for you by noon at the latest, Senhorita."

"That would be wonderful. Call me when it is here. Oh, and then would you also call my friend to meet me in the lobby? Senhorita Tahaly Sanji, in 402." Tahaly Sanji was the name Raini had chosen to travel under. Kat chose Elinor Rigby

"Certainly, Senhorita Rigby."

"Perfect, thank you."

She rejoined Deacon and the manager escorted them to the suite then immediately began to give them the obligatory tour of the rooms. Deacon interrupted the performance, thanked him with a generous tip and sent him on his way. "I thought he'd never leave."

"Deacon," she said, while smiling wickedly from the doors onto their private terrace, "the sun is about to come up," she said stepping outside, "and this uniform is feeling tight. Would you be able to help me with it?" She tossed the blue jacket with the gold captain's stripes carelessly to a nearby chaise.

"Absolutely, just hang on for a second and I'll be right there."

The air was deliciously warm and filled with the fragrant scent of hibiscus and oranges. Kat drank it all in as she looked around. Their privacy on the terrace was complete. The sun was just beginning to spread a hint of pale pink, purple and orange over the mountains. Not only had she not slept since yesterday, she had lost six hours. Jet lag was going to be a bitch, as she was bone tired. But she had made a promise and she intended to keep it. He quickly locked up and began to remove his tie as he headed for the terrace. "Tell me something," he said at the door.

"Anything," she said, reaching for his shoulder. "What do you want to know?"

"Do you think ... you'll ever wear this uniform again?" She brought him closer.

She stroked his cheek gently and kissed him. "No, I don't think so," she said, anticipating some sort of impending wardrobe failure. Her hand returned to his shoulder to give him some room to work. "What did you have in mind?" Choosing to act rather than trying to explain, he ripped the shirt open letting the buttons fly off like popcorn. "Oh-ho!" She laughed. "Well, that was easy, wasn't it?"

"Shush," he said, as he gently brushed the shirt off her shoulders while kissing her neck. She practically purred with pleasure.

He undid the button at her waist, then the zipper, letting the weight of the uniform trousers do the work.

She stepped out of them. "I apologize for the underwear," she whispered softly. "If I'd know we were going to experience this much turbulence, I would have worn something that would be easier to remove."

"It doesn't matter," he said, between little kisses. "As long as they come off.”

They made love until the room filled with light. As she lay there glistening with sweat, Deacon got up to close the curtains. “Are you tired?” he asked.

“Exhausted,” she replied, and drifted off into her dreams.

While she slept, surrounded by all that luxury, natural beauty and warmth, Kat was pulled down into a terrible nightmare with a frightful new twist. Someone was after her, of course. Someone was always chasing her in these dreams. She had been captured again, stripped to the skin and tied to a table. ‘I’ve taken everyone you have ever loved,’ Jäger said, and they appeared, slaughtered at her feet. ‘And now he is going to gut you like a fish.’ Then Jäger’s monster troll approached with his knife, grinning manically, and stabbed her belly.

She screamed and Deacon was there instantly and took her in his arms. “What’s wrong?”

She was crying and trying to catch her breath. “They killed all of you.”

“No Kat, we’re alright.”

“Yes, they did, everyone I ever loved.”

“Shush, Kat. You’re safe now, I have you. It was just a dream.”

“Everyone, everyone,” she sobbed, as she buried her head in his neck.

“It was just a dream. Everyone is fine, Kat. Shush.”

Breathing heavily, she tried to regain control. “Oh god, I’m so sorry Deacon, I didn’t mean to scream I...”

“There’s nothing to be sorry about. You’re safe now and it’s alright, everything is going to be alright,” he said.

And she knew he believed that too, but something deep inside her told her that it was more than just a dream, that nothing would ever be right again. “I love you so much, Deacon.” She kissed him. “I hate to put you through this.”

“Kat, I understand. You just try to focus on what you have to do. It will all work out in the end. You’ll see.”

“Will I?”

The phone rang. Deacon released her, so he could roll over to reach for it but he checked his watch first. It was 12:57. "That's probably about your car." He picked up the phone. "Olá" he said, as Kat lay back. "Yes, one moment please." He handed her the phone.

"Olá" she said, her voice was still tremulous.

"Bom ja, Sra. Rigby. "It is I, the concierge. I have a beautiful car for you, it is waiting out front. I will call Senhorita Sanji, Yes?"

"Thank you. I'll be down in twenty minutes."

"I shall tell her, Senhorita."

"Thank you, and how much do I owe you?"

"It is the very best car I could find."

"I'm sure it is. How much?"

"Altogether it will be fifty thousand euros, Senhorita."

The only thing that mattered now was the mission. "Fine," she said, and gave the phone back to Deacon and he placed it in the cradle.

"All good?"

"Yup."

"How much does he want?"

"Fifty thousand euros."

"Have you got that much cash?"

"Yes, I'll go to a bank tomorrow to get some more though."

"You make it all sound so matter-of-fact," he said, letting his frustration show.

"Excuse me?"

"You just woke up from a terrible nightmare, you're exhausted, and I can tell you're frightened, Christ, I'm terrified for you. And now you're just going to head off to god-knows-where to do god-knows-what, like it's just another day at the office. Couldn't you just let it go? We're safe, Kat and nobody knows you're here."

"They'll find me, someone always does. It's gotta stop, Deacon. Don't you see that?"

"What I see is that maybe you don't want it to stop."

"Oh fuck, Deacon," she said, letting her anger flare this time. "That's unfair. Of course I want this to stop. That's why I'm doing this. I'm trying my best to make this work, us work. I want what we had in Toronto. That's all I ever wanted. A family with you, Sara and me." Her tears were hot and stung her eyes. He wasn't looking at her, so she turned his head to look her in the eye. "That's all I want, Deacon. Please believe me."

"I do."

"But it can't happen until this is over."

"I know you're doing your best. It's just ... hard, you know?"

"I know." Kat kissed him, then got dressed.

∗∗∗

While sipping delicious coffee after their lunch of baked almond sole, and garden salad, the concierge approached with the keys for her car. Kat handed him the package of money she'd wrapped up in the morning newspaper. He bowed and was about to leave.

"Senhor, can I have a moment?"

"Si, of course."

"I wonder if you could recommend a boutique hotel in Saville hotel, somewhere in the center of the old city?"

"Oh yes, I know only the best place, a boutique hotel." He hurried off to get her a brochure. Presenting it to as if it were a precious gift he said, "It's very beautiful, very exclusive."

"It looks perfect."

"Am I going to make reservations for you?"

"Yes please, a suite for two, with two queen-size beds, thank you."

"Certainly, Senhorita." He left with his money.

Not understanding a word of Portuguese Deacon asked, "What was that all about?"

"I asked him to make a reservation for Raini and me in Seville."

"That sounds sensible. Why don't you let me take care of the hotel in Seville for you?"

"Deacon that's lovely of you to offer, but the moment we leave this table we cannot be connected in any way until this is over."

He could see the vehicle the concierge supplied. "Tell me, why you want the Spanish plates?"

"An old car with local plates won't attract any attention," she said, then finished the last sip of her coffee.

"Right, of course."

"Sweetie, listen to me. We will do our very best to be careful. No unnecessary risks, or anything like that. And if we do get in over our heads, then I'll call you to save me like always. How does that sound."

"Sure, that sounds great." He certainly didn't sound as if he thought that sounded great, but what could he do about it?

She cradled his face in her hands and kissed him. "I love you, Deacon. Don't ever change, promise?"

He let out a hint of a laugh and said, "I never will." He lay the linen napkin down over his plate. "So, does this mean you two are off now?"

"I'm afraid so."

He stood up. Kat and Raini did too. He asked, "Will you call me even if you don't need to be rescued?" Raini felt that was her cue to leave them alone and went into the lobby.

"No. We have to concentrate on finding the imposter. Deacon ..., will you promise me something?"

"Kat, I think I know what you're going to ask me. Don't worry about Sara. I will love her and look after her forever. And Rosario too, though they'll probably want to have lives of their own someday. They'll be fine no matter what, I promise. Just worry about yourself now and be safe."

Raini joined her at the hotel entrance. "Ready?"

"As I'll ever be," Kat said.

"Senhorita Rigby," said the concierge. "I have made the reservation for you at the Corral del Rey hotel, in the old quarter of Seville. Here is the address and some instruction to get you there."

"You're wonderful, thanks." They walked outside with their backpacks.

"I hope the car he got us is comfortable."

"Me too."

"Have you got the computer with you?"

"Yeah, it's in here." Raini patted her bag. "It's all charged up and I got an adapter plug for it from the desk. We're good to go."

The valet was waiting for them out at the hotel's beautiful mosaic paved courtyard. Beside him was a pale blue six year-old, Ford Mondeo liftback with Spanish plates. "How is this, Senhorita Rigby?"

"It looks perfect. Is the gas tank full?"

"The tank is full, yes Senhorita."

Kat chose the route with the least amount of exposure, taking the divided highway A2 south from Lisbon to Faro, then the A22 east to the border. There they would cross the bridge that spanned the Guadiana River from Monte Francisco into Spain. And she fervently hoped that it would be clear sailing from there to Seville.

Chapter ~ 17

There was a moment at the border crossing, where it appeared as if the border guards recognized Kat as Anita Franco. They started by having them get out of the car and were prepared to take it apart looking for contraband. But it turned out that they were just being difficult. Perhaps a bribe would help. Kat left two-hundred euros on the seat as she got out smiling brightly. Before they began a thorough search, she started telling them how wonderful it was to be back in Spain. She noticed that the money was gone. "It's like coming home," she said, "After all the problems we had in Portugal." That was like music to their ears, the search and examination of their passports was forgotten, they were welcomed home, and sent on their way.

"That was easier than I thought it would be," said Raini.

"You never know what you're going to run into here. A little money can go a long way."

The rest of the drive was uneventful, just two stops for gas and coffee and to switch drivers. They reached Seville at a quarter past four, just in time for rush hour, joining into the lighter stream of traffic heading into town. It was like entering any large city, with characterless suburban homes on either side of the highway hiding behind tall sound barriers, graffiti decorated.

They crossed the Guadalquivir River and the Grand Canal, then immediately felt the city close in on them. The exhaustion from too many miles traveled with too little sleep made the transition a little overwhelming.

Seville's inner city was a maze of narrow canyons of densely packed apartment buildings, perched above a seemingly endless parade of small shops. The sidewalks were crowded with people, but as they went deeper into the old city the character of the buildings changed again. They were forced to depend on the GPS on Raini's phone and the simple map the concierge gave Kat to find their way around.

The buildings were smaller, some, centuries older, and more interesting. It was exhausting to navigate around the unpredictable one-way streets as cobblestone paths meandered through quiet neighborhoods.

At last, they reached the hotel on a street so narrow, that Raini had no idea what to do with the car. Kat suggested they just leave it at the front door and let someone inside deal with it. The problem was solved when a young man immediately came out. "Welcome, Señora Rigby e Señora Sanji, I will take this for you. Your room is ready, just check in at the desk."

"Thank you."

"When you need the car again, call the desk and we will bring it up for you."

"Thank you again," Kat handed him ten euros then went in to be greeted by another young man with a big smile. It seemed that the concierge had told him all about the wealthy women he'd sent to him. He had been anticipating their arrival and their room was ready.

He took their bags and escorted them upstairs and accepted ten euros. The concierge had been right, the suite was lovely, the beds were comfortable, and the bathroom had a terrific shower. They both took showers then Kat hung her damp towel over the edge of the tub and stretched out naked on her bed.

"Do you always sleep naked?" Raini asked.

Kat didn't reply because she was asleep the second her head hit the pillow.

Raini couldn't settle so she sat on her bed and watched the TV.

After their rest, they went out to a nearby restaurant for dinner at ten. Using the mealtime to calm herself, Kat ate the simple food like a zombie and drank the red wine. Raini wanted to talk about what was ahead of them, but Kat kept the conversation light and talked about Sara and Deacon. It was close to midnight when they finally found their beds and both women fell asleep immediately.

***

Their hotel was close to a branch of Barclays Bank, so that was their first stop the moment it opened. Kat withdrew money from one of her numbered accounts, taking the maximum amount one could without alarming the banking authorities. The process had practically become automatic for her. When they got back on the street, Raini asked, "Where to next?"

They had left all their luggage at the hotel in Portugal, so they needed clothes. "Shopping." The phones came out again and they looked up shopping in the area. "What we want to do is blend in."

Raini had been noticing what the women were wearing and said, "That seems simple enough, we'll dress like them."

"Then that's the plan." They were surrounded by shop icons. "It looks like we can get everything right here," said Kat.

They picked up what they needed for a couple of days and wore some of the new things out of the shop. Everything old was left in the changing rooms. "That's done." Raini looked at her watch.

"Let me see," said Kat, putting her hand on her friend's wrist. "Hey, it's a quarter after twelve."

"Yeah, you've been up for almost five hours. Do you need a nap?"

"If you're going to be a wise ass, I'm going to start looking for something to hit you with."

"Sorry."

"I was going to say it's lunch time, then we should get going."

"Right."

"Let's head back to the hotel, there has to be a restaurant between here and there. Then we can ask the guy to haul out the car and then blow this popsicle stand."

Taking the quickest route back according to the GPS, it took them down a very narrow street across from the Iglesia de San Isidoro. It ended in a small neighborhood square. It was more of a wide fork in the road, than a square. The lane to the right led into a community of modern looking townhomes.

Turning to the left would take them to a busy street only a couple of blocks from the Corral del Rey hotel.

"We'll head down that way," said Kat.

Raini quickly felt uncomfortable. "Kat, people are watching us, and I don't think it's a case of casual curiosity either. They're definitely looking unfriendly. I don't like this."

Kat couldn't see what Raini was talking about. "What do you see?"

"Well for one thing, there's that sign on the post over there."

Kat looked over at it. "Aw shit." The red circle meant no entry, below that was the declaration, Excepto Residentes.

"And, I really have a bad feeling about those two guys behind us." There were two twenty-something males perched on a couple of concrete road barriers across the little square. One was staring at them looking puzzled, the other seemed to be preoccupied with his cell phone.

Kat looked over her shoulder and saw that not only were they both staring, but one of them was pointing at her and telling the other to do something. "Oh, now that's not good. What's wrong with me? I should have spotted them right away." She was turning away just as the friend snapped her picture with his phone.

"Let's go," said Raini.

"No kidding. Down that way." Acting as if they hadn't noticed a thing, they began walking. "We can't go back to the hotel now."

"We have to, the computer is there with all the research I did to find Hedda Jäger."

The picture the man captured was a good clear profile of Kat, but he was disappointed that the other pretty girl was not in the frame. He was going to take a picture of her too, but Raini had turned her back. Anyway, he was happy enough with the candid shot that he had. His friend, the pointer, was interested in that woman too, but for a different reason. He asked the photographer to send it to his phone, the transfer was very quick.

That face was unmistakable, a face that any policeman with eyes in his head would recognize, on-duty, or off.

While Kat and Raini had left the restricted community, the photo stayed behind with the cop. He made a quick call, gave his report, then waited for instructions. It only took a few seconds for his superior to react.

The photo was forwarded to the CNP's Seville office, and his orders were to follow them wherever they went, but not to engage. He wasn't armed, so he had no intention of taking on Anita Franco.

He put the phone back in his pocket, pushed off the post and started after them. He walked close the wall on the dark side of the lane, thinking he was being discreet. Tailing two experienced field agents was something that took finesse and experience and like the gun, those were two things he did not possess. He may as well have been holding a sign saying, 'I'm following you.'

Kat was feeling foolish. She should have been sharper, her instincts were off and her reactions slow. Luckily, Raini was tuned into the possibility of the danger and her warning gave them some time.

"I'm sorry, I should have picked up on them right away," she said.

"You're tired and stressed."

"That's no excuse."

"It's not your fault, Kat. Let's just get out of here."

Reading between the lines, what Kat thought she heard was Raini saying, 'You're ten years older than me, so what did you expect?' Even if there was no rebuke intended, the result was crushing. Kat felt that she had let Raini down and was determined not to let it happen again. It was time to take charge again. They were too close to the hotel, so without letting on that they knew they were being followed, they led him away. Walking down the Calle Don Remondo, Kat casually flagged a cab. The policeman saw that and was afraid he'd lose them. Cursing he ran back to get his motor bike. It took him precious seconds to find them again. By the time he did, they were blocks ahead. He only just spotted the cab as it turned the corner heading west.

Kat opened her phone and could see the general layout from the GPS and knew the canal was off in that direction. She asked the driver to take them over the Puente de S. Telmo. "Si, señorina."

While they were crossing the canal, Kat handed the driver twenty euros and told him that a jealous old boyfriend was following them, and they had to get away from him. "It would be a big help if you could stop over there at the amusement park just long enough to let us out. "Then, if you could head north and keep going as far as you can?"

"Si, señorina. No hay problema."

She drew out a hundred more and handed them to him. "You are a very kind man," she said, as they prepared to bail out, "Muchas gracias." The policeman was threading through traffic as quickly as he could without killing himself and caught a glimpse of the cab up ahead on the bridge.

Preoccupied with avoiding the surprise door openings on parked cars and other drivers in his way he lost sight of the cab, just for a moment. The cab stopped and the women got out. He missed that entirely and when he looked up again, there it was moving over to the left.

In that few seconds, Kat and Raini had made a smooth exit into the park and hid behind a tree. The cab driver did just what she'd asked. He pushed right back into traffic and at the next intersection turned left.

They waited behind the tree and watched as he sped by. When he was out of sight, they flagged down anther cab. The young policeman spotted the cab, relaxed, and followed it at an easy pace.

The hundred and twenty euros Kat gave the driver encouraged him to take his role in the diversion very seriously. He drove northwest out of the city and up the A8077. In a half hour, he had gone all the way to Castilleja de Guzman. He had family there and called ahead to say he had some money and wanted to take them out to lunch.

Their second cab continued to the next bridge, the Puente de Triana, and crossed back over the Canal de Alfonso XIII taking them a little closer to their hotel.

Concerned that there was still the chance of a tail, they had him drive on a bit further. They made one more stop to see what was happening behind them while they window shopped. It was clear, so they hailed a third cab to take them back to the hotel.

Having taken well practiced precautions they were sure they were safe for now. They'd bought some time to make a clean exit. Up in their room Raini tapped into the police radio signal on her computer and listened to the evolving dragnet. "Jesus, listen to this. The CNP brought in a helicopter to chase the cab."

"How far out is he taking them?"

Raini laughed. "He's still going. Oh, they will *not* be happy about that."

"I'll try to remember to send them a sympathy card. Now we have a little time to get out of here. They have our description now, so let's change again and I'll call for the car." The man who parked the car said it would be out front in fifteen minutes.

That gave them some time to pack the boots and coats away in the backpacks and put on their new cross trainers, jeans and sweatshirts.

Pulling up a map, they looked for a route out of the city that would keep them out of the search area. The exit path seemed complicated, but it would be safe. Raini put the computer in her backpack. "I'm ready."

"Alright then, it's … ten past one. So, if we hurry, we can be in Nerja in about three hours," said Kat, "so let's bail."

***

Chapter ~ 18

The German Ambassador to the UN lived in a very exclusive and quiet part of Hamburg on Elbchaussee, a beautiful, narrow, tree-lined street. A popular route for the residents to make their way down to the river for a stroll along the shore.

When compared to some of the neighbors' houses it was unremarkable, just another old German family residence. With a low iron fence, a tall, trimmed boxwood hedge, and thick bushes of oleander, it was almost hidden on the south side of the street. The perfect front lawn, the beds of bright white hydrangeas and deep red roses were the pride of the woman who cared for them, Frau. Von Grimmelshausen.

Surrounded by her beautiful gardens, the property stretched down to the edge of the River Elbe. Its back yard ended at a fence atop a steep slope, a natural barrier separating it from the paved public path that bordered the river and was shaded by magnificent old trees.

All was dark on the night they arrived, shrouded under heavy rain clouds that hid the moon. The erratic showers kept puddles full as tiny rivers flowed in the gutters.

The streetlamp's pale-yellow light offered the only illumination for the street. They were dimmed by the rain and reflected off the ripples in the puddles.

In addition to the iron grates on the windows, there was a small complement of security guards protecting the house.

Out front on the street, the guard was absently counting his paces between driveways. Dashen would turn around after every sixty steps and count another sixty on his way back. He was up to four-thousand-six-hundred-and forty-three, a third of the way through his seventy-seventh round trip. When he reached one hundred, he'd go inside and tell the lazy bastards to get off their asses and move outside.

The second man patrolled the path at the side of the house, from the street to the shore. Jon was cold and miserable, and he hated his life. With his head tucked into the collar of his jacket like a turtle, he imagined being inside, warm and dry with a sausage and a stein of beer. That was all he cared about. How much longer did he have he wondered and looked at his watch. Near the edge of the river on the foot path, the third man, Jacob, was on his cell phone, on a sex chat line, as he walked. He was immersed in a hot conversation with a sixty-two year-old fat woman. Because of her sexy mellow voice, Buffy sounded young, playful and beautiful.

Toby, the guard in the back yard, was facing the house with his back to the river. A soggy cigarette dangled from his lips, his eyes were locked on the second-floor window on the right, the one with the light on. That was the eldest daughter's bedroom. She was a beauty, like her mother. A few minutes ago, she'd stood at the window with nothing on staring out at the river. All he really saw was a dark silhouette, but it was enough for him. The light was still on, and he was betting that if it happened once, it would happen again.

Two men were inside on a break. Thomas and Felix had been sitting in the kitchen for an hour, eating sandwiches and talking quietly about what they'd rather be doing.

Upstairs the family was quiet and sounds of sleep drifted down the stairs. It well after midnight and as far as the men were concerned, the night was theirs.

Holt Von Grimmelshausen had been born to wealth and power, a descendent of a very old German family with strong political connections reaching back as far as memory could record. He was a calm, competent man who was a great asset to his country. He took his responsibilities very seriously, but he always made time for his family. He had just come home from New York and now lay happily with his wife Linda. His two teenaged daughters Signe, a precocious fourteen-year-old, and Christina, seventeen, were in their rooms, Signe was asleep, Christina, was still up trying to read a few pages of a dull book, hoping that would help her drift off.

Because of the rain, walkers had stayed away in droves. The rain had eased, but did it matter? Guard duty on the deserted shoreline was boring in the extreme and Jacob paced the pavement, his mind focused on what Buffy was whispering in his ear. With no moon, he and the others were basically working blind and what happened out on the river was of no interest to them.

***

The time was 12:18 and the *Kristen,* one of the many barges plying the waterway that night, slowed to a stop and the captain quietly let down its anchor. It's deck light winked out moments before four black clad figures slipped over the side into a small black skiff. The oar had been wrapped with soft cloth, so they wouldn't make a sound in the oarlocks as they rowed to the shore. The weather suited them perfectly, their night vision goggles got all the light they needed from Christina's bedroom window. Before they beached their craft, the guard on the path turned and saw them approach. He dropped his phone, opened his mouth to raise the alarm and was silenced by a double tap to the head from Hedda's gun.

Pulling the boat up onto the beach, they crouched low, moved forward and split up at the path.

Brans moved quietly up the hill and took out the smoker watching Christina's window, then he climbed the fence into the back yard. Fritz stopped the miserable turtle on the side path with a bullet through the top of his head, then he joined up with Brans and headed for the veranda on the back of the house.

Bonweld and Hedda continued up the side path to the street. Hedda caught up to the man who was completing lap number seventy-eight and shot him twice in the head. Bonweld dragged the guard's body off the sidewalk, leaving him under the oleander.

When the way was clear Hedda gave the signal over their coms to breach the house. Bonweld went over the gate on the driveway, straight to the front door and set to work with his lock picks. The men in the back went to the back door and found it unlocked. They made their way quickly through the dining room to the kitchen and waited.

Tag Fritz listened at the door and hearing the guards talking on the other side, held up two fingers. Brans bumped into the sideboard rattling the silver.

The guards' conversation stopped immediately. Thomas thought that Toby had made the noise coming in for a break. He called out quietly, "Toby, be more careful, ja? You'll wake up the whole house." He laughed and took a bite of his sandwich. Toby didn't answer. Thomas turned looked over his shoulder and took the bullet under his right eye. Felix died in the same instant with a slug through his ear. The bottle he was opening for Toby crashed to the floor.

The gunmen froze, waiting to hear if the noise woke anyone. Presently, they heard the footsteps on the stairs. Werner Brans cautioned his partner to stay while he went out into the hallway.

Christina had been listening to the chatter and trying to ignore it, but the broken bottle was too much. She was on her way down to give the men a piece of her mind. While tying her robe, she prepared what she would say to them. While her mother slept, she was the mistress of the house and she was angry.

She arrived at the landing midway down and was turning the corner when she saw him.

Brans was standing at the foot of the stairs pointing his gun at her and he put his finger to his lips. She was so startled to see a stranger with a gun pointing at her she obeyed without question. Smiling, he fired the shot into her chest. A short puff of air left her lips as the bullet passed through her slight body and slammed into the wall behind her and she dropped lightly to the floor.

Fritz heard that distinctive click of the pistol's suppressor, the thud of the slug hitting the wall, and the tinkle of the brass as it hit the floor. He came out to see what Brans had done. When he looked up and saw her body, he knew instantly how Hedda would react.

Brans was already on the stairs halfway to the landing. "You fool, she'll kill you for this." Just then the front door opened behind him, and Hedda entered with Olaf right behind her. Seeing the young woman brought her to the brink of a scream. She glared at Fritz who shrugged and pointed at Brans. Judging by what he had just done, she knew what Brans was going to do next. Without a care for the noise, she stormed up the stairs to stop him, but she was too late to save the other child. Brans was in the doorway with a cruel smile on his face. Beyond him, Signe lay still beneath her blood-stained blankets.

Hedda grabbed Brans' shoulder and spun him around to face her and glared at him. Unmoved by what he had done, the grin remained, and he simply stared back at her.

Without any hesitation, she pushed the barrel of her gun into the soft skin under his jaw. His expression instantly changed to defiance. But it was short lived. She pulled the trigger and the top of his head opened like a volcano, spraying the ceiling with blood, bone and brain. By this time Fritz and Olaf were behind her. The primary target and his wife had apparently slept through it. Their room was down the hall, the door was closed, and the ambassador was snoring softly. Hedda was consumed by rage at this point.

"I made it abundantly clear that his family was not to be harmed. This is intolerable," she growled, "We are done here."

At the sound of a door opening, her head snapped around to see Linda at the end of the hall wide eyed with terror. Hedda had only a moment to look at her, but it was enough to make an impression she would carry with her the rest of her life.

Linda was a slightly older version of herself, a classic beauty. She was just how her mother might have looked had she been allowed to live beyond thirty-five. But Hedda only had a moment before the vision was shattered.

Linda saw Brans' gory mess and instantly assumed that the assassins had killed her daughters. She began to scream.

Olaf Bonweld reacted instinctively, firing two shots into her head cutting off the cry. As she crumpled to the floor, Holt von Grimmelshausen bolted from their room and reached for Linda, shouting, "No, no!" he looked up and saw them staring at him. "What have you done?"

Olaf fired again, twice, placing both bullets in a tight group in his forehead. He collapsed over his wife. It was Hedda's turn to scream, but it came out more like a roar of frustration and anger. This was not at all what she had come to do. The contract was difficult enough to accept. Killing his family was too much.

Bonweld and Fritz didn't know what to make of her at this point. She had just killed their comrade. Granted, he had disobeyed her orders, but then so had they. Fritz felt no allegiance to this woman, if she had lost it, then perhaps it was time to cut and run. Bonweld was coming to the same conclusion. Neither man thought it wise to leave her alive. Hedda had processed the situation much quicker than they had and by the time they decided what to do, she shot them both. She took a moment to consider how she would leave this and chose to just walk away.

She descended the stairs in a rage so hot that she felt sick. She knew who to blame for this. They were Siggi's men, loyal only to him. He had told her as much and ordered them to do just what they had done. He probably told them to kill her too. Siggi had just outlived his usefulness.

****

Almost twenty minutes after leaving the barge, Hedda returned and was met by the barge captain Lars Güotter. She tossed him the painter and climbed aboard. "You were fast," he said. "Where are the others?" Naturally, he was curious about the fate of her men, but she stormed by him without answering and went below. "Hedda?" He followed, demanding to know, "What happened? Where are the men?"

Lars Güotter, was a coarse, bull of a man hardened by forty years of moving illicit cargo up and down the river. A pirate in the truest sense of the word and she didn't trust him at all. She simply said, "They did not survive. Now, do your job and get us away from here."

He'd expected more of an explanation than that, but the riverman was a pragmatist, he hoisted the anchor then went to the wheelhouse and pushed up the throttle. Bringing the barge about Güotter steered it back to his temporary port. She stood behind him watching him closely. He spoke to her without bothering to turn around. "I suppose that in your line of work death on the job is a fact of life, ja?"

"In this job, there is no place for stupidity," she replied angrily. "No one is immune,"

"So, it would seem that they displeased you in some way." Till that moment she hadn't realized that his loyalty was also with Siggi Kraft. His tone set off warning bells in her head. He was a serious threat now. She had to deal with him before he had a chance to turn on her. But she couldn't handle the boat herself. It had to wait until the trip was finished.

192

The question now was would he wait before he attacked her? Their destination was only a few minutes away, a small shipping port across the Elbe and a short distance up the Este River. Practically next door was the Flughafen Hamburg Finkenwerder where she had landed her small Baron G58 the previous afternoon.

When the skipper had tied up at the dock, he returned to the cabin. Standing in the doorway at the stern of the barge he blocked any chance of her getting by. She was waiting for him midship at the galley, leaning against the counter with a cup of tea in her hand.

"So, now it is done. It is time to complete our arrangement."

"You have been most efficient Güotter. How about some tea first?" She held out his cup. He approached to take it, but instead of handing it to him she threw it in his face.

The scalding tea made him jump back covering his face with his hands. That left him open and vulnerable. She brought up her gun, but he was tougher than she'd anticipated and slammed the gun from her hand with his huge fist. She jumped back out of the way of his next blow as the weapon went clattering to the deck. In an instant, her knife was in her hand and she plunged it into his chest.

She discovered that it would take more than that to cut him down.

Nearly blinded by the boiling tea, he pushed her away and charged with the knife still buried in his chest. He slammed her against the hull grabbing handfuls of her hair and smashing her head against the hull while slamming her ribs with his knees. But she fought back. Scratching and kicking, she tried to drive him away, but it hardly made an impression on him.

She got her hand back on the knife and pulled it out of his chest and instantly stabbed him repeatedly, her arm moving like a piston, stabbing him until his chest was shredded.

The wounds let out a torrent of blood, and the floor became slippery with it, but he still had the strength to throttle her.

Güotter had his calloused hands around her neck, squeezing her throat with a vice-like grip. Her ribs were aching, probably one or two were broken. She was bleeding from cuts in her face and an open wound on the back of her head. Blood stung her eyes, and she couldn't breathe. She was losing focus.

Desperate to end this before she died and still holding the knife, she drove her arm up between their blood-slick bodies and rammed it through his jaw, tongue and into his brain.

The grip slackened immediately, his massive bulk was still pressed against her, crushing her into the rough planks of the hull. Then his feet slid back in the blood, and he dropped down to his knees at her feet.

She pushed him away and yanked the knife from his head, then let him fall back. When he hit the deck, there was enough force to shake the barge.

She didn't have the strength to clean the barge. The police would find her DNA everywhere. The evidence would have to be dealt with some other way.

There was a shower in the skipper's head. She stripped off and stood under the meager flow until the water went cold.

She had left a small bag with the clothes and the wig she wore for the flight up to Germany in the guest cabin. After laying them out on the bed she carefully placed the soiled clothing in the case and washed again before she dressed.

Güotter was already beginning to stink. Thankfully there were still hours of dark left, but she had to work quickly. There were canisters of kerosene in the engine room. She brought them up to the galley and stuffed a rag in the spout of one as a wick, placed it next to the gas stove and lit one element. Next she emptied the other cans around the deck and furniture. Finally, she put a frying pan on the burner and dumped in a container of corn oil and filled that container with water and placed it in the pan.

It would take time for her timer to work, but she had no idea how much time it gave her, so she hurried out onto the deck and went ashore.

Moving as quickly as she could she walked just over three kilometers to the airport. Each step was torture. The effects of the punishment she had just endured would take a long time to heal. Her face was swollen and bruised, her lip was cut, a cut above her eye kept bleeding and the eye was blackened.

The broken ribs made every breath feel like swallowing razor blades. There was no way she could hide what had happened to her.

The pan of oil began to boil and melt the plastic container. The burning plastic ignited the oil and released the boiling water which then sent splatters of burning oil all over the galley.

The kerosene exploded, the propane exploded, and the barge became a fire ball on the river.

Hedda was a third of the way down the road when there was a mighty WHOOSH and *BOOM* as the old wooden barge went up like a funeral pyre. Glass shattered and licks of flame reached out of the cabin's windows, and hatches. By the time she reached her plane she heard sirens wailing in the distance. She arrived none too soon. The dock house was burning. Finally, the flames reached the fuel tank and there was a second larger explosion blowing pieces of the barge across both rivers.

Climbing into her aircraft, with no one around to question her, Hedda went through a cursory check list started the engines and took off. There was no one in the tower at that time to ask her who she was, or where she was going.

Before she climbed through the clouds, she saw the flashing lights of fire trucks racing to the dock. The flames were diminishing as the barge began to sink, and with it every scrap of evidence to tell them that Hedda Jäger was there. When she landed, nobody had bothered to read the name she used on their manifest, but eventually someone would.

When they did, Anita Vargas Franco would be blamed for another scene of horrible murders.

She flew an hour and forty minutes southeast of Hamburg to her secret fuel stop. It was a small, uncontrolled grass strip she'd discovered while planning this assignment. Optimistically it was called Oschersleben Flugplatz Oschersleben Airfield). She'd arranged to have cans of fuel there waiting for her under a tarp.

It was a monumental struggle to fill the wing tanks and she was forced to take several breaks before she finished. It all seemed so simple when she planned the fuel stop. Then, she was counting on the men to do the heavy lifting. All she had was a hand pump to transfer the fuel.

With that done, Hedda removed the stick-on vinyl registration numbers that hid the real ones on the tail and wing. By the time she climbed back in to fly home she was in agony and exhausted. Taking off in her condition, would be suicide.

She thought about it, but she wasn't quite ready for that kind of punishment.

Postponing the inevitable, she stretched across the back seats and fell asleep. Nearly four and a half hours later she forced herself out of a light sleep. It wasn't enough, but it would have to do until she got home.

Her small plane settled on the Malaga runway at 11:35 am. By then the Hamburg police were all over the crime scene. The press was running with the grizzly story of a massacre. There was no motive to report yet, but that would come out in time, and it would be sensational.

The police in Spain were keenly interested in their findings and confirmed through photographs that the three dead men were the same killers who worked with Anita Franco in Madrid.

Why had the assassin killed her own men?

Speculation ran ramped. The familiar photo of Anita Franco was featured across Europe on early morning TV and the front pages above the fold of practically every paper in the world.

Hedda was deeply disturbed by what happened. It was an off feeling to have an emotional connection with the women in that house, something she had never felt before. Was that what empathy felt like?

The reign of terror was over. She was done with the senseless killing. She felt true regret, not just for herself and the injuries she had suffered but for what she had done.

Hiding the bruising and her shame behind dark glasses and a head scarf, she went to the car lot. She looked haunted and exhausted. Slipping behind the wheel of the old Ford, Hedda struggled to fit the key into the ignition. As she made her way out of the parking lot she thought of her mother. She thought of Linda too. It was hard to separate them now. Home was still a long way away, up the dangerous road that had taken her mother's life.

Expecting that at any moment she too would make a fatal mistake and plunge into the sea like she had. Maybe that would be for the best. Was she really thinking of suicide now? The kilometers drifted by as if she were in a dream.

***

The general was having second thoughts; things had gotten out of hand in Europe. Sooner or later it would all come back on him.

"Capt. Gradin, will you come in here please?"

"Sir."

"I heard a report that Gen Ramsey Hershoff has disappeared. Do you know anything about that?"

"Only that he was being brought in for questioning, Sir."

Wolfson jumped and screamed "What? On whose orders?"

"Sir, I don't know, Sir."

Staring at the man, Wolfson looked for a tell, but he couldn't be sure if he saw one. "OK Captain, can you tell me who brought him in?"

"I'm sorry, Sir. I don't know anything about that. Perhaps Senior Special Agent Song knows what happened, Sir."

Wolfson was sure the man was lying to him now. He knew Song. He was a good man following in the footsteps of Paul Devlyn. Shifting the blame on a good man was practically an admission of guilt. But he couldn't do anything about it now.

"Sir, if I may, I'm really sorry about the way things turned out up there. Katrina Fernando's death is a tragic loss for us all."

Disregarding the false sympathy Wolfson said, "Have they recovered the bodies yet?"

"Apparently her apartment was a vault built within the building They've had to cut through heavy steel doors. The interior was completely disintegrated, and they haven't recovered any human remains yet, but they're still sifting the ash. We may never know what happened in there."

"What's happened to the agent Song sent up there?"

"That would be Special Agent Raini Hanamansingh. She disappeared, Sir."

"Like Hershoff disappeared?" Wolfson said.

"I don't know about that, Sir. Song lost contact with her. But she did call in after the fire. She was in Toronto at a police station. She refused to be brought in for a debriefing. As I understand it, Sir, she refused to come in at all and is now considered AWOL. We have agents looking for her now."

"What the fuck is going on here. Why wasn't I told about this four days ago?"

"I'm sorry, Sir. I thought you knew."

"I want to know what happened to her, Gradin. I want to know about Hershoff. I want to know about all of them and I want to know about them now!"

"Yes, of course, Sir. Will there …?"

"Shut the fuck up Captain. There is still a chance that Fernando is alive.

She's no fool, and it's obvious to me at last, that she was ready for an attack and made a back door. If she is alive, then my bet is that she has gone to Europe to hunt down the imposter. Alert our people over there to be on the lookout for her."

"But Sir ..."

"Captain, the whole premise for thinking she could be the assassin is because that woman can do pretty much anything she wants. Don't underestimate her, if she's alive trust me, she's on her way to get whoever it is who's calling herself Anita Franco."

"So, you don't think she's guilty, Sir?"

"I know she's not guilty. I thought I made that clear."

"Yes, Sir. What are the rules of engagement, Sir?"

"So, we're talking about ROE's are we? When did we go to war with our retired agents?" Gradin chose not to contradict him. It seemed that he had forgotten that it was on his orders that they were to apprehend by any means necessary. "Alright, I'll say it again. If she's alive, she is to be apprehended and detained. I don't want anyone to harm a hair on her head. Is that clear?"

"But, Sir, your orders were ..."

"I need you to be clear about this. If she's headed for Europe, then she's going after the assassin. If she is killed because of a misunderstanding, then where is that going to put us?" Gradin's face was a blank. "Alright then I'll tell you; it would put us in Leavenworth. Our people are simply to apprehend and *detain*. They are not, I *repeat*, *not* to engage the subject with deadly force."

"Understood, Sir."

"I'm putting that order in writing, Captain. I'm calling 66 and telling the commander personally and you are going to send him my orders. Clear?"

"Sir."

"You make sure our people get it, or so help me God, if you fuck it up Gradin, I'll see to it that you'll be plucking penguins in prison at the South Pole. Everyone is to be made aware that this is my official position. Clear?"

"Clear. I'll make certain, Sir."

Wolfson sat down and typed out the orders, printed two copies and handed one to Gradin. "Now, get the fuck out of here and do your fucking job!"

He thought that by making that statement for the record, it would cover his ass if the tactical team actually terminated her. He called the commander of the 66 Brigade and explained what might be happening and faxed him the orders he had just written. As far as he was concerned, he'd done a fairly good job of CYA and Manx would see to it that he was in the clear.

***

Raini followed Kat as they walked down to the lobby carrying their backpacks. The car should be out front by now, Kat thought. There was no need to hurry, it would just draw attention to them if they did. They were quietly discussing the drive to Nerja as Kat stepped onto the mid-way landing. It all seemed to happen at once.

Just as the lobby came into view, she saw a large man in a dark suit speaking to the clerk. There was no doubt in her mind who the man was. He had 'Federal Cop' written all over him. She stopped and signaled Raini to back up and stay out of sight.

The cop had been holding a photo in his hand and talking quietly. She couldn't hear what was being said, but she didn't need to. The clerk was nodding and pointing at the stairs.

The cop turned to look and forced Kat's hand. Kat practically flew down the last few steps. Raini moved down to back up her partner and saw Kat go into a gymnastics floor routine like she had never seen before.

The cop saw her but couldn't possibly react in time. She did a forward somersault off the stairs, landed on her left foot and went straight into a cartwheel, a back flip and then as she turned in the air above his head, she aimed her right foot high on his chest. Her hands were clenched into tight fists her eyes grimly focused on her target and she came down on him with amazing force. His eyes widened as her heel connected and he was thrown across the far side of the room and hit the wall. He went down hard and stayed there on the tile floor.

Kat had landed on her feet ready to take him on if he got up, but that wasn't going to happen. Descending the stairs, Raini drew her gun, her attention was keyed on Kat, but out of the corner of her eye she caught a flicker of movement.

Outside on the street was a second man, basically a clone of the first. His weapon was out and trained on Kat through the window.

"Window!"

Kat dove out of the way as the cop fired, almost emptying his clip. The bullets smashed through the glass smashing into the tiles and tracing the path where she'd been a nanosecond ago.

Before Raini cleared the stairs to take a shot, the Fed. charged the door with his shoulder, not realizing the door was a pull, not pushed. He slammed into it so hard he smashed his shoulder and hit the heavy door frame with his head. He too went down dazed, but not out.

"Were you hit?"

"No. You?"

"I'm good." Raini looked on in amazement as the guy got up and shook it off. He backed up and fired the last bullet in his mag into the door's brass work and charged again with the same result. This time he was out cold. Einstein had a phrase about what had just happened. "We cannot solve our problems with the same thinking we used when we created them."

Einstein also said, "The definition of insanity is to attempt the same thing a second time expecting a different result."

The man was an imbecile. Raini looked at Kat and they both shrugged. Opening the door they saw him come to and reach for his radio.

Raini punched him on the jaw which sent him back to dreamland and snatched his radio.

"Are you okay?" asked Kat.

"Just peachy, thanks," she said, with her gun pointed at him, "and fucking amazed. How the hell did you do that?"

"I watched a video once." Looking down on his crumpled body she suggested that they didn't have to worry about him for a while. They both turned to face a new threat when they heard an engine revving and the noise echoed as if it was in a tunnel. Thinking it was an approaching police car, they trained their guns in that direction.

Their car poked out of a door less than three meters away and when the valet saw the guns, he screamed and bumped into the wall on the other side of the narrow lane. When it stalled, he jumped out, and ran off like a rabbit leaving it in gear.

"You gotta hand it to the kid," Kat said, "he's got great timing." With a running jump she slid over the hood and scrambled into the driver's seat.

Raini hopped in beside her as she restarted the engine, backed up, yanked the steering wheel all the way to the right, shoved the gear shift into first, stepped on the gas, popped the clutch. The car slid 90° and with a slight crash and tinkle the car was pointing in the right direction, after having completed a seemingly impossible standing right turn.

"Jesus! Wonder Woman much?" her partner said, astonished.

Kat wasn't paying attention to her, she just floored it and sped away.

"Our exit plan is out the window now. Get your phone out, I need you to figure out where the hell we're going," she said, as she speed-shifted into third.

"Okey dokey ... Ah ... where did you learn to move like that?"

"I taught defensive driving at Eagle's Nest."

"What you just did there ..., *that* was *not* defensive driving, and I was talking about what you did to that cop inside. Those were Cirque du Soleil moves."

"Jesus, Rani, focus will ya! Where are we going?"

"I mean you were incredible."

"Raini! Where do I turn?"

"Uh sorry, uh, next block, turn left."

She made the turn and since there was no one chasing them, she immediately slowed down. "They found us a lot faster than I thought they would. "How did they do that?"

"A house to house search? They probably have the city closed down now," said Raini.

"It sure turned to shit in a hurry."

Raini had been running on adrenalin and it was beginning to fade. Now she was scared. "How are we going to get out of here?"

"Did they get a look at you?"

"What does that matter now, they both saw you."

"My point is ..." she down shifted for a turn, " they don't know you, and they don't have a picture of you. I think you'll be safer if we split up."

"I'll be ... w-what? No! That's not going to happen!" she put her phone away. "I won't leave you, Kat."

"Listen to me Raini. We have to split up. They'll be looking for two women now and I just fucked up this car. We'll be spotted in no time and they're going to shoot to kill. So, you are getting out."

"Kat, no!"

"Shut it," she snapped angrily. "I need you to do this. Now open my bag."

"What? Why?"

"You'll need money. Take out five thousand."

"No."

"Will you stop arguing with me?! Take the five thousand. Hurry, we haven't got much time."

"Kat, please, I can't leave you."

"Yes, you have to. Use your training, Raini. Think about what we are doing, alright. If we are going to survive this, we have to split up now and meet again later. Come on, it's in that pouch." Raini opened the bag and found it. "Finally. Now take five." Again, Raini hesitated. "Aw Jesus, Raini, don't be so fucking stubborn and listen to me! You're going to need money for emergencies, so take it!"

Finally, Raini put the money in her bag. "So, I've got the money, what's the plan?"

"Yeah, it's really simple. I'm going to stop at the end of the next block, you get out, stay calm, and act like you're on vacation. Get yourself to Nerja however you can and please, don't get caught."

"I'll do my best."

"Yeah, I know you will. We'll meet at the Balcón de Europa. Got that?"

"Nerja, Balcón de Europa, got it. So, you're not giving up?"

"Hell no, we're partners now! And I need you to be there with me. But you have to get there on your own. Get to the bus station and take the first bus to the coast. Marbella probably. Then make your way up to Nerja. When you get there, take a cab to the Balcón, get some ice cream, find a bench, and wait for me."

"OK."

"Take a cab to the bus terminal and Raini ... *stay calm*. I'll see you soon, I promise." She pulled up at the curb. "Now go."

Raini paused. "Kat,"

"Fuck! What now?"

"Please don't get caught."

"Goddammit woman, you're killing me here! I'll see you in Nerja. Now get out of the fucking car!"

***

Chapter ~ 19

During Hedda's flight back to Spain, the images of that terrible incident of Linda von Grimmelshausen played over and over in her mind. That woman she helped to murder began to mesh with her mother's death. It was almost impossible to separate them. As she drove up the road from Malaga, she was twisting the two deaths together in a whirlpool of despair.

How she got home and managed to get through the security system without setting it off was a miracle. It was automatic and the memory of doing it was lost in the blistering sun. Thinking that she was going mad, Hedda dragged herself into the house at ten to one that afternoon. The familiar surroundings should have made her feel safe and in control again, as it used to. It wasn't working this time. Things had gone too far.

She poured the first of many glasses of vodka while she filled the bathtub with ice water, then she stripped down and immersed herself in it, hoping to numb the pain. The physical relief was slight and did nothing for the pain that was torturing her mind.

Ten minutes was all she could stand. She dried off and stood shivering in front of the full-length mirror wincing at the sight of her battered body. It looked like she'd been flogged, then run over by a bus.

An application of makeup to hide the bruising on her face helped. Binding her ribs with a wide tensor bandage didn't.

She dressed in a loose t-shirt, jogging pants and ballet flats. Then wearing sunglasses and holding the bottle of vodka in one bruised and scraped hand and her glass in the other, she went out into the garden. This had always been one of her favorite places. The sun had begun its slow decent, the sky was cobalt blue with streaks of small white, wispy clouds rimmed with gold, and the shadows across the wild and angry mountains painted them with a beautiful dusky purple. As beautiful as it was, she found no peace in her surroundings anymore. Haunted by those visions of the carnage in Hamburg, she weaved around the orchard, constantly draining her glass and refilling it. Finally, drunk and bitter, she stopped at a row of spreading pomegranate trees to refill her glass and found the bottom of the bottle. Flinging it away she screamed, "Fuck!"

Her phone rang. She hadn't remembered putting it in her pocket. "Now what?" As she took out the phone she glanced at the time, it was right on 4:00 pm. Had the call been scheduled? She looked at the caller ID and whispered, "Shit."

✱✱✱

The clerk called for the police and ambulance. Both arrived a few minutes later. It was obvious that neither man was going to regain consciousness for quite some time. While the medics carted them off to the hospital the police conducted interviews with the hotel employees. "What did they look like, describe them for me." The valet identified Kat from that now famous photo.

"They looked the same too, very tall, slim, long black hair. This one in that photograph was older. The other woman looked very much the same, but she was Indian."

"What else can you tell us?"

"The car they were driving, it was an Opel sedan, and it went that way," he said, pointing to the right. He described the car.

"Anything else?"

"They both had guns."

"Did they threaten you?"

"Oh yes, I thought they were going to shoot me." He paused as another memory came to him. "Oh, the car!"

"The Opel?"

"Yes. I hit the wall when I brought it up, so there is damage to the front of the car." He pointed to the bits of broken taillight on the street. "It had some damage to the left rear corner too."

A BOLO was broadcast across the province. With the description of the car, it shouldn't be too hard to find.

The federal officers finally woke up, but unfortunately neither man had a good look at the women. Nothing was added to the investigation, and the visit added a great deal of time to Kat and Raini's escape. If it wasn't for the cellphone picture, they wouldn't have been certain at all that it was in fact Anita Franco. Now the whole city was on alert. Calls went out to every station saying that they were armed and dangerous. If encountered, they were to be approached with extreme caution. Also, they were authorized to use deadly force if necessary. The Guardia Civil set up roadblocks to seal off all routes leading out of Seville.

***

As soon as Raini was out on the curb, Kat sped away and turned up a very small one-way street. Another right turn and then a quick left. She drove on a few blocks and stopped. With the backpack over her shoulder, she abandoned the car and started walking. Around the corner was a small Honda scooter with the key in the ignition. She climbed on kicked the engine to life and sped away.

Coming to the edge of the old city, she ditched the scooter and began walking again, unsure of what she was looking for.

There was a street market with goods of all kinds laid out on long tables under a cat's cradle of wires and colored lights. Happily, she discovered that she was the only customer, and the woman didn't recognize her. Kat looked for nondescript clothes, but it was a waste of time. Because it was all trashy 'hip' styles she made a quick change of plan. In no time she found some things that were both warm and colorful; a pair of denims torn at the knees, red knee-high boots, a tight Madrid football t-shirt and a sheepskin lined, pink, nylon windbreaker with **Golpea esa Cosa** (Hit That Thing) written on the back. She chose something to clip up her hair; it had a hummingbird on a hibiscus flower attached. Then she added cheap false eyelashes, shameful red stick-on nails and makeup. The woman liked the cash, smiled wickedly at her choices and gave her a bag. Satisfied, Kat walked away with her disguise under her arm. A few blocks on she found a tapas bar, located the washroom, and went in to change. After applying the makeup, eyelashes, the fake fingernails and wig she packed away her nice new things and dressed in the trashy garments from the street market. Everything was too tight, too bright, and made her look like a hooker. It worked. She put a thick coating of eye liner which made her eyes look dead. She added blue eye shadow that was absolutely the wrong color for her complexion and black eyebrow pencil.

A heavy layer of ruby red lipstick on her lips and a little too much rouge on her cheeks completed the disguise. After she pinned up her red hair over to one side with the flower hummingbird combo, she looked at the result. "Yikes!" There was no question that she looked like a working girl who was severely colorblind. Bravely, she hurried on her way. So far, she was lucky to be alive and desperately hoped that Raini had been lucky too. The luck seemed to drain away a few blocks further on. She ran right into a police blockade. Guardia Civil Officers armed with submachine guns were checking every car, bike and pedestrian that went by.

She stood back out of sight and leaned against a wall, wondering how she was going to do this. That was when providence smiled upon her once again. Actually, it was more of a leer than a smile. It was supplied by a sad looking man in his sixties. He approached and asked for a date.

"Señor, do I look like a hooker to you?"

He smiled lecherously, latched onto her arm and said, "Are you not all whores when the money is right?"

She could have clocked him, but then again. "A philosopher, alright lover-boy, how about we go to my place? It's not too far from here."

He was about four inches shorter than she and his attention was completely devoted to her very tight t-shirt. For him, it was as if the police didn't exist. Interestingly, the Guardia seemed to feel the same way about them. She and her trick crossed the road and walked a few blocks further on without being disturbed.

Then with a jerk, she steered him down a tree lined street. He began to complain. "My feet are killing me," he said, "are we getting close?"

"Only a few more blocks lover."

He became anxious. "You said it was close!"

"Then I lied, didn't I?" she said.

That did it. His swaggering demeanor vanished, he apologized for his mistake, disengaged from her arm and ran away. As she did up the windbreaker she called after him, "I see your feet are feeling better, lover-boy."

At the next street she flagged down a cab which took her to the east end of the city. She got out and began walking again. After a bit of a stroll, she found a powerful new BMW motorcycle parked in a line of Ninjas, Hondas and mopeds.

She used her knife to break into the ignition and took the Avenue la Paz out of the city. Luckily, she made it through Montequinto without encountering another police check point.

✶✶✶

At the speed she was going, the lining of the ridiculous windbreaker couldn't keep her warm enough as she headed east on the highway. She was cold, tired and very hungry. The bike needed fuel anyway and she needed to rest. Nearing a Repsol truck stop with a restaurant, Kat decided to risk it.

She filled up the tank first, paid cash for it, then parked the bike under the restaurant's awning. With a quick scan of the room through the window, she couldn't see any obvious threats, so she went in. There were three guys spread out in booths along the edge of the room at the back. The men were staring at her like she was some sort of a zoo animal. She assumed they belonged to the Pegasus 1 big rigs outside.

She could see the balding short-order cook in the kitchen behind the pass through. He was too busy preparing food to notice her come in. There was an overweight guy with a bad combover reading the paper. He had his feet up on another chair. The manager, she thought. What gave him away was the white shirt and black tie. Plus, the fact that he was sitting behind the till and he studiously ignored her.

The waitress, a slim, nice looking red-head in her forties, watched Kat walk in, but her interest was nothing like that shown by the truckers. She had been waylaid by one of them attempting to pick her up. Now she had an excuse to break away from Señor Boring and do some work. There was an empty booth by the door nearby, which backed against a solid wall. There was also a heating vent above it with lovely warm air blowing down. Kat shed the jacket and sat down hoping to thaw out. The truckers eyes began to bulge. "Hey animals, calm down," the waitress said, and approached Kat with a warm smile. "Cold?"

"Frozen. It's colder on the road than I expected."

"I can see that. You need a warmer coat. I'll get you some hot coffee to warm you up. Anything else?"

"Yes, ... maybe a cheese omelet and toast?"

"Bueno, I'll be right back with some coffee."

"Thanks."

As soon as she left, the parade of pitiful propositions began. One by one, the truckers came over as if they'd rehearsed the show. They squeezed right up next to her, all smelly, unshaven, fat and soft. It made her cringe. They must have just seen the same Antonio Álvarez movie because they all used his tired old pickup line. If she wasn't so cold and depressed it would have made her laugh.

She tried to ignore them. The last thing she needed now was some drooling oafs hitting on her. The waitress chased the first one away when she brought Kat's coffee. When she returned with the omelet, she told the next one to smarten up and get back to his table. "Can't you see that the lady wants to be alone? What's the matter with you men?"

"She's no lady." The manager didn't get involved; he barely lifted his head. The cook watched the pantomime from the pass through, laughing quietly. When she put her fork into the omelet, the third man wandered over. The only difference in his approach was that he was super aggressive, ugly and mean. "Go away."

He treated that as an invitation to put his arm around her, then got busy with his hands. A loud gagging sound caught everyone's attention as the man's hands went to his throat and a loud bang as his head hit the plate breaking it and spoiling her omelet. Then he seemed to just slip off the seat and slide across the floor. Everyone saw that. No one actually saw how she did it, but it frightened the hell out of the truckers.

While he was trying to pick himself up from the floor, she pushed the remains of her plate away and headed to the washroom to hide. She stayed in there long enough to get rid of the makeup and change back into the clothes from the morning. The truckers had used that time to pay their bills and flee.

Feeling better, she returned to her booth and the waitress came over with the coffee pot. "You look much better Señora. And may I say, that was truly one of the greatest performances I have ever seen in this place," she said. "I suggested that the man who ruined your omelet leave a hundred euros behind to pay for another. He didn't argue. Are you still hungry?"

"Yes. That would be very nice, thanks."

***

Siggi sounded disgusted "You are drunk!" All the pretense of the willing employee was gone.

"What do you want?"

There were two things weighing heavily on his mind and he could have shared both of them with her. The first was an interesting development which would make her heart sing. On the downside it would certainly bring an end to his plans. The other was something he could use to lord over her and push his plans forward. He chose to play to his advantage.

"The reports from Hamburg are upsetting."

"I can't disagree with that. How did you hear about it?"

"I have a friend in the Hamburg police. What possessed you to kill them all?"

"I didn't. Your freaks did that."

"They are who I'm talking about! That was incredibly stupid! Why?"

She pretended to ignore the insult. "Why? Because they shot the girls and their mother. Something I had specifically told them not to do."

She gulped down the last of the vodka and the glass chased after the bottle. "I told them to leave his wife and daughters alone. It sounded simple enough. Leave them alone. But no. They killed them all."

"That was the job!"

"No!" she shouted, then immediately calmed down. "No, you don't give the orders, Siggi, I do. The job was to kill the Ambassador. That was the job."

"They were witnesses!"

"You fucking idiot. Dead witnesses are useless. The point was to have living witnesses."

"Did you have to kill the captain?"

"Why not? He certainly wanted to kill me. So did the others. In fact, wasn't that one of your orders, you snake."

"Nonsense. You are delusional."

"Nonsense? Siggi, you are a dead man."

"Don't be so stupid, Hedda, I have you in my pocket. One call from me and your little impersonation comes to an end."

"I'll see you soon, Siggi." And with that she ended the call. She knew what was coming and she couldn't do it drunk. Staggering back to the house she stripped off and plunged back into the ice water.

***

That development Siggi had withheld from her ... that little bit of news that could have changed her life, was that her brother was alive. Edward had been working in Berlin when the Golden Fortress was bombed. Frightened that the authorities might be looking for him too, he moved to Paris, and legally changed his name. Having met the conditions regarding education and professional practice, he was allowed to practice law and opened his own firm.

He kept his head down and settled into his new life paying little or no attention to what was going on beyond Paris.

Then, that familiar name and photo appeared in the news. Anita Franco was on the rampage again. He had met her and thought that she would have been dead before the missile hit and killed his uncle.

Wondering what to do about this revelation, he hid himself away in his apartment fearing that she might track him down.

After the massacre in Germany, he couldn't stand the suspense, and had to do something. Remembering the security service his uncle had utilized, he decided to call to see if they could provide security for him. His call was put through to Siggi. "Of course, we can provide you with security. Edward, you have my personal guarantee that the assassin will never find her way to you."

"Thank you. Have you had any contact with my sister."

"Hedda? No, I'm sorry, Edward. She must have done as you did. She could be anywhere in the world. I will begin looking for her for you, if you like."

"I am not a wealthy man, Siggi, I couldn't possibly afford to pay for such a search."

"I wouldn't dream of taking money from you, Edward, it is the least I can do to help you rejoin your sister. All I need is time."

"Again, I must thank you. I won't forget your kindness and loyalty to my uncle."

"Think nothing of it my boy. The moment I find your sister you will be the first to know."

***

When she came back with the omelet, she had the coffee pot too. "I'll bring you a flan too if you want, he paid for it." she said, pointing to the man behind the cash. "Can I freshen your cup?"

"Thanks. Will you tell me something?"

"Sure."

"Why are you being so kind to me." She took that as an invitation to sit down, which surprised Kat.

"While you were in the washroom, some policemen came in asking about a woman." Kat stiffened. The woman patted her hand to calm her. "Oh, don't worry the truckers were far away before the police arrived."

"What did the police want?"

"You, of course," she said simply. "They showed me your picture, a very nice one too and you really haven't changed a bit. You are still a very beautiful woman, Anita. Ha! Some women have all the luck, eh?"

"I'm not feeling very lucky at the moment." Kat was finding the suspense a little hard to deal with. "What did you tell them?"

"I told them there hadn't been any women in here today The boss and the cook said the same thing,. They asked me about the bike. I said it was mine, so the cops moved on."

Kat let out a sigh of relief. "I appreciate that, thanks for telling me."

"Sweetie, I know that you are in serious trouble, but I can tell just by the way you acted with those men that you are not the one they want."

"How would you know that?"

"I can tell. If you were the assassin, those truckers would be dead, and so would the rest of us."

She sat back and smiled. "You know, I remember it like it was yesterday. You were such a sensation when you left Ibiza." She laughed with only a smile. "The Happy Widow of Ibiza. My God, half the men in Europe were in love with you. Half the women wished they were you. I myself among them. The assassin would never have that effect on people."

Kat was incredulous. "I am so flattered that you would say that. But how can you be so sure?"

"I know you killed those German criminals; everyone knows this. But they were bad people."

"Yes, they were."

"And I have heard a rumor that you are some kind of secret soldier, yes? The way you move, I can see that. You don't have to say anything, I know. You don't take crap from any man; I see that too. You are strong and powerful, but I can tell you have a soft heart, Anita. You are not a killer like her. That woman who uses your name, she destroys people. I have seen her picture on the television, the images from Madrid. Don't they see that she is nothing like you?"

"I wish the authorities could see what you see."

"Oh, my dear, they are all men. They don't see who you are, or who she is; they only see what they want to see. This … this other woman, she knows that, and she uses it," the waitress said. "I admire you, Señora, you are very brave. I know this also. If I can help in any way you have only to ask.”

Kat's attention was drawn to the activity out on the highway. The police had set up a checkpoint since she came in.

“What is it?” she asked.

“They are being very thorough out there. If they stop the trucker I hurt, he will tell them about me. That will mean trouble for you.”

“Don't worry.” Traffic was beginning to back up in both directions as the police looked through every vehicle before sending them on their way. “He was gone before they set up the roadblock. There is a service road that goes to the town the long way. That's the way he went.”

She paused for a moment to study Kat. “Señora, You look so very tired. There is a small room in the back where I sleep when the diner is empty. Why don't you go there and rest? A couple of hours will do you good.”

“Thank you again, but I ...”

“I know, I promise you; you will be safe back there.”

“I can't believe how kind you are, thank you.”

“We women must look out for each other, no?”

“You are not the first to tell me so.”

Kat slept for almost two hours and when she came out to pay her bill, the waitress pushed the manager away and said, “I will take care of this.” He may have been the manager but clearly the waitress was the one in charge. He simply nodded and took his newspaper to one of the booths. “You owe nothing, Anita.”

Kat smiled. “Thank you very much, but I must pay you something for the room. Money is the least of my problems.”

“It is the men who trouble you, yes?”

Kat shrugged. “What's your name?”

“Elizabeth Gutierrez.”

“Give me your hand, Elizabeth.”

Puzzled, she asked, “Are you going to read my palm?”

"No." Elizabeth chuckled and held out her hand. Kat placed a one hundred euro note in it then gave it a gentle squeeze. "For the room."

"You are too generous, Señora, but thank you. Go with God."

With a sad little smile Kat said, "Your God and I are not on speaking terms, Elizabeth. But thank you, adios."

With the warm coat she bought in Seville just a few hours ago, she got back on the bike and headed for the service road Elizabeth mentioned. That shopping trip with Raini felt like it happened a lifetime ago. Avoiding the highway, she headed for town, all the while keeping to the service road that Elizabeth had mentioned. It took her through farmland and at the side of the road was a car for sale. She rode in and found the farmer by a shed behind his house. They talked for a bit, came to an arrangement and she finished the trip to Nerja in an old Fiat 124.

***

Hedda wasn't too drunk to know her limitations. She showered and threw on a skirt and top then emptied her safe, putting bundles of cash and her passport into a tote bag, along with a gun, a suppressor and a large box of 9mm ammunition.

She had no doubt that Sigismund Kraft's call had been his way of saying goodbye. He'd probably activated the solution to his problem before he made the call. His killers were already on the way. Of that, she was certain.

When they would arrive was uncertain. Did she have time to get away? She passed a mirror and paused. Looking into the glass she saw herself as if for the first time. If she had been a dog on the road in her condition it would have been a mercy to put it down. There were loose ends to tie up, but she was finished.

There was one other certainty, Siggi would die before she would.

The difference between Hedda and Kat was that her self-destruct system was designed to kill lots of people. There were just a few little connections to make then she would walk away from her father's house for the last time.

Zürich, Switzerland was her next destination. Siggi might have thought that her survival was impossible. But did that mean his defenses would be down? If he was thorough, and being Swiss it was likely that he was, in addition to attacking her house, he may have boobytrapped her planes in Malaga. But would he have made plans to be far away from Zürich. She couldn't trust them now, so she phoned ahead and chartered a jet under a corporate name to take her to Zürich.

When she was done preparing the reception for her uninvited guests, she hiked up the road to the new highway, turned on the system with her laser remote and then called for a cab to take her into Nerja.

First stop was the auto dealership Lessarggro where she hired a car to get her to the airport. She boarded her chartered business jet and flew to Zürich before the sun was down.

***

Chapter ~ 20

Siggi asked. "Is it done?"

"No, sir. There was a delay at the airport. We are about to begin our descent into Malaga soon."

"What? You should be on your way back by now."

"Our flight was delayed, some problem with the hydraulics, so we had to wait for a different plane. We should be landing in about fifteen minutes. Have your new instructions? Should we abort?"

"Damn," he grumbled quietly. He had not anticipated technical difficulties and factored them into his plan. Give or take a minute or two, they were supposed to arrive as he ended the call. He checked the time, 6:56. There was a chance that she was too drunk to think. She may have done what she said she was going to do and they would catch her sleeping. Though, knowing her as he did, that wasn't likely. He would have to arrange for protection at home.

"No, stick to the plan. I have arranged transport for you. Pick up the cars at Auto Lido rental. Make your way there as fast as you can and make sure you take care of the target. As soon as you are done with her, come back to me. I may need your protection."

"How many guards will there be?"

"None as far as I know, I told you that. You should have no trouble at all if you go in hard and don't waste time."

"Then why did you send twelve men? I could have done this alone."

"Don't try to second guess me, Lexi. If you want to be paid, then do your job."

"Yes sir." He closed the connection.

***

Raini's bus trip ended in Malaga without any difficulty and renting a car to complete the journey was just as easy. Nerja, she discovered, was no longer the small town Kat had described. Following Kat's advice, she left the car near the highway and took a cab to the Balcón de Europa. The driver left her at the plaza, which was as close as he could get. There was an odd little brick booth selling ice cream. She laughed and bought a Negrito to work on while she waited for Kat. Then she began to wander around looking for that bench Kat had promised would be there.

The Balcón wasn't busy, it was siesta time, but it was definitely a tourist town with practically every building in the area having a restaurant or a bar on the main floor. As she wandered along the plaza, she got the impression that she might be the only one out there under sixty. Down on the beach below the Balcón was a different story. In view of the hotel under the Balcón there were dozens of half-naked young people on the east side sunbathing. There was a sign warning of a rip tide, so no one was in the water.

She walked to the end of the platform and looked out across the Med. A bank of heavy clouds hugged the horizon, and one might imagine that they were looking at Africa.

Time slipped by like sand through her fingers and still she stayed on the bench Kat remembered.

It was a quarter past seven and all she could do was buy another Negrito, sit back down to wait and hope that Kat would join her soon.

***

It was his turn to be afraid now. He knew better than anyone what Hedda was capable of and now that she was gunning for him, he had to do something drastic and risky. He dialed Guy Papain's number in Paris.

"Oui"

"Edward, I have some wonderful news."

"Siggi is that you? Have you found my sister?"

"I have indeed, and I expect her to arrive here at my house in Zürich at any moment."

"Then I will make my way over to you at once. What is your address?"

"That's wonderful Edward." Siggi gave him the address and directions. "It is easy to get confused about how the streets work on the mountain. People are always getting lost."

"I should be able to get there later this afternoon."

***

Kat was surprised to discover how much Nerja had changed. It had grown so much she didn't recognize anything other than knowing that the sea was down there to the south. Just as Raini had done earlier, she found a parking space by the highway, then took a cab to the Balcón. That part of the town at least hadn't changed that much.

As she walked out onto the deck of the viewing platform, the memories of the place finally returned.

She spotted her partner on the bench taking advantage of the shade under the tree and looking quite relaxed.

Relieved, she smiled. Raini was right where she was supposed to be, eating ice cream just like she said she should. Raini was looking off to the south.

Gracelessly, plunking herself down on the bench near her, Kat immediately slid up to Raini, leaned over and said in a deep husky voice,

"¿Puedo tomar un bocado?" (Can I take a bite?) Raini turned around so quickly that she dropped the ice cream. Kat grabbed it before it landed in her lap "Whoops, be careful!"

"Jesus Kat. Are you trying to scare me to death? Holy shit. I ..."

"Sorry, did I freak you out?"

"Oh you think? Yeah ya did, bitch!" She laughed.

"Then you should be more vigilant."

"Bite me."

"No, but I will bite this." She took a bite of the ice cream. "Say, the view is something, eh?"

"Yeah, it's a great. Fuck no! I've been so worried sick about you."

"You have no idea how good it was to see you sitting here."

"Did you have any problems?"

"An old guy in Seville and some truckers at a truck stop asked me for a date. Do I look like a hooker?"

"Why?"

"Well, there are at least four unhappy Spaniards and a bunch of police who think I do." Kat took another bite and found the chocolate core.

"Doesn't surprise me."

"Oh really? Who's the bitch now?"

"Yeah? So, give me back my cone."

She popped the remainder in her mouth and said, "I'll go get you another one."

"Don't bother, I've had three already."

"Three?"

"Kat, I don't want to split up again. This was torturous, so don't even try it again, OK?"

Kat put her arm around Raini's shoulders and leaned her head against hers. "Did you know they have a fiesta in the streets down here every year?"

"Why no, I did not know that." Her eyes twinkled. "Wow, the things you teach me are truly impressive."

"Stick with me kid, I can show you stuff you won't see with anyone else."

"Like what?"

"They have fireworks and parades." Her stomach growled. "I'm hungrier than I thought."

"Me too. That's why I ate all that ice cream."

"OK, I know a good restaurant near here. And if it's gone, we'll find another one."

"That's a plan I can sink my teeth into." They headed for the main block of buildings. "So, the women and girls get all dolled up in fancy dresses and come down here. They dance and sing to the Flamenco guitars all night long. They put up a bit of a midway out here, a merry-go-round ..., oh, and they have a cart that makes the best fresh potato chips. A lot of the locals make a point of being out of town during that weekend." Kat looked around at the town that had become more like Torremolinos or Benidorm, than the small fishing town she once knew. "It just goes on and on."

"What goes on and on, Kat?" The carefree act she was putting on wasn't fooling Raini. Hell, it wasn't fooling Kat either.

"I thought I could get right back into this, but I'm not that person anymore. None of this makes sense to me. I mean Deacon was right, why am I even here? I don't know why I thought I could fix this."

"I get that things are different for you now, Kat. You've got a daughter and a man who loves you. You left a wonderful, peaceful life behind and jumped into this nightmare.

"It's only natural that it would freak you out a bit. But you're here now and I know you can do this."

"I have to, don't I?"

"Yes, you do, and I'll do whatever I can to help you." They walked a little further. "Do we go up to Fragiliana now?"

The level of tension had been so high that it was necessary to let some of that pressure off. The only way Kat knew how to do that was with a little humor.

"Oh, gawd no!" she practically shouted. "If Hedda is up there now, then she can wait for an hour, don't you think? Food first, then we will put an end to the villainy."

"I'm so glad you're here, Kat. I was afraid I'd never see you again."

"I know, Raini. But so far, we've been very lucky. Anyway, yada-yada-yada, I'm starving."

***

There was an air off finality surrounding that meal, as if it could be their last. Possibly it was just more of the tension building up inside them. Or was it the feeling that coming face to face with Hedda could turn out to be a terminal experience for all of them.

During the drive up into the foothills, it became increasingly apparent that finding the farm might be much more difficult than they anticipated. It was after eight and they had less than an hour of sunlight left.

There were so many roads without names that split off from the Avenue de Andalucía. The farms and villas were hidden away in a maze of terraced fields and irrigation channels on both sides of the ridge.

Kat was driving while Raini was using Google Earth on the laptop. She'd entered the address, but the program couldn't pinpoint it.

They turned down several roads on the west side of the ridge, but nothing matched up with what they saw in the photograph.

It was getting late when they came to the large traffic circle and Kat was surprised that there was a new housing development up on the right. "Shit, this is nothing like it was when I was here last time." There was only one sideroad left to search.

"It had better be down there, because I don't want to go through this again, I'm getting car sick." She pointed to a parking area on the west leg of the highway leading out of Fragiliana. "I'm going to turn around and park it over there."

They got out of the car and walked to the edge. The valley was at its deepest there and there were only a couple of houses visible. Kat saw something at the bottom, a private road that led off into an orchard. It was the first orchard they'd seen all afternoon.

Raini said, "Those are orange trees, aren't they?"

"That's what they look like."

"And the others?"

"Small pomegranate trees."

"Do you think that's it?" asked Raini.

"I think it is. I wish we could see the house from here." It took a moment to make a decision, then she said, "Yeah, we're going to have to go down to make sure."

"On foot?"

"No, it's too far. We're going to have to drive down. Keep your eyes open for surveillance equipment."

Kat pulled back onto the road and was about to turn onto the sideroad but had to slam on the brakes to avoid a collision. Three cars roared around the traffic circle cutting her off. Without hesitation, they sped over the crest of the hill and caught air before they disappeared into the valley.

As far as Kat could tell, each car had four black figures inside and there was no denying that they knew exactly where they were going.

"Maybe we should have a peek," Kat said.

"You think?" Raini remarked sardonically.

They got out and ran to the edge to see what the men were doing. By the time they could see what was happening, the auto trio had reached the bottom and was turning onto the private lane.

"Are they finally after her now?"

"You mean the police?" Raini asked.

"Did they look like police to you?"

"Ah ..., no?"

"Correct. That was a kill squad."

"Yup," said Raini. "What are we going to do now?"

"We're going to follow them."

"Wait, what? Are you serious? What if they *are* cops? We'd be handing ourselves right over to them."

"Why would cops be going after Hedda?"

"OK, another good point. But then does it matter who they are? Cops or otherwise, they're not on our side, are they?"

"True, but we're not going to learn anything by standing up here."

"I beginning to think you're certifiable. You know that?"

They ran back to the car and drove into the valley but more cautiously than the others. The cars were still obscured by the terrain, but they marked their progress with clouds of dust as they turned onto the orchard lane. There was a substantial stand of trees blocking the view of the house, but what followed seemed to prove that they were in the right place.

Automatic gun fire erupted. Kat stopped. "Whoops! Now that doesn't sound friendly at all."

Judging by the noise, there were a dozen weapons firing together. "Apparently somebody else doesn't like the lovely Hedda." She was preparing to reverse up the hill when the sounds were swallowed up by a big explosion. "Holy shit, what just happened there?"

The first was quickly followed by second and a third; then it seemed as if the whole valley erupted in a huge succession of detonations.

"Down!" Kat shouted, and she pulled the parking brake on as they ducked down and covered their heads. The shock wave rolled over them like a freight train, pounding the car back. The ground shook as the fireball rose a hundred meters into the air.

Dense black smoke billowed up and was carried down the valley toward the sea. "Are you OK?"

"What? Um ..., yeah, I think so. You?"

"Yeah. Jesus, I did not see that coming." She sat up and looked at the devastation. "I think we should go down there."

"Ah ... no! Is that a good idea? I don't think so."

"There may be some survivors. We need to know what happened."

Raini was about to continue with her objection, but Kat's stare stopped her.

"Fuck it ..., alright, since you insist."

Kat released the parking brake and moved carefully down to the lane. The charred remains of the house were visible through the flames. All three of the cars had been thrown by the explosions and were engulfed in the inferno. An old unidentifiable bit of twisted metal lay at the bottom of a crater perhaps three meters deep and twenty across.

"Another car perhaps?"

"Could be." No one was moving. "Kat, we can't risk going any further. What if there are unexploded ordinance?"

"It looks like anything that could explode did."

"OK, That's one way of looking at it. Then again you could be full of shit. The police can't have missed that and they'll be on their way. We'll be cut off."

"I don't care now, Raini."

"Jesus Christ, if they ..."

"If there are survivors, I have to know what happened. We need that information. Who are they? Who sent them?"

"If she was in that house then she's gone. It's over, Kat."

"I don't think she would have done this if she was inside. Trust me, I know a self-destruct protocol when I see it.

We need to know what happened." Kat looked back up the hill and said, "There's no one home at the house back there. Let's go back and leave the car in their car port."

"Then what?"

"You stay there. If the cops come, wait till they've gone by and then bug out."

"We've been through this, Kat. We are not splitting up again. Park the goddamn car and let's do this thing together."

Kat had to agree, so she backed up and parked in the car port. As it turned out, people were not inclined to run toward the disaster. Even the fire department seemed in no hurry to save the day.

The women ran down using a rift cut into the hill as a path to the orchard. For a moment, they took cover behind a small concrete shed with tools and a small Kubota tractor inside. When they felt it was clear, they sprinted across the dirt road to the driveway and closed in on what was left of the house.

Body parts were spread around the courtyard, a couple were still burning. It seemed that no one had survived. But then, Kat heard a low groan coming from the far side of the first car. "Well, someone is still breathing. Come on."

The man was in bad shape, a large splinter from the house lodged in his side. Kat lifted the hood from his face. His breathing became a little easier. His clothes had melted onto his body and his exposed skin was terribly burned.

"Try to hang on, help is on the way."

"Er hat uns aufgestellt. Sie wusste, dass wir kommen würden." (He set us up. She knew we were coming.)

"Obviously, she knew you were coming," Kat said, "Speak English, who sent you?"

His eyes couldn't focus on her. "Kraft. Kraft sent us to kill her."

"Who is Kraft?"

"She ..., she knew. He could have warned ... us. He must have known she would ..., she would ... do this."

"Was it Hedda Jäger?" Raini asked.

"Ya. Jäger."

Kat was still trying to find out who sent them. "Who is Kraft?"

It took him some time to control his breathing, his features distorted with the pain. "Sig ..., Sigismund ... Kraft." He coughed up blood as the name came out. "He knew."

"So, who the hell is Kraft?

"Sigismund Kraft ..." His voice strained and weak.

"Wo finde ich diesen Mann?" (Where can I find this man?)

He kept trying to swallow as he choked of the blood. "Zürich ..., Kroner ... Agentur, Züri-- ..." Kroner... Agency, Züri-- ...) the word hung unfinished as his life sank into the dirt and his dead eyes stared up through the smoke-filled sky.

Kat stood up. "So, all we know now is that she set this up because she knew they were coming. And the man who sent these guys down here is Sigismund Kraft."

"He said Kroner agency, didn't he?"

"He did, yeah."

"That's not much is it?"

"It was enough."

Raini didn't understand that comment. "Tell me."

"The Kroner Agency was in Zürich, It was Jäger's intelligence network. I thought it was destroyed when Kroner died. Maybe it just grew another head called Kraft. She knew Kraft would be sending people down to kill her. This was our luck at work again. I think she's headed to Switzerland to kill Kraft."

✳✳✳

Chapter ~ 21

CNP Agent Carmona had arrived by helicopter in the dark. While viewing the devastation, he was wondering aloud, "How is it possible for the police to take a photograph of Anita Franco in Seville while at the same time she was in Hamburg murdering the family of a diplomat?"

"Sir?"

"That was clearly her image on the off duty policeman's phone, was it not?"

"Yes sir."

"And yet the name on the document at the Hamburg Airport was Anita Franco. She was there and three of the bodies in the house were her crew from the Madrid murders." He called the inspector in charge of the investigation in Hamburg about this inconsistency.

The inspector asked him, "Had any of your witnesses identified her before they were shown the photos?"

"No. As far as I know, they were shown the photo right away and they all said it was the woman at the hotel," Carmona said. "What about your witnesses?"

"The controller at the airport did not call us until he read the name on the receipt for the landing fee again this morning. My officer showed him the photo your people sent us."

"And ..."

"He said the woman looked like her."

"Looked like her?"

"Yes, but I didn't get the impression that he was certain about it. I am sensing that you are having doubts as well."

"I can only confirm that the woman we know as Anita Franco was in Seville this morning. There has been an incident on the Costa Del Sol. Our investigation has only just begun but the owner of the house was one Hedda Jäger, a German national," said Carmona.

"Ja, I know that name."

"You should," Carmona said pointedly. "Ähern Jäger was the leader of the Rote Faust group some years ago."

"Ja of course, are they related?" the German inspector asked.

"I will have to check to be certain, but I think there must be a connection. The reason I mentioned her was because my agent in Malaga discovered that yesterday, Hedda Jäger flew out of Malaga in her private plane with three men. She filed a flight plan listing the destination as a small airfield in Germany." He paused for effect.

"Yes, go on," urged the inspector.

"Flughafen Hamburg Finkenwerder. She returned early this morning, alone. And this evening three vehicles containing twelve men stormed her property. It appears that the house had been rigged with explosives. Those men drove into a mine field."

"Were there survivors?"

"No."

"Was Anita Franco in the area at the time?"

"There were no witnesses." The Spanish National Security agent waited for his German colleague to work it out.

"It is probably simply a coincidence, and the two incidents are unrelated."

"I strongly doubt that."

"Alright, then I wonder if you would you be able to send me a photograph of Hedda Jäger? I would like to show it to my witness."

"Of course. There must be one available somewhere."

Was it possible that they had been looking for the wrong woman? Finding Hedda Jäger suddenly became a priority. They quickly traced an abandoned car she left at the Malaga airport to a car rental agency in Nerja. The man who served Hedda confirmed that it was she, and said it looked as if she had been beaten badly. He had a photocopy of her driver's license. Carmona sent that to his friend in Germany. Eventually they found out that she had chartered a plane to Zürich.

***

Edward's flight touched down near the end of the day and the cab he hired found Siggi's address without difficulty. Siggi met the young man at the door with a gun in his hand.

"Ah, Edward, how nice to see you again. Please come in."

"What is going on, Siggi? Why the gun?"

"We live in dangerous times, Edward, very dangerous times."

"I am well aware of the danger. Do you think they are after you as well?"

"I am sure she is. She could be here at any minute now."

Edward was puzzled. "Who are you talking about?"

"Hedda, I'm talking about your sister." He was acting quite nervous now, all pretense of control had been shucked away. "Come in further, away from the door. Yes, that's it, now move into the living room and have a seat."

Edward remained standing. "You are afraid of my sister, why?"

"Because, she said she was going to kill me. That, I should think, would be sufficient cause."

"So, you intend to kill her?"

"I do, but I want her to see you before she dies."

"And you expect me to just stand by and let you do this?"

***

Kat and Raini had been traveling east on the main highway for almost an hour before Agent Carmona arrived at Hedda's house. They'd been silent most of the way, neither had much to say after what happened at the Jäger farm. The imperative now was to find Kraft before Hedda did and they had no idea if that was even possible.

Raina eventually broke the silence. "You still haven't told me how we're going to get to Zürich. We're not driving there in this thing, are we?"

"No, we're going to fly. There's an airport in Almería. We can charter a plane there."

"You're kidding right?"

"No, I'm not kidding."

"I think that's a bad idea, they'll spot you getting out of the car at the airport."

"You'd be right, if I was going to show my face. But I'm not. Anita Franco has one trick left that she's never used before."

"Oh, and what's that?"

"I got that stupid nickname from media after my new millionaire 'husband' died. I was wearing a bright sun dress not the traditional black widows do. I never gave it a thought at the time, but the Spaniards were scandalized. A reporter dubbed me the Happy Widow of Ibiza and it stuck. I think it's time I went into mourning. I'll wear black from head to toe and just sit quietly, while you rent the plane."

"Oh well, of course, how could that possibly fail? Where are you going to come up with this black outfit?"

"There's a town not too far away. We'll shop there."

"We? So, I have to wear black too."

"No, but something business like, You'll be my companion during my bereavement. You'll look great in a grey suit."

Raini folded her arms and stared out the window. "Wonderful."

"Come on, it'll work, you'll see."

Kat turned off the highway and found the main boulevard through the downtown section of el Ejido. It was a fair-sized town, not far from their destination, and she expected that there'd be a place to get what she needed but at that hour nothing would be open. They stopped at the Grand Hotel Victoria booked a room and planned to do their shopping in the morning.

They found the perfect shops with everything they needed. That included two suitcases for their backpacks. Before they left, Kat asked the shopkeeper if there was a limousine service in town. There was, and the woman phoned to hire one and had it meet them in front of the store

They finished the trip to the Almería airport in a long black chauffeur driven limousine. Raini arranged the charter and surprised the agent by paying cash while Kat sat by silently, looking very sad. That part required no effort at all.

***

The time they spent in the air was busy. The two-and-a-half-hour journey was the first time they could stop and plan for the next phase. Raini went online to find out who Kraft was. To their surprise there was no bio, no photographs, nothing about the man at all.

"It's like he doesn't exist. Kat, we don't have much time, and I've got nothing to work with. It's a big city, and saying he's in Zürich was not that helpful."

"It's not that big, but yeah, you're right."

"So how are we going to do this?"

"Christ, I wish I knew. After I got what I needed from Kroner I moved on to the primary objective which was to find Jäger. I thought the CIA would deal with that."

"Where were you when they found Kroner's agency?"

"Italy."

"Italy, yeah that's not helpful." She thought for a moment. "I'll try to dig up the CIA file then."

"How can you get access to that system?"

"I still have a friend there. It would be easier if M-CI had a file on it. Do you know if they worked with the CIA?"

"Yes, someone from Devlyn's team."

"Do you know who?"

"No, sorry."

"Never mind, it doesn't matter. I'll start with my friend." Raini remembered an email account her friend used. She returned the message a minute later and they began to write back and forth. *"Is that really you, Pooky?"*

"Hey Rainbow, what's up? I heard you were off the reservation."

"She calls you Rainbow?"

"Oh, did I forget to mention that? I'm gay. Yeah, we'll talk later." Kat was about to comment but decided to wait to Raini was ready.

"I'm in trouble, Pooky. A long story. Can you get some info for me."

"I can try. What do you need?"

"Looking back to Rote Faust, specifically the investigation the company did on the Kroner Agency."

"How much time can you give me?"

"All I've got is an hour."

"WHAT! I'll do my best. Do you want the address?"

"Please."

"OK."

Kat read the last response. "Won't she report your contact?"

"Oh, no doubt about it. For a twisted sister she's a strait and I 'd trust her with my life."

"You just did."

"Uh huh, I did didn't I. We'll just have enough time to get the Zürich and destroy the computer before they can trace the IP address."

"They're that slow?"

"No, but she's a really good friend."

"It makes no difference to me, you know."

"What are you talking about?"

"I don't care if you are a lesbian or not."

"And, I don't care that you're straight. Fuck, who am I kidding? Yeah, I care OK? And I care more and more every day."

"Jesus Raini..."

"No don't say anything, please. Don't ask don't tell."

"A bit late for that, don't you think?" Raini shrugged.

Forty minutes later Pooky wrote back and had a lot of information.

"Kroner's office was in District 6, right in a residential neighborhood. There was a reference to the M-CI report. An M-CI agent reported that the office had been evacuated before they arrived. There was evidence of recent activity, and they arrested a suspect for questioning because his name was found on a scrap of burnt paper, but released him, lack of evidence."

"So that's it?"

"Hold on a sec, there's more in the CIA's file. Oh, this is interesting. They have included something that the M-CI agent left out of his report. It says, the special agent entered the building before the Company's agents got there. They're being cagey here. It says, he may have had contact with one of Kroner's people, who is identified in the report as S.K."

"Sigismund Kraft!"

"No doubt. It alleges that the agent removed valuable evidence, and that he allowed the suspect to escape."

"Does it give the name of the agent?"

Raini sent that question. The response was frustrating.

"The CIA report says that M-CI withheld that information. They said they would conduct further investigations into the agent's possible wrongdoing."

"Did they?"

"No. The CIA kept on investigating but came up with nada. They believed there was a mole in M-CI who was able to bury that information. Good luck Rainbow."

"She is a true friend. What are the chances that the mole is someone from Devlyn's team?"

"It has to be. So here it is, right after I left for Italy, someone spoke to S.K. at the Kroner Agency, then S.K. escapes."

"So, Kraft must have turned the agent."

"That's got to be it."

"Kat, you knew them all, does anyone of them fit the profile of a turncoat?" asked Raini.

Kat sat back and rubbed her forehead. "Shit. It's been staring us right in the face. We both know who the mole is, don't we?"

"Nunez."

"Yeah, it's gotta be him, he was leading the kill squad. This makes me sick to my stomach." Kat sat in silence for a while. "That confirms that all along we've been played by people on the inside who are working for Kraft."

"And Kraft has been supplying information to Hedda Jäger. No wonder Hedda knows so much about you."

"Oh shit, I just thought of something. Remember I found Hedda's address in the white pages online?" Kat nodded. "I wonder if I could find Kraft's address there too. While I look this up, could you ask the attendant to bring me some coffee, please."

"Sure. Let's hope this pans-out quickly," Kat said. "When I get back, I'm going to call to rent a car for us."

Raini went to the web directory for Zürich and when Kat returned to her seat, Rain showed her the address. "I don't know why I didn't think of that before. Jesus, it was that simple?"

The hostess came down the aisle with a tray. "Here is your coffee ladies."

"Thanks," Raini said, grinning triumphantly.

"We have got to destroy that laptop," Kat said.

***

They made good time to Zürich Airport and after going through a very abbreviated customs and immigration check, which, in deference to Kat's bereavement, was handled respectfully. Kat asked the car rental agent for instructions to get from the Unterlandautobahn to the intersection of Scheuchzerstrasse and Langmauerstrasse. The rental agent gave her a map of Zürich and marked the route with a yellow highlighter. Then he escorted them to a medium sized Mercedes parked near the front door.

Kat was anxious to find Kraft before Hedda had a chance to kill him. Realistically though, it was more likely that he would already be dead. It was also likely that Hedda would be long gone, probably somewhere off the continent. The world's a big place and she would have to throw around a lot of money to mount an effective global search.

It was hard for her to feel any optimism about how this would end.

The neighborhood was complicated. There were no parallel roads in that part of the city. It was charming to be sure, but very confusing. None of them ran in a straight line and many of them changed names inexplicably at the end of a block. To add to the confusion, the street signs were not always visible, and the roads began to snake unpredictably as they drove closer to the top of the hill. His address was at the eastern edge of District 6, on the side of Zürichberg.

After considerable frustration they found the street. The houses on the right side were elevated at least three meters above the road. Most were semidetached with stairways reaching up from the street or from short driveways.

Several of the houses were, to some degree, obscured from street level by lush gardens, and some had garages built right into the hill. As they drove slowly up the tree lined street, they saw a tall woman walking gingerly down the steps from behind a large cypress. She was favoring her left side, wore dark glasses, and a scarf covering her head.

She paused at the gate and looked down the road watching them as they approached. The design pattern on her blouse was odd, it looked like a blood splatter.

"Is that blood all over her shirt? Oh Christ, that's gotta be her."

"Shit," Raini immediately made the connection, "he's dead. We're too late."

"I don't care about Kraft now, if we can catch her then I'm free."

Clearly alarmed, Hedda hurried through the gate to get to the car in the drive. She was moving like she was in a lot of pain.

"What do we do now?"

"We stop her," Kat growled, as she raced to get behind Hedda's Mercedes and slammed on the brakes just as she was backing out.

Hedda turned and glared at them through the rear window.

Kat was about to get out when Hedda moved forward and then put the car in reverse again and stepped on the gas.

Raini said, "Holy Shit!" She shed the seatbelt and leapt into Kat's lap just as Hedda's car rammed into them. Their smaller car went skidding across the street to the far curb. The damage to Hedda's Mercedes was relatively slight, but the rented Merc was a write-off. Very nearly trapping Raini's legs, the door had caved in, crushing the seat. The suspension system broke, leaving both wheels on the left side lying flat on their rims. Hedda accelerated, fishtailing up the hill then drifted out around the corner.

"Get off me!" yelled Kat furiously. In seconds Hedda was gone, but they could hear the sound of screeching tires drifting through the corner, then squealing away on the road above them.

Raini moved back onto the crumpled seat as Kat jumped out. Frantic to give chase, she ran to the VW Golf behind them and, using the butt of her gun, smashed the driver's window, unlocked the door and climbed in. While she was pulling down the ignition wires, Raini knocked on the passenger window.

Kat unlocked that door then went back to the wires. Raini hopped in as the engine came to life. Kat jammed the shifter into reverse, accelerated backwards then pulled up on the emergency brake, yanked the wheel to the right and, as the car drifted around a hundred and eighty degrees, she released the brake. With perfect timing Kat shifted into second gear and floored it, and the chase was on.

"Where?" Kat shouted.

"First corner, right," Raini told her.

The Mercedes had the advantage of speed, but Kat was able to compensate with the car's agility and her skill. She put the Gulf sideways as she came to the curve and maintained the drift all the way around, gaining precious seconds.

Just over the crest of the next hill they saw Hedda's taillights as she braked to avoid a head on collision.

She was way ahead, but Kat sped by the terrified driver in the oncoming car, red-lining with every shift and closing the gap. They snaked up the hill at terrifying speeds. Again, they lost sight of Hedda's car as she caught air on the crest of a hill, but only for a moment. Her skid marks left a trail and they followed it, gaining more ground.

Hedda had turned left at the next intersection, another sweeping switch-back turn. Kat was closing fast now as they continued to climb. They blasted under the tram bridge with a small, angled car chugging along making the steep climb. The passengers watched in astonishment as the two cars raced by underneath them.

There she was, just making a right turn up ahead. This time, it was a hairpin switch-back turn. Hedda was going too fast and she lost control, hit the curb and nearly tipped over.

Touching the retaining wall at the top of the door frame saved her. She had to reverse to get back on the road. Off she went again with some serious damage to the door and the left front fender. The jagged metal was rubbing on the tire and slowed her down.

She'd lost valuable time.

Kat was practically breathing down her neck.

When Kat was an instructor at Eagle's Nest she had trained for this kind of driving. She taught students how to do it on dangerous mountain roads in California. While she was driving with utter confidence, Raini was terrified. All she could do was hang on.

Now the Volkswagen was right on the Mercedes bumper. They raced up the hill, catching air at the crest, just missing a collision with a small tour bus pulling a trailer. Sparks were flying as they landed and the chase continued, bearing right at the fork in the road. Hedda picked up speed on the long straightaway, but frustratingly, the Golf couldn't keep up. Near the end there was a hard left and another sharp right.

Hedda was going too fast to set up for it, and oversteered, but Kat had plenty of time to prepare, and gained on her.

Hedda was leading them into the woods, up Batteriesteig and over the top. They roared past several cars filled with families heading for the zoo.

Again, they caught air as they started down the other side. The cars passed dangerously close to a group of hikers. They scattered in panic. More sparks and screeching tires, accompanied the sound of overrevved engines as they blasted through an intersection where three roads crossed. Cars were coming at them from every direction, but Hedda kept right on going. People swerved out of the way and off the road, forcing Kat to brake to avoid colliding with one car that misjudged everything and drove into her path.

"Aaaaaaa!" Raini screamed, as fenders touched, glass and plastic shattered and scattered across the road, and Kat kept on going.

The road curved to the left above the Zürich Zoo leading up to another 'T' intersection at Orellistrasse. Hedda had been making a lot of mistakes, she was exhausted, and in terrible pain. Taking too much time to decide which way to turn, she went straight off the edge, catching air once more, landing nose down in the parking lot of the Sorel Hotel

Zürichberg. Her chest slammed into the steering wheel breaking ribs as people scattered. Her car careened out of control, sideswiping the cars that had just exited and began spinning. Slipping through a gap in the parking curb at the edge of the lot, it plunged over another short drop and rolled ending right side up with the passenger door against a tree. Stunned, winded and gasping for air, she sat for a moment unable to think what to do next.

Kat wouldn't let up for a second, she followed the Mercedes through the parking lot, over the mini cliff, skidding to a stop near the back of Hedda's car.

Hedda opened the door and began to run, heading back to the hotel but she could only take a few steps before she collapsed, her energy drained. Unable to ignore the pain any longer, she had fallen to her knees and lolled over onto her side.

Kat launched herself from the Volkswagen to chase her but there was no need to run now. Hedda reached out her arm trying to hold up her gun. Kat easily took it from her hand and tossed it aside. She could see how much pain the woman was in and shouted, "Enough Hedda!" Then her tone softened as she sat down beside her. "Enough."

Hedda began sobbing. It was the release of all the pent up hatred and anger she had been storing since that day when she thought her brother had died.

Kat became overwhelmed, the feeling she had now was totally unexpected, she felt compassion. "It's over Hedda, it's over."

"No ..." she cried, desperately. "No! Never!" Hedda pulled her skirt up to her thigh and drew the knife from a sheath strapped to her leg and tried to stab Kat.

Kat simply batted it away. "Hedda, whatever it was that you were trying to do is over. Please, stop now."

Hedda didn't have the strength to continue, her arms fell slack at her sides, she coughed, and blood filled her mouth. The broken rib had shifted and pierced her lung.

"Oh god!" Kat held her shoulders. "What's happening to you?"

"I ..." More coughing and more frothy blood.

"Your lung has been punctured." She turned to her friend. "Raini, she's bleeding internally. Call for an ambulance."

Hedda looked down at the blood that covered her chest. Very quietly she said, "Anita, Karma is a bitch, don't you think?"

"We're getting help," said Kat.

"No," she coughed. "No don't, Anita. It's too late for that."

"I won't let you die. You can't die. Raini!" Kat shouted.

"It's not up to you this time, is it Anita?"

"Hedda, I'm not Anita," she said plaintively, "I'm Katrina Fernando, Anita was my undercover name."

"Well, it doesn't matter who you are now, does it? It's too late for both of us. You've almost killed off my entire family." She choked on the blood in her throat and coughed, sending a shower of blood from her mouth.

"What do I dial ..., 911?" Raini asked

Hedda shook her head and sagged against Kat. Kat held her against her chest with Hedda's head resting on her shoulder. Her voice was fading. "There's no more time."

"It's 144 here," Kat told Raini, the urgency had gone from her voice as she gently brushed the hair from Hedda's face.

"I don't need your sympathy, Katrina."

"I didn't want any of this, Hedda."

"But I did. You know ..., I ... couldn't ask ... for a better ending. They ..." she coughed, "will have you now. I have won."

"Is Kraft dead?" Kat asked.

"Yes, but I didn't kill him. He was dead when I arrived." She coughed, winced in pain, and gasped for air. "But ..." she coughed more blood, her eyes rolled back, and she struggled to stay conscious. The siren's faint ring drifted across the distance. Hedda put her hand on Kat's chest and lifted her head. "You ..., you will be blamed, Katrina."

"Was it worth all of this, Hedda?"

She smiled and winced in pain. It all flashed through her mind, and she could feel Kat's heartbeat against the palm of her hand. She looked into Kat's eyes and whispered, "Was I wrong?" She lapsed into unconsciousness and her head fell back and thinking that she had died, Kat slowly lowered her to the ground.

Rani was by her now and had heard every word. "Is she dead?"

"I don't know, but she has destroyed me. It's over for me, Raini." She looked up. "You have to get away now, I'll stay with her."

"Kat, they're not going to wait for explanations. They will just shoot you." Kat looked at her as if to say she didn't care. "Come on, we have to go."

The ambulance was rushing up the hill and before long they could see it heading right for them. "No, I can't run anymore."

"Yes, you fucking can! Jesus Kat, think of Sara. Look, you have no choice! I told you, we are never going to split up again. Do you hear me? Now get up on your fucking feet and come with me now, or so help me I'll die here with you. Kat! " Raini demanded an answer, "What's it going to be?"

The police cars would not be far behind and Hedda's last word rang in her head like a huge bell. "But ..."

"No buts! You're coming with me right now!" She pulled on Kat's arm. Reluctantly, she got up and Raini forced her to run back to the car, took the wheel and drove down towards the city.

Raini drove right by the ambulance as she slipped into the cat's cradle of streets in Kraft's neighborhood. They passed two police cars racing toward the crime scene but they never gave them a thought.

Shortly they entered a commercial area. Raini spotted the streetcar tracks on Vorderberg and had an idea. She backed into a parking space on Keltenstrasse and urged Kat to move with her. They hurried across the intersection to the platform just ahead of an approaching tram and boarded by the rear door. The car was practically empty, so they took their seats at the back as the tram pulled away.

They sat in silence for a few blocks, just trying to let their hearts slow down. While Kat was reliving the tragedy on the hill and sinking into the abyss of depression, Raini was planning their escape. She heard the police cars coming their way and froze, but Kat showed no reaction at all. The patrol cars raced by as the tram innocuously trundled on.

At last Raini broke the silence saying, "Kraft was a fool."

"Why."

"He underestimated Hedda."

"Yeah, he sure did, didn't he," Kat said. "I wonder who else underestimated her?"

Raini looked at her, but this time she saw what she had missed before. "Oh fuck, you're covered in blood, Kat. I don't know how anybody could have missed that. We have to get off right now."

"I can't move."

"Kat, listen to me, we have to move now. Come on stand up." When the tram slowed at the next stop Raini practically carried Kat to the exit. "We have to get off and get another car."

"How? We left everything in the Mercedes. I have no more money. No clothes. Raini it's hopeless."

"You still have your passport, don't you?"

"It's in my bra."

"Okay, good. That's all we need. We can deal with the rest later. Now come on, the tram's stopping, we have to get off now." Kat was slow to move. "It's not over!" she growled in Kat's ear. "Do you hear me?" She dragged Kat down onto the platform.

"What's the point now?"

"Sara, Sara is the goddamn point!" She looked across the street and saw The Library for Business Administration and had an idea. "Listen to me. It's not over until I say it is. We'll steal a car if we have to but first I have to find you some clean clothes."

Kat looked down and saw the blood as if for the first time. "Shit, look at me. How can you stand to Stay with me now? I'm finished, Raini. She's dead and I may as well be."

"We are not giving up. I am going to get us out of here. Have I made myself clear?"

"Why?"

"Because I love you."

"Raini ..."

"It doesn't matter if you love me back Kat, I was in love with you before we even met and I don't regret a second of it.

***

Raini snuck Kat into the library and hid her away in a stall in the public washroom. Then it took some doing but she managed to convince Kat to give her the access code to her bank account.

She withdrew twenty thousand euros, bought new clothes and a few extra things for her friend, and rented a car. She wasn't sure if Kat would be in the stall when she returned, but her friend had barely moved a muscle in all that time.

Kat was almost catatonic, so Raini helped her wash off the blood and fix her hair then dressed her in an elegant pant and blouse outfit. Then after stuffing her stained clothes in the waste basket they calmly walked out to the street. She had parked the executive size Audi close by and before long they were heading out of the city on the highway.

All she wanted to do was get out of Switzerland, so she drove northwest without stopping for anything. When they crossed into France, she pulled into a fuel station to fill up and bought some sandwiches and coffee.

"Here," she said, handing Kat a sandwich, "eat something."

"I'm not hungry."

"Eat it anyway." Kat just let the food sit there on her lap as Raini stared at her. "Alright, I don't get it, OK?"

"What?"

"We came all this way to catch the woman. People have been chasing us, shooting at us, you burned down your own place because of her."

"Are you angry with me?"

"Angry with … huh … No Kat, I'm not angry … well I guess I am I suppose, but all you did was comfort her. I don't get it. Why?"

"Why what?" Kat reached for the coffee and had a sip.

"You, you … No, I'll start again. She was a terrible vindictive woman. She did everything she could to destroy you. How could you feel any compassion after what she had done."

"I know, but when I saw how badly she'd been beaten I … I, I'm sorry."

"Yeah, me too. Eat the sandwich, it'll make you feel better."

The 'why' Raini couldn't understand, grew out of Kat's persistent depression. It seemed to become more powerful with that name, Anita Franco. It was her demon that had devoured Hedda. All the negative feelings she'd been building up throughout her life had crystallized in that horrible thing. In some bizarre, twisted logic when Hedda took on that name she had somehow been consumed by that demon and Kat felt responsible.

Raini had no idea what was going on in her head and probably wouldn't have understood it if she did. All she could see was that her friend was unable to save herself, so she had to take charge to save them both. Kat took another bite and wiped her mouth with the back of her hand.

"Are you feeling better?"

"Should I be?"

"Fuck it." They were on the move again. "Kat, we're looking for an exit to take us north." She shoved the map at her. "Help me to find some place safe."

"Where are we going?"

"All I know is we're going north. I need more than that, so get it together and focus. Where are we going?"

Kat forced herself to concentrate. Scanning through the possibilities in her mind, she eventually said, "Luxemburg, we can get a flight off the continent from there."

"Would Deacon be able to come and get us?"

"I don't think I should even ask him."

"Kat, he loves you. We need help and he wants to help, so please, just ask him."

"I'll think about it."

✳✳✳

Deacon could fly into Luxemburg without raising suspicion. It would be just like he did in Lisbon. That thought eased Raini's mind a little while she was driving. Kat was navigating their way to the tiny country using secondary roads to avoid police and traffic cams.

After four hours on the road, Kat was still in a sort of fog, and she still hadn't contacted Deacon. "Look, I'm serious, would you please pick up the phone and call him? If we don't call him until we get to Luxemburg, we'll be waiting around all day and someone is going to spot us." Raini was hoping that hearing Deacon's voice might help clear Kat's mind. Finally convinced, Kat made the call.

She put it on speaker phone. "Deacon."

"Kat, oh Jesus, are you alright?"

"Not really, no. Things have turned to shit here, but we're alive and on the road in France, heading for ..."

"No, don't tell me."

"What's happened?"

"I've just seen it on TV. The American news is already showing it."

"Showing what?"

"What happened in Zürich. People were filming it on their cell phones. The woman died, Kat."

"I'm not surprised."

"Before she died, she said she was Jäger's niece. She said that's why you came after her."

"That's not true, you know I went after her because she was posing as Anita."

"I know it, Kat, but…they recorded what she said. She was incoherent, speaking in Spanish one moment, and German the next. It was all jumbled up and hard to understand. It looked like she wanted to confess, but she died before she could get it out. People are saying that you killed her and a man named Kraft. Did you know anything about him?"

"Only that he worked for her, and he must have betrayed her. That was why she wanted to kill him."

"But they're saying that you killed him."

"I didn't, but never mind that now. What's happening with you?"

"Don't worry about me, Kat, but they've identified Raini now. Her picture is on the tube beside yours."

"Jesus."

"The Americans have given her up. They say she's a deserter and she's wanted for treason."

"This just keeps on getting better and better."

"They have a description of the car you stole, the Volkswagen. Are you still driving it?

"No."

"Good. Kat, apparently everyone is now convinced that you are the assassin." Though it shouldn't have come as a surprise, she was stunned and just sat there as the French countryside flashed by.

"Kat, please talk to me."

"Deacon, I'm sorry. I don't think there's any hope for us now." Raini looked at her and stopped the car. Her hands dropped to her lap as if it was a sign that she had given up as well.

"Kat, maybe you could negotiate a surrender. I could have a lawyer take care of that. You don't have to die."

"She told me that it was over for both of us." Though Kat was speaking to Deacon, she was saying it to herself.

"It's not over, Kat. I spoke with someone today, an American agent. He said he knows you. He said the only way to stay alive is to give yourself up."

"Who was agent?"

"What?"

"Deacon, did he give you his name?"

"Yes, Nunez, Jamie Nunez. He said he'll see to it you won't get hurt."

"Wait, is he there with you now?"

"Yes, he's listening in."

"Oh god, Deacon. I'm sorry, I have to go now. Look after Sara for me and tell her that mommy will always love her."

"Kat I ..."

Marketers had been using MAC locaters for some time to log people who had seen their ads. Kat knew that the Six-Six-M-I had been utilizing the MAC address locaters all over Europe. They'd been planting the scanners wherever they suspected enemy agents might be working. If a device with a MAC address were to drive by a scanner, embedded in say, a road sign or a store front for example, it could identify that device and its location.

Did we pass any billboards or road signs while I was talking to him?"

"There's been nothing like that on this road."

If they had pinged the phone they could have figured out what part of France it was in. If there were cameras on that road he'd probably have already seen all the cars with two women driving and identified theirs.

She took out the battery and threw it out the window, then removed the SIM card, broke it in two, and sent it after the battery. Finally, further down the road, she tossed out the phone.

***

The special team, aka Nunez's Goon Squad as Raini like to refer to it, had located the phone somewhere along the French German border. They needed access to US military equipment, so they immediately headed for the airport then flew on to Stuttgart.

On their way, Nunez bypassed Special Agent Song and contacted Capt. Gradin directly. What he wanted was a helicopter to continue their pursuit.

Gradin had been manipulating Wolfson for some time, often by hiding orders and requisitions forms in stacks of documents that the general had to sign. Wolfson trusted him, so when Gradin wanted to get something through, he'd just pile it on, knowing his boss wouldn't bother to read them all before signing them.

"I have some orders and requisitions for you to sign, Sir."

"What orders?"

"To continue the search for Gen Hershoff and a few standard transfers of personnel and equipment in Europe, Sir. The usual stuff."

"Hold on there, what makes you think he's in Europe."

"There was a sighting at an airport, and they figured that he might have gone over to help Fernando."

"That meddling old bastard. Very well, let me have them," Wolfson quickly went through the short stack and handed them back to Gradin.

"Thank you, Sir."

"If you hear anything about Hershoff, I want to know about it."

"Yes, Sir."

"Very well."

With the general's signature on orders, Gradin sent the requisition to the 1/10th Special Forces Group stationed at U.S. Army Garrison Stuttgart. The request was for a Blackhawk and two pilots mentioned by name, chosen from his list of insiders.

The pilots, CWO-3 Ronny Majors and CWO-2 Neil Rutledge, were soldiers he had recruited but until now, had never used. He called them to let them know what was expected of them and nothing more. They geared up and were running through the pre-flight to be ready to go when the Nunez team arrived.

1/10th Special Forces Group, Stuttgart

The UH-60A was ready for lift off when the special team walked out onto the pad. Nunez checked it out and smiled when he saw the two M-60 GP 7.62 mm machine guns mounted underneath.

They would tear a target to shreds in seconds. He found that the image of Fernando's body disintegrating before his eyes quite appealing. Then again it would be too quick. Where was the fun in that? No, he had to think of something else.

Hanamansingh meant nothing to him, he could just let one of his men eliminate her. But that bitch who embarrassed him in Zürich had to suffer. He'd think of something in the air on the way to Metz, France.

"Have you been briefed on the mission?"

"Yes Sir, Gradin filled us in, so we're good to go."

"That's what I like to hear. Good men." Nunez returned to the bench at the rear and while he watched forests and mountains drift by below, his mind turned to entertaining ways to kill the Kat.

***

Part 3

Chapter ~ 22

Raini pulled off the road at the next intersection. "You need to tell me, what are you thinking, Kat?"

"That we are completely fucked."

"Agreed. What do you think of his idea?"

"I don't think there's a lawyer on the planet that could stop someone from killing us. The Goon Squad would want to be the first in line to do that unless the police shoot us on sight.

"Agreed. Is there any place we could go where we wouldn't be shot on sight?"

Kat thought for a moment then said, "Well, there's always Canada."

"We wouldn't be able to get on a plane."

"Then there's England. Hedda didn't kill any British mucky-mucks, did she?"

"Not that I am aware of. Hey, the bobbies don't carry guns."

"Old news, Hon. Terrorism changed all that a while ago. But then again, England probably would be the safest place. I just hope they hate us less there than people do here."

"Do you think Nunez will find us?"

"Yup, He's on his way here right now."

"Yeah, I suppose he is. Shit!"

"Don't worry about him. It'll take time to get to a plane in Portugal and then fly up here. Then he'll have to find someplace to land, then get transport and ..."

"Yeah, OK I get it. So, we're going to England. How?"

Kat studied the map and came up with a route. "OK, beyond that traffic circle up ahead there's a ramp onto the highway. We head west to Paris then to Calais, how does that sound?"

"And what if they see us on one of those goddamn cameras on the highway?"

"I don't see what choice we have."

"Yeah, OK, let's go to Calais."

"We're French tourists now. We'll ditch the car and take the Chunnel across to England."

"Now that sounds like a plan."

"I sure as hell hope it works. You've been at it for hours, It's my turn."

Kat drove around the traffic circle to the A-4 then took the ramp heading west toward Paris/Thionville. She easily merged into the light traffic and moved over to the middle lane following the signs to Calais. Raini was thankful for one thing. The call had cleared the cobwebs. Kat had her emotions under control. Even so, it was another indication that Kat had lost her edge. Kat had too much to lose, and that made everything harder.

The younger fugitive was at the wheel again when they reached the port city. She turned off the highway heading into the city center along the Rue des Prairies, a one-way street in a rather depressed part of town. Kat had wanted to leave the car somewhere where it was certain to be stolen, but the chances of finding a cab along that street were slim.

So, Raini kept going until the street opened onto the Boulevard la Fayette. That looked more promising. She turned right and found some street parking in front of a flower shop. Leaving the car running, they walked a couple of blocks west to find a clothing store. They knew that they'd be under constant observation by security cameras.

With that in mind, they spent some time shopping for anything that would hide their faces and help them blend with the tourists.

Just up ahead, they discovered Texti, a small version of Walmart with cheap summer clothing. They emerged a half hour later with the best they had, hiking boots, broad hats, sunglasses and small travelling bags with toiletries and a change of everything. "What do we do with all this money?" asked Raini.

Kat thought about that for a moment and then said they could stash it in a loaf of bread. It seemed like an odd idea, but they hollowed out a large loaf, rolled the cash up inside then carefully fit a plug of bread in the end. Kat smeared a tiny bit of pâté and cheese on the torn end to make it look like lunch.

They took their time walking back to the spot where they left the car. As expected, it was gone.

Raini flagged down a cab to take them to the Eurotunnel Terminal. There they found out that it would have been easier had they made a reservation beforehand.

They bought tickets for the train leaving in two hours and then got in line for the security and customs check. The line was full of people eager to get home to England as well as European tourists. The inspection of documents and luggage at security was intense but, at the moment, they were looking for contraband and terrorists. They didn't seem to be interested in apprehending an assassin. There were no photos of her posted anywhere, and when the customs agent told her to take off her sunglasses, he didn't bat an eye.

Since both women were obviously American to the core, the questions were minimal. Nobody cared about them, and they got on the train without incident.

Twenty minutes later the train arrived in Folkestone. Merging with a tour group trying to look as if they belonged, they made it off the train and chose the little bus that was heading to the Royal Norfolk Hotel across the tracks.

At the desk Kat asked about rental cars. "Are you checking in dearie?"

"We haven't made a reservation. Is that a problem?"

"Oh, not to worry about that, luv," she said, assuming they wanted a room. "We'd never turn away such a lovely couple of Yanks. I have a cozy room with a queen size bed and a bath/shower en-suite."

"That would be perfect," said Raini, affectionately slipping her around Kat's and leaning her head on her shoulder. Kat glanced at her, and Raini squeezed her arm lovingly.

"I thought it might," said the woman, with a conspiratorial grin and nod.

***

There were no clues to tell them in which direction the women may have gone. Nunez racked his brain for a while waiting for inspiration to lead them to her. He took a guess. "Head west. The best chance to get away would be to get off the continent. I think they'd go to England; the English are less inclined to shoot first. Airports are out, so they'll probably take the train across from Calais to Folkestone. That's where we'll pick up their trail."

"We're going to need to take on some fuel if we're crossing the channel," said Ronny Majors.

"Is there a fuel station nearby?"

"Yes, there is, we're about ten miles out now. I'll radio ahead and have them standing by."

"Good."

***

Kat had picked up a road map of England and some tourist guide books at the train station and spent some time overnight planning where to go before they turned in. They needed a place to hide for a while to give them time to figure out what to do.

Romsey was her choice because it was small, two-and-a-half-hours away and far away from London. One of the guidebooks featured that area, so she stuck her finger on a nice-looking hotel right in the center of town and called ahead to book a room.

***

After the surveillance was pulled away from his hotel, Deacon was done sitting there doing nothing but worry. Jim and Janet knew people stationed in the Canadian and American facilities in Germany. Through them, they found out some interesting things about the movements of the special team.

"We heard that they left Lisbon for Stuttgart, picked up a helicopter there and then flew back to France. They must have picked up their LKL."

"What does LKL mean?"

"Last known location. They were way too late."

"Well, that's a relief, but where did Kat and Raini go?"

"We haven't heard any official reports about them at all, not since Zürich. So, we have no idea. They could be anywhere."

"Oh god, I hate this. I need to know that she's safe."

Jim said, "We'll find them, Dr. Loats, it takes time."

Janet was going over the relevant things she knew about Kat. She remembered a name Kat had mentioned some time ago, an agent from Europol.

"Jim, did Kat ever mention a guy from The Hague to you? I think his name was Henrick Something."

"Wait a second, yeah. The one she met on her way back from ah ... where was it now?"

"St. Petersburg, yes, that guy, Henrick ..."

"Ah Henrick ..., De Jonckheer, yeah, Henrick De Jonckheer."

"What a memory. I wonder if he's still with the agency. Let's see if we can reach him." She got the number for Europol and left a message. "It is urgent that I speak with him."

"May I tell him what this is concerning?"

Janet and Kat had talked about her first experience in The Hague and that he was the first person to refer to her as a tiger. "Yes, it's about an endangered tiger that has recently disappeared." Janet gave her cell number for a call back.

The news that the Goon Squad was on her trail was disturbing and Deacon hadn't been able to help her at all. The last thing in the world he wanted to do was let her down, and now he believed that he'd done just that. Why did everything have to be so damned difficult?

He called in his reserve pilots before checking out of the Olissippo Lapa Palace Hotel, then they went to the airport to wait for Henrick's call. Europol must have been part of the search for Kat because Henrick called back while they were in the car heading for the airport. He had gone off on his own and was using a new phone. "I had assumed that you would have heard the news."

"What news?" asked Janet.

"The Spanish authorities have found new evidence that vindicates Kat. The woman who died in Zürich was the assassin after all. The manhunt is over."

"Oh-my-god, I can't believe it. Damn, it wasn't on the news, she doesn't know that."

"I haven't been tuned in. Perhaps the media has not been given the latest reports yet. But it will come out in time. They've been spotted at the Eurotunnel Terminal; they boarded the train to England. The authorities in England will no doubt find her and tell her she has nothing to fear now."

"That is very good news, Henrick, thank you. Oh, hold on for a second Henrich."

"You have thought of something?"

"Yes, If they see the police coming for them and they don't know they're in the clear, then they would try to get away. That could turn out badly."

"I agree. What do you propose we do?"

"It would be very helpful to get it on the news ASAP. Flood the airways and make sure they hear it."

"We can try that. I'll see to it that there is an immediate press release."

"Thanks again, Henrick."

Deacon seemed more concerned now. "If they don't know about this turn of events, how do we communicate with her?"

***

Their investigation had been restricted to Germany and Spain. 6-6 M-I had been keyed into the Spanish CNP and dutifully informed Wolfson the moment Hedda died. Now he knew that the Spanish Security Agency had been communicating with Germany's. The evidence showed that Kat had been exonerated.

When the truth about Gen Wolfson's involvement at the very least he'd be charged with obstruction, and he'd be cooked.

If Kat was dead, it might all go away.

Fearing that the media would pick it up, Wolfson asked the President to intervene requesting that the investigations in Spain and Germany be kept top secret claiming national security concerns.

Interpol became aware through a source in the German National Security Agency and Europol had been silenced. The Swiss and French authorities were concerned. Clearly for some reason the Americans wanted this revelation kept under wraps. They couldn't imagine how this had anything to do with US National Security but agreed to the US blackout. MI5 was briefed by the CIA and asked to treat it as Top Secret and they blacked it out as well.

The media was kept out of it leaving Kat and Raini at the mercy of Britain's police protocols in pursuit of felons considered armed and dangerous. Wolfson had effectively cleared the way for his special team to pick her up anywhere in the British Isles.

***

The White Horse Inn was a plain looking three-story building with a whitewashed facade. The stables at the back had been converted into large suites and Kat and Raini took one of them planning to stay four nights. Just down the one-way street from Market Square was the Lloyds Bank. The proximity to a supply of funds was handy but the stash hidden in the loaf of bread was more than enough to cover their needs for now. They needed clothes again and a new computer, but first they needed lunch. They found a computer store and Raini chose the laptop while Kat picked up a couple of pay as you go phones. Then with their electronic needs satisfied, they shopped for clothes. It started to rain while they were in the shop necessitating the purchase of raincoats and umbrellas. The weather kept them close to their rooms for the next four days, giving them some time to rest in safety.

***

On the fourth day the rain stopped and gave way to sunshine. With a clear sky above, they evolved a rough idea of how to get back to Canada. It had a few wrinkles that Kat needed to iron out over the phone. That was problematic. Anything she said could possibly trigger an algorithm in the NSA's global monitoring system.

Of the billions of calls, it would single her out and lead the authorities right to them. That meant they had to leave Romsey to use the phone. It was possible to stay in the rooms for the remainder of the week, so they left their things locked away and drove south to Lyndhurst.

They were heading for New Forest National Park. Its isolation would give them some cover to make the call. Kat tapped in Ramsey Hershoff's number.

Raini said, "Turn on the speaker." Kat obliged.

"Hello." A man answered. "Who is calling please?" She was stunned into silence "Hello?" he repeated, "Who is this?"

Raini jumped in putting on a Punjabi accent, "Ah ..., hello this is Sandra, am I speaking to the owner of the house?"

"No, what do you want?"

"I am calling from Trans America Duct Cleaning Service we are conducting a special..." She shrugged not knowing what to say next. Kat roller her eyes. "...a special offer ... offering today ... in your neighborhood and..."

"I'm not interested. Please take this number off your call list," he said, then hung up. Kat pressed the cancel button.

"So, I guess he didn't need his ducts cleaned," Raini said. "Who were you calling?"

"Either Ramsey or his wife Bernice. One of them should have answered the phone. I have to assume that something has happened."

"What if she was there and just let a friend handle the calls?"

"Oh, that's just perfect, Goddammit." She dropped the phone on the floor and was about to stomp on it.

"Wait. Stop!" Raini pushed her foot away. "What are you doing?"

"They're going to trace the call."

"Who, Bernice's friend?"

"What if it was the FBI? It wouldn't be a stretch to say they've already located us."

"If they did, then we'll be someplace else in a minute, right?"

"Oh ... right." Kat moved her foot and picked up the phone. "If the bastards have Ramsey, then he's as good as dead. This is all my fault!"

"Don't say that. Look, you've got to pull yourself together, Kat, or we won't survive this. I need you at a hundred percent."

"You're right, I'm sorry … I…" The phone rang and she just about to drop it again. "Fuck!"

"Answer it." It kept ringing, "Kat, please answer it."

"They must have located us the instant the connection was opened."

"Perhaps, but like I said, we won't be here when they show up, will we? Don't you want to know who it is? I think we owe it to ourselves to find out, don't you?"

"Why not" She opened the connection. "Hello."

"Hello, you just called the Hershoff's number, who are you?"

"No sir. First tell me who you are."

"I'm Special Agent Adam Brennan, FBI."

"Well Special Agent Adam Brennan, FBI, I want to speak to Bernice Hershoff."

"I am acting for Mrs. Hershoff. If you have any demands, you can tell me what they are. I am authorized to see that they're taken care of. But first I want proof of life."

"So, someone does have him."

"Yeah, so now it's your turn. Who are you? Are you Katrina Fernando?" He waited. "Alright, listen Katrina, General Hershoff has been missing for several days. We believe he was taken away by people in the Army. What do you know about that?"

"Nothing, but I can guess."

"Alright, guess."

"Just so you know we are in the middle of nowhere and we'll be someplace else as soon as this call is over."

"I understand."

"OK, There's a mole in M-CI, I believe it is Special Agent James Nunez. Actually, it might be a cell possibly led by him. He's been chasing us all over Europe. He's the one who set me up and chased me out of Toronto. Speak to Major General Wolfson, Fort Belvoir, Army Intelligence. Nunez couldn't do anything without Wolfson's knowledge."

"Then we'll talk to Wolfson, got it. Now don't hang up there's some …"

Kat ended the call and tossed the phone out the window. "Happy? We have to go right now." Raini just sat there. "What?"

"No, I'm not happy. I think you should have listened to what he had to say."

"I could guess what it was."

"Kat, I don't think you could. I want you to call him back."

Kat was angry now. "Forget it. Let's move it."

"OK but think about it. Things may have changed."

***

Brennan was frustrated and just stared at the phone for a few seconds. "Did you get a fix on that phone?" Jim Daniels was looking at the GPS screen and the dot at the center of the radiating rings marked where Kat had been.

"Yeah, they're in southern England. Our system picked up a ping off towers in the Lyndhurst area. They're in the New Forest.

"Do you think she was telling the truth?"

"I don't think there's any doubt, and that Indian accent must have been Special Agent Hanamansingh. If they are still in hiding, then there's a chance they don't know."

"So, what do we do?"

"I'll call her back." The phone kept on ringing on a path in the New Forest. "She ditched the phone." Brennan called it in.

The Director of the FBI notified his counterpart at the CIA about what Kat had said concerning MGen Wolfson. After that, he called the head of Scotland Yard to warn them that Kat and Raini didn't know it was over yet, and to approach peacefully with extreme caution." OK, what's bothering you, Jim?"

"I don't know, Adam. Why would she risk calling here?"

"Like Mrs. Hershoff said, Fernando is like family, she was worried about him. Now she's pretty sure he's dead."

Jim Daniels banged his hand down on the table in frustration. "And that's why you believe the story she just handed you?"

"Yup, no question. Right now, we have a couple of innocent women, professional soldiers who are capable of bringing a lot of hurt down on some people if they feel trapped. When Fernando answered that phone, she was reaching out for help. What's going on over here is something that we need to bring to a peaceful conclusion."

"Fine," said Daniels, "Then I think we should take her advice and have a chat with that General Wolfson."

✳✳✳

Chapter ~ 23

The Shell Station at the edge of the New Forest was their first stop for fuel on the way back to Romsey. The patch of dirt opposite the pumps was filled with lorries, parked two abreast, and more were parked on the shoulder further along. All the fuel bays were occupied, and people were out of their cars talking. Raini was at the wheel and Kat just sat there staring off into the distance. Raini nudged her gently and said, "Kat ... Kat are you in there?"

Kat was jolted out of a flashback. "What's happening?" Instinctively her hand went down for the gun she no longer had.

"Whoa, whoa slow down. Nothing's wrong." She rested her hand on Kat's. "Are you OK?"

"No." She looked around at their location "Where are we? What's going on?"

"I just pulled in for fuel. There's a line up, so it's going to take a while. I'm going in to get something to eat. Do you want anything?"

"Sure, what do they have here?"

"It's Micky D's. They've got stuff."

Kat smiled. "Then I'll have some stuff and a Coke."

The people around the pumps talking excitedly. "Two orders of stuff with Coke. I wonder what they're talking about over there?"

Raini drove by them slowly with the window open but couldn't hear any details. People were talking at the restaurant too.

She parked close to them and listen.

"... and the police are looking for them everywhere," said a woman.

"Aw shit. Did you hear that?"

"I'm not dying for a burger now."

Raini rolled up her window. "What are we going to do now?"

A truck emerged from a small underpass that led to the other side of the highway. Kat consulted the map and saw that it joined another road heading south to Burley. "How much fuel have we got?"

Raini looked at the gage and said, "About an eighth of a tank, why?"

"Burley isn't that far. We'll fill up there and then find a way back to Romsey."

"Should we be going back there?"

"Christ, I'm not thinking. No, you're right. Fuck!" She paused trying to think of a plan but couldn't think. "Just head down there and maybe we'll find a place."

"Wonderful. Cross off another collection of nice clothes." Raini wheeled the car under the highway. "At least I brought the computer." They proceeded down the narrow country road to Burley, found fuel, then continued south on Station Rd.

To avoid a bike rally, she turned off the main road and ran right into a police checkpoint. It was just outside of Wootton. Manned by two unarmed local constables. She threw it into reverse and did a very reasonable approximation of a 180 turn.

"Whoa, nice work," Kat said. "Now where?"

"Now we scare the shit out of some cyclists."

One of the constables ran to his car and started chasing them. Raini went right and kept heading south honking the horn as she flew by the bikers.

They were in a developed area and neither woman cared where that took them. Halfway to Bashley they heard the familiar sound of a heavy helicopter coming from behind.

"Oh, holy crap, whose is that? Can you see it?"

"No," said Kat, "but I know what it is. We can forget about the Brits taking us prisoner, that's a Blackhawk."

Suddenly it was right above them and swooped in low enough to push the car down with its rotor wash. It turned sideways in front of them trying to force them to stop.

The cabin door was open and two of the six men inside were seated on the deck with their feet hanging out and their guns, a couple of SIG Sauer MPX, pointing at them.

Raini wasn't sure what to do now. "Are they bluffing?"

"It can't land and block us. Drive under them."

"You're kidding right?"

"If they don't get out of the way we all die. Keep going and put your foot down!"

"OK." Raini floored it, scooting under the helicopter. "Where are we going now?" Raini shouted over the noise.

"South."

"Then we're pretty soon we'll be running out of England," Raini warned. "How did they find us so quickly?" The Blackhawk was staying with them, at about fifty feet off the deck.

Kat was feeling very vulnerable as she looked up at it, wondering if they might just be trying to set up for a sniper to take a shot. "I don't know. Maybe the FBI told them."

Raini drove as fast as she could to New Milton. The officers were still back there, but the traffic closed up behind them allowing Raini to put some distance between them. "Kat, *where* am I going?" she pleaded.

"Jesus! Uh … just … just keep on this road." Kat pulled out the map and scanned their options. "We're here, we have Barton on the Sea ahead."

"Wonderful, we're going for a swim."

"If we stay on this road, we'll pass a golf course."

"We haven't got time for this. I have to turn somewhere."

"No. The chopper will have landed on the course waiting for us, so we can't go that way."

"Fuck! *Kat*, tell me where to turn!"

"Wait, if we go left down at Lymington Rd. then we just have more small towns and tourists all the way to Bournemouth."

"I need a fucking decision!"

"Give me a second here."

"Left, or right? Tell me now!"

"Right!" Kat said, "Go right!"

Raini made the turn onto Ashley Rd., went around the traffic circle, then carried on down Old Milton Rd.

Kat crumpled the map in her lap, with her voice expressing her emotional exhaustion she said, "Slow down, Raini. That's the ocean ahead of us, slow down. I for one don't want to do a Thelma & Louise."

"Neither do I."

***

She slowed and pulled into a parking space at the curb. Across the sidewalk was an appliance store with a few customers near the front.

"What do we do now?"

"Just get out. We'll leave the car and wait for the police to come and get us."

"Speaking of which, what happened to the one that was chasing us?"

"I don't think we need to worry about him, he called ahead. Look down there." Down the way they'd set up a blockade in front of a small white building, the sign above the door read, The New Milton Advertiser & Lymington Times.

The head reporter, photographer, managing editor and the publisher of the Lymington Times, poked his head out to see what was going on, then disappeared. A minute later he was back with his camera to record everything. The police had begun evacuating people through the back doors of the shops.

Kat got out and crossed the sidewalk to the wall of the appliance shop. Raini followed her looking down the road. Police cars were already blocking it off. "It won't be long now."

Cops were positioning themselves behind the cars with their guns aiming at them.

"Oh goody," Raini said, "we've found the British cops with guns."

"Lucky us," Kat said, and they put their hands up. "Do you think they're going to arrest us or just shoot us?"

"Just at the moment, I don't really care."

Raini closed her eyes. "I have to pee."

Kat took Raini's hand and held on to it as she closed her eyes. "Do you mind."

"Are you kidding? I need a little hand holding." Raini looked down the street the other way where they saw two more police cars pull into view at the junction of a residential lane. In no time the tiny English town resembled Tombstone at high noon.

The silence was unbearable.

The suspenseful quiet was shattered by the screech of a bullhorn. Then a high-pitched male voice blared up the street. "This is Chief Constable Merking of the Milton Constabulary. I'm advising you to throw down your weapons and remain where you are with your hands raised."

"Is he kidding, Kat? Doesn't he see that we're right here with our hands up?"

"Give the guy a break. Maybe he's been waiting a long time to say that."

"You are too kind sometimes."

Several officers wearing body armor and carrying riot shields moved towards them. A few had shotguns, some had automatic weapons. They seemed to be eager to do battle.

They were rushed from both ends of the block and squeezed between the riot shields. Then, brutally grabbed, they were thrown to the pavement and held down with knees on their necks. The police pushed them into the concrete with more force than necessary, pulled their arms behind their backs and cuffed them with nylon pull straps. Yanking on their wrists, they violently dragged them to their feet thoroughly frisked.

The search was painful, pointless and maliciously degrading. "No weapons detected. Clear!" one man shouted.

A police van sped up and they were goose-marched into the street then shoved in the back and belted onto their seats. Only then did the wizened little Chief Constable Merking make an appearance.

"See that their feet are restrained as well, will you please. I shouldn't like to be kicked."

Nylon straps were placed on their ankles and around the uprights under the seat. "Ah, much better. Thank you." Regardless of the precaution, he remained on the street. Carrying a light metal clipboard box under his arm, he swung it out and flipped it open to consult the photos inside. Taking one out he held it up to compare it with Kat's face.

Her cheek was scraped and bruised from the take down, but he made the identification. Then consulting the back of the photo, he said, "Excellent. Ah ..., it would seem, Ms. ah ... Anita Franco, aka ... ah ... Elinor Rigby. Elinor Rigby yes, very drole. Anita Franco, you are nicked. It took a small-town constabulary to bring your diabolical reign of terror to an end." For a fraction of a second he attempted a smile. The attempt failed miserably.

"And ah, this would be the American traitor, Special Agent Raini Hanamansingh. I am pronouncing that correctly, am I not?"

"We gave ourselves up you skinny little, self-important, misogynistic shit. The brutality was unnecessary," said Raini.

Without looking up from his clipboard he spoke dismissively. "A typical American response, I suppose. Well Ms. Hanamansingh, you're nicked too."

He recited the British version of the Miranda, replaced the photos, flipped the metal lid over with a snap and tucked it under his arm. That, apparently, indicated that he had completed the official part of the arrest. He moved away and spoke briefly with two of his officers then took a phone from one of them. As he spoke, he turned and looked at Kat and Raini and seemed genuinely put out.

When he returned the phone, he had a few more words with his officers then came back to the truck.

"I have been in contact with our friends at the Yard and it seems that the charges of murder against you both have been dropped. They believe that the assassin has been apprehended in Zürich."

"Oh-my-god. Then if you know that, then why haven't you let us free?"

"Because I have been informed by a gentleman with US Military Counterintelligence that the Yard has it wrong."

"That's ridiculous, who told ... Oh, it was Special Agent Nunez wasn't it."

"As it happens, yes. It is no longer my problem, Ms. Fernando. I've done my bit, so it is of no interest to me at all. They can sort you out in London. Have a pleasant journey, ladies. You may take them away now constables."

"Now wait a moment ... please. Nunez leads an American Black Ops team. They've come to kill us. You can't hand us over to them."

"I am not turning you over to them. As I have said, I am sending you to London. Good day to you."

✴✴✴

Chapter ~ 24

The trip to London was up the M-3 and went smoothly enough as far as their guards were concerned. They were approaching the sign for the Winchester Exit when they passed three black Range Rovers idling on the shoulder of the road. The moment that the police van went by, the SUVs pulled out into traffic and pursued them. A minute later they overtook the prisoner van, boxed it in on three side, and closed in tight.

"What's this now?" asked the driver, Const. Sid Cox.

"Bloody hell. I don't like the looks of it at all, Sid," said Const. Archie Raddon. "I'll call it in. He looked at his watch as he picked up the mic. They'd been on the road for nearly three quarters of an hour and Raddon was afraid that it would take at least that long for help to arrive.

"You'd better be quick about it; I don't think we have much time."

"I'm doing as best as I can, mate. Keep your eyes on the road. And while you're about it, perhaps you could take out your weapon."

Worried, the guard turned on his radio, "All units, all units, this is Prisoner Transport 5568 om the M-3 to London, in the vicinity of ..." he waited to read the next sign, "yes, ah ..., the Park & Ride at the Otter Bourne Rd Overpass. Mayday, Const. Raddon calling, mayday, come in."

He repeated the call twice, and in the seconds between each call he checked the dials, "Hello dispatch ..., anyone in the vicinity of the Otter Bourne Overpass, Mayday, mayday," he said, becoming seriously frightened. "This is Cost. Raddon transporting prisoners to London.

We have an emergency. We are being hijacked. Do you copy, over? Respond! Jesus Sid, this isn't working!"

"They must be jamming the radio," said Sid.

Archie tried again, "Hello, hello, is anybody receiving this?" There was no response. Until the radio ominously crackled to life. "Good afternoon gentlemen."

"Who's this then?"

"There's been a change in plans. We are going to do a prisoner transfer just up ahead. We'll be there in just a moment. If you cooperate, no harm will come to you. Do you understand?"

"We can't do that," the guard said. "This is official police business. We have called for backup, and they will ..."

"No one is coming to help you, Archie. This is your only warning. Tell Sid to follow the lead car to the ramp and then hand over your prisoners. If you cooperate, you'll live ... if you don't you'll die. Your choice."

"Oh, for Christ's sake, Archie," said Sid Cox, "We're giving these murdering bitches to them, and that's the end of it."

"Alright." Archie clicked on the mic. "Yes, we'll cooperate. They are all yours, mate, and welcome to 'em."

"Perfect. This will all be over in no time."

Kat and Raini had heard the exchange and Kat shouted, "For-god-sake, don't stop. They're going to kill us all."

"That's not our problem. Now shut it."

"No, they're going to kill *all* of us!"

"I said shut it!" Cox shouted.

Traffic was very light on the three-lane highway, and no one seemed to pay any attention to what was happening. There was no activity at the Park & Ride.

The policemen saw the helicopter up ahead, parked on the grass of the Hockley Link traffic circle. "Jesus, look at that. These blokes are Yank military."

"They're a kill squad," Kat said. "Believe me, if you stop, you're dead." As they neared the ramp they saw armed men, dressed in black from head to toe, standing in the road by the Blackhawk. "Do you reckon she's telling the truth, Archie?"

The big side door was open and there were more men inside with their automatic assault rifles at the ready. "Bleeding hell!"

The small procession stopped, placing the police van right in front of the helicopter door. "I hate to say, I told you so, but you've killed us all."

The three men from the Range Rovers got out and converged on the van. The man from the lead car went to the driver's door. The man from the side car positioned himself at Sid's door. The one from behind opened the back doors and using his Ka-Bar, cut the straps that bound their ankles and the belts that held them in their seats. "Get out."

Kat and Raini obeyed, Kat couldn't help noticing that all the men were wearing sport parachutes and jump helmets.

The leader signaled from inside the chopper for them to hurry. Kat and Raini were rushed up to the cabin door, two men quickly pulled them inside then placed them into the two center seats facing the rear. Kat looked at the man in the corner with pure hatred. The three men behind hopped in and sat at the back beside him covering them with their guns. While the fourth went up to the crew seats behind the pilots and strapped in. As soon as they were inside the two men covering the van moved to the front and opened fire, killing the policemen, then boarded the chopper and it immediately lifted off. The last man in closed the door then took the seats directly behind Kat and Raini.

"I don't suppose that General Wolfson authorized you to do that," she said.

"He said, and I quote, 'by any means necessary.'"

"What about them?"

"I didn't want anyone reporting how this acquisition went down."

"Acquisition? You son-of-a-bitch, that was murder."

He stood, stepped over to her, leaned forward and slammed his fist into her solar plexus. She doubled over gasping for air. When she recovered, he said, "When we first met you told me to call you Senior Special Agent Fernando. Do you know what I'm calling you now bitch? I'm calling you Dead." He laughed.

"Is that why you're doing this Nunez?"

"Yeah, for the sheer pleasure of it."

"Words fail me."

"Oh, give it to me, bitch, give me all you got, because this is the last chance you'll have."

She could have done without that bit of information, but she kept her expression neutral. She didn't want him to see how frightened she was. She looked at Raini and saw that she was probably trying to do the same thing. That made Kat wonder if her expression was as unconvincing as Raini's.

"Your people just killed two policemen and they know we're innocent. You're all cop killers now. The Brits are not going to be thrilled with you at all." To which he said nothing. "Alright, tell me something."

"What?" he asked, clearly enjoying himself.

"This can't just be about losing face, years ago. What's this really about, eh? What do you expect to gain by killing us?"

"You know, I'm glad you asked, because if you can't figure it out, then I doubt anybody else will be able to either."

"So, there is something else going on."

"Uh huh," he looked at his watch then spread his hands as he shrugged "We've got some time to kill and since you're already dead I'll tell you. I've been wanting to tell someone anyway. While you and your little band of heroes went off to take down the evil Herr Jäger, the rest of us were supposed to go back to our original stations. Well, I ditched my partner and stayed behind to check out Kroner's intelligence service. What a surprise that was. I was expecting one of those expensive hi-tech offices in a building in the center of Zurich. But it wasn't like that at all. Instead, it was some little rathole above a gas station. I mean fuck, talk about low profile. Nobody could have guessed what was going on up there.

"I met this guy coming out of the building, so I asked him who the tenant was upstairs. He played it cool at first, said he had no idea. But I figured that he was lying, so I put a gun to his head and asked him again. He admitted that he worked upstairs, said that he was the #2 guy in the operation. He was a real salesman; you know what I mean."

Kat figured she knew who he was talking about. "So you met Sigismund Kraft."

"You know about him, do you? Well of course you do, you killed him didn't you."

"No, as a matter of fact I didn't kill anyone."

"Now that's funny." He shared his grin with the other guys, and they didn't look like they found it all that funny. "Anyway, when I told him I had the #1 guy, he got very talkative. He said, rather than killing him, I should join his organization. You know as it turns out, I'm really glad I didn't cancel his ticket."

"So, you turned into a traitor as well as a terrorist."

"A traitor? It was just business. I called in some friends," he said, indicating his men, "and the business became very profitable."

"You've been working for Kraft this whole time?"

"Not working for him, bitch. We're partners."

"Is Wolfson in on it too?"

"Wolfson? He hasn't got a clue. I've been leading him around by the nose since Zürich. I've got people working in his office, in JAG, all over the place, Army, Navy, Air Force."

"So, you think no one has figured out what you were doing."

"Because they haven't. We're in control. We let them see what we want them to see."

"If it was just business as you say, why did Hedda kill all those people?"

"They were getting in the way, asking questions. Siggi figured out how to get Jäger's niece to take them out."

"You're a slug."

The men chuckled over that. Nunez bristled, and shouted, "Shut the fuck up." then turned back to Kat. "It was a shame that someone killed him. Now I have to find a replacement."

"You've deluded yourself into thinking you're in charge. Wake up, Nunez, someone's pulling your strings. Haven't you figure that out yet? You're an expendable flunky, like your boys here."

"I'm nobody's flunky," he snapped.

"Oh please, spare me. You're a fuck up, Nunez. You couldn't run bathwater."

Touching the transmitter on his shoulder he said, "How long before we get there?"

He listened to the reply in his ear bud.

"Copy that."

"Get where?" she asked.

He looked at the man beside him and nodded. That man nudged the one beside him. Looking at Raini he nodded. The man beside him got up and pulled her to her feet. "Wait, what are you doing?" Kat asked.

"It's payback time. You like Hanamansingh, don't you, Fernando? I bet you do. She's pretty hot, right guys?"

"Don't be a fool Nunez, if you kill us, they'll find you and we both know what that means." He ignored her. "No, stop! Nunez, stop it right now."

"Oh, you'll love this. Do you want to know what my first job for the syndicate was?"

"No."

"I'll tell you anyway. I was the one who took out Helmut Kroner. Everyone thought he was flying back to Washington with your old fuck-buddy, Devlyn but I got him first."

"Look, I'm sorry, I believe you now. You're the boss. Please let her go!"

"I love to hear you beg. So, I did Kroner first, put a bullet in his brainpan and then you know what I did? I interrogated Devlyn. Oh, it was very messy. That's how I got to know all about you. He told me everything …Then I told Jäger. Yeah, that was me. And I made sure he still thought you were Anita Franco. I said you were coming after him. I told him you were pregnant. Oh, he was going to have such fun with that. "He told me how he was going to gut you like a fish. I was surprised he let you go to do that hit in the States. I mean, that whole Mogilevski thing came out of nowhere. Big mistake for him, but it turned out alright for me."

"You win, you've paid me back, now let Raini go."

"I'm going to let you both go, don't worry about that. Lee, get ready to open the door." He took out his Kay-bar and slashed the nylon strap on Raini's wrists then slammed the knife into the deck. "Spread her out," he said.

Desperate to save her friend. "What do you want? Anything and it's yours. You want money? I've got billions now and it's all yours if you hand us over."

"It's too late for that Tiger."

"No, it's not. You can still give us to the cops and get away clean with a billion US."

"Oh, we'll get away clean, don't you worry about that. Too bad you and your Paky girlfriend won't be around to see it."

"Killing us will only prove that you are the traitor. Your fingerprints are all over this. The only hope you have is if you give us back to the English."

The guy on his right looked like he was beginning to question the plan, which gave Kat some hope. "Listen to me. You want to get rich right? I can make you rich." She strained to think of a figure that might change his mind. "I'll pay each of you fifty-million if you let her live." That got them thinking. Nunez was obviously giving it some thought. "Cause you're the boss, I'll double it for you."

"Stop bull shitting, you don't have that kind of money."

"If you really knew about me, you'd know that it's true. Harm left me Eagle's Nest.

How do you think I could afford to rig my apartment to self-destruct like that?"

"Nah, you're desperate, you'd say anything …"

"I own Eagles Nest. Surely you are connected enough to know what that is. I'll make you all billionaires. How does that sound?"

"Nunez, I want to be a billionaire," said the guy holding Raini.

"What you want is a fucking brain, you moron. There's no way she has that kind of money. The moment we let them go she'll rat on us and tell them everything? I don't think so."

"Oh, come on, you know the police won't believe a word we say."

"She's right," Raini said. "You could return the helicopter to wherever you got it, and no one would know."

"They probably think we killed the cops back there. They're going to shoot us on sight. But, if you go through with this, they'll definitely be coming after you."

"Sorry no sale, girls."

"We told the FBI about you, Nunez …, you and your boys. If you take my offer, you could all go where they'd never find you."

"I don't believe you."

I called Ramsey Hershoff's house. The FBI answered the phone. Ramsey is missing. Does that ring a bell? Is he dead? Did you kill him? I told the agent that you did. Special Agent Adam Brennan. If you take a pause and call him, he'll confirm it."

"He touched his ear bud, "Yeah?" he paused to listen. "Feet wet in two. Get her over by the door."

The door was opened, and a blast of cold air filled the cabin.

"No!" Kat shouted. "No, please don't do this!"

Raini was trying to fight them off, but they knocked her feet out from under her and dragged her back to the door on her knees.

"You can't do this," pleaded Kat.

"Wow, I love hearing you beg."

"I wasn't lying about the money. Please ..., let her go and..."

"Why sure thing, Kat. That's just what we're going to do."

She was inches away from the opening facing Kat and Kat knew there was no hope left. It was over for them. Raini knew it too. She struggled against the men, but they stretched her between them and edged her back so that her feet dangled from the door.

Wide eyed, Raini glanced over her shoulder and all she could see was sky. She looked back at Kat, terrified. Kat's face was going to be the last thing she would ever see.

"Nunez!" Kat screamed, tears streaming down her face, "Please bring her back to me!"

"This is all on you, Fernando!" He raised his gun.

Raini wanted to scream, but with death so close, she didn't want Kat to think her weak. As much as she wanted to cry, she wasn't going to utter another sound. Staring into Kat's eyes, she let her mind drift.

Maybe her people were right, she thought. Maybe God was out there, and maybe he would actually reach down from the sky grab her by the hair and pull her up to heaven. Was there ever a time when she actually believed that? What was the point now? Her eyes were fixed on Kat. Kat was her sister, her efforts had all been for her, her sister, her spiritual twin. She drew her strength from that.

Kat wanted to grab her and pull her back, she tried to get up, but the man slammed her against the seatback. She stared at Raini.

Raini closed her eyes.

Nunez fired.

Her head snapped back as the bullet drilled a hole into her skull and she dropped out of the door and was gone in an instant. Kat froze. She couldn't breathe. She just stared into that empty space.

Raini's body hit the icy water of The Solent Delta as if it was concrete and was crushed on impact. No one bothered to see if she made a splash, a thousand feet below. She floated to the surface and was carried away by the tide.

Kat had closed her eyes and lowered her head as she sobbed. Closing the door became symbolic of their lives ending. What she had witnessed left her hollow, a void that was quickly filled up with anger. Nunez looked at her, without remorse. He was that boy who tortured small animals. "What ...?" he asked. "Did that upset you? You are such a fucking hypocrite, Fernando. I know what you've done to your enemies. You bragged about snapping that old man's neck. Kraft showed me the recordings from Kroner's house."

"Shut up!"

"I saw those men die in Kroner's office."

"I said, shut up!" But he didn't stop.

"You piled the dead like cordwood in the front hall, didn't you?"

"Shut up!"

"I know what you are, Fernando. I saw how you tortured Kroner. I've *seen* you in action, bitch. Remember? You, *you* are the monster here, not me." She had nothing more to say. "What, no threats, no promises?" Still nothing. "How disappointing."

He pressed his com, "What's our position now?"

"Feet dry in thirty seconds," said Ronny Majors.

"See that? I'm on a roll here."

Two minutes later he said, "We're coming to the drop zone now."

"Very well, set the autopilot and give us the countdown." As they closed in on their destination the men stood up and checked their parachutes in preparation for the jump.

They listened as the pilot began his countdown. Majors and the co-pilot, Neil Rutledge, had unbuckled their restraints and opened the doors. Nunez leaned over Kat for one last barb.

"Just so you know. On this southwest heading you are going to fly another four hundred miles out to sea and by then I'm told, this bird will be sucking fumes. You're going to splash down out there somewhere in the North Atlantic.

"Think about it. Just try to imagine what's going to happen to you then. Try to imagine how your daughter is going to grow up without you. She'll never know what happened to you. Air Sea rescue may look for you out there, but all they'll find will be wreckage, because something big and nasty is going to rise up and eat you. In a week or so, no one will remember you at all."

"I'm going to kill you, Nunez."

"Are you really?" he asked, with a smug and superior sneer. "Well, I find that very hard to believe."

The bird was cruising along smoothly at a hundred and thirty-five knots. Majors made a quick course change, turning west by southwest. He set the trim and switched on the autopilot, then said, "Go, go, go." He pushed opened the cockpit door and bailed out; Rutledge was right behind him.

"Well ..., say hi to the fishes," Nunez laughed, as the other men dove out, then he moved to the door.

She moved too, and he turned back with his right hand holding the top edge of the opening.

"Maybe it'd be quicker if you just follow us out." He started to laugh again but cut it off in surprise when she got up from the chair. "What?" he asked, with a stupid grin. "Are you really going to jump after all?"

"No. But then, neither are you," she snarled.

*✶✶

The Strike team landed on a pasture in the gently rolling hills south of Bowcombe. Ben Wheelwright, a local man, had been waiting for them with a small tour bus on Bowcombe Rd. He'd parked in the field access lane leading up to their LZ. It was hidden from the road behind a hedge and tree, but they had no problem spotting it from the air. The plan was coming together just like Nunez said it would, except for one thing. Nunez wasn't going to land on the LZ. Wheelwright said he saw a man plummet to earth beyond the trees, perhaps a mile away. They gathered their chutes up, stuffed them on the bus then went to find him. Nunez had done a face plant in the middle of a ploughed field on the west side of the road. His chute hadn't been touched. "The poor bastard never tried to open it," said Rutledge.

Teller turned him over and said, "Well, I'll be fucked. That bitch wasn't kidding."

"What do you mean?" the co-pilot asked. The pilots hadn't heard Nunez deliver his pathetic monologue, or Kat's threat just before they jumped.

"Fernando said she'd kill him," explained Teller. "If she says she's going to do something, it gets done."

Teller was in command now, so they all looked to him. "Alright, the plan still stands. Stevens, you and Holt load him into the bus, he's coming with us. We have a schedule to keep and we're running behind, so let's get a move on!"

The driver pulled out onto the road and drove north again through Bowcombe and Newport to Cowes at the mouth of the River Medina. They arrived just in time to join the line up to get onto the last ferry to the IOW Car Ferry Terminal in Southampton. Before long they were headed up the A3 to London.

Mr. Wheelwright made it as far the tunnel at Hindhead. Sticking to the Nunez plan, Teller suggested he take a slight deviation from the Tunnel Way to a road that led over the top of the mountain. It ended at a picnic spot where they stopped for a rest. As soon as the man left the bus he was shot in the back of the head.

The body of Nunez joined his in a shallow, woodland grave.

They turned around and went back to the A3, through the Tunnel Way and continued to Heathrow.

✳✳✳

Staying back to taunt her was a bad idea. If he had been paying attention back in Zürich when he first met her, he would have known that when she said she was going to kill someone, they usually died. In one stride, she closed the distance between them and kicked him on the chin. His head snapped back hard against the rear bulkhead. The jump helmet gave him some protection. At least it kept him conscious. But he was stunned, off balance, His jaw was crushed and hung loosely on his neck, and he'd bitten off the end of his tongue. "Do you believe it now, asshole?"

With a wide eyed, bewildered expression he swung his arms trying to regain his balance as blood oozed from his gaping mouth. He staggered a step too far to the right and whoosh, he was gone.

Putting her shoulder against the door, Kat leaned out to see if his chute opened. It didn't. She watched him tumble and twist, his arms and legs flailing until he made a hole in the plowed field. It didn't come close to making up for what he had just done, but he'd never hurt anyone else. Her uncanny ability to deal with an enemy was just one of the things that Nunez should have known about.

Also, it might have ended quite differently if he had known she wasn't kidding about the money. There was one other thing about Kat that he overlooked. That oversight of where she had trained, ensured that he would not survive but that she would.

Kat had trained as a combat pilot in a Blackhawk, just like this one. Piloting a helicopter had been Kat's all-time favorite job.

She looked back at the knife he'd left behind embedded in the deck. Getting down on her knees, she turned her back to it and sliced the nylon straps away.

Rubbing her wrists, she made her way to the cockpit and lowered herself into the chair on the right. Again, tears for Raini began to stream down her cheeks as she strapped in and looked over the instruments. There was plenty of fuel and the instruments showed the systems were functioning normally.

She looked at the Manson collective (the control lever for the left hand) and confirmed that the Blackhawk's four-axis, fully coupled autopilot was set trimmed and working properly. If left alone, it would have guided the ship off into oblivion without any help from a pilot. Her stress level was through the roof, and she had to get her breathing under control before she disengaged it.

Nunez counted on that function to seal her doom, yet it was the contributing factor that helped to save her.

Then, taking hold of the collective and the control stick, she took it off auto. Using the GPS to get her bearings, she swung the bird around and aimed for Portsmouth.

Once she had her heading, she moved the collective to her desired altitude and rpms, then tapped the trim and left it there. The island was only eleven and a half miles across and it was another four miles across the delta to England's terraferma. It wouldn't take long to get to the port.

The course she chose wasn't the one they had taken down to the jump zone. She reasoned that Raini's body might have drifted to the west in the tidal current. She hoped her new course might overfly that area where Raini landed. If she was going to have any chance of spotting her, she'd have to slow down and get much lower.

She throttled back to seventy knots and dropped down, automatically falling into the familiar rhythm, she guided the Blackhawk just above the trees to the coast.

As the shadow of the helicopter crossed over the north shore at Ryde, all she could think of was Raini. She dried her eyes and began scouring the surface. She just wanted to find her. After that, she'd give herself up and let whatever happened happen.

Skimming the surface as she did, the sparkling reflections off the waves became hypnotic, sending her into a sort of waking dream. A dream that touched on a lifetime of regrets.

Watching Raini die was the last straw. It tore her open, exposing every terrible thing that had ever been done to her, every terrible thing she'd seen and every terrible thing she had ever done. The only thing in her entire life that wasn't tainted by ugliness was Sara. Maybe she should have jumped out the door and followed Nunez into hell.

Realistically, there was no chance of finding Raini, Though Kat realized that she couldn't just move on.

The faint sound of a ship's horn alerted her to a danger she hadn't seen coming. She instinctively pulled up and over, just before she slammed into the bow of the Fishbourne Ferry.

The search was over, it wasn't just about her own life now, she was putting others at risk. She had to concentrate, to focus on what she was doing before she killed someone else.

She climbed to two hundred feet without changing speed and focused on reaching the mainland.

***

There was a good chance that as she neared the harbor, they would try to contact her on the radio and order her to identify herself.

If she didn't respond, they'd take her for a hostile and shoot her down. She put on the headphones and switched the radio to a military frequency to listen for air traffic controllers in the harbor. No one was hailing her, nothing was happening, no ground to air missiles, no RPGs, nothing.

She was closing in on the mouth of Portsmouth Harbour and still there was no reaction from the naval base. She slowed to twenty knots before she passed the old fortifications at the harbor entrance with no idea what do next.

People on the beach by Square Tower stood up and pointed as the Blackhawk flew by. They were used to seeing the aircraft of the Royal

Navy, the Merlins, Lynx and Sea Kings, but this American bird was a novelty.

She'd never been to Portsmouth and had no idea where she was going to land. There was an open area beside the HMS Victory.

That might work, she thought.

She'd found a spot to land, but before she started her decent an RN Lynx swung in on her left side. She felt it before she saw it, the pilot was staring at her and there were two men at the open door. One was pointing a .50 Cal heavy machine gun at her and the other had her in the sights of his L129A1 Sharpshooter rifle.

She raised her hand in greeting.

They did not wave back.

A second later she felt the disturbance of another aircraft on the right. A Merlin came along with a similar set up of weaponry pointing at her. Her radio crackled to life and the pilot of the Merlin said, "US Army UH-60 2597, you have violated UK restricted air space and are being placed under guard.

Follow us up and do not attempt to break formation, or you will be shot down. Do you copy that?"

"Copy that," said Kat, and complied.

"Identify yourself."

She thought she might ease their minds if she also told them what she had been. She said, "This is 2597. My name is Colonel Katrina Fernando, US Army Counterintelligence, Ret'd. I am alone, and, as far as I know, unarmed. I'm all yours."

"2597, stand by." During the pause Kat looked at the men who had their guns trained on her. Because of their helmets and goggles it was impossible to read their expressions, but their potential was clear enough. "2597, to clarify, what did you mean by, 'as far as I know'?"

"This is not my bird, and I didn't see what it was packing. The weapons system has not been engaged and my finger is nowhere near the trigger, that's all I meant."

"Copy that." He decided not to mention the two machine guns mounted on the airframe. "What is your fuel situation?"

"I have just over two hours of flight time remaining."

"Very well 2597, increase your speed to one-two zero knots, climb to four thousand feet and follow me."

The Merlin began to climb, and Kat followed with the Lynx maintaining its position beside her. Their heading was west by northwest, they were taking her to the Royal Navy Air Station Yeovilton about a half hour away.

***

Chapter ~ 25

Deacon asked his pilot to get them to London ASAP. On the flight over, they received the news that Kat and Raini had been arrested on the south coast and were being transported to London when they were hijacked. Jim called ahead to arrange for a car to be waiting for them at Gatwick. When they arrived, the news was full of reports about the hi-jacking of a prisoner transport and the murder of two policemen. Although the murders were attributed to Kat and Raini as Nunez had expected, Deacon had to accept that they were too late. A black Rolls was standing by at the airport and Deacon nearly broke down the moment he saw it. It made him think of a hearse. Jim helped him into the car and said, "If Nunez was going to kill them, he probably would have done it when they stopped the transport. Don't give up, sir. There's still a chance that we'll find them alive."

"I appreciate the thought, Jim. I hope you're right. Where did they say she was arrested?"

"A town called Milton."

"Alright, find out where that is and take us there. Maybe we can find out what really happened."

***

Kat was guided to the helipad on the south side of the Royal Navy Air Station by two ground control personnel. Nearby, an armed detail of six men was waiting in combat gear with yellow Royal Navy Police vests over top. The pad they directed her to was 1 of 9, the furthest from the buildings.

She touched down first, then the Lynx set down on the pad just to the north of her. She powered down immediately, unstrapped, and then waited with her hands up. A Chief Petty Officer was right there at her door with his L85A1 assault rifle aimed at her head. An ordinary seaman came forward to open her door, then stood back keeping her covered with his weapon.

"Step down slowly if you please, miss," the sergeant ordered. In the tight light blue cotton pants and t-shirt, it was easy to see that she wasn't armed He beckoned her away from the helicopter, so she followed him. "Turn around and put your hands on your head, please," he said. Then taking her arms one at a time he placed handcuffs on her wrists behind her back. When she was secured the commander of the Merlin landed beside her.

A transport came around the eastern end of the hangers and she was put inside with three guards. The vehicle turned around and returned to the cluster of buildings from which it had appeared.

On the other side of the hangers, they turned onto Taranto Way and drove to the single-story building at the corner of Plye Lane. It was an open-concept office at the front and behind the back wall that divided the building, there was an interview room and a holding cell. She was taken to the interview room and cuffed to the table. Her female guard with two chevrons on her sleeve stayed in the room to watch her.

***

Their flight to Washington wasn't scheduled to leave until the following morning, and the Strike Team's plan had them booked into rooms at the Ambassador Heathrow Hotel, close to the airport in Feltham.

They stopped in Esher to leave the bus in the parking lot behind the Waitrose Store on High Street. So that they wouldn't all arrive at the same time, they split up and took cabs to the hotel. So far, almost everything was going to plan.

***

Kat was kept waiting for hours on an unforgiving, steel frame chair, behind a two-legged steel table bolted to the floor and the outside wall. She asked for water but other than that Kat had nothing to say to the guard. She sat silently in the corner and never took her eyes off her for a second. It was creepy. She closed her eyes and tried to sleep. It didn't work.

It was a gloomy little room, lit by a single, low watt bulb secured inside a heavy wire cage. There was a very small, frosted window high up on the wall to let in a little sunlight. She wondered about the color scheme. The navy blue and dingy white walls could have symbolized the ocean and the sky. Maybe they were the RN colors. Whatever it was it didn't matter, because it just added to her depression and feeling of hopelessness. Suddenly the door opened without warning. Startled she jumped up and withdrew to the wall but being anchored to the table she couldn't go far.

She stood, bent over with her arms stretched out as three people walked in.

"Leading Rate, would you assist the prisoner back into her chair, please?" The corporal rushed over and forced Kat to sit. "Gently now, Leading Rate. We mustn't be cruel."

The speaker was the man in plain clothes, so she assumed he was a detective. "Thank you, Leading Rate, that will be all." The corporal saluted and left. The sergeant-whatever, who greeted her out on the pad was the second man in, and behind them a woman. She was also a Leading Rate. Kat thought she might be there to ensure that the prisoner wasn't abused during the interrogation.

"We didn't mean to startle you. I'm sorry for that and the holdup," the detective began, "I had to come up from our office in Portsmouth. It's been rather a busy day."

He sat on the outside chair, the sergeant-whatever sat by the wall. Kat wasn't familiar with their badges of rank and had to wait for the introductions to find out what they meant. The sergeant turned on the recorder. "Thank you, Chief Petty Officer. Time is ..., 17:38 hours, WO1 Harcourt, conducting the interrogation of suspect, Colonel Katrina Fernando Ret'd. Also present is, CPO Featherstone and Leading Rate Cantor."

"Oh," Kat said, "you're a Chief Petty Officer. I was wondering what the crown meant."

"Then you are familiar with my rank?" WO Harcourt said.

"Yes, I was a Chief Warrant Officer 2nd level, before the promotion."

"Were you really?" said Harcourt. It rang a bell for him, but the memory took a moment to come into focus. "Oh, of course, a Yank helicopter pilot. Well, that explains one thing at least."

"What's that?"

"Your facility with the machine. I was told that for a civilian you were quite good. As I said a moment ago, I've been very busy. I'll need a moment to look at the charges. Give me a moment, will you?"

Harcourt opened the folder he'd brought. He scanned the first two pages. "Very interesting. Alright, for the record, you are charged with criminal trespass over a British military installation and being in the illegal possession of a military aircraft.

Have you anything to say regarding these charges?"

"Am I going to be allowed to speak to a lawyer?"

"Sorry, not for the moment, no. Questions?"

"In that case then, I suppose not."

"Splendid. Just to confirm your identity, you are Ms. Katrina Fernando, is that correct?"

"Yes."

"You're an American, obviously, and yet you had a document in your pocket that says you are Elinor Rigby. A Beetles fan no doubt. So, who are you really? And where exactly are you from?"

"I am truly Katrina Fernando, a Canadian citizen now, living in Toronto."

"Really, a Canadian now? You do get around, don't you? But your country of origin is America, is it not?"

"Yes, I was born in Los Angeles, California."

He checked that off. "Thank you. Can you explain this strange document for me?"

"I'd rather not."

"I see." He cleared his throat and looked to the CPO for some non-vocal communication then back to Kat.

Just to clarify, you mentioned in your first radio transmission and just a moment ago that you are a retired major Is that correct?"

"No, I was a lieutenant colonel."

"Of course. You said you were with Army CI, did you not?"

"Yes."

"That would be the US Military's Counterintelligence." She nodded. "So, you were a special agent. Attached to which unit?"

"I was a Senior Special Agent, with the Six-Six-M-I."

"Excuse me?"

"Sorry, the 66th Military Intelligence Brigade, Wiesbaden, Germany. Although I served in field offices in Rome and briefly in The Hague then Brussels."

"Thank you. It's quite a leap from a CWO-2 to major. How did you manage that?"

"It was a field promotion," she said, not feeling the need for details.

"A helicopter pilot too."

"I was trained as a combat pilot, yes, though I never served in that capacity."

"I see. And why not?"

"The training was to augment my capabilities to work with Special Forces."

"There was other training to augment your capabilities then, I assume."

"Yes."

"I see. Now, you are aware, are you not, that you were wanted for murder?"

"Yes."

"This states that on Monday, April 22 you telephoned Mrs. Williams-Blake in London, identified yourself as Anita Franco then said that you had been contracted by her husband to murdered her. She said that you killed her husband instead."

"I had no contact with that woman or her husband."

"Then she was lying?"

"No, she was telling the truth, but it wasn't me who called her."

"You told her she needed to go to his house to feed the dog. Is that correct?" Kat looked at him incredulously but said nothing. "A silly question I know but humor me with a response."

"No, I did not call Mrs. Williams-Blake and I didn't murder her husband. I was in Toronto on April 22 with my daughter and her nanny."

"And you have proof of that?"

"I believe around that date I was negotiating the purchase of a building. So, there would be a record of that with my Foundation, the Harmon Toucksberry Foundation, the vendor was there, Fred Christakos, and his lawyer, Thom Demopoulos, among others."

"We'll check that out."

"I also have a murder to report. My friend, Raini Hanamansingh, with whom I had been traveling, was just murdered earlier today, over the Isle of Wight. She was also a special agent with CI, on assignment in

Toronto at the time, observing my activities and reporting back to CI command on a daily basis."

"We'll have to check it out but that sounds like you didn't do it."

"The killer was the late Hedda Jäger, a German woman who used the name Anita Franco as her alias, one that I had used some years ago on a mission. She died in Zürich a number of days ago."

"Yes, we know about Hedda Jäger."

"What? Then why did you ask me if I killed that woman's husband?"

"Uh, I needed to hear you confirm that." He flipped through the file. "We received the report from Europol on May 10 I believe."

"What? May 10? All this time we've been hiding because we were sure everyone in Europe was trying to kill us. And ... and ... nobody made any attempt to communicate with us?"

"Uh ..."

"If everybody *knew* this, then why the hell did that ridiculous little prick in Milton arrest us?"

"He didn't know, and witnesses said you were resisting arrest."

"Witnesses, what witnesses? They evacuated the town while we were standing on the sidewalk with our hands up. Then the cops charged in and jumped on us. I can't believe this. They threw us down and crushed out faces on the pavement. That's where I got this." She pointed to the swelling bruises and the scrapes. "This is bullshit."

"Chief Constable Merking tells a different story."

She was so angry she began to cry. "Well then, he's a liar as well as a fucking prick. Listen, because of him my friend, a wonderful young woman, was shot in the head and dumped out of the helicopter. Because of him, two of his policemen were murdered by the side of the road. Mr. Harcourt, if there's anyone who needs to be in restraints it's that guy, Chief Constable Merking."

"Perhaps, but to be fair the Royal Navy played no part in this ..."

"To be fair? To be fair? There's nothing fair about this. Someone sent a kill squad after us. They nearly killed my daughter and her nanny in Toronto. Since that failure they have been following us through Europe. Raini and I have been running for god knows how long and then the goddamn Chief Constable Merking handed us over to them. "Did I mention that Nunez shot Raini and left me bound up in the helicopter heading out to sea? They wanted me to just sit there for four fucking hours until the bird went Bingo fuel and crash into the ocean. If everyone knew I wasn't the assassin then please tell me, Mr. Harcourt. What could possibly be fair about any of that?"

Harcourt put his pencil down and closed the file. "Please remove the restrains, Leading Rate. Thank you." It took him a full two minutes to find his voice again. It was low and filled with regret. "No, there is nothing fair about any of that. I am deeply sorry. I can't imagine what, if anything, could be done to compensate you for the suffering you've endured. That is way beyond my pay grade, I'm afraid."

Again he paused, and the silence extended for minutes. Kat offered nothing to assist him. "Ms. Fernando, if I may. All I can think of now is to promise we will do whatever we can to find these people who took you and your friend from the police and see to it that they are brought to justice. Can I ask you to help me with that?"

"Yes!" she said emphatically.

"Who was the leader of these men who took you?"

"Special Agent Jamie Nunez, US Army Counterintelligence."

"Excuse me, are you saying that this was your own service that did this to you? A military operation?"

"Nunez said he was acting for a criminal organization that had infiltrated the Military. But to do what they have done would have required orders from the top, G-2 General Wolfson."

She gave Harcourt the short version of their hunt for Hedda Jäger and what they found when they tracked her down from the mountains of Spain to Switzerland. And finally, how the team had jumped from helicopter over the Isle of Wight. They listened without comment and when she was done Harcourt asked, "This Nunez character, are you quite sure that he didn't survive the jump?"

"His chute didn't deploy. People generally don't walk away from a four-thousand-foot free fall."

***

Milton police refused to comment on what happened to Kat and Raini, so Deacon asked to be taken to Portsmouth. They got three hotel rooms right together and turned in, but none of them slept.

***

Harcourt put down the phone then leaned back in his chair as he prepared his thoughts. He had the name of the Chief Inspector at Scotland Yard who was handling the murder of Williams-Blake and put a call through to his office. He left a message informing the Chief Inspector that he had talked to witnesses in Toronto who confirmed that Katrina Fernando was in Canada when the murder occurred. He also mentioned the so-called kill squad and suggested that they should be on the lookout for eight men, two of which were helicopter pilots. Kat had told him that they were not part of the original team, and she didn't know where they came from."

"All Americans though?" She nodded and then she said she remembered two names, Perez and Holt. "No first names?"

"No."

During the second interview Harcourt opened with, "Please allow me to sound foolish, but I don't understand something."

"What's that?"

"There were so many witnesses who swore they saw you, so much evidence against you. I even saw photos of Anita Franco and I would have sworn that they were unquestionably of you ...,"

"Yes, they were of me."

"Really?"

"They were taken six years ago on the earlier mission I mentioned."

"Then how could they all be wrong? Were you and that German woman so much alike? Was that what made it possible?

"What can I say? She went to a great deal of trouble to create an illusion. People believe what they want to believe, see what they expect to see and the more that illusion is reinforced the stronger the belief.

"The police wanted them to believe it was me. The people who wanted to catch the assassin, wanted it to be me. They were convinced that it had to be me and wouldn't accept anything else.

The police only showed pictures of me. They were shown on television every day all day long. I was the only suspect they would accept." Tears began to stream down her face.

"I am a Mexican American, and in America, it seems that if the authorities want a wetback, or a black person to be guilty, then they're going to find that Mexican or a black person guilty. They'll try to get the right one, but it doesn't always matter to them. It's sort of like that song, if you don't have the one did it, convict the one you have."

"Don't you think that's a rather harsh statement?"

"Really? Have you ever been to America? Tell me you don't have a race problem here in Briton."

"I wish I could. Ms. Fernando?" he waited. "Ms. Fernando, please."

"Sorry, I ..., just give me a second, please." She struggled to hold back the tears and get her breathing and her pounding heart under control.

"Are you alright?"

"No! I'm not alright, I'm not in the least bit alright…"

"Of course. I can see that. Under the circumstances, although you've satisfied my concerns regarding the illegal possession of the helicopter and criminal trespass, the Navy has cause to hold you as a hostile."

"Figures."

"Quite," he said regretfully. "I'll report back to my superiors in the morning. I expect that all charges against you will be dropped very soon. Then your business with the Royal Navy will have been concluded. Until then, I must detain you. I do apologize."

"Then what?" Kat asked.

"Presumably, you will be released into the custody of the civilian police until the murder charge against you is dropped. I can't say what will happen after that."

"I understand. Thank you, Mr. Harcourt."

"I see no need to lock you up. I'll ask the commandant to put you up in the visitor's quarters until you are released. Leading Rate Cantor, will you see that Ms. Fernando arrives there safely."

"Yes, Sir."

He looked at his watch again and said, "That concludes the interview. Time, 21:25."

∗∗∗

Chapter ~ 26

Kat was escorted to a room provided for visiting flight crews. "You should be comfortable bunking in here for the night."

"Thanks. What's your name?"

"Liz."

Kat found it interesting that the two women who showed her to a safe place to sleep were both named Elizabeth. "I'm Kat."

"Cheers, Kat."

"Listen Liz, I hate to put you on the spot, but I'm heading into day three in the same underwear. Do you think you might be able to get me some underwear and socks?"

"Oh sure, yeah, I think I could manage something from the PX in the morning. If you can wait that long, that is. Oh, do you need something to sleep in?"

"No, I'm good, thanks, but if you could some undies that would be great, thanks a lot."

"Cheers."

"Oh, are there towels in the shower room?"

"Yeah, right in there, help yourself. If you need anything at all Kat, I'll be right outside your door. " She fell asleep around four.

✦✦✦

The local news media carried the story as if it were a national emergency, and the papers hit the streets early that morning. They began by reporting that the helicopter was stolen by terrorists from an American Base in Stuttgart, Germany.

People jumped on that, and accusations, rumors and denials began spreading like wildfire. How could something like this happen? Was this another potential incident like 9/11?

Commentators, experts on terrorism and critics of American security policies were abuzz. It was going to be a 'talking heads' field day, which forced the Royal Navy to release a statement. It was to remind the residents along the southern coast that RNAS Yeovilton was responsible for maritime security against terrorist threats.

'A Westland Super Lynx from the WMF (Wildcat Maritime Force) and a Merlin from the RN's Commando Helicopter Force were on the job, patrolling the area at the time of the incident.

'Due to security concerns, no further details would be released during an ongoing investigation.'

***

As Deacon sat in his hotel room in the Residence Inn trying to comprehend what was going on, Jim and Janet were following the developing story on television. Suddenly Janet burst into Deacon's room. "Quick Dr. Loats, turn on the TV. They've got Kat. She's alive!"

"What? … Oh-my-god where? Where is she?"

"Yeovilton, wherever that is." The amateur video of the apprehension of the single aircraft invasion over the harbor was picked up by the BBC. Jim came in just as the item was starting again. News outlets throughout Great Britain ran the story continuously as if it was the only thing happening.

And as usual, the 'talking heads' spoke of the implications to the fragile global status-quo and warned of what might follow. They had no details of what proceeded the incident, or who was piloting the helicopter other than it was a middle-aged woman. The command at RNAS Yeovilton was getting tired of repeating that they were not issuing any further statements at this time.

"So, we don't actually know that it was Kat who was flying it"

Janet was adamant. "Who else could it be?"

"Janet's right. They took her to Yeovilton. We'll present ourselves at the base and ask to speak with someone who can tell us what's going on."

"Great, let's go." He stood up excitedly and reached for his jacket. "God. Maybe this horror show is finally over."

"Think positive thoughts, Dr. Loats. It'll be OK. We'll get her back."

***

The remainder of Nunez's team gathered in the hotel's lounge for an impromptu meeting to discuss what they'd heard in the news. "How the hell did she fly the helicopter back to Portsmouth?" asked Fen Stevens.

"We should have killed the bitch with the other one," Jan Peters added. Teller raised his hands, "Jesus Christ will ya keep your voices down. Come on outside everyone." They moved out to the parking lot away from the building. "Look, I know this looks bad. Nunez fucked up big time, but we have to pull it together and get off this berg."

Gill Baker said, "That won't do us any fucking good now. The idiot ran off at the mouth telling her everything. You think she's not spilling it all to the Navy cops? We're completely screwed."

"We don't know that."

"No? Are you willing to bet our lives on that? What are we going to do about this?"

Teller got their attention again, "Guys, we're done fucking around. The woman can identify us, so ..."

"So, you want to eliminate her," Perez said, finishing his thought.

"Yeah."

"That is the craziest thing I've ever heard, except for giving up the billion dollars she offered." Perez challenged. "They've had enough time to get the whole story out of her. Face it, it's over."

"Yeah, maybe she's talked but maybe they don't believe her. The Brits don't know she's been cleared. They'll probably be keeping her on the base until some honcho comes up from London tomorrow."

"And you know this how?"

"It stands to reason. She's an international assassin. They're not going to let some local yokel steal their thunder again. One of us is going to go in and take care of her."

"You are out of your tiny fucking mind?" Holt growled. The others watched Teller react.

"You're right, one guy can't do it alone, I need two volunteers. What about you, Holt?" He already knew how he'd answer.

"Whoa, that's suicide, pal. Count me out."

"OK, is anybody going to volunteer? No takers? Look, you guys said you wanted this cleaned up, I agree, so what's it going to be?" Teller waited. "Fuck cowards. Come on, who's going with me?"

Perez stood by his side. "Fuck it. I'll go with you."

Teller smiled. "Good. We'll need some ID to get us through the gate."

Perez hadn't thought of that. "Where are we going to get those?"

"Don't worry about it, Lenny. I've got that wired. The Brits are a bunch of pansies. We'll walk in through their front door, kick some Limey ass, and bug out." He put his hand on Perez's shoulder. "We'll be in and out before they know what hit 'em.

The rest of you clowns are in the clear, she doesn't have your names, so split up, get over to the airport, get on the plane and go home. Don't do anything stupid, you hear me?"

They all nodded. "No problema Boss."

"OK, I'll contact you when we get back home."

The likelihood that the Brits would be able to stop them seemed pretty slim. Teller spoke to Majors separately. Would you and Rutledge hold up for a second? Since you guys are heading back to Stuttgart there's one other thing that I need some help with."

"Look if you want us to go with you to get back the Blackhawk, then forget it," said Majors.

"Oh hey, no-no, Perez and I can handle that. I'll be happy to see you off. But we need to get some technical information about the Blackhawk. Come up to my room so we can pick your brains."

"Yeah, OK, no problem."

"Great. This won't take that long." They didn't speak in the elevator and held their questions until they got into Teller's room. Teller walked over to the table by the window, set his bag down and unzipped it. He had his back to them.

"If we get a chance to get near the chopper, I want to blow it up. You know like where should we set the charges? I was wondering what your thoughts were on that."

"You don't need any diagrams from us, just toss in a grenade," said Majors.

"Yeah, I figured that's what I'd do. Actually, what we really need are your IDs," he said, as he turned. He fired the shots so quickly that neither man had a chance to react. The silencer kept the murders quiet. Perez was caught off guard. "Holy fuck, what did you do that for?"

"We need their IDs to get onto the base. I thought being pilots would be just the thing."

"Couldn't we have just asked for them?"

"These fucking guys weren't part of the original team, and I didn't trust 'em," he said, putting the gun back in his bag. "We'll have to replace their pictures, but that won't be so hard. Come on, help me move these guys into the bathroom."

He lifted Major's body by the armpits and dragged him out of the room. "So much to do, so little time."

Chapter ~ 27

Kat spent the night with Lr. Cantor on the door. In the morning, another young Lr with the Royal Navy Police arrived with two suitcases and handed them to Cantor. Kat had just stepped out of the shower and wrapped a towel around her to answer the door.

"Morning Liz," said Kat.

"Good morning, Kat. Slept well, did you?"

"No, but thanks for asking. Come in."

"I'll just put these things on the bed for you, shall I?" The Yank looked awful, but who could blame her, thought Liz. "There you are Luv. See if there's anything you like in that."

"Thanks, oh, and thanks for the breakfast tray, Liz."

"Cheers." She put the brown paper bag on the bed.

"Wow, a toothbrush, terrific."

"Yeah, and toothpaste, a razor and deodorant. No bra I'm afraid, but I got everything else, you'll need. Just pick what you like, and I'll take the rest of it back."

"This is very kind Liz, thank you. I wish I could pay you for these things, Liz, but..."

"Not to worry, Kat. The sergeant at the PX just gave them to me and said they were a gift from the CO."

"Really, well I'll have to remember to thank him."

"I'm really happy that I could help you out …." What followed was an awkward pause. "Well, I should let you get dressed now. When you're ready the WO would like to have a word with you. I'll say goodbye to you then. I'm off duty now, Leading Rate Jefferies will be out there to escort you to the office."

"Goodbye Liz, and thanks. I'll be out in a couple of minutes."

The helicopter was undergoing a thorough forensic examination, but apart from the tip of his tongue, the Nunez team had left very little to prove that they were ever there. The exceptions were significant. The knife Nunez had stabbed into the floor was still there with identifiable prints on the grip, as were the two sets of nylon manacles. The ones he'd removed from Raini were covered in her blood. The ones Kat removed herself remained with the knife. There was also a large blood splatter on the rear bulkhead where the tip of a tongue was found. There was also blood on the outside of the door. It all told the story of what happened over the Isle of Wight.

The Ferry Service in Portsmouth received word from one of it ships crossing to the island. A passenger had reported a body in the water. A Royal Navy Rescue Sea King HU5 was sent out, and just after 8:00 it located and retrieved Special Agent Raini Hanamansingh's remains and took them to HM Naval Base Portsmouth. Later the body was transferred to the MOD morgue at Queen Alexandra Hospital in Cosham. Harcourt had asked to see Kat so he could inform her that Raini's body had been recovered. He was waiting for her by the barrack's door and spoke quietly, almost in a whisper as he told her about the recovery. She closed her eyes for a moment. "Thank you for telling me Mr. Harcourt."

He escorted her across the compound to Commodore Scott Kipling's office and, Kipling greeted her with a gentle handshake. "Good morning, Ms. Fernando, I'm sorry to be meeting you under such unfortunate circumstances. You have my deepest sympathies for your loss."

"Thank you, Commodore."

"Mr. Harcourt has been telling me some details of the ordeal you have been through. I can't imagine how you must be feeling. Would you care to sit down?"

"Thank you."

"I'm sorry to say, Ms. Fernando, that it isn't over yet. Mr. Harcourt has a favor to ask."

She turned to Harcourt. "If you are willing, I'd like you come with me to identify her body. We should be back by mid-afternoon."

"Alright, but before I do that, would it be alright if I tried calling home?"

He looked at his watch and said, "They are five hours behind us there, so you might be waking them up."

"Yes, but I have to talk to Rosario, my daughter's nanny."

"Of course. How old is your daughter?"

"She's four."

"A busy age. Come with me, you can call from the admin. office. I'll have to stay in the room with you, you understand."

"Of course. Thank you."

Rosario answered the house phone without thinking who it might be. Her reaction to the sound of Kat's voice was very telling. "Oh-my-god, Kat! How are you? Oh-my-god, I can't believe it. I heard that you were captured in England."

"Yes, but I'm alright, Rose. How is Sara?"

"Sara is fine, she misses you terribly, of course. She's having difficulty settling at night and has been very quiet, but otherwise she is fine."

"I'm glad to hear it. What about you?"

"I've been worried sick. Will they let you come home?"

"Yes, I think so, but not right away. Rose .... Raini is dead, she was killed yesterday."

"Oh." Her voice dropped to a whisper. "Kat, I am so sorry."

"Me too."

"Deacon has called a few times to try to reassure us, but I don't think he believed we would ever see you again. Have you told him yet?"

"No, not yet, I don't know where he is."

"Don't worry, he'll find you, I know he will. We love you and we're just thankful that you're safe."

"I know, I love you too. Give Sara a big kiss for me. Goodbye."

She was dreading the experience that lay ahead and the drive to Portsmouth was uncomfortably quiet. The day was a dark grey at the outset and the rain began to fall softly as they left the gate. It grew progressively heavier the closer they got to the coast, and it seemed to match her mood precisely.

WO Harcourt took her to the hospital's basement morgue. The doctor, a Naval officer, and the civilian pathologist were there for the postmortem. The doctor lifted the sheet and, in deference to Kat's fragile emotional state, held it so that only part of her face was visible. Still, there was that ugly hole above her eyebrow and the shooting replayed in Kat's mind. She quickly looked away.

"Is this your friend?" Harcourt asked.

"Yes, that's Raini Hanamansingh." She spoke so quietly that the doctor nearly asked her to repeat it, but Harcourt cut him off.

"Thank you, Ms. Fernando." The trauma suffered from the impact had been so great, that it no longer looked like the friend she had known.

"Gentlemen, could you give me a moment alone with her, please?"

"Oh… uh … Of course, we'll just be outside the door."

"Thank you." When she was alone with Raini, she found her hand under the sheet and held it gently. "I love you. You had the strength to carry on when I had given up. You were the brave one, the best of us all and I will carry your friendship with me for as long as I live." She covered Raini's hand again, closed her eyes and turned away.

Opening the door, she went to Harcourt and took his arm. "Would you take me back now?"

"Yes, of course."

The sky had gone so dark it was almost like driving at night. Kat was focusing her attention on the reflections of the headlights on the rain-soaked highway.

Harcourt had been harboring a question raised by her reaction to seeing the body and couldn't hold it any longer. "I could see that she meant a great deal to you." She didn't speak. "You blame yourself for her death, don't you? You shouldn't."

"No? I shouldn't have brought her with me. None of this should have happened."

"You're right, none of this should have happened. But you did not cause any of it. Surely you must see that?"

"All I know is that she is dead. Almost everyone I've ever loved is gone, my husband Harm, George, even Devlyn, Sara's father. For all I know Ramsey Hershoff is gone too ... and now Raini. How can I live with this?"

"That does not make it your fault, Katrina."

"If not mine then whose fault is it?"

"Everyone should be able to see that now. Especially you."

She had no words to respond, instead she just stared at the yellow and red reflections on the rain-soaked highway.

When they returned to the airfield, Harcourt asked Leading Rate Jefferies to escort her back to her room.

"Thank you," she said.

"I am sorry to have made you do that."

"I understand, Mr. Harcourt, It was good to be able to say goodbye."

"Get some rest, and we'll talk later."

It was a short walk across the road to the enclosed residential area off Corporate Rd. Her billet was in the second barracks building, looking north out onto Heathcote Rd. The umbrella had barely served its function in the heavy downpour, and she was soaked to the skin. Taking the stairs to the third-floor room she sat, soaking wet, at the small desk and stared out through the haze, focusing on the field on the far side.

The only thought she allowed herself at the moment was to wonder what those soggy, ghostly white blobs were. "Sheep, that's what they are, sheep." Kat was trying without success to push the image of Raini from her mind, she cried.

***

As Kat changed out of the wet clothes, an RN sedan from Portsmouth arrived at the west gate. Due to the rain, it had been a quiet day with little traffic going in and out. The solitary sentry stood at attention in his rain gear, water dripped from his cap onto the end of his nose and ran down his chin. Recognizing the blue car turning in, he signaled for the car to stop by the barrier and walked up to the window. "Afternoon Farmer, what have you brought us today?"

"Afternoon Kenny, I have a couple of Yanks in the back. I understand they've come to take possession of their helicopter."

The guard leaned down to look at the two men in civvies. "Well, good afternoon gents. May I see your identification, please?"

"Captain Majors and Lieutenant Rutledge, 1/10th Special Forces Group, U.S. Army Garrison Stuttgart," Teller said, both quickly flashing their IDs.

"Thank you, Sirs." The guard consulted his clipboard then leaned down again. "You don't appear to be on my list of visitors, so if you would just wait in the car over by the hut, I will contact the watch commander." He looked to his left and said, "Just pull it over to the siding for me would you, mate."

"Uh, Cpl Kenny, is it?" Teller said.

"Yes, Sir, what can I do for y-- ..."

Teller lifted his Beretta with a suppressor and shot the guard in the face.

Then he fired two shots into their driver through the back of the seat. He opened the trunk and dragged the guard's body to it and dropped him inside. Perez quickly followed with the driver then got behind the wheel. He backed up and went around on the right side of the guard post.

Perez kept on driving by the Rec. Center then turned right, onto the road that ran parallel to the runways. On the right were to concrete pads, one was a fenced in area for the flight service vehicles. The other pad was a larger area for staff. Perez pulled into a space close to the taxiway and stopped the car. They continued the Admin. Building on foot. It wasn't far but the rain had become heavy and by the time they got there they were soaked through.

A young sub-lieutenant looked up, startled to see civilians just walk in unannounced. "Excuse me gentlemen, may I help you?" he asked, as he got up from his desk.

"Yeah, I certainly hope so. I'm Captain Majors, 1/10th Special Forces and this is my copilot, Lieutenant Rutledge. We've come to pick up our helicopter."

"Have you indeed? May I see your IDs, please." They handed over the documents and stood back dripping water on the tile floor. "There's nothing on my schedule to indicate your arrival. May I see your orders please, Sir?"

"Yeah, no-can-do, Lieutenant. We got them over the phone. No hard copy."

"How irregular." He stared at them assessing the situation. "Captain, this is not what you Yanks refer to as casual Friday."

"What?"

"You are out of uniform, and I'm wondering why that is."

"The lieutenant and I were on leave in Portsmouth when we got orders to come up here and fly it home. This was a vacation, so we didn't come with our uniforms in the bags. I hope that doesn't upset you too much, lieutenant."

"It's sub-lieutenant, Sir, and we were informed that the American pilots detailed to retrieve the aircraft would be arriving tomorrow on a One-Three-0 (C-130 Hercules) from Stuttgart. I have received nothing to indicate any changes to those orders."

"Well, isn't that just typical. Obviously, there's been a SNAFU in Stuttgart."

"How unfortunate for you, Sir. Regulations prevent me from allowing you to go any further without the proper authorization. I'm afraid you've wasted the trip in the rain. Where is your driver, he's still on the base I assume?"

"Oh, don't worry about that, he's not going anywhere."

"I'll call security and have you escorted back to your transport."

The sub-lieutenant picked up the phone and then dropped to the floor with two rounds in his forehead.

The Duty Officer, Group-Captain Gordan, appeared as the sub-lieutenant went down and was about to duck away.

"Hold up there buddy-boy."

The group-captain stood stock still facing the gunman. "Was that entirely necessary?"

"No, but who gives a shit? Come closer." The young man moved forward. "You have an American woman in custody. Where is she?"

"I don't know what you are talking about."

"You'll either tell me or end up like the sub-lieutenant here."

"I ..."

"What's it going to be Skippy? Where is the woman?"

He looked down and reconsidered. "She is in Barracks 2, I believe, room 305."

"Thank you. Now was that so hard?" Teller said. "Who else is in the office?"

"There are several personnel in the area. I suggest you put the gun down and give it up."

"That wasn't what I asked, was it? In this building, how many?"

He paused before answering. "Just the two of us."

"Better." He fired two into Gordan's head. "Alright, we head to Barracks 2 and look for the room with a guard posted outside."

"What about them?"

"Forget them. We want Fernando."

"But ..."

"I said forget them. Come on!"

They had been gone for less than a minute when Lt. Cdr. Leggatt came out from the offices and saw the men on the floor. There was no point checking for signs of life, so he went directly to the phone and called for a Station-wide Alert. "Two officers down. Hostiles in the compound, armed and dangerous."

The alarm sounded, the Marines scrambled into action and all the buildings went on lock down. Sailors and Marines flooded out fully armed in combat gear to protect the airfield, hangers and shops.

Teller and Perez were out in the open running as the station locked down. They made it to the side of the Common building without being seen, and their position, though exposed, was obscured by the rain. They kept running to Albion Rd. and saw the sign for Barracks 2 across the street. There were Marines moving through the parking lot behind them and more rushing away from their position to the north. They hadn't been spotted yet.

"Right, there's the sign for Barracks 2. Shit. I see three buildings. Which one is she in?" Perez asked.

"How the fuck should I know?"

No one knew where the hostiles were heading, or why they were there, so the defenders were spreading themselves out to cover the maximum area.

"Well, we can't stay here."

Teller looked down the street. "It's clear, cross the street and go between the first two buildings."

They ran and took the path between the shrubs and the barracks that faced onto Albion. When they reached the courtyard, Perez pushed his back against the block wall and closed his eyes.

"Holy Christ! Another fucking problem, there are four buildings not three. How are we supposed to search four buildings?"

The courtyard was completely empty. Teller started to scan the windows, looking for signs of habitation. "Tell me, what do you see?"

"Nothing."

"Anybody in the windows?"

"Not that I can see."

"OK." Teller's attention was drawn to the building across the north side of the courtyard. There was a small blue sign with white text on the wall by the east door. Barracks 2 - Visiting Pilots Billeting. Pointing, Teller said, "There. She has to be in that building."

"You're going to bet our lives on it?"

"Have you got a better idea? Come on, let's get it done."

"You first, Ron. I've got your back," said Perez.

"You're all heart."

"Hey, this was your fucking idea man, not mine."

"Yeah, if I ever have another one like this, just shoot me, OK?"

"Oh, Teller my friend, count on it. Go. I'll cover you."

He ran across the courtyard, splashing through the puddles and slippery grass then slammed into the door.

It was locked, of course, but the place wasn't built to withstand an invasion. He stood back and fired at the lock then pushed it open. Once inside he turned and signaled Perez to cross.

They had the small foyer all to themselves. Teller saw two sets of muddy wet shoe prints heading for the stairs. One a large man's boots the other were made by a woman's shoes. "What did I tell you?"

With their guns raised, they moved to the stairs. There was a short set of steps to the landing of the first floor. The fire door was locked. "OK, we just follow the tracks."

Silently, they began to ascend the staircase, stopping at each landing to see if there was anyone above them. The doors on each landing were locked.

If there was a guard on her door, he may have missed the sound of the front door being breeched, but he wouldn't miss the sound of them blasting open the door on his landing. Teller did some quick math. The extended magazine in the butt of his SIG 226 held twenty rounds, he had fifteen left and two more mags in his pocket. Perez hadn't used his gun yet. What were the odds of getting out of this alive with only 115 rounds? He hadn't thought about it before, but now, having come this far, the stark reality was impossible to ignore. Their chances were probably zero.

"What are you waiting for?"

"Fuck off! I'm trying to think."

"Too late for that shit, pal. Do something!"

Teller aimed at the lock. "Ready?" Perez nodded. Teller squeezed off a round into the lock and pulled the door open.

∗∗∗

When Deacon's Rolls drove up, the Marines at the gate were in full battle dress and prepared for a fight.

Two APCs (Armored Personnel Carrier) were blocking the road beyond the gate with their .50 Cal. machine guns trained on them. Deacon felt very uncomfortable.

Even before Jim turned off the road, a sergeant with a crown patch above his stripes stepped away from the small squad of Marines and moved toward them, ordering them to stop with the palm of his hand. Holding his submachine gun ready, he walked out to confront them.

"You'll have to keep on going, sir. We're on lock down 'ere. Nobody gets in, or out."

"I can see that sergeant," Jim said calmly, "but, my employer has an appointment with the Commandant."

"Well, his lordship will just have to put it off till another day, won't he? The Commodore isn't taking any callers today. Now off you go, there's a good lad."

The back window of the elegant car rolled down and Deacon reached out his hand holding his phone. "Sergeant," he said. "I have the Commodore on the phone, and he'd like a word with you, if you don't mind."

The sergeant's eyes shifted to the phone then locked onto Deacon's face. By his expression, Deacon could tell that he was less than thrilled to take the call. He walked to the back window and took the phone. "Color Sergeant Nevil, Sir?" He listened for a moment. "Yes, Sir. Two men and a woman."

He listened. "Yes, Sir." He looked up at the sky as if hoping the rain would cool his frustration. "May I see some identification please, sir?" Deacon handed him his passport. "Thank you, sir." He opened it and studied it carefully. "And these are your personal security people?"

"They are."

"I'll need to see their IDs as well, if you don't mind." Deacon collected them and handed them to the sergeant. He looked at them just as carefully, then handed them back.

"Just one moment, sir." He raised the phone to his ear. "Yes, Sir, all Canadian passports. Dr. Deacon Loats and bodyguards Ireland and Cotter." He listened again.

"Sir." Another pause, then, "Yes, Sir." He handed the phone back to Deacon then turned to Jim.

"Right, you can drive through to the next checkpoint for a vehicle inspection."

"Copy that," said Jim.

That earned him a look of scorn from the sergeant before he continued, "When you are released, just follow the road straight ahead and continue around the bend. There will be Marines there to guide you the rest of the way. Do not deviate from the route I have described to you. Do you understand?"

"Will they be standing in front of a building?" Jim asked.

In addition to being angry, the Color Sergeant was miserable standing out in the cold rain. "Don't worry, sir, you won't be able to miss 'em." He stood back from the car and called to the man on the gate, "Oy, Lark! Open it up and let this vehicle pass. I want it searched thoroughly for weapons and explosives."

"Yes, Color Sergeant." He unlocked the chain link gate, pushed it open, and signaled for them to proceed.

Another Marine stopped them at the APC, where men looked under the car with extended mirrors. Two others opened the doors and inspected the inside. Studying the three carefully, the corporal of the guards spoke as if he were addressing a group of delinquents.

"Now, mind yourselves in there, sir. We have orders to treat all strangers as a threat. There are two gunmen on the loose and they've already killed four of our men. Clear?"

"As crystal, corporal," said Jim.

"Right then, you are cleared to proceed to the next checkpoint. Off you go."

They drove along to the big curve by the tennis court then up to the traffic circle onto Kutching Rd. A Marine at the driveway of the pavilion waved them in and pointed to the front door. A sergeant was waiting for them and opened Deacon's door.

"Afternoon, sir." The man said, pleasantly, "I'm Sgt Woolly, if you will come with me, the Commodore is waiting inside."

His tone was quite different from the greeting they got from CSgt Nevil.

Jim began to open his door, but the sergeant stopped him. "No, sir. You two will remain in the vehicle … for your own protection. The Commodore will speak to Dr. Loats alone." Jim closed the door and the sergeant turned back to Deacon. Now Dr. Loats, if you would step this way, please."

Judging from the decor of the Commodore's office, he had no time for the unnecessary trappings of power. A few group photos on the walls of squadron pilots, some shots of helicopters and publicity shots from the air shows RNAS Yeovilton put on each year. He displayed models of aircraft currently operated by the Naval Air Squadrons on a shelf and his aircraft, a Lynx, on his desk. It was particularly interesting to Deacon that there were no photos of him. The senior officer stepped out from his desk and came to meet Deacon at the door. He was a short, trim man brimming with energy and he was angry. He extended his hand to Deacon. "Dr. Loats, how-do-you-do, I am Cdre Scott Kipling. Please, have a seat."

The Commodore waited until Deacon was sitting before he returned to his chair behind the desk. Deacon couldn't help noticing that his computer, monitor and keyboard had been set aside and, in their place, close to hand was a Glock. "I was sorry to hear that there have been casualties. Do you know who the intruders are?"

"No. It is a highly dangerous situation. You said you have some information pertaining to this woman we have in custody? How do you know her?"

"Commodore, I'm hoping that the woman you have is either Katrina Fernando or her partner, Raini Hanamansingh, either way I know the women and I have come to help them."

"We have not released any names. How would you know who we have?"

"The fact is I don't, sir. The woman was described in the news only as an American. What they didn't say was that she was either a former or current special agent with US Army Counterintelligence. Please, I have to know, is it Katrina?"

"What is your relationship with this woman?"

"Thank God, it is Katrina." His eyes closed and he heaved a heavy sigh of relief. "She and I are ..., well it's a long story. But I am the guardian of her daughter, Sara."

"I see. Yes, it is Katrina Fernando."

"Can you tell me if she is safe?"

"As far as I know she is. She is under guard in her quarters. Do you know who these people are who took her?"

"I believe that they are members of a special team sent by Counterintelligence to kill her."

"You can't be serious." Deacon nodded, gravely. The commodore's phone rang. He snatched it up. "Yes!" he said sharply.

"Sir, WO Harcourt here. I've sent a tactical squad into the Barracks 2 compound. That's where Ms. Fernando is, I'm betting that's where they're headed."

"Are they any more casualties?"

"No."

"Thank heavens for that. Are there any people still in the other barracks?"

"I believe so, yes, Sir. But not in the building where we put Ms. Fernando. She has one sentry with her."

"Alright, carry on and secure the building."

"Yes, Sir."

He put the phone down and said, "It seems that the special team has located Ms. Fernando. Our people are going in after them."

"She isn't alone in there, is she?"

"No, she has one guard, a Royal Navy Police officer, he's a good man."

"If she was armed, she could defend herself."

"We couldn't possibly allow a guest to have a weapon."

The Commodore's phone rang again. "Yes?" His eyes widened as he listened. "Right, well let's make sure they don't leave the building." He put the phone down.

"Mr. Harcourt was correct. The patrol found the lock on the door of Visiting Pilots Billeting has been shot away."

Deacon couldn't believe that he had found her alive, only to be there at the moment of her death. It was like reliving the horror of the attack on his house in Mulmur. Except that back then, she was with George Flynn.

321

✳✳✳

Chapter ~ 28

Leading Rate Jamil Jefferies was standing outside her door prepared to fire on whomever came through the door. He'd heard the lock being shot off on the front door. The gun may have had a suppressor on it, but the metal lock didn't, and they made an awful clang coming off.

"Jeffries," Kat said, speaking through the door, "what's going on?"

"I don't know for sure, Miss. But I think someone just broke into the building."

"Are you armed?"

"Yeah, of course I am."

"What are you carrying?"

"What? Uh ..., I got an MP5, why?"

"Do you have anything else?"

"Yeah, I've got my side arm, a Glock 17. Why are you asking what guns I got?"

"Because you need my help. Give me your sidearm."

"What? Not bloody likely."

"Jeffries, I'm afraid that you might not be ready for these guys."

"I'm a Navy Policeman, Miss. I know what I'm doing."

"I'm sure you do, Jeffries. I'm just saying that the men coming after me are commandos, specialists. You can't deal with them on your own. Please, open the door and come in here. If they see you, they'll kill you and they'll know where I am."

"That ain't right. I ain't a coward, I have to hold my position."

"It's Jamil, isn't it?

"Yes, Miss."

"Jamil, please come inside. I'm really frightened."

"No, I can't leave my post."

"Jamil, I … I don't want to die alone. Please come inside."

"Christ." He hesitated then gave in. "Yeah, alright then." He opened the door and backed in, keeping his eye on the corridor.

"Thanks, now give me your Glock."

"What? Are you insane? I'm not going to hand over my weapon."

"Jamil, give it to me, or I will take it away from you." She was standing quite close, and he moved to turn his machine gun on her.

"There's no way in hell that … Oh fuck!"

She got by his machine gun, had him on his knees and upholstered his Glock before he knew what was happening. "I'm sorry, Jamil. I have way more experience than you do." This said while holding his own gun to his temple. "Now please, don't make a fuss about it. You are perfectly safe with me. They, on the other hand, would kill you in a second then I'd be next, and I don't want that to happen."

"Jesus! Now, how the hell did you do that?"

"That's not important. Get up, put the machine gun on the bed, sit down on the chair and behave yourself." Her voice was kind and soft, like a mother calming a kid with a sugar high. She hadn't hurt him physically, but the take down was so fast that she definitely bruised his ego.

"Alright, but you're going to have to show me how you did that sometime."

She picked up the MP5 and put the single point sling over her shoulder.

"If we live through this, Jamil, maybe I will."

"What are you going to do now?"

There was a sharp bang from the corridor. "I'm going to ask you to hide in the closet."

"What! You've gotta be kidding me. I ain't …"

"There's no time." She pointed the Glock at him. "Move."

"OK, sure, I'm going." He moved from the chair to the closet. "But I don't think you're going to shoot me."

"I just want you out of the way, Jamil." He squeezed into the small space. "And please be quiet."

She closed the closet and went to stand behind the door. Presently she heard footsteps just outside. She placed her foot so that when the door opened it would stop short of 90°, then widened her stance in preparation and selected single shot.

It happened very quickly. A bullet shattered the lock and the door burst open and banged on her foot. Perez led with his gun. Holding the barrel of the MP5 against the door, Kat's hand lashed out grabbing his left hand and pulled him into the room.

He turned the gun toward her and fired blindly. At the same time, she sent a slug through the door into his ear. He immediately dropped at her feet with a big ugly hole in the side of his head.

Without hesitation, she stepped back and crouched out of the way. Another instant later the spot where she'd been standing was filled with holes as Teller emptied his clip through the wall, then retreated to the stairs.

She stepped over the body selecting automatic fire and flew out into the hall spraying the corridor with fire. He just made it to the door and was gone.

Kat wasn't done. She chased him to the stairway and was met by rapid fire. His gun made a heavy clicking sound as the rounds spat out of the tube. But the suppressor couldn't hide the cracking sound as the hot ammo broke the sound barrier and dug chunks out of the cinder block walls. He dropped his second spent mag on the landing, reloaded, and took off covering three steps at a time.

She followed more cautiously, keeping her back to the wall and her gun trained on the space ahead as it came into view. Her foot swept aside some of .45 shell casing that littered the steps, and the noise was followed by three quick shots that struck the wall just behind her.

She fired back. Her shots were amplified by the stairwell chamber and echoed down to the cellar.

Before the echo faded, she heard a single shot down at the bottom. He'd taken out the lock of the main floor door. A heartbeat later the door above her opened. She spun and was about to fire but saw Jamil Jeffries. He had the dead man's gun. "I told you to stay put."

"That was never going to happen, Miss. I got your back now."

"OK, toss me another clip and stay close. He's gone to the basement." She reloaded and began to move down. Jeffries moved with her like they'd done this before.

She stopped, realizing that she'd behaved like a man would have done in that position and felt ashamed. She'd underestimated Jamil. "I'm sorry, I shouldn't have doubted you. Hang on." She lifted the sling over her head and handed the MP5 back.

"That's OK, Miss, I understand." He had a silly grin on his face.

"Here, let's trade," she said, handing back his Glock too. "I'd prefer a SIG."

"Cheers." He handed her the gun and they continued.

"Thanks."

"Seeing how you took that bugger down was amazing."

As they came to the main landing, the exterior door burst opened, and Harcourt stormed in with four Marines in tow. Kat dropped the gun and threw up her hands. Harcourt took in the situation immediately and said, "No, keep it. Where have they gone?"

Jeffries answered for her. "Down there, Sir."

Kat picked up the pistol and moved to the stairs. "I think he's alone. We left his partner upstairs in my room."

"Dead?" asked the Warrant Officer.

"Oh, quite dead, yes Sir," said Jeffries.

The Marines were fresh, well trained in how to deal with the situation, so they took the lead. "Gentlemen, I want him alive if possible."

"Aye, Sir."

The men carefully cleared the rooms one at a time and eventually found Teller on his knees in the utilities room. His gun was on the floor and his hands were on his head, fingers laced. "I surrender, don't shoot."

They brought him out into the hall and pushed his down on his knees again. Harcourt looked at him with disgust. "Do you recognize this man?"

"Yes." She handed Harcourt the Sig. "I don't know his name, but he's the one who held me back when Nunez shot Raini."

Harcourt handed Jeffries gun to him. The Marine sergeant checked Teller's weapon. Looking down at Teller Harcourt said, "Which one of you shot the sub-lieutenant and the group-captain?"

"That was Perez, not me."

He looked at the murderer with utter contempt. "Why don't I believe you?" Turning to his officer. "And Leading Rate Jeffries, what in God's name, was she doing with a weapon?"

"Sir, she ah ...."

"I'm sorry, I surprised him and took it."

"You let her overpower you?"

"Sir, I did nothing of the sort, Sir. She just put me on the floor and took it from me. But you wouldn't believe how fast she is. Sorry Sir, I ..."

"Never mind Jeffries." He looked a Kat, remembering the long drive in the car alone with her, thinking that he had everything under control. It was quite upsetting to realize how wrong he was. Kat was looking at the floor trying to pretend that she was invisible, but it wasn't working. Everyone was looking at her now. "Right. Sergeant, would you please call in to say we have apprehended the intruders and cancel the lock down."

"Yes, Sir." He made the call and they all listened to the response. "Sir, the Commodore requests ..."

"Yes Sergeant, I heard the message, thank you. It seems, Ms. Fernando, the CO would like a word."

***

The Commodore stood as soon as they came through the door. Kat saw Deacon and ran to him "Deacon. Oh, Christ, Deacon, she's dead. They killed Raini. I ..." she threw her arms around him and buried her face in his neck and wept.

"I know, I'm so sorry, Kat." He let her sob and just held her. "Tiger, it's over now. I just thank-god you're safe."

"Dr. Loats, this is Warrant Officer Harcourt, RN Police. He has been handling the investigation for us."

"Sir."

Deacon reached around Kat and shook his hand. "Hello, how are you Mr. Hardcourt?"

"Much better now, Dr. Loats."

Commandant Kipling said, "Would you and Ms. Fernando have a seat for a moment. This shouldn't take too long."

"Mr. Harcourt, would you fill me in on our current situation, please."

"Yes, Sir. We have one man in custody and another man down. Killed by Ms. Fernando, I might add."

"She did?" He was astonished and bewildered.

"Yes, Sir. When she realized that she was in danger she overpowered her guard, took his weapon and shot the man. In doing so, I believe she saved Leading Rate Jeffries' life."

"I see. Well, this is rather awkward, isn't it? It appears that we owe you a debt of gratitude, Ms. Fernando. Ah, let's put aside the ah ..., awkward part shall we."

"If I may, Sir, Ms. Fernando was no longer a prisoner at the time."

"Uh huh, well thank you for that, Mr. Harcourt. You will deal with your man I assume."

327

"Yes, Sir."

"Very well. Ms. Fernando, after thoroughly checking your story, we are now convinced that the statement you gave to Mr. Harcourt was born out by the evidence. Therefore, your flight over Portsmouth did not constitute a threat against Great Britain, and the Royal Navy has dismissed the charges against you. I am very pleased to inform you that you are now free to go."

"Thank you, sir."

"And please accept our deepest sympathy for your loss, and the trials that you endured at the hands of this terrorist group."

"Thank you, sir. May I ask, what will happen to Teller?"

"Mr. Harcourt will take Teller into custody. He will be charged with murder, among other things, and then he will be bound over for trial. We'll let the Ministry of Defense take care of the details. I understand that their IDs were false."

"Yes, Sir. The prisoner has identified himself as First Sgt Ron Teller and the other man was Cpl. Lenny Perez."

"These documents look quite authentic; I wonder how they obtained them? A mystery for another time, perhaps.

This awkward situation between America and Great Britain remains to be settled at a level much higher than this office."

The commadore stood. "Regrettably, Ms. Fernando, the unfortunate matter of the murder in London persists. Though it is clear that you are innocent, the civilian authorities have requested that we inform you to turn yourself over to them when you leave here.

"I suggest that you drop in at Scotland Yard at your earliest convenience. Dr. Loats will, I am sure, offer to drive you to London.

Now if you will excuse me, I have other matters to attend to." Kat and Deacon stood. Goodbye Ms. Fernando, Dr. Loats and good luck."

***

Chapter ~ 29

The two-and-a-half-hour trip to the capitol gave some time for Kat to decompress and be held by Deacon. Jim on the other hand had a nightmarish time fighting London's traffic to Westminster. Looking ahead, Deacon had booked rooms at the Corinthia Hotel on Whitehall Place for an indefinite stay. The location was just a few minutes away from New Scotland Yard.

Had security at 10 Downing Street, or Buckingham Palace known who was checking in down the street they might have taken issue with his choice of hotel.

***

News traveled at the speed of light and the moment he heard about Teller and Perez, Cpt. Gradin set about covering his tracks. He made a call to an operative in up-state New York, a specialist in problem solving for the syndicate's eastern branch. The specialist was contracted to locate and eliminate the remaining members of the strike team, Jim Holt, Fen Stevens, Henry Lee and Gil Baker. Without any trouble at all he accomplished that task in less than twenty-four hours.

***

Because of the Bank Holiday they had to wait until Tuesday to make the appointment with Deacon's lawyer. The first opportunity was on the afternoon of the 21st, a Wednesday, at the offices of the firm he retained when he was setting up his London Office. He had met the Barrister who handled criminal cases several times at various functions and Deacon felt sure he could trust him to handle Kat's case. The plan was for Kat to surrender herself to the Yard with him beside her.

Since it was close, they had a quiet fifteen-minute walk to Queen Anne's Gate. Jim led the way and Janet followed behind as inconspicuously as possible.

No one paid the slightest attention to Kat as they strolled hand in hand along the Palace of Whitehall. She was struck by the number of buses that crowded the street and had only momentary glimpses of the monuments that were in the middle of the boulevard, celebrating those who fought in the wars. She saw an inscription on one which set her off. It read, 'To the Glorious Dead.' That made her stop.

"What is it?" asked Deacon.

"I was just wondering what it is about dying that makes a soldier so glorious. I mean, in that war, until the moment of their death they didn't matter to their leaders, they were cannon fodder.

Ordinary people, farmers, laborer's, office workers, sent into battle because they were disposable. If they'd lived, they'd just come home and continue being ordinary, wouldn't they?"

"Kat ..."

"No," she said, passionately, "I know. I get it, OK? That's what soldiers are supposed to do, isn't it? They are supposed to die or fade away quietly. For what? Honor and glory? Who is going to remember Raini Hanamansingh?"

In the silence that followed, she heard every civilian's reaction.

"I'm sorry. Don't pay any attention to me, I'm just feeling angry and sorry for myself. I didn't mean it."

"Yeah, you did, and that's OK. And you're right, she deserves more."

"They had no right to kill her. She deserved to live."

"I know, and you do too." He had a feeling he knew what was going on inside her head. The biggest threat she faced now was herself. That frightened him. "You can always talk to me, Kat. You do know that don't you?"

"Yes, I know, thank you. No, I'm good, really. You don't have to worry." Then, he asked himself, why do I feel that I should worry?

They walked the rest of the way through small flocks of tourists in silence.

***

The Barrister's offices were in an elegant old yellow brick Georgian building in the heart of the ancient city. It backed onto the courtyard of the house on Brigade Walk in St. James's Park. Buckingham Palace was just there outside his window, and one of the Royals occupied the house behind.

When they reached the office, Jim stayed outside while Kat and Deacon went up the steps to the elegant glass and mahogany door. The gleaming brass kickplate and latch suggested the significance of what lay beyond. Janet followed a few paces behind.

Before Deacon could knock, Percy Archer opened the door. "May I help you, Sir?" he was an elderly man in blues and greys with a row of medals, and his regimental crest on his breast pocket.

"Dr. Loats for Sir ..."

An attractive middle-aged woman swept out from the offices on the right, wearing a business suit and a no-nonsense expression. She interrupted his introduction.

"Thank you, Percy." Her voice was crisp and edgy. "I'll take it from here." The doorman saluted and retreated to his chair by the door. "Good morning Dr. Loats."

"Hello Mrs. Shelton. This is Katrina Fernando and my assistant Janet Ireland."

"A pleasure."

"Mrs. Shelton is Sir Torban's Head Clerk, the manager and administrator of the offices and, I am told she runs it with an iron fist."

The woman smiled appreciatively and said, "Yes, well someone has to keep these hamsters on the wheel. How do you do Ms. Fernando. Ah, Ms. Ireland, would you please go with Percy? He will show you the way to the barrister's lounge. Percy, if you please." He got up from his chair and signaled for Janet to follow him. "Thank you."

Janet looked at Deacon for instructions and he said, "Thanks, Janet. We'll be fine now."

"Yes sir." she followed the doorman down the hall to the left.

"Dr. Loats, Ms. Fernando, Sir Torban is expecting you. This way please."

Sir Torban Heath was nothing like the man Kat had been expecting. Upon entering the great man's room, Kat discovered that her knight-protector had no shining armor.

He looked up from his desk and removed his half glasses, "Ah, Deacon, my boy. You can't imagine how surprised I was to receive word that you were coming in." He looked drained, and it seemed to take some effort to set the glasses down on the desk. He stood as if he expected the floor to shift, then assumed a slight smile as he came around the desk to receive them. "A pity that it is under such unfortunate circumstances."

Kat was disappointed by her first impression. Yet, he was an interesting looking man. His bright inquisitive eyes peered out at her from beneath two hedge-like untrimmed eyebrows. He was heavy-set and somewhat stooped, with pale skin and ruddy cheeks.

She placed him in his late sixties, and she guessed he'd be about medium height if he stood up straight.

"It was good of you to see us on such short notice, Sir Torban."

"Nonsense, it's absolutely lovely to see you any time, dear thing." Self-consciously, he combed back his unruly greying hair with his fingers, to no noticeable effect. So far, she thought, he seemed to validate the uncomplimentary portrayal of the affected upper-class Englishman.

"I take it this is your friend, Ms. Fernando," he offered his hand to her, and, as he did so, he smiled, showing his yellowed and slightly crooked teeth.

His handshake was soft and powerless, and she wondered if that was just an affectation or a sign of weakness. "Hello, my dear. Oh Deacon, she is absolutely stunning, as advertised, what a lucky boy you are."

Kat raised an eyebrow as her level of irritation began to climb and looked at him reproachfully.

He gave it back to her with a look that said, 'give it your best shot, sweetheart' then he smiled. "Deacon has mentioned you frequently on previous occasions." Deacon blushed.

Turning her attention away from him she looked at the surroundings. He had been working when they came in, but you wouldn't have known it. Nothing seemed out of place. A leather-bound desk blotter was positioned in front and center and a closed file lay beside it.

A fresh pad of paper was set carefully in the center of the blotter and beside it an expensive looking fountain pen was placed perfectly parallel to it.

There even seemed to be an order to the way he placed his glasses on the pad.

Maybe Deacon's description of the 'A' type personality with a keen legal mind, was accurate was after all. It was a handsome room, well organized, of course, and as comfortable as a gentlemen's club lounge. Perhaps her first impression missed the mark. She looked at him as her opinion evolved.

Sir Torban clearly enjoyed the way she studied his space.

"A lovely room, isn't it? It was my great-grandfather Sir Geoffrey Heath's office, then my grandfather Sir John, took over the firm. I succeeded my father, Sir William, when he retired. It has been a rare privilege to work in it. I wouldn't change a thing. Oh, please ..., take a seat. Shall I have some tea brought in?"

"Not for me thank you," said Kat. Deacon declined with a slight hand gesture.

"Uh hah. Well then that will be all, thank you Mrs. Shelton." She left closing the door behind her. He made a half-hearted attempt to tuck in his rumpled white shirt, held roughly in place by his overworked suspenders.

His suitcoat along with his black robes and wig hung on a cloak stand that had been hidden behind the door.

"You must forgive my appearance," he said, tugging at his tight flyaway collar to loosen the ceremonial tie, "I've just come from a rather taxing session in court." He sat down and picked up the pen and gently unscrewed the cap. Placed it down carefully he folded his hand on the desk and said, "Shall we get straight to business? "Now, I have been following the news, along with everyone else, and am aware situation vis-a-vis regarding the murder of Samuel Williams-Blake.

While the truth concerning your involvement in that incident has been made abundantly clear, the case against you seems to be mired in bureaucratic intransigence. If I am to cut through this incomprehensible buffoonery, it would be helpful to hear the story from you."

She spent the better part of an hour relating her experience that began with the phone call from Ramsey Hershoff. Heath interrupted occasionally with questions and wrote down everything she said in his unique shorthand. When at last her story was finished, he screwed the cap back onto the pen and set it down as before.

"A disturbing account indeed," he said. Staring at the pages he pursed his lips and combed through the untidy mop of hair with his fingers, then leaned back in his chair.

None of them spoke again for a considerable period. Deacon was getting restless, stood up and paced to the window. Heath sat forward, laid his hands on the desktop and looked at Kat. Then he too got up, walked around the desk and sat down in the chair that Deacon had vacated. Perched on the edge of the chair he faced her and said, "It has been my pleasure to have enjoyed a long and relatively successful practice. Thus far, it has been defined by all manner of cases, both simple and complex." He stood up quite suddenly, bristling with anger. "But never ..., have I encountered anything like this. This whole diabolical business is beyond alarming. Katrina, allow me to say how truly sorry I am at the loss of Ms. Hanamansingh. What a terrible tragedy it is in a long list of tragedies."

"Thank you."

"The brutality of it all! I mean, my God! It is simply incomprehensible."

"What is our next move, Torban?" Deacon asked.

"What?" He looked at Deacon with surprise as if drawn out of some other place.

"How do we proceed from here?"

As if changing gears to address the problem directly he said, "Yes, of course. Well, my friend, this will need to be put before a judge. Once the evidence proving my client's innocence is laid at his feet the charges will be dropped. Of that, I am certain. Now, what happens in the interim is of concern to me, as is Katrina's security."

He returned to the desk, absently picked up the pen and fiddled with it while he formed his thoughts. "I have some influence at the Yard ..., Chief Superintendent James Gardener is a friend. I would like to invite him here to meet you."

"If you tell him I'm here," Kat cautioned, "they'll surround the place with a SWAT team."

"I didn't bring her up to London to be slaughtered, Torban."

"Oh, there will be no slaughter whilst I stand between you and the police, I assure you. Though I do agree, it is indeed likely that a tactical squad will arrive with him." Then with a smile he looked out the window and indicated the building across the courtyard. "Having said that, my Royal neighbor to the north would take a very dim view should the police resort to violence so close to his home."

"Well, that's something I suppose." Deacon was too tired to process this. "Is there any chance your friend won't cooperate?"

"I think I can count on our friendship to afford us the courtesy of a peaceful transition. The safest place for you, I believe, Katrina, is in the protection of Scotland Yard. If that is agreeable to you, then I shall endeavor to call him now." Kat agreed. "Splendid."

Sir Torban asked his partner, Patrick Goodfellow, to come in and add his thoughts to the discussion of her defense while they waited, and Mrs. Shelton sent in the porter with tea and biscuits.

***

Part 4

Chapter ~ 30

While on a training flight, the crew of a UH-72A Lakota spotted a body floating in the marsh of Nanjemoy Creek. A Coast Guard MH-60 Jayhawk Helicopter was dispatched to recover the body and it was taken to the Naval Medical Center in Portsmouth, Virginia.

About all they could say for certain was that it was male in his seventies and had been in the water for some time. There were bits of rope embedded in the skin at the wrists and ankles suggesting that the body had been weighted down. Cause of death was a small caliber bullet wound to the head.

The FBI was informed and arrived with their own ME. The age and body type suggested that it was their missing general. Later that week a DNA sample confirmed that it was BGen Ramsey Hershoff, Ret'd. His wife was informed, and the story led the national news.

***

Since talking to Kat from the Hershoff house, and tracing the call back to the New Forest, FBI Agent Brennan was convinced that she was telling the truth.

Finding Gen. Hershoff's body in close proximity to Quantico and Fort Belvoir, suggested that the kidnappers could have come from either facility. Kat's reference to Gen Wolfson strongly favored the connection with Fort Belvoir.

And after receiving the transcript of the confession from Special Agent Ronald Teller that confirmed it. The organization had spread like a cancer through the military.

Special Agent Brennan was sent over to question Teller and in return for a plea deal, the killer was eager to turn on the syndicate. He had identified the members of his team and said that two pilots had been sourced from the 1/10th Special Forces Group, U.S. Army Garrison Stuttgart. "What were their names?"

"I don't know, they weren't part of the team."

"Were they not the identities you used when you entered the Royal Navy Air Station?"

….. "Yeah, I suppose so."

"You suppose so? You just lied to me Mr. Teller so your plea deal just flew out the window. Now, who sourced them for you?"

"I don't know, the orders came from Virginia."

The FBI soon had the requisition signed by MGen Wolfson for a helicopter to be assigned to Special Agent Nunez. "Did the orders came from MGen. Wolfson?"

"Yeah, they came from Wolfson. Everything came from him." Teller told them where they could find the kill order, written in Wolfson own hand. He was ordered to destroy the document, but Nunez suspected that it might come in handy and stashed it away in his apartment between the pages of John le Carré's novel, *Tinker, Taylor, Soldier, Spy*.

Brennan returned to Washington and brought him in for an interview. Wolfson came in with his JAG lawyer Col. Bill Manx. He was there to see that his client didn't fall into any federal legal holes.

"Agent Brennan, before I let my client answer any questions, I'd like to know what sorts of things you are looking for."

"As I'm sure you know that we have evidence of several crimes, that have taken place, here ... as well as in Canada and Europe. We have sworn statements from several witness, as well as confessions by persons being held in Britain, that have linked these crimes to Military Counterintelligence personnel."

"May we have access to these witness statements?"

"No, we are not releasing anything for the time being. The purpose of our investigation is to determine where these crimes originated, and to uncover the person or persons responsible."

"I see. Is my client being interviewed as a suspect in any of these investigations?"

"I'd think that was rather obvious, Col. Manx. As the commanding officer of M-CI is ultimately responsible for the activities of his agency, he would be the first person we would like to talk to. Now General Wolfson, are you familiar with Retired General Ramsey Hershoff?"

"Of course, Ramsey and I have been friends for many years."

"Was he a close friend and associate?"

"He is and a vital resource in the work we do at M-CI."

"You are aware that he was discovered floating in the Potomac with a bullet in his head?"

"What? No, I did not know that. When did this happen?"

"I find it interesting that you, as the head of Army Intelligence, were not aware that a close friend and colleague had been kidnapped and murdered virtually on your own doorstep. The Washington papers have been full of it."

"I … I have been…"

"You don't have to answer that General. Agent Brennerman…"

"That's Brennan, Mr. Manx.

"And it's Colonel Manx, Agent Brennan. As I was saying, I am inclined to believe that you have no evidence connecting my client with any of these allegations, and therefore, I am instructing him not to answer anymore of your questions at this time."

"Interesting. Is there any reason why your client is reluctant to help in our investigation?"

"My client and I are going to leave you now and if you have anything further to ask, I suggest you put your questions in writing and send them to my office. Goodbye Agent Brennan."

"Col. Manx, sit down please. I'm not finished with you yet. As I said, we have certain evidence that connects M-CI with these crimes. One rather pertinent piece of evidence …" he sorted out the order bearing Wolfson's signature. "… is this requisition for a helicopter to be provided for the transportation of a team of M-CI special agents."

Both men on the opposite side of the table maintained a stony silence.

"That helicopter was involved in quite a list of crimes, beginning with the misappropriation of government military equipment. The use of said government military equipment in the commission of the crimes of illegal entry into a foreign country, fraudulent claims of military authority, kidnapping and murder."

"Let me see that document."

"Certainly." He passed it across the table.

"That's an awful lot of bullshit to attach to one requisition."

"I think the salient point to concentrate on is the signature that approved the transfer of the helicopter."

Manx saw the signature then looked at the general. "That looks like a forgery to me."

"Does it? Oh, I think we'll discover that it is in fact genuine, and that we have the testimony of the general's adjutant, Capt. John Gradin, who witnessed the general signing it."

Manx looked stricken. Was it an act? If it was, then it was a very good one.

"Gradin is a liar, I have never seen this document before," said Wolfson, and he shoved it back across the table.

"OK, so that's your word against his." Brennan placed a photocopy of the handwritten orders he gave to Nunez. "And is this a forgery as well?"

"I … h … how did you get that?"

"Were you aware, Sir, that by the time that requisition for the helicopter was received in Stuttgart, European authorities had cleared Katrina Fernando of any involvement in those assassinations?"

"Don't answer that." said Manx.

"No, I ... I was not aware of that."

"As your counsel, I implore you to shut the fuck up!"

"Well, I think that's enough for now anyway. MGen. Tucker Wolfson I am placing you under arrest for conspiracy to commit murder, to being an accomplice before the fact to ten counts of murder and two counts of attempted murder.

"As your lawyer is present at this time, I will waive reading you your rights General Wolfson and suggest to you that the next time we speak, you either listen to him or you tell the truth. If you would stand, please.

Special Agent Daniels, cuff the prisoner."

***

Kat was restless, so Deacon suggested they go out for a walk along the river. They had been out for well over an hour and she'd hardly said two words.

"Are you alright, Kat?" She didn't respond. "Kat?"

"Sorry, what did you say?"

"I'm worried about you. Are you alright?"

"Yeah, I suppose."

"You haven't said a word for over an hour. Is there anything I can do?"

"Why don't you tell me that you can you bring back the dead."

"Kat, come on."

"No." She shook her head and fists and quickly walked ahead a few steps, then stopped. "Damn ... I'm sorry, Deacon. I didn't mean to snap at you." She looked out at the river. "No, there's nothing anyone can do. I ... I just need time."

"Wouldn't it help to talk about it?" They were surrounded now, caught in a crush of tourists converging on the bus tours kiosk at the corner of Westminster Bridge Rd. and Victoria Embankment.

"Please, not now." She looked up at the chariot driven by the Celtic Queen Boadicea with her daughters beside her and thought of Sara. She couldn't seem to get away from tragic stories of mothers and daughters. "I need to get away from this crowd, but I don't want to go home yet. Can we just keep on walking?"

"Sure, anything you want."

How ridiculous it was, she thought, to call a hotel, home. She hadn't had a real home in a very long time. She'd come close to it a couple of times, at ENA with Harm, in that lovely house overlooking the Pine River Valley in Mulmur, and then the safe house on King Street. But they were gone, and she was sick to death of it. Exhausted by the never-ending instability and danger.

As they passed the Battle of Britain Monument, she saw an unoccupied bench. "I'd like to sit down for a little while, if you don't mind."

"Not at all," said Deacon. The sat in silence for a moment looking across the river at the London Eye turning slowly. "Kat."

"Yes?"

"I did something the other day and I wanted to keep it as a surprise, but I think I should tell you about it now."

She wasn't sure if she should sound happy of be frightened. "What have you done?"

"As soon as you left, I had Rosario and Sara moved over to my house."

"I knew that. Wait ... Oh god, Deacon, are they alright?"

"Yes, they're just fine. Rosario told me that Sara has had a terrific time in the garden."

Kat smiled and her shoulder seemed to relax. "She loves that garden. Thank you."

"This morning, I sent my plane back to Toronto to fly them here to join us. They should be here by dinner time. I was hoping it would make you feel better."

Now that was exciting, and now she was happy. "Really? Oh Deacon, thank you, thank you so much." She stood up almost trembling with excitement. "Oh, I can't see them like this. I have to shower and change." She looked around her as if seeing London for the first time and it made her feel very small. She looked back the way they had come and saw the plain clothes officer who'd been assigned to keep an eye on her since they left Sir Torben's office. "This is wonderful, Deacon. Thank you."

"You are most welcome."

"Do you feel like a boat tour?" she asked.

"What, now? I thought you wanted to rush back to shower and change."

"You're right, I'm just so excited, I can't believe it." She was able to see him clearly now and was surprised by how tired he looked. "Oh gosh Deacon, I'm sorry, All I've been doing is thinking about myself and here you are completely exhausted. We'll go back so you can have a lie-down."

"If I'm going to go to bed in the afternoon, then I'd like to do something far more interesting than have a nap."

"Deacon Loats! You are a maniac." She couldn't believe it, but she actually felt like doing something 'interesting' too. "Do you honestly think you have the energy to fool around?"

"OK, so maybe we could just neck for a while."

"Sometimes you can be a very funny guy."

"Was that a no?"

"God-no, it's a *yes*, but I won't be surprised if you fall asleep on me." They got off the bench and headed back to the Corinthia.

"I can't imagine a nicer place to fall asleep."

"You boob-men are all alike."

He placed his hand on her shoulder. "You know that I'm hopelessly in love with you, don't you?"

"I feel the same way about you." She placed her hand on his and squeezed it tightly. "Deacon," she said quietly, "I want the three of us to be a family. Can we do that?"

He stopped in mid stride. "Does that mean you'll marry me now?"

She kissed his cheek. "Yes, let's get married. Let's do it here, tomorrow when Sara and Rose are here."

"That's a great idea. I'll set it up, but now there's something else I want, something more substantial than a kiss on the cheek." he said and got another kiss. "Thank you."

"I love you, Deacon."

***

The policeman followed them at a distance. He'd correctly interpreted what had just happened and decided to give them some space. He looked around for someone who might be watching his couple. It appeared that they were good to go. No red flags no one had shown any interest in them at all.

But he missed something. A tall man with his coat collar up and his hands in his pockets. He had been watching Kat and Deacon from the Thames wall. He had also spotted the plain clothes policeman.

***

Chapter ~ 31

The doorman in the tasteful grey and black livery doffed his top hat and smiled as he saw them approaching. He reached for the door, and he said, "I hope you had a pleasant walk."

"Yes, thank you," said Deacon, beaming widely as he followed Kat through the door. He was more tired than he thought and moving slowly. The concierge looked up from his podium and greeted them. Kat took the second set of steps to the lobby, turned, and smiled back at Deacon as she walked along the hallway to the elevators. The was glass table in the center of the hall and at the center of that was a large vase with a gorgeous display of white flowers. Deacon was just coming to the steps holding on to the handrail. She stopped to open her purse, so that she could find the room key to operate the elevator.

She heard something so familiar that made her heart stop.

It was the sharp snap of the hammer of a gun with a suppressor, a sudden exhale, and the tinkle of the casing bouncing on the stone floor. She spun around to see the concierge fall. "No!" Then right after that a second shot and Deacon hit the floor. She moved towards him. "Deacon?"

"Stop right there."

Deacon groaned in terrible pain. The bullet had destroyed his knee. She looked up at the shooter. "What are you doing?"

He was staring at her, his face flushed with victory. "You have the nerve to ask me that? You killed my uncle, and then you murdered my sister."

"Edward?"

"Oh, so you know who I am. Then you know why I am here."

"Edward, I didn't kill Hedda, I tried to help her."

"You expect me to believe that? I saw you chase her from that bastard's house. No Anita, I know you killed her, and you thought you killed me too, but here I am." he moved closer.

"Wait, you were at Siggi's house? Then you saw what someone had done to her. Did Siggi do that?"

"Hardly, he was dead before Hedda arrived, I saw to that. He was playing games, he knew I was alive, but he didn't tell her. He planned to kill me before she got to him. I was supposed to be the distraction to give him a chance to beat her at her own game. He hadn't counted on me to be able to defend myself. I didn't hear Hedda when she came in, I was upstairs. It wasn't until the cars crashed out on the street that I knew what was happening."

"Listen to me, Edward, everyone knows that Hedda was the assassin."

"You love this man don't you."

"Edward, please."

"Don't you!"

"Yes."

"I thought so." He aimed his gun at Deacon.

"Don't do it, Edward, please, don't shoot him."

He fired a second shot into Deacon's head. Kat screamed and sank to her knees.

She looked from Deacon's lifeless body to Edward, her lips parted as if to say something, but no words came out.

"Yes, look at him. Fill your heart and your mind with the knowledge that his death is on you." He was giving her time to think about it, probably the cruelest thing he could have done. Of course, she thought about it. He was right too, she thought.

They all died because of her. A violent death had been inevitable for her, she had known that almost from the beginning, but she thought

Deacon would outlive her that and Sara would be his daughter. She heard him before she saw him. The DI she hadn't met but knew he was near came racing into the lobby. "Police! Drop the weapon and raise your hands!"

"Anita, your time is up."

"Freeze! Put your gun down, or I will shoot!"

The sound of Police officer's gunshot filled the hall but it was an instant too late. Edward's folly couldn't be stopped.

The bullet that pierced her chest was fatal, though not instant. She did hear the shot that would take her life which would answer that question she had so many years ago. And she heard the shot that ended Edward's. Not a thought was wasted on her killer. There was only regret that her curse had, as she feared, led to Deacon's death as well.

DI Gadsden raced to her side and held her, hoping that something could be done to save her. Her last thought was of her daughter only enough time to say, "Sara."

The bullet had done too much damage and he was just in time to see the life drain away. He lay her down as the crowd gathered, horrified, shocked and sickened.

***

Epilogue

Rose and Sara arrived in London hours after the shooting, unaware of the tragedy, still ex-cited to see her and Deacon again.

For Rosario, the end was devastating but not unexpected. For Sara, the shock of it left her numb, unable to speak a condition that would continue for more than a year. With the love and caring that Rose had promised, she would recover and they would continue living in Deacon's pal-ace. Sara would grow up to be the absolute image of her mother in every respect save for the color of her eyes. They were blue just like Paul Devlyn's were, the father she never knew.

With an excellent education, some guidance from Rose, along with the help and advice from her mother and stepfather's staff, Sara would keep the businesses and foundations going. Eventually she would become an astrophysicist. The spirit of her mother, taken from her far too soon, will live on in her.

But that is another story for another time.

The End

The Author

Canadian writer Hugh Russel and his wife Cheryl make their home the house that he designed and built (mostly by himself), in the beautiful forested, hilly part of the Niagara Escarpment. About an hour and a half north west of Toronto. It's far enough away from the city to breath the clean air, enjoy night sky and the four seasons to their fullest. Yet close enough to it, should they ever feel the pressing need to go there. There is not question, they have found the perfect place to live play and work.